THE STOCKHOLM RUN

Ken Lussey

ARACHNID PRESS

Other books by Ken Lussey

Thrillers featuring Bob Sutherland and Monique Dubois
and set in Scotland during World War Two:
Eyes Turned Skywards
The Danger of Life
Bloody Orkney

For younger readers:
The House With 46 Chimneys

First published in Great Britain in 2022 by
Arachnid Press Ltd
91 Columbia Avenue
Livingston EH54 6PT
Scotland

www.arachnid.scot
www.kenlussey.com

All rights reserved. No part of this publication may be reproduced, stored in a retrieval system or transmitted in any form or by any means, electronic, mechanical, photocopying, recording or otherwise, without the prior written permission of Arachnid Press Ltd.

Copyright © Ken Lussey 2022

The moral right of Ken Lussey to be identified as the author of this work has been asserted by him in accordance with the Copyright, Designs and Patents Act 1988.

Except as set out in the author's note, this is a work of fiction and any resemblance to real persons, living or dead, is entirely coincidental.

ISBN: 978-1-8382530-4-2

Cover design and photography by Carolyn Henry.
Cover map of Stockholm sourced from Discusmedia.com.
Printed and bound in Great Britain by Inky Little Fingers Ltd,
Unit 3, Churcham Business Park, Churcham, Gloucester, GL2 8AX.

For Maureen, who came with me to Stockholm.

PROLOGUE

It might still have been March, but the ferry from the old town to Djurgården was busy. The early Sunday afternoon crowd of families and couples, both young and old, was such that Werner Lippisch found it hard to identify watchers or followers. It ought to have been easy to spot anyone who didn't fit in, anyone like himself, but he knew that anyone interested in him would have taken care not to be obvious. It could be the young couple so apparently in love over by the railings on the far side of the vessel, or even the rather severely dressed woman talking in Swedish to the small blonde girl whose hand she was holding. With people milling excitedly around on the deck there was no way of telling.

Werner realised he'd been in the city for just over a year. How different things were now. The Stockholm he had first encountered had been firmly in the grip of the tail end of the worst winter that anyone could remember, a winter whose effects were felt right across Europe. The city, the entire continent, had experienced three exceptionally cold winters in a row and when you looked into people's eyes back then you got the sense they'd had enough. At the time Werner had found that ironic, humorous even. He'd come directly from Berlin, where the winters had been just as bad, but where people were also starting to come to terms with real privation, with growing casualty lists from the Eastern Front, and with the realisation that their city was not as safe from British bombing as they'd been assured it was.

Stockholmers in March 1942 might have had unusable harbours and solidly frozen waterways around their 14 islands, but their street and shop lights were switched on at night and the only air-raid warnings were rehearsals for an eventuality that, so far at least, had never happened.

A year later and many essentials were rationed in Stockholm. But bumper harvests the previous autumn had ensured that no one would starve, and the mild winter and early spring that followed had brought the city back to life much earlier in the year. There was still a chill in the air and the trees had yet to leaf but, those things apart, the blue skies of this March Sunday could easily be mistaken for early summer. Little wonder that Stockholmers seemed so determined to enjoy themselves. Little wonder the Djurgården ferry was so full.

When the ferry berthed in the shadow of the Gröna Lund amusement park, which had opened to accommodate the unusually early-season pleasure seekers, Werner joined the throng of people who surged onto the island. The crowd thinned out as those visiting Gröna Lund turned off, and there were fewer people around by the time he'd walked the half a kilometre or so to the entrance to the Skansen open-air museum park. He knew he could have taken a tram from the city centre to Djurgården, but the idea of the ferry had somehow appealed.

Having paid his admission to the park, Werner rode up what he'd been told was the longest escalator in Europe, opened just before the war by King Gustav V, to the raised plateau on which most of the elements of the park were located.

The man he was due to meet should be waiting for him in Seglora kyrka, the lovely old wooden church that had been moved in its entirety to its current location in 1916. Werner had picked the meeting place. He had visited Skansen once before, the previous summer, and felt the church would give them both a degree of privacy and security. If it was quiet, they could talk in the church, admiring the magnificently decorated ceiling. Alternatively, especially given the weather, they could walk through the park as they talked. Briefly, at least: what needed saying wouldn't take long.

The interior of the church seemed dark after the sunlight outside. The door, in the base of the south side of the tower, gave access to a vestibule, which in turn led through to the broad nave. As his eyes adjusted to the gloom, Werner again realised just how beautiful this place was.

A man was seated in a pew near the front of the otherwise empty church, at its far end. He turned round and stood as Werner entered. Werner felt a flood of relief. He knew Peter Bostock by sight, occasionally glimpsed across busy Stockholm cafés or restaurants. This was the man he wanted to talk to.

'Hello, Mr Bostock, I'm Werner Lippisch. I'm with the Bureau Wagner.' Both men smiled at the euphemism widely used to describe the Stockholm office of the Abwehr, the German intelligence service.

As they shook hands the other man replied. 'As you know, I'm Peter Bostock and I work in the British Passport Control Organisation here in the city.' This was the very transparent cover used by the British Secret Intelligence Service for its operations abroad. 'Let's talk here. Take a pew.' Bostock smiled again.

Werner had been right. The meeting didn't take long. He then left. The darkness of the church meant it took a little time to adjust to the sun shining into his eyes as he emerged. Too long, as it turned out. Two pistol shots were fired into his head from close range by someone standing to one side, just outside the church door, and Werner was dead before his body hit the ground.

By the time Peter Bostock reacted to the sound of the shots and reached the doorway, his pistol in his hand, there was no one in sight. No one still living, anyway: Lippisch was all too obviously beyond help. Bostock holstered his weapon, realising how it would look if he was seen there. He then stepped over Werner Lippisch's body and made his way as quickly as he could without drawing attention to himself towards the exit of the park.

*

Margaret Forsyth knew she should have been grateful, but that was easy to forget. She'd been told that the year before, two guards up here on the top of the old tower had, on separate nights, suffered from frostbite. This had been her first winter in Scotland and everyone said how mild it had been compared to previous years but even now, in March, it didn't feel mild.

Her older sister Alice had it easy by comparison. She worked on permanent nights, helping build parts for Spitfires in an old motorcycle factory in their home city of Southampton. Alice at least enjoyed relative warmth while she worked and could go home to her own bed, even if her husband John would never again share it with her. Perhaps, Margaret thought, Alice didn't have it quite so easy after all.

Margaret tried to sink further down into the large turned up collar of her greatcoat, pulling her scarf tighter to help keep her ears warm. She looked up, admitting again to herself that the beauty of the night and the setting was some compensation for the cold. The full moon shone down from a nearly cloudless sky. She knew that if the moon hadn't been so bright, she'd have been able to see the arc of the Milky Way with total clarity. The absence of artificial light in the blackout brought with it many problems, but it was good for stargazing.

To keep her circulation going, Margaret stamped her feet as she walked round the top of the flat roof of the keep. Almost flat, anyway. The sloping roofed room that could have given shelter was locked, to prevent guards spending their nights there rather than keeping a lookout. She could have climbed up the narrow steps of the little circular turret that gave an extra ten feet or so of elevation, but the steps were narrow and uneven and at night that didn't seem a great idea. The view over the parapets was enough to lift her spirits anyway. The most outstanding feature in the view lay only a couple of miles to the north-east. In the moonlight the Forth Bridge, which she thought looked at its best from this angle, was strikingly prominent.

If you followed a rather convoluted train of logic, Margaret was only here because of the bridge. She'd been told that one of the first Luftwaffe air raids on Britain had been on the River Forth in October 1939. She'd heard different accounts of whether the target of the attack had been the bridge itself, or nearby warships in the river, or the dockyards at Rosyth. But whatever the reason for the Luftwaffe's visit that day, an immediate response had been to move a squadron of barrage balloons from England to help protect the area. Dundas Castle had been requisitioned to serve as the squadron's headquarters because, from this viewpoint, you could look out over the whole area that its two dozen balloons defended and gain an immediate impression of whether their teams of operators were doing their jobs or not.

Air raids were much fewer and further between these days, with the most recent Luftwaffe attack anywhere within miles of here having happened the previous August, over seven months earlier. But there had been an air raid on civilian targets up in the north-east a month before and they could be back here at any time. Everyone serving on 948 Squadron knew how important it was to maintain constant vigilance.

During the previous year, the men serving on barrage balloon squadrons across Britain had been increasingly replaced by women, on a supposedly scientific basis of fourteen women of the Women's Auxiliary Air Force taking the jobs of ten men of the Royal Air Force, who could then be deployed elsewhere. What this meant in practice was that even the squadron's headquarters had become an increasingly female establishment and that tended to make it a pleasant enough place to do your bit for the war effort. Until very recently, anyway.

The views were a little less spectacular in other directions, taking in woods or the farmland that now covered much of the parkland that she had been told existed before the war.

Immediately to the east, the view extended out over the dark roofs of the much later parts of Dundas Castle, built in the first half of the previous century. To the south of the old tower was the stable court with, beyond it, slightly rising and rather overgrown ground that would have been attractive if the grass had been tended over the preceding few years. Growing in from the right-hand side of the view, extending almost from the corner of the stable court until it became lost in the woodland to the south-west and more distantly to the south, was a mass of rhododendrons.

As she looked, Margaret though she saw movement on the slightly irregular edge formed where the rhododendrons met the overgrown parkland. She could see nothing through her binoculars and decided she must have imagined it. Then something moved again, and she realised she was looking at someone making their way very slowly towards the castle while trying to keep in the shelter afforded by the rhododendrons.

The squadron's sentries patrolling the grounds now always went in twos, a change deemed essential for their safety. Margaret had seen a pair to the north of the castle but couldn't see any to the south or west. She was sure that this was just one person, acting in a way that no sentry ever would. She walked rapidly over to the turret, which served as a head for the spiral stairs descending into the tower. Inside the door she picked up the phone mounted on the wall, desperately hoping that the orderly officer was awake and equally desperately hoping that it really was a person she had seen, rather than a fox or a badger.

*

It was just her luck that the orderly officer tonight was Flight Lieutenant Dean, a portly man in his late forties who, she assumed, had remained with 948 Squadron because anything more active, or overseas, was judged to be beyond his levels of fitness and commitment. She couldn't reach him on the phone, so ran down the full height of the steps in the old tower and then into the main castle buildings, a task made no easier by the encumbrance of her greatcoat and rifle. Dean wasn't in the duty office. It didn't take Margaret long to decide the next best place to look was in the kitchen, where she found him eating a sandwich. A 'mid-duty snack,' he called it.

He did at least take her report of a possible intruder in the grounds seriously. They met two of the recently arrived women on the squadron coming in from a patrol of the grounds through a rear entrance near the kitchen. The women said they'd seen nothing suspicious, but it turned out this was the pair Margaret had seen to the north of the castle, and her sighting had been on the opposite side. Both had Sten submachine guns and Dean ordered them to follow him and Margaret. He then led the way through the castle's main entrance hall, which Margaret always thought must have been a lovely place before the war, and out of the front door.

The area in front of the castle was used to park many of the squadron's vehicles so the view across to the rhododendrons was largely obscured.

'It was over that way, sir.' Margaret made her way between parked lorries and cars until she could see the edge between the overgrown parkland and the rhododendrons where she'd spotted the intruder. She couldn't see anyone now.

'Look!' One of the other women, Margaret thought her name was Harris, was pointing. 'Over there, by the edge of the bushes.'

Margaret looked and, in the moonlight, could see a dark figure, still partly in cover from the edge of the dense mass of rhododendrons, moving away from them towards the visible skyline.

'Halt! Stand still or we will fire!'

The volume of Dean's bellow surprised Margaret. She could see the figure had heard, for it paused, looked round as if to assess how far away they were, then set off for the skyline again, this time at a run.

'It's up to you, Forsyth,' said Dean. 'You're the only one here with a rifle. You've got to take the shot.'

'But it must be 200 yards sir.'

'And getting further every moment. Fire or I'll take your rifle off you and do it myself, which would be pointless as you're a better shot than I am. Remember what happened to Mallory. This must be the man who did it.'

Margaret dropped to the ground and raised the rifle to her shoulder. She'd put a round into the breech as they'd left the castle. She lined the primitive sights of the Lee Enfield on the figure, realising there was no time to adjust for range. She moved the safety catch to off, breathed out and squeezed the trigger.

She didn't see what happened next because of the effect of the muzzle flash on her night vision, but she heard Harris scream, 'You've got him!' Then, 'No, he's getting back up!'

'Take another shot, Forsyth,' said Flight Lieutenant Dean. 'No, too late, he's over the skyline. But you definitely got him. Well done, that was great shooting.'

Margaret wasn't sure how to feel, except perhaps pleased that she'd not seen her shot hit the figure. Then she remembered Barbara Mallory and felt a pang of regret that she'd not killed the intruder outright.

CHAPTER ONE

Group Captain Robert Sutherland, 'Bob' to his friends, drove himself to work that morning. It might have been a Monday, but he'd been in the office on Saturday and again on Sunday morning. He'd been doing the job long enough to realise that keeping up with the paperwork was never going to be his forte, so time in the office when it was quiet and with no distractions was an ideal way of catching up. To an extent, anyway.

He'd thought of going to see his parents the previous evening but hadn't much liked the idea of visiting them on his own. Nor the idea of having to explain why he was on his own. If he was honest, he'd felt at a loose end all weekend and more than a little lonely. A trip into Edinburgh the previous afternoon for a walk round Holyrood Park hadn't really helped.

It never took long to drive from the bungalow in Featherhall Crescent in Corstorphine to the base the army had built around the fine old country house at Craigiehall after requisitioning it at the beginning of the war. When Bob had taken command of the northern operations of Military Intelligence 11 the previous October, he'd inherited from his predecessor, an army colonel, a suite of offices on the first floor of the extension added to the original house in the 1820s. Much of the main house was used as a headquarters by Royal Artillery and anti-aircraft artillery units whose operational elements were scattered along both banks of the Firth of Forth and on islands in the river.

That meant that he didn't need to worry about mundane matters like catering and accommodation for the junior staff in the office and, overall, the arrangement worked well. There had been a slight chill in the relationship with their hosts over the festive season when the head of Bob's army team, Captain Anthony Darlington, had highlighted a series of shortcomings in the security at Craigiehall. But improvements were made, and it had been accepted that this was part of MI11's job.

As he showed his pass to the guard at the main gate, Bob reflected on the recurring part that Craigiehall had played in his life. His parents had moved to nearby Cramond when he was ten. At that time, the big house had been empty and abandoned and Bob, like many local children, had enjoyed exploring the extensive grounds. When Bob was about fourteen the house was renovated and reoccupied, and forays into the grounds had to be undertaken with much more discretion. His parents had told him when Craigiehall had been converted into a hotel in 1933, and a year or two before the war he'd stayed there with a young lady he'd met through the Auxiliary Air Force. He'd chosen the location for their illicit weekend mainly because he'd wanted to know what the interior of the house was like. In the event he found the two-night stay extremely uncomfortable. Not because they were pretending to be married: everyone did that. Rather he spent his time worrying that a fellow guest or member of staff might recognise him and tell his parents that he'd been in the area without calling in on them.

Bob parked as usual near the main entrance to the house and climbed the stairs to the MI11 offices, returning the salute of an army sergeant who he encountered in the upper hallway. He put his head round the door of the general office to find it empty. The sound of typing led him a little further along the corridor to his own outer office.

His secretary, Joyce Stuart, looked up as he entered and smiled. 'It's quiet, isn't it group captain? I can see from the work you got through that you had time on your hands over the weekend. With most people away this week I sent Lorna and Alice for an early and long tea break with Private Jenkins. It's less distracting if they chat in the canteen rather than here.'

Joyce Stuart was a stereotypically Edinburgh lady in her fifties who was the very model of efficiency. Bob had long since given up trying to get her to call him by his name.

'Is the place entirely empty?' He'd been about to go on to ask Joyce if he was right in thinking that Taffy Jenkins, now the office's only specialist driver, had become close to Lorna McIlroy, the older of the two typists, but held back, thinking the question would make her uncomfortable.

'Not quite. Captain Darlington is in the army team's office. I believe Sergeant Potter is following up the visits they made last week to Redford and Dreghorn Barracks in Edinburgh while the captain writes his reports. You know where everyone else is.'

Bob offered his thanks before going into his office, closing the door behind himself. He normally left it open but had half a mind to try to phone Monique. Then he realised she'd not welcome the call if she was busy.

Instead, he looked at the pile of papers in his in tray and sighed. He thought he'd made progress over the weekend, but it seemed that however fast he cleared the largely pointless material that found its way into his tray, there was always more waiting to replace it. Sometimes he missed the clarity and simplicity of the life he once lived, in which nothing mattered except shooting down your opponent's aeroplane before he shot down yours.

A clarity and simplicity, Bob reminded himself, that he'd pushed a little too far on the evening of the 1st of November

1940, at huge personal cost. He was lucky to have survived. And he was lucky that people whose opinions mattered had decided he had the skills to do the job he was doing now, which allowed him to make his contribution in a very different way. Part of the contribution he was expected to make as deputy head of MI11 – an irksome part for him, but important in the eyes of the people he reported to – was ensuring he kept on top of the paperwork. He sighed and shuffled through the top half dozen documents before selecting one that looked interesting and placing it on the desk in front of him.

Sometime later a knock on the door brought Bob back to the present from a document he'd discovered further down the pile in his tray, a long report his boss had written about the activities of MI11 in southern and central England, Wales, and Northern Ireland, the parts of the UK Bob wasn't responsible for. He knew he'd have to produce something similar for northern England and Scotland.

'Hello, come in.'

Joyce put her head round the door. 'You have a visitor, sir. He says you'll be pleased to see him.'

She swung the door open, and a figure Bob knew well entered, a broad smile on his face. It had been a while since Bob had seen his father in his police uniform.

'Dad, what brings you here? Joyce, meet my father, Superintendent David Sutherland of the Edinburgh City Police. Dad, meet my amazing secretary, Joyce Stuart.' Bob saw Joyce blush and realised it may have been the first time he'd praised her in that way.

'Can I get you both a cup of tea?'

'Does that suit you, Dad?'

'Yes, please. I'm intending to convince you to leave with

me in fairly short order, but we have time for a cup of tea.'

While waiting for their teas, Bob enquired after his mother and his younger sister Pearl, who was working as a nurse in Edinburgh.

As they sipped their drinks, David Sutherland sat back in his chair. 'Is it always this quiet here?'

'Anything but. I've probably told you before, but I've got three teams of two men, each focussed on one of the three main services and manned by an officer and a non-commissioned officer from that service. You'll remember I told you we stirred up a hornet's nest in Orkney in November when we turned up mob-handed and uncovered large-scale problems of corruption and worse in the naval establishment there.'

'When you nearly got yourself killed, twice, according to Monique? Yes, I do remember that.'

'My deputy, Lieutenant Commander Michael Dixon, also heads up the naval team and is flying up to Orkney this morning with his sidekick and with the RAF team to make a return visit to see how things have moved on since then.'

'Is Dixon the one who got involved with that hotelier's daughter up there?'

'Betty Swanson? Daughter of the late and deeply unlamented Edward Swanson? Yes. I think that Michael hopes they can reach an understanding during the visit and that she'll agree to move down to Edinburgh. It's not breaking a confidence, well not seriously, to say that he took an engagement ring with him in her size. I don't know how much of the story I told you, but thanks to her father's activities, a quarter of their hotel was owned by everyone's favourite Glasgow gangster, Willie Shand, an arrangement managed by my equally late Uncle Frank. How is Mum coping with Frank's death, by the way? I do feel guilty about it.'

David Sutherland put his teacup down on its saucer. 'I think the loss of a brother is always hard, but the circumstances of his death, especially the idea he was going to kill you, made it easier for your mother to come to terms with. Anyway, is the Willie Shand link why I hear you've been spending time with your old partner-in-crime Lieutenant Jack Callaghan of the Renfrewshire Constabulary?'

'You really do have eyes and ears everywhere, Dad. Yes. Some subtle pressure was brought to bear to persuade Mr Shand to buy the three-quarters of the St Magnus Hotel in Kirkwall that he didn't already own from Betty, and for a fair price. I think she intends to set herself up in a rather smaller-scale business in Edinburgh, though the idea is that, in the short term, she and Michael can use the second bedroom at the house in Featherhall Crescent.'

'And where's Monique?'

'Ah, yes. I was wondering when you'd ask. She's in London.'

'Is something wrong? Your mother has high hopes for you and Monique. As do I, for that matter.'

'Does she really? How much of Monique's story have you told her?'

'Everything I know, with one small exception. I omitted the bit about Monique threatening to kill your Uncle Frank in a particularly unpleasant way in the police office in Kirkwall.'

'But the stuff about her being a dancer who once had a cocaine habit, and her spying on the Russians and the Germans for SIS, and her coming ashore in Scotland as a German spy, and her becoming widowed from highly unsuitable Russian and German husbands? You told Mum all that?'

'Yes. I think what mattered most to her was that I also told her that Monique had saved your life at least twice, by my count.'

'Good God, Dad. How did she react?'

'She said something about it making a refreshing change for a woman to have lived such a full life by the time she was 30. She er...' David coughed and smiled. 'She also said you were going to have to make a real effort to keep Monique now you've found her. Which brings me back to the question you avoided a moment ago. Is something wrong?'

'Not personally, Dad. Not between Monique and me. But MI5 had an operation go tragically wrong in Scotland last month. Though Monique had nothing to do with it, indeed, she didn't know about it until last week, she has become involved as an MI5 officer "on the ground" so to speak. She went down to London last Friday to try to make sure that nothing of the sort ever happens again. She'd previously visited the area where the problem arose, and I know she was angry about what had happened.'

'What did happen?'

'I'm sorry, Dad, it would be betraying personal and professional confidences to tell you.'

'Come on, son. My security clearance is every bit as high as yours. Remember that the head of Special Branch in Edinburgh reports to me.'

Bob didn't choose to challenge his father's assertion about security clearances as that would truly have been betraying a confidence, but he did see the point of what his father had said.

'Very well, Dad, but this is strictly between you and I.'

'Of course.'

'Much earlier in the war two German spies came ashore

from a U-boat on the north-east Scottish coast, much as Monique and her ill-fated companions were landed off the same coast by seaplane. They turned themselves in to MI5, who kept the whole thing totally secret and ran them as double agents from an address in Aberdeen.

'Roll things forward to the beginning of the year, and some bright spark in MI5 suddenly decided that they needed to reinforce the deception of the Abwehr, the German intelligence service, by asking them to provide cash and equipment to allow their "spies" to continue operating. The idea was for the Germans to drop supplies by parachute onto a beach near Rattray Head and that is exactly what happened, in the early hours of the 20th of February.

'So far, so good. The problem was that the Luftwaffe decided to go one better. They decided to provide cover for the aircraft making the supply drop by mounting air raids on nearby Fraserburgh and Peterhead, places that were both heavily attacked earlier in the war. A single bomber attacked each and in Fraserburgh a young boy was killed while asleep in his bed. These were the first air raids on targets in Scotland for months and it's difficult to avoid the conclusion that they only happened because MI5 thought it would be a nice idea to reinforce their deception. Frankly, it could have been far worse. The attack on Fraserburgh, though only by one aircraft, caused widespread damage and there could easily have been far more than one fatality.'

'I can see why Monique was unhappy,' said David. 'Did she visit Fraserburgh?'

'Yes, she got the early train last Wednesday morning, using her MI11 role as cover and taking the junior member of my RAF team with her. Ostensibly they were checking up on the security of the anti-aircraft defences in the area. Monique is normally pretty thick-skinned, but I think that what happened got to her a little. She was also angry that it had taken three weeks for those in MI5 who were responsible to accept the reality of what had happened and tell their senior officers. She got back late on Thursday night and as I said, she's been in London since Friday. Other than a very brief phone call to me here on Friday afternoon to say the aircraft I'd arranged for her had got her to RAF Northolt, I've heard nothing from her. I think she intended to talk to those directly involved on Saturday and have meetings with more senior officers yesterday. After that, I don't know.'

'You have to feel for the poor boy and his family,' said David. 'But there is a war on, and these things do happen.'

'That's true, Dad, though I'm not sure that makes it any easier. But you didn't come here to ask after Monique. What's up?'

'It might be easier if I show you rather than tell you. If you've got any troops who've not gone to Orkney, you might want to involve them. What we've found is really rather odd and I think it falls within your area of competence rather than mine.'

CHAPTER TWO

It was only a couple of miles along narrow roads and Private Taffy Jenkins had no difficulty keeping up with the police driver of the car Bob's dad was using.

'Have you any idea what it's about, sir?' asked Captain Anthony Darlington, sitting with Bob in the back of the car.

'None at all,' said Bob. 'I just know we're going to Dundas Castle, a little south of Queensferry. My father was rather mysterious about it, but I don't think he's any interest in wasting our time, or his own for that matter. I've been trying to think why the name of the place rings a bell. I think there's a Royal Air Force unit based there. If I remember correctly it's used as the headquarters for a barrage balloon squadron protecting this part of the Forth estuary from air attack.'

They approached the castle along a narrow drive through heavy vegetation that emerged into a more open area. They came to a halt alongside the police car, parked amongst a varied collection of RAF vehicles in front of the castle.

Bob looked out of the car window. 'You know, Anthony, I spent a large part of my childhood within a few miles of this place, but this is the first time I've ever been here.'

'It must have looked nice before the air force parked this lot in front of it, sir. Especially on a beautiful day like this one.'

Despite the vehicles, Bob could see that Dundas Castle was an attractive building made of grey stone. To his inexpert eyes, much of it looked to date back to the 1700s or 1800s and it had a nicely imposing frontage at the end they'd approached from, with a longer, pleasingly asymmetric, face looking out over the vehicle park. At the far end was what looked like it had started life as a grand stable block extending forwards from the rest of the castle. As they'd approached, Bob had also caught a glimpse of what seemed to be a much older and taller part of the castle, slightly behind and beyond the rest.

Bob got out of the car and saw two men approaching his father from the main door of the castle. He and Anthony Darlington walked over to join them. One of the men was in civilian dress but still looked like a policeman. The other, a heavily built flight lieutenant, saluted as he saw Bob.

'Let me do the introductions,' said Superintendent Sutherland. 'These gentlemen are Group Captain Sutherland and Captain Darlington, both with Military Intelligence, Section 11, based here in Edinburgh. Bob, this is Inspector John Nicholls, and this is Flight Lieutenant Dean, who is the adjutant of 948 Squadron, based here at the castle.

'Flight lieutenant, would you start by telling us what happened last night? I know we talked earlier, but I'd like MI11 to hear it directly from you.'

'Of course, superintendent. It was a few minutes after 2 a.m. this morning. The guard posted on top of the keep, the oldest part of the castle and the place with the best views, Aircraftwoman 1st Class Forsyth, thought she saw someone approaching stealthily along the line of the edge of the rhododendrons over there.' He gestured. 'She and I came out to look, accompanied by two other guards who had just returned from patrolling the grounds on the other side of the castle.

'We saw a person heading back up the edge of the rhododendrons towards the skyline and not far short of it.' He pointed again. 'I assume he'd heard us come out of the castle's front door and decided to make himself scarce. I shouted out a command for him to stop or we would fire. He obviously heard, for he paused and turned towards us, then turned back and ran. Forsyth was the only one of us with a rifle – the other two had submachine guns and I had my service revolver – and it was a couple of hundred yards range, so I ordered her to fire at the intruder. She lay down over there and took her shot. She scored a hit, for we saw him fall. But then he got back up and disappeared over the skyline while she was still blinded by the muzzle flash from the first shot.'

'That's remarkably good shooting at night,' said Anthony Darlington.

'Yes, she's an excellent shot, which is why she'd been issued with the rifle. She's been able to provide us with venison on several occasions over the winter. Last night was clear and it was a full moon, which helped, but you are right, it was fine shooting.'

'It makes you wonder why he stayed in the open,' said Anthony. 'If it had been me, I'd have burrowed into the rhododendrons when I heard you come out of the castle.'

'I've wondered that, too,' said Dean. 'But those rhododendrons are seriously overgrown and very dense. I'm guessing he knew that and decided his best chance of getting away was to follow the line of the edge of them. If he'd hidden in the vegetation he might also have been trapped there if we'd mounted a serious search; unable to move without making lots of noise.'

'I have to ask,' said Bob, 'didn't it cross your mind to fire warning shots before actually shooting at the intruder?'

'Yes sir, it did, but only very briefly. The intruder was so close to the skyline that any waste of time would have allowed him to escape. There's another factor too, which you should know about. Until last week it was the norm for our sentries to operate individually. In the early hours of last Tuesday morning a member of the squadron, Corporal Barbara Mallory, was attacked and severely injured while patrolling to the east of the castle, close to the wooded area you can see over there.' Dean pointed.

'She was struck on the side of the head by what we've been told from her injury was probably a hammer and she must have known she was being attacked because she screamed. This brought two other sentries to the scene quite quickly. As they approached, they saw someone making off into the trees. They didn't know what they were dealing with, so didn't fire their weapons. Then they found Corporal Mallory. Both later said that it looked as if someone had been trying to remove her clothing when they were disturbed. At the time, the sentries were mainly concerned about summoning help to treat her obviously severe head injury.'

'How is Corporal Mallory?' asked Bob.

'Nearly a week later and she's still in a coma and no one can tell us if she's likely to come out of it, sir' said Flight Lieutenant Dean. 'I'm sure you'll understand why, in very similar circumstances, I thought it best to issue the order to open fire immediately and worry about asking questions afterwards.'

'Were the police informed of last week's attack?' asked Bob.

'Yes, and the RAF Police Special Investigation Branch, but neither were able to find anything of use to help track down the attacker.'

'Have you contacted the Special Investigation Branch this time?'

'The flight lieutenant was going to this morning, Bob,' said his father, 'but for reasons that will become clear, I suggested that it might be better to involve you.'

'What became of the intruder last night?' asked Bob.

'That's where it gets strange,' said his father. 'John, can you fill us in on what we've found, please?'

Inspector Nicholls looked pleased to have been asked. 'We were called immediately after the shooting but were unable to do much in the dark. At first light this morning we undertook a thorough search of the area. We found blood on the ground where the intruder was shot, and then an intermittent trail of it, as if they were trying to stem the bleeding but finding it hard to do so. We also found, snagged on a branch at the edge of woods not far to the south, a green woollen cap comforter. We'd arranged for a sniffer dog to be present in case we found anything that would give a scent. The cap comforter enabled the dog to follow a trail, complete with more blood, for a little under half a mile to a wooded area on the far side of that hill you can see to the south. Then the trail disappeared, until we literally stumbled over something quite unexpected.'

'What did you find?' asked Bob.

'This is very much a case of "seeing is believing", Bob,' said his father. 'If you can get your driver to follow my car, we can save a bit of a walk.'

Bob and Anthony returned to the car, which then drove off behind the police car. After a short distance Private Jenkins pulled off the side of a road running south from the castle, coming to a halt on a broad overgrown verge, still behind the police car. The verge was defined by a metal fence that ran parallel with the road.

Another police car and a black van were parked on the equally broad, and equally overgrown, verge on the opposite side, which came complete with a matching metal fence. Bob followed the others through a gate and along a grassy track that led slightly uphill towards another gate visible against the sky, a hundred yards or so to the west. This stood at the tail of an expanse of woodland that seemed to occupy the line of a ridge and extended back the way they had come. Looking in that direction, Bob realised he could still see Dundas Castle.

Beyond the second gate the track curved round the end of the woodland before heading north up its far side, while the ground dropped away to the west towards a loch that Bob could glimpse between trees.

Inspector Nicholls saw him looking. 'That's Dundas Loch down there, while the rising ground to the north-west of us is Dundas Hill. We turn off the track here and head into these woods on the right-hand side for 50 yards or so.'

As they entered the woods Bob saw two policemen and a man in civilian clothes standing together and talking. The civilian was smoking.

The inspector continued, 'The trail, which we followed from the north, disappeared here. But the dog wouldn't let it be and kept trying to dig up the earth just over there. When we took a closer look, we found a hatch, covered in vegetation, and carefully counterweighted to open and close easily. That's it, beside my men.'

'What's under the hatch?' asked Bob.

'See for yourself, Bob,' said his father.

Bob walked over and peered down into a square, brick-lined shaft that seemed to be a dozen or more feet deep. He thanked a constable who had offered him a torch and climbed down a substantial wooden ladder, telling Anthony Darlington to follow.

At the bottom he found himself at the start of a brick-lined passageway that headed, he thought, parallel with the line of the ridge. He looked up, and saw a substantial ceiling made of secure-looking corrugated metal, apparently bolted onto some sort of frame above it. To make progress it was necessary to squeeze past a brick wall that partly obstructed access. Beyond it, the passage opened out, with brick walls giving way to concrete. An opening on the right gave access to what smelled, and then looked, as he shone his torch into it, like an ill-ventilated latrine.

Beyond this the structure assumed the form of a very much more substantial version of the Anderson shelters that gave protection against air raids in so many gardens up and down the country. Corrugated iron, though when Bob reached to his left and tapped it, it seemed much thicker than normal corrugated iron, formed an arched roof and walls. When Bob shone his torch at the floor, he could see it had been formed from thick planks or possibly railway sleepers. There was furniture in the room and wooden boxes were piled up against the wall on his right. In the centre of the room was a wooden table surrounded by four chairs. The left-hand side of the room was taken up by two sets of bunk beds. The far end wall was made of bricks and there was a doorway in it leading to another passage, this one apparently lined with the same corrugated iron as the main structure.

Bob was about to go and find out what was beyond the doorway when something, he wasn't sure what, caught his attention. He shone the torch at the far bottom bunk and could see it was occupied by a man wearing an army greatcoat with no visible rank or other badges. The man lay on his right side, facing towards the wall. Bob could see he had been shot in the back, but just to be sure reached over and felt the side of his neck. The man was dead and from the temperature of his skin he had been dead for some time.

Bob was about to shout out that he'd found a body when he realised that his dad was already well aware of it. This man was going nowhere unless carried. No wonder his dad had been happy to chat over a cup of tea in Bob's office.

Bob heard a movement from behind and swung his torch round to see Anthony Darlington, also carrying a torch, entering the main room followed by Bob's dad. Another noise preceded the emergence through the doorway ahead of him of Inspector Nicholls.

'It seems that we've found the back door,' said the inspector.

'What the hell is this place?' asked Bob.

'We were rather hoping you might be able to tell us, Bob,' said his father.

'I think that perhaps I can,' said Captain Darlington.

*

The squadron commander was, the adjutant said, on leave in southern England, so they gathered around the wooden meeting table in his office in Dundas Castle. Bob looked around and saw that there were maps covering most of one of the walls, while two windows looked out onto the grounds to the east of the castle. The walls flanking the door from the main entrance and around to the fireplace were occupied by wooden bookshelves, largely empty. They waited until a young aircraftwoman served tea and left, closing the door behind herself.

'I'm assuming your people had a chance to look at the body before we arrived, Dad,' said Bob.

'Yes, the police surgeon said the cause of death seemed to be a single gunshot wound to the back that caused major internal damage. He'll take a closer look later but doesn't expect that opinion to change. In his view it was a miracle that the man was able to get up after being shot, still less make it back to the bunker we found him in. He seems to have died quite soon after he got there. I decided we should leave him there to give you a better idea of the way in which he'd holed up. We're removing the body now.'

'Do we know who he was?'

'No, that's part of the mystery. We initially searched the body for evidence of identity but found nothing at all.'

'No identity discs, sir?' asked Captain Darlington.

'No, absolutely nothing, I'm afraid. We will obviously search the bunker thoroughly, but for the moment all I can say about the dead man is that he seemed to be in his forties, had dark hair, was perhaps a little over average height, and he was wearing an army uniform.'

'I couldn't see any rank or unit badges on his greatcoat,' said Bob.

'It was difficult to be sure without moving him, but there didn't seem to be any on the battledress uniform he was wearing underneath it either,' said his father. 'Which leaves us with a mystery body in a mystery bunker. Captain Darlington, you said you might know something about the bunker. This would be a good moment to enlighten us.'

Bob looked across the table at Anthony Darlington He'd poached the captain to join MI11 on promotion the previous October. Bob knew that he was 26 years old, having celebrated a birthday in February, and that he had impressed while serving as a junior officer in an infantry unit in France in the retreat to Dunkirk in 1940. He'd then been very highly rated at the Commando Basic Training Centre at Achnacarry where he'd been sent as an instructor after the discovery of his talent for unarmed combat and knife fighting, which was where Bob had met him. The captain had fitted in well since joining MI11, rather better than he had himself, Bob sometimes thought.

Darlington looked like he was working out where to begin, then turned to look at Superintendent Sutherland. 'I'm not sure what it was like in Scotland in 1940, sir, after Dunkirk, but in southern England it was absolute chaos. Far more of us had escaped from France than ever seemed possible, but we'd left virtually all our vehicles and equipment behind us. Everyone expected the German army to turn up on the beaches of Kent or Dorset or Norfolk or wherever at any time; under skies darkened by German parachute troops. We'd seen how shockingly effective blitzkrieg warfare could be and had to assume that the Nazis would find a way of overcoming the barrier of the English Channel. As we now know, it didn't happen. With hindsight I think that was partly because of the strength of the Royal Navy, and partly because of the group captain and his colleagues in Fighter Command, who prevented the Luftwaffe gaining the control of the skies over southern England that the Nazis needed to counter our naval superiority and mount a successful invasion.

'But at the time the threat was so real and imminent it felt like a looming physical presence. My unit, the 5th Battalion of the Gloucestershire Regiment, suffered serious casualties in France and the immediate task was to build it back up to operational capability, something the surviving senior officers succeeded in doing quite quickly despite shortages of everything from boots to ammunition. We were then assigned to man coastal defences in Cornwall.

'One day, just before Christmas 1940, I was summoned to see my lieutenant colonel and told I was being posted to an unusual unit and that I should report to a place called Coleshill House in the Vale of the White Horse immediately after Christmas. I didn't want to leave the regiment but was told I should consider my selection as recognition that I had done well and that, in any case, I had no choice. I suppose that was the start of a rather irregular career path for an army officer that now finds me working for the group captain in MI11.

'Coleshill House, it turned out, was the training base and operational headquarters for the Auxiliary Units then being formed across areas of England and Scotland considered vulnerable to German invasion.'

'I've never heard of them,' said Bob. 'What do they do?'

'I think I have,' said his father, 'though only vaguely and not for quite some time. I assumed they'd ceased to exist after the threat of invasion diminished. Carry on, captain, you've got me thoroughly intrigued.'

'Auxiliary Units were set up from the summer of 1940 with the support of Winston Churchill. They were intended to be established and to operate in total secrecy. They formed "operational patrols" of between four and eight men who were highly trained and equipped: certainly at the time I was posted away from Coleshill House in late 1941. At one level the units looked and acted as if they were part of the Home Guard, but in terms of command structure they were separate. This did allow them a plausible cover for their activities, though.

'Their role was, put simply, to prepare for a German

invasion and when it happened, go to ground and let the invasion roll over them. Once the immediate fighting had died down, they would emerge at night to operate as guerrilla units, harrying the enemy. To allow this to happen, each patrol had an operational base and what we saw a little while ago was a typical example of one. They were constructed in total secrecy, sometimes by the Auxiliary Units themselves, but more often by units of the Royal Engineers who specialised in the job. If necessary, curious locals were given a cover story that it was an ammunition or supplies store or a sewerage works being built, but I think that for the most part the operational bases were excavated and prepared without anyone in the area knowing what was happening.'

'That's interesting,' said Flight Lieutenant Dean. '948 Squadron took over Dundas Castle in November 1939. I was with the unit at the time. I do recall some work being done in that part of the estate the following autumn by the Royal Engineers. Something to do with improving the water supply for the castle though I remember the commanding officer at the time thought that was odd as we'd not complained about the water. Are you saying we've had a secret commando unit based in our back yard ever since then?'

'Not actually a commando unit, but a highly trained and equipped group of men, yes.'

'But it's March 1943,' said Bob. 'The last time anyone seriously believed the country was going to be subject to a large-scale invasion was quite some time ago. Are you saying that these Auxiliary Units are still active, under our noses and without anyone knowing about them?'

'I don't know, sir. As I said, I moved on in late 1941. But from what we've seen today, it appears that they may well have some sort of continuing existence.'

'I'm finding this quite remarkable,' said Bob. 'We've got clandestine military units operating on our patch and knew nothing at all about them?'

'That was rather the intention, sir.'

'Yes, I can see that. It seems to me that our top priority must be to identify the man who was killed last night and to find out if he was operating alone or with others. The idea of some sort of guerrilla unit operating to its own agenda within a few miles of Edinburgh sends chills down my spine. Do you know how they were, or are, commanded in Scotland? How many other operational patrols might there be?'

'Across Britain, we set up literally hundreds of patrols, each with its own operational base. My main area of interest was southern England, so I really can't help on the number or their organisation in Scotland. The Auxiliary Units in England operated under the guise of a couple of Home Guard battalions, though they weren't units you'd find on any organisational chart of the Home Guard. As for a reporting line, I don't know, but I would imagine that they report to the army's Scottish Command.'

'It may be time for me to make a phone call to Edinburgh Castle then,' said Bob. 'My point of contact in Scottish Command is the deputy commander there, Brigadier General Sir Richard Blackett. Let's see if he's heard of the Auxiliary Units. Do you have a secure phone I can use, Flight Lieutenant Dean?'

CHAPTER THREE

Bob had great confidence in Private Jenkins' driving, just as he had in Anthony Darlington's map-reading. But for whatever reason, the journey had taken rather longer than he'd expected from his initial scrutiny of a map on the wall of the squadron commander's office in Dundas Castle.

They'd swept past the queue of vehicles waiting for the ferry to take them across the Queensferry Passage, claiming military priority. In the face of a protest from an army major also wanting to be at the head of the queue, Bob had simply pulled rank. Bob had stayed in the car on board the *Queen Margaret,* while Anthony and Taffy walked to the side of the deck to enjoy their cigarettes.

Since taking up post in MI11, Bob had never commented when someone else lit up, but his colleagues seemed to have drawn their own conclusions about their new boss quite quickly. He never smoked cigarettes and was a self-declared 'pipe man' who never lit his pipe, in fact he wasn't sure where it was. The truth was that he just didn't like the sensation of smoking cigarettes. His colleagues had simply stopped smoking around him, which he found a pleasant change in a world in which it was the norm to be breathing in someone else's smoke in just about every confined space and in many open ones.

Brigadier General Blackett was a man who Bob found hard to read and he'd not sounded particularly pleased to be called out of a meeting to the phone that morning. Having heard what Bob had to say he had, however, told him what he needed to know. The barest minimum he needed to know, certainly, but enough to be going on with. The man he needed to talk to was a

Major Brian Spottiswood and the place he needed to go to talk to him was called Melville House, which could be found towards the northern side of Fife. The brigadier had agreed to get someone to make sure Spottiswood knew Bob was coming to see him without telling him why.

Now they just needed to find Melville House.

'The railway bridge over the road in the last village was right for it to have been Collessie,' said Anthony, looking at an Ordnance Survey map that the RAF at Dundas Castle had given him. 'That will make this place up ahead, in these woods, Monimail. We need to turn right in the centre, Taffy. If we get to a church we've gone too far.'

'It would make life a lot easier if they put the road signs back, sir,' said Private Jenkins.

'True,' said Bob, 'but it seems that's not the only relic we're still living with from a time when we all thought we were about to be invaded.'

The two guards at the barrier they encountered at the start of the drive to Melville House had clearly been told to expect Bob, which he thought was a good sign.

Bob leaned forwards in the back seat as they approached, better to see through the windscreen. 'Wow! It seems to be our day for visiting the unknown great houses of central Scotland. I'm not sure what I was expecting, but this place seems enormous.'

Melville House was an extremely imposing four-storey stately home clad in harling. Their approach gave them a rear corner view of the house, which from this angle seemed almost square in plan. Off to the left as they approached was what was probably originally a farmstead and as they got closer Bob realised that there was an outlying two-storey building set forwards from the left-hand corner of the main house as they were looking at it. Bob wouldn't have minded betting it had a matching counterpart on the far side.

A group of half a dozen men in army uniforms and carrying rifles was walking across the grass near the road towards what Bob recognised was a firing range, some distance to the north of the house.

'At the Commando Basic Training Centre, they'd be running,' said Captain Darlington.

The guards at the gate had clearly phoned ahead to let the occupants of the house know that Bob had arrived. As Taffy parked between an army staff car and a lorry opposite what seemed remarkably grand for a back entrance, a tall man aged about 50 and wearing a major's rank insignia on the epaulettes of his army battledress emerged and walked over to meet them.

He saluted, then shook Bob's hand. 'Hello sir. I'm Brian Spottiswood. Would you mind confirming who you are?'

Bob showed the major his pass. 'Group Captain Sutherland, from MI11. This is Captain Darlington, who works with me.'

'Thank you, sir. You'll understand that I had to check. I must admit I've never heard of MI11. Are you what happens when MI5 gets added to MI6?'

Bob laughed. 'I'm rather surprised I've never heard that joke before, major, but then I've not been in post for all that long. We are all part of the same family, but MI11 is much smaller than our better-known siblings. We look after military security. I must admit in return that until today I'd never heard of the Auxiliary Units. Is there somewhere we can talk?'

'My office is on the ground floor. Perhaps you could follow me? Your driver can get a cup of something warm and a bite to eat in the canteen in the basement.'

After tea had been served by a soldier wearing an unadorned and anonymous army battledress uniform, Bob found himself looking round a room that had seen better days. It occupied one corner of the ground floor and had windows on two sides. The wood panelling that lined the walls had once been magnificent but was now faded and stained and in need of a lot of care and attention. There was a wood fire burning in the fireplace. The desk, table and chairs were military issue and looked totally out of place in their surroundings.

Major Spotswood saw him looking around. 'I tend to think of it as "military utility", group captain.'

Bob smiled. 'To be honest, I was thinking that you are the first army officer I've ever met who didn't cover his office walls in large maps.'

'A large map of Scotland with a series of small red dots on it might be something of a breach of security, in the circumstances, group captain.'

'Yes, very true.'

'Though I've never heard of MI11 before, it was made clear to me by his aide-de-camp that Brigadier Blackett has heard of you, and that I am to offer you every cooperation. What can I do for you?'

Bob told the major what had happened at Dundas Castle and what they had found. 'I appreciate the need for security, but we badly need to know who the man is who was killed last night. More widely, I need you to fill me in on the background to Auxiliary Units in Scotland. Clearly no one realistically believes we are likely to be invaded now, so what's the rationale for keeping them in being and how widespread are they? I find the idea of highly trained and well-armed guerrillas wandering round my patch a slightly unsettling one. I should add that Captain Darlington here has provided me with some of the background as he spent much of 1941 at Coleshill House, helping set up units in southern England.'

The major looked at Anthony. 'It's possible our paths crossed.'

'I think they did, briefly, sir. I reported to Lieutenant Colonel Bruce "Screw Loose" Whitworth. I suppose if your surname coincides with a standard for screw threads, and if your leadership style is borderline psychopathic, then you risk having an unflattering nickname. I heard he was killed in a training accident involving a hand grenade not long after I left.'

Bob realised that the major had been setting a test for Anthony, which he had passed.

The major turned to look at Bob. 'Very well, group captain. I'm ordered to be open with you and that's what I'll be. I'll take you down to the basement where we keep our organisational and personnel files presently to see if we can identify the man who died. I'll also try to arrange for you to speak to the captain who commands the units in the Edinburgh area and south-eastern Scotland. For the moment, however, it might be most useful if I fill in the Scottish dimension of the picture that I imagine Captain Darlington has painted for you and bring it up to date with developments over the past year.

'Melville House serves as the Scottish headquarters of, and training centre for, the Auxiliary Units. I suppose that even though the threat of invasion was effectively countered by the Royal Air Force's victory in the Battle of Britain in the summer and autumn of 1940, the high priority given to establishing, training, and equipping Auxiliary Units carried on throughout 1941.

'By the end of that year we had about 100 patrols

established across Scotland, with heavy coverage down the eastern side for obvious reasons, but also as far afield as the Outer Hebrides and Shetland. In all we had some 650 men serving in Auxiliary Units in Scotland at the end of 1941. Nominally we formed, and continue to form, 201 Battalion of the Home Guard, but we've always operated entirely separately from that organisation.

'No one who was involved was under any illusion about what would become of members of the Auxiliary Units if there was an invasion. Even the most optimistic projections were that members would be hunted down and killed within a few days, or at most a couple of weeks, of emerging from their operational bases. There is a separate part of the organisation, the Special Duties Branch, intended to allow covert communication in a country under Nazi control, but the operational patrols would have been entirely on their own with no communications links to anyone else. In effect, to volunteer to join an operational patrol was to volunteer for a suicide mission and all our men were fully aware of that.' The major looked at Anthony Darlington, who nodded.

He continued. 'If you could characterise 1941 as continuing growth despite the diminishing threat, then 1942 might be summarised as a year of keeping ourselves hidden behind a cloak of secrecy and hoping that no one in power realised or remembered just how much resource we were consuming against an eventuality that, to be honest, no one any longer believed was likely to arise.'

'You are being very frank with me, major.'

'There's no reason not to be, sir. Sooner or later reality was bound to catch up with the Auxiliary Units. For the last year or so, efforts have been made to avert the inevitable by redefining

Auxiliary Units as an anti-raiding force, but that was never very convincing, even to those of us on the inside. It's not widely known, but there was a raid by German commandos on the east coast of northern Scotland last September. It was exactly the sort of thing that we were trying to convince the War Office that the Auxiliary Units could counter, but in the event the Germans were rounded up by regular troops garrisoned in and around Inverness. The Auxiliary Units in the area, and there were a few, never got off their starting blocks, partly because we were hiding behind our veil of secrecy and no one involved in dealing with the problem knew or remembered we existed.'

The major looked at Bob. 'You don't seem very surprised to hear that, sir.'

'I have to admit that I'm one of those who overlooked the existence of the Auxiliary Units when the Brandenburg Regiment came knocking on our doors dressed as Polish soldiers.' Bob blushed as he remembered that they had, literally, knocked on his door, and who he had been with at the time. He briefly wondered what Lady Alice Gough was doing now. His embarrassment caused him to proceed more bluntly than he had intended. 'I was the one who stood in for King George and who shot their commanding officer.'

'Ah, I see.' The major smiled. 'In one sense you didn't do us any favours, sir, but congratulations nonetheless.'

Bob could see that what he had said was news to Anthony Darlington too. 'You are giving the sense, major, that reality, as you put it, has now caught up with the Auxiliary Units.'

'That's correct sir. It's always been the case that anyone volunteering for the Auxiliary Units was exempt from call-up to the mainstream armed forces. For some that was an incentive to join, though we have always tried to weed out anyone applying simply so they could shirk military service. Increasingly over the past year we've seen the opposite happening, with our most able and fittest members leaving the Auxiliary Units so they could do their bit in the more regular services. This has led to a serious decline in numbers, to the extent that some patrols are down to only a couple of men, and often the least motivated or fit. We are still trying to recruit to fill the gaps but it's an uphill struggle. If this had been eighteen months ago, there would have been several groups of recruits or existing members undergoing training here at any given time. At the moment we have just one small group of recruits here and a slightly larger group of existing members. As a result, we do rather rattle around in the house these days, with parts of it seldom used.

'What I suspect will turn out to be the final nail in the coffin came last month when a report commissioned by the War Office led to the cancellation of the exemption from call-up for members of Auxiliary Units. This effectively means that any current members who are between 18 and 51 years old and not in a reserved occupation will be called up for service. It's already starting to happen. What this means, as with the mainstream Home Guard, is that our pool of potential recruits is now confined to those aged over 51 or under 18, or those in reserved occupations and as such exempt from call-up.'

'Thank you for being so open with me,' said Bob. 'Can we turn to specifics? What can you tell me about the operational patrol operating from the grounds of Dundas Castle?'

'Off the top of my head, nothing other than to confirm that there is one. Perhaps you'd care to follow me, and we can find out together.' Major Spottiswood led Bob and Anthony out of his office and down to the basement of Melville House. A locked door at the end of a corridor opened to reveal more steps going down to a lower level, and another door, this one apparently made of metal and protected by a combination lock.

'There have long been stories of tunnels associated with Melville House,' said the major. 'We did find this underground chamber which might have been something to do with one of them. Either way, with a bit of work it's proved an ideal place in which to keep our more sensitive files.'

'I understand why your security is so tight,' said Bob after they'd passed through the thick metal door into a small room with an arched stone ceiling. One wall was lined with eight metal four-drawer filing cabinets. 'Presumably, the information kept down here could have compromised the entire operation?'

'That's right, sir. I did try to get them to install pipes with explosives under the floor of this room, but that was deemed to be over the top and perhaps prone to an unfortunate accident.' He gestured at a wooden box on top of the filing cabinet nearest the door. 'That's my alternative in case German paratroopers ever land on the lawn. There are half a dozen phosphorus grenades in there. I've no real idea if I could destroy the files in these cabinets with them, but I'd certainly be prepared to give it a try. Files for the Edinburgh area ought to be in this one.'

The major spent a few moments dialling in the combination needed to remove the security bar from the front of the cabinet he'd pointed at, then a few more hunting through the next to bottom drawer.

'Here we go.' He held up a brown cardboard covered file marked very prominently in red on its front and rear covers, at top and bottom, with the word 'secret'. He turned and opened the file on a small table set against the other side wall of the cellar.

'It seems that the patrol based in the grounds of Dundas

Castle is down to just two established members and that one of them has been in hospital and then convalescing at home since a fairly serious stroke early in December. We are keeping him on the books, so to speak, more because we think it gives him something positive to aim for than because we really believe he will recover fully enough to take up his duties again. A third long-standing member left to join the navy last November and another left earlier in the year. There are, in addition, three young volunteers and an older man who could be assigned to the patrol and who have undergone some initial training, but it seems in the balance whether that patrol is now sustainable or whether it will have to be merged with another in the area. The situation is made worse because the last established member of the patrol may himself be subject to call-up under the new rules. According to the last report on the file, written two weeks ago, it's not clear whether his job in the clerk of works' office at Edinburgh Castle would be considered a reserved occupation or not. It seems a case had been made to exempt him from call-up, but a decision, at that point at least, was still awaited.'

'That rather narrows things down, doesn't it?' asked Bob. 'All I can really tell you about the man whose body we found was that he seemed to be in his forties, had dark hair and might have been a little over average height. Would that describe the last active member of the patrol?'

The major turned back to the cabinets. 'Personnel files are in the last three cabinets. The man we are interested in is called Edgar Ross, so I think he should be in the one at the end.'

The major again dialled in a combination to remove a security bar from the front of the cabinet. 'The personnel files each have a small photograph. This is Edgar Ross, who in Home Guard terms is serving as a sergeant.'

'We didn't see him at his best this morning,' said Bob, 'but that could well be the man we found. His hair colour and age of 43 is right. Can we take some notes from the file, home and work addresses and so on, so we can do some digging?'

'In the circumstances, of course sir. I hope I can go one better, though. The man overseeing the Dundas Castle patrol, and all the others from the English border up to the River Forth, is Captain John Elphick. He's past normal retirement age but came to us with a wealth of experience including active service in the Great War. He was promoted from the ranks back in the early 1920s and has done an excellent job, both when the Auxiliary Units were being set up and now when we are trying to manage their decline. He will know Edgar Ross well. It was his most recent report that I was drawing on in telling you about the Dundas Castle patrol just now.'

'Is he based here?' asked Bob.

'No, sir. He works from an office in Redford Barracks in Edinburgh. I'll try to get him on the telephone from my office. I should warn you that he's often out and about, visiting his patrols, so I can't guarantee I'll be able to raise him immediately.'

Bob looked at his watch. 'If you can, then it might expedite things if we can put him in touch with Inspector Nicholls in Edinburgh. If he could go and identify the body in the mortuary while we are driving back to the city, it would give our talk with him a much clearer focus. It will take us a little while to get back.'

'Yes, we are rather out of the way, sir. We normally suggest that visitors come by train. The station at Ladybank is only a few miles to the south.'

In the event, the major was able to contact Captain Elphick

in his office and found him happy to help as much as he could.

The major escorted Bob and Anthony back to the car, where Taffy Jenkins was waiting.

As they drove away, the sound of gunfire could be heard from the firing range. 'I can see how it's come about, sir,' said Anthony, 'but I do find this lingering existence of the Auxiliary Units quite strange.'

'I agree,' said Bob. 'Right now, though, I'm regretting we didn't have time to join Taffy for a bite to eat.'

'No sooner said than done, sir,' said Private Jenkins from the driver's seat. He slowed the car and reached down into the front passenger footwell, then passed a brown paper bag back to Anthony Darlington, who was sitting next to Bob in the back seat.

'What's that?' asked Bob.

'Corned beef sandwiches for both of you from the Melville House canteen, sir, and a couple of not very nice chocolate bars. But you know what they say about beggars and choosers. I've got a thermos of tea in the boot, too.'

CHAPTER FOUR

When he was shown into Bob's office, Captain Elphick saluted as Bob walked over from his desk to meet him. The captain was not what Bob had been expecting. He looked to be aged about 60 and was about average height and wiry in build. He had a large grey moustache and a black patch over his right eye that was held in place by a cord round his head. The surprise was in what he was wearing. Given the informality and anonymity of the uniforms Bob had seen being worn by everyone he'd encountered who was connected with the Auxiliary Units, the last thing he expected was a man in what seemed to be an old-fashioned cavalry officer's uniform, complete with highly polished Sam Browne belt and holster, long brown leather boots and riding breeches.

The captain's uniform was immaculately pressed, in a way that made Bob's feel decidedly second-hand in comparison, and the man was wearing an impressive collection of medal ribbons, only some of which Bob recognised. Bob saw the captain's glance shift towards the ribbons on his own tunic before he smiled and reached out his hand.

'Captain John Elphick at your service, sir.'

'Hello, I'm Group Captain Sutherland and this is Captain Anthony Darlington, who heads up my army team. I am responsible for the northern operations of Military Intelligence Section 11. As you know, we are looking into the death of a man found this morning in a bunker in the grounds of Dundas Castle. Take a seat and we'll get some tea.'

After Joyce had served tea, Anthony turned to their visitor. 'Were you able to identify the body in the mortuary?'

'Yes, it was definitely Sergeant Edgar Ross. I understand he was shot in the back after failing to obey an instruction to stop by sentries at Dundas Castle. A bloody silly way to go, if you ask me, and worse still if he was, as they suspect, behind the attack on a sentry there last week.'

'What can you tell us about him?' asked Bob.

'Ross had been with the Auxiliary Units since we first started to set up in the area in late 1940. He showed promise, so was promoted to sergeant to become the senior man in the Dundas Castle patrol. He seems to have been an effective leader over most of that time. The patrol had six members early in 1941 though this fell to a core of four by early last year. But the best of the other members left to join the regular army last March, and another long-standing member joined the Royal Navy in November. That left just two, and Edgar's only remaining comrade suffered a stroke last December and is highly unlikely to return to duty.'

'That left Sergeant Ross on his own?'

'Yes, I instructed him to mothball the operational base at Dundas Castle and attach himself to another patrol that operates to the south of Edinburgh. This has an operational base in countryside near Newtongrange and is manned by miners from the nearby collieries. He has only occasionally shown up for gatherings of the Newtongrange patrol. I'd been trying to decide whether it was worth assigning some new recruits we have - a very precious commodity these days - to revive the Dundas Castle patrol or whether to close it down entirely. His response to his temporary reassignment was leading me towards deciding on the latter course of action.'

'Weren't you in a position simply to order Sergeant Ross to commit himself to the Newtongrange patrol?' asked Anthony.

'A little diplomacy tends to go a long way in dealing with irregulars, especially irregulars who are virtually all asking whether the reasons why they joined the Auxiliary Units in the first place still have any relevance. Morale is an issue right across the patrols, but there are two reasons why I was treating Sergeant Ross particularly carefully. Some who know me would say uncharacteristically carefully.'

'Major Spottiswood told us about the doubts over his exemption from call-up since the rules were changed last month,' said Bob.

'Yes, sir. Ross had for some years worked in the clerk of works' office at Edinburgh Castle. He was exempt from call-up because of his work with the Auxiliary Units, and the question was never asked whether he would be exempt anyway because of his work at the castle. I understand that the man he reported to, the clerk of works, is exempt. The castle had made a case for Ross's exemption, but last time I checked, last week, no decision had been made.'

'You talked of two reasons,' said Bob.

'Yes sir, I did. Edgar Ross had been apparently happily married to his wife, Mary, for over twenty years. They had no children, but I never had the sense this was something that worried him. You will probably recall the outbreak of smallpox in Edinburgh in November last year. There were over twenty cases in all, and five people died. One of those, tragically, was Mary Ross.

'It was obvious that this had a huge impact on Sergeant Ross. He once talked to me of her being his reason for living, but seemed to bottle up his feelings most of the time. Given this coincided with the reduction in the core membership of the patrol at Dundas Castle from three to two, which became just one the following month, I'm sure you will understand why I was prepared to handle Ross with kid gloves and overlook his lack of commitment to the Newtongrange patrol.

'What is worrying me now, to be brutally honest with you, sir, is that if I'd been firmer in my approach he might have been left much less to his own devices. The man I've known for the past couple of years would never assault a woman. I'm wondering if I gave him so much leeway that he was able to have some sort of breakdown without anyone noticing. Which leaves me feeling rather responsible for what happened to that corporal at Dundas Castle last week and to Edgar Ross himself last night.'

'I'm sure you did what you felt was best for him at the time,' said Bob. 'None of us can ever hope to do more than that. Let's remember that he would have been in daily contact with colleagues at Edinburgh Castle who would have been much better placed than you to tell if he was heading off the rails because of his wife's death.'

'Thank you for saying so, sir, though that doesn't make me feel any happier about the situation.'

Bob turned to look at Anthony Darlington. 'I think we have the broad picture, but still need to tie up details. The day is getting on, but I'd be grateful if tomorrow you and Gilbert Potter, calling on Inspector Nicholls for extra pairs of hands as necessary, could mount a thorough search of the operational base at Dundas Castle, and of Sergeant Ross's home, which,' Bob looked at notes he had taken at Melville House, 'is a flat on Slateford Road. It's on this side of the city centre, so I suppose would have been ideally placed for getting to both Edinburgh Castle and Dundas Castle. You should keep a lookout for anything that seems odd, and in particular anything that ties him to the attack on the corporal last week. I'd also be grateful if you could speak to his colleagues at Edinburgh Castle and check whether he might have kept anything significant there.'

'Yes, sir, of course.'

'I think that's about everything, Captain Elphick. I'm very grateful to you for identifying the body and talking to us about Sergeant Ross. I'll make sure we let both you and Major Spottiswood know if we find anything else of significance.'

'Thank you, sir, but there is something else I need to discuss with you.'

'What's that?'

'I've been asked to talk to you, and at your discretion your colleague, about a related matter that might help complete the picture for you.'

'You've certainly got my full attention, captain.'

'I should say that I've been told to ask you not to discuss what I'm about to tell you with anyone outside the military intelligence community. It shouldn't be mentioned to the police, for example. And I'd particularly ask that no word of what I am about to tell you finds its way back to Major Spottiswood. He would consider it a grave personal betrayal on my part and it would become impossible for me to continue to work with the Auxiliary Units.'

'Please continue. You can count on our discretion.'

'Thank you, sir. I should start by saying that when the War Office decided to establish the Auxiliary Units in the summer of 1940 they were already rather behind the game. As early as February that year part of the Secret Intelligence Service, MI6 if you prefer, was already putting in place plans that would come into effect in the event of a German victory in western

Europe and an occupation of the United Kingdom.

'This involved establishing a communications network operated by small cells across the length and breadth of the UK. It was closely based on the highly effective spy network that SIS had been operating in Eire. The network is so secret it has never been given a name of its own, but it was initially formed under the deliberately misleading guise of SIS's "Section VII", which is their accountancy branch, and that's the name that has stuck ever since.

'In addition, from May 1940, SIS started highly secret recruitment for what they called their "Section D Home Defence Scheme". The HDS, as it was known, was intended to operate as a guerrilla army in an occupied UK and to pick up the baton once the initial resistance offered by the Auxiliary Units had been suppressed by an occupying force. Perhaps not surprisingly, the idea of SIS running its own unofficial army within the UK gave people pause for thought. The scheme was quite quickly halted, with elements being used to bolster the Auxiliary Units, the regular Home Guard and the "Section VII" cells, which quietly developed to form what would become a national resistance organisation within an occupied UK.

'What you need to know is that although the threat of invasion has diminished hugely, to the point where the future of the Auxiliary Units is in considerable doubt, so far at least that has been much less of an issue for the SIS Section VII cells: which remain largely in being and are highly equipped and highly motivated.'

'Do these Section VII cells exist across Scotland as well as England?' asked Bob.

'Yes sir. But unlike with the Auxiliary Units, you will never find a centralised set of records telling you who they are, or where, or what they do.'

'What's your role in this?' asked Bob.

'I'm the Scottish coordinator for the Section VII cells, reporting back to SIS in London. My role overseeing the Auxiliary Units across part of the country is a perfect cover for what I do. The persona I create of a caricature chocolate soldier is intended to dispel any thoughts that I might be anything else. Brian Spottiswood has been a very good friend and would be absolutely appalled if he knew what I'd just told you. I sometimes wonder what I'll say if I bump into him in some distant part of Scotland where, as far as he's concerned, I'm not meant to be. Those I report to in SIS are, on the other hand, fully aware of and entirely supportive of my role with the Auxiliary Units.'

'On a strictly need to know basis,' said Bob, 'the captain and I could probably have done our jobs without hearing what you've just told us.'

'I agree, sir. I'm told that there's a new spirit of openness and cooperation sweeping across the previously deeply byzantine and untrusting world of the military intelligence sections in Whitehall, but that alone isn't why I've been instructed to brief you about the Section VII cells.'

'Why, then?' asked Bob.

'Until her death, Mary Ross had been a member of a Section VII cell. I don't believe she ever told her husband, but his absences in connection with his own clandestine duties allowed her to make a significant contribution. After she died, two of her fellow cell-members visited the Ross's flat, when we knew Edgar would be absent, to look for anything incriminating she might have left there. They had already been inoculated for smallpox because of their contact with Mary at the time she fell ill, and that's something the captain here and the police might need to consider before searching the flat, though I understand transmission of the disease is normally from person to person. Anyway, nothing incriminating was found but you are going to have the opportunity to be much more thorough.'

'You want us to keep a lookout for anything relating to Mary Ross's Section VII work during our search,' said Anthony, 'and keep anything we find from the police.'

'That's it, exactly,' said Captain Elphick.

'I can agree to that,' said Bob.

'I'm having some difficulty digesting what you've been telling us,' said Anthony Darlington. 'I spent most of 1941 at Coleshill House helping establish Auxiliary Units across southern England. Are you telling us that the whole thing was pointless because the Secret Intelligence Service had got there first, but without anyone thinking to tell us?'

'Not at all, captain. If the Germans had invaded, then there's a real sense of "the more the merrier" in terms of resistance to them. There would certainly have been plenty of scope for the Auxiliary Units to do what they were trained to do.'

Bob thought he could see where this was going. 'I suppose from SIS Section VII's point of view, it would have been ideal to have the Auxiliary Units active in the aftermath of an invasion because they would have distracted the Nazi's attention from the real resistance.'

'That's right, sir,' said Captain Elphick. 'It would never cross the Germans' minds that we might be so uncoordinated as to be operating two entirely separate resistance organisations. Once they'd rounded up the Auxiliary Units, they'd have thought that was the job done and it would have taken the pressure off the Section VII cells.'

'My God,' said Anthony, 'so from the SIS point of view the operational patrols were nothing more than decoys?'

'I'm afraid so. Though from a War Office perspective their role remained as important as ever, until the threat of invasion effectively disappeared.'

'I can see why Major Spottiswood would be unhappy,' said Anthony.

'I think he'd probably kill me if he knew of my dual role, and no, that's not a joke.'

'Thank you for telling me, captain,' said Bob. 'And please pass my thanks back to whoever asked you to let us in on the secret. Before you go, do you mind if I ask you a personal question?'

'I suppose that depends on what it is, sir, but no.'

'What happened to your eye?'

Captain Elphick reached up to touch the patch over his right eye and smiled. 'Ah, a souvenir of China. My unit was part of the international force put in place to protect Shanghai's European Quarter in 1927 when the Chinese civil war got underway. One night in a dark alley, in a part of the city I really shouldn't have been in, someone threw a dart at me. This was the result. I've tried a glass eye from time to time, but frankly feel more comfortable with the patch. Why do you ask, sir?'

'I lost the sight in my left eye when I was shot down at the beginning of November 1940. The eye still functions, but a wound in my left temple cut the optic nerve, leaving me functionally blind on that side.'

'Judging by your medal ribbons, you got a few before they got you, sir.'

'Officially the number is 22. By my count it's 24. But the loss of three-dimensional vision got me grounded. I have slowly adapted and even more slowly returned to flying, though only in daylight. At night I find it impossible to judge depth. After a gap of not far short of two years, I shot down a Luftwaffe intruder I met by chance off the coast of Caithness last September but misjudged my attack to the point where I nearly collided with it. You've had longer to get used to the loss of sight in one eye. How have you adapted over time?'

'It's difficult to remember timescales, sir, and I've never piloted anything in my life, so can't really comment on that. As far as driving is concerned, which is the nearest experience I can offer, I found I was increasingly better able to cope over a period of time, a few years I think, and then I reached a plateau and have stayed at that level since. I drive a lot in my job, in both of my jobs, and still find it quite challenging in the blackout at night.'

'Yes, I avoid night driving when I can. Anyway, thank you again, captain, and I'll make sure we keep you in touch with what we find out about Sergeant Ross. I'll also let you know if we find anything relating to Mary Ross's work with Section VII.'

After Bob had shown Captain Elphick out, he returned to find Anthony sitting at the meeting table.

He looked up as Bob entered. 'Have you ever wished you could un-know something, sir? It's not pleasant thinking that I spent nearly a year of my life setting up, in effect, decoys for the Secret Intelligence Service.'

'I know what you mean, Anthony. Can I leave this to you and Sergeant Potter tomorrow, as we discussed? Make sure that you are both inoculated against smallpox before going near the flat, and mention that to Inspector Nicholls, too. As for now, I think it's about time we called it a day. How are you finding living in the officers' mess here?'

'Now some of them have started talking to me again after I highlighted their security problems, I'm doing fine, sir. As far as smallpox is concerned, I'm pretty sure I was inoculated against it before being sent to France at the beginning of 1940, but I'll check, and I'll talk to Gilbert to make sure he's been inoculated too.'

'OK. Goodnight then.'

CHAPTER FIVE

Bob was a great fan of having daylight saving time in place all year round, and a double dose of it in summer. It meant that the evenings seemed so much lighter than he remembered from before the war.

It also meant that although it was after 7 p.m. he could drive back to the bungalow in Featherhall Crescent knowing he had over half an hour before the sun set and over an hour before it became dark. You paid for the light evenings in the mornings, of course, but somehow Bob just preferred it this way.

Having parked his RAF staff car on the street outside the bungalow, he unlocked the front door and knew immediately that he wasn't alone.

'Hello Bob!' Monique had obviously heard the front door and came out of the lounge with a broad smile on her face.

Bob grinned and looked at her. She was, like himself, 30 years old. In fact, she was seven months younger than him. She was dark haired and classically beautiful in an attractively flawed sort of way. But there were times when, especially if she was caught unawares, her eyes could take on a slightly haunted look. Bob knew enough of her story to understand why that was. There was no sign of that right now, for which Bob was profoundly grateful.

'When did you get back?' he asked.

'Less than a quarter of an hour ago. I had my last meeting very early this morning and then caught a train from King's Cross a little before 10 a.m. It's a lot slower than flying but first class wasn't too crowded. I got a taxi from Waverley Station. The journey wasn't that bad, really.'

'I could have organised a flight from Northolt.'

'I know, Bob, but I hadn't been sure until this morning that I'd be coming back today. Yvette sends her regards, by the way.'

Yvette was an MI5 friend of Monique's whose West End flat she, and on one occasion she and Bob, stayed at in London. Bob hadn't told Monique that Yvette had shown an overt interest in him during their stay, quietly offering to put him up if he ever found himself in the capital on his own. Bob had always tended to stay at the RAF Club on Piccadilly when in the city on his own and on the one occasion he'd spent the night in London since meeting Yvette, he had made sure he stayed well away from both her and her flat.

'How did the visit go?' he asked. 'I could see on Thursday night that what had happened in Fraserburgh had upset you a little.'

'I suppose I'm back to my more sanguine norm now. To my mind the problem was mainly about the failure of those running the operation to be honest with their senior officers in MI5 after they'd realised what had happened. It seems they were unaware that when the Luftwaffe parachuted Stan Harrison into Scotland at the end of September last year, they tried to mount a diversionary air raid at the same time on Aberdeen but failed to find it because of cloud conditions. It was in my report about that operation but for good reason not many people had seen it. If those involved had known what had happened on that occasion, they might have realised in advance that their call for an air drop of supplies could also lead to a diversionary raid.

'But they didn't, so can't really be blamed for what happened. As I said, though, their decisions after the raids are more open to question and have led to their being given rather less responsible roles within the organisation until they have proven their judgement and ability. Nothing can bring that little boy back, though.

'The local parish priest told me that earlier in the war that north-eastern tip of the country was attacked so often that it became known as "Hellfire Corner". He said that Fraserburgh had been attacked over 20 times, and Peterhead even more. It was the easiest part of the country for Luftwaffe units based in Norway to reach, and the hardest part to defend. These latest attacks were a huge shock to the local population because they came after such a long gap. Anyway, changing the subject, what have you eaten?'

'Nothing since some corned beef sandwiches Taffy Jenkins acquired for Anthony Darlington and me during a visit to Fife earlier today.'

Monique took a step back. 'Your uniform's getting loose.' She reached out to press a finger against the left-hand side of his chest. 'Even your pistol's becoming a little less visible under your jacket. What were you planning to eat tonight if I'd not been here?'

'I thought I'd walk up to the fish and chip shop on St John's Road.'

'Is that all you've been eating while I've been away?'

'Friday night, yes. But Saturday night and last night I dined in the officers' mess at RAF Turnhouse.'

'That's something, I suppose. Although I didn't know what time you were getting back, I telephoned the North British Hotel as soon as I got in and, as we're regulars and they are quiet tonight, they were happy to reserve a table for dinner in your name. If you get yourself sorted, I'll telephone for a taxi.'

'I could drive.'

'You could, but I fancy some of their very nice champagne and don't really want to drink on my own. I don't think either of us wants to drive back in the blackout after a few glasses of bubbly.'

*

'Why do I get the sense you don't like Yvette, Bob?'

They'd been shown to their table in a dining room at the North British Hotel that was indeed 'quiet' and were enjoying their first glasses of champagne. As on previous visits to this Edinburgh institution, dominating the eastern end of Princes Street and towering over the city's Waverley Station, Bob noted that although wartime regulations now controlled the maximum price of restaurant meals, there was no such control over drinks prices.

'It's not that I don't like her, Monique.'

'What is it, then?'

'If you want the honest truth, it's that I find her just a little predatory.'

Monique choked back a laugh, clearly trying not to spill her champagne. 'Why would you think that?'

'Since you ask, it's because when we stayed at her flat, she took me to one side and said I was welcome to stay any time I was in London on my own.'

'Oh dear, Bob, you are priceless. Did you think she was trying to steal you away from me?'

'It did feel that way, yes.'

'Please don't take this personally, Bob, but you really aren't Yvette's type. Her tastes are more, how can I put this, sapphic in nature.'

'You mean she's a lesbian?'

Monique laughed again. 'I'm sure I've told you this before, Bob, but for a senior officer in British intelligence you really do need to work harder at keeping your thoughts from showing on your face. To answer your next two question and save a lot of time, yes, Yvette and I did have a relationship for a while after I first joined MI5 from SIS, but it was over before I met you. And no, when I stay at her flat, I sleep on my own. I've got you now and this weekend she had a nice young woman called Susan staying, who she recently met working in a shoe shop not far from her flat.'

'I'm sorry, Monique.'

'For being so transparent?'

'No. Well yes, partly. But mainly for wondering about you and Yvette.'

There was a pause as the soup they'd ordered for their starter was served.

'I do love you, you know, Bob. You needn't have worried about me and Yvette, or anyone else for that matter.'

'I know, Monique. I just sometimes feel a little out of my depth with you. I think it seems that way to others, too. I had a visitor turn up at the office this morning. It was my father.'

'A social call?'

'No, it was about a shooting at a RAF barrage balloon squadron headquarters near Queensferry. But in passing he said he had high hopes for you and me and that my mother did too.'

'I seem to remember telling you once, not long after we met, that no mother was going to be attracted to the idea of her son jumping into bed with a recovered cocaine addict who had slept her way round Europe by the time she was eighteen and could speak the languages of all the security services that actively wanted her dead. I know I told your father the outline of my story, but he's very much a man of the world.'

The main course was lamb with roast potatoes and vegetables and again there was a pause in the conversation while it was served.

'It seems that Dad has told Mum most of what he knows about you.'

'Oh, no! Really? He agreed not to tell anyone.'

'It seems he made an exception for Mum. According to him, he told her everything except for your threat to blow Uncle Frank's balls off in Kirkwall.'

'That's a shame. I was quite getting to like your mother.'

'It seems it's mutual. According to Dad, her reply was that it was nice to hear of a woman who had lived such a full life by the time she was 30. She apparently went on to tell him that I needed to make a real effort to keep you now that I'd found you.'

Monique was silent, looking down at her half-eaten main course. When she looked up, it was to wipe tears from her eyes with her napkin.

'I'm sorry, Monique, I didn't mean to upset you.'

'You're not upsetting me, silly. That was a lovely thing to hear, but so unexpected.'

When he and Monique had moved into the bungalow in Corstorphine together a few months earlier, it had felt like a terrifying leap in the dark to Bob. Now he felt on the verge of another.

'Monique, you said something else to me not long after we met. We were at Dunrobin Castle, and I was trying to persuade you to see me again after you returned to London.'

'I did see you again and look where we are now.'

'You said that your effect on the men you'd known was such that you'd made it a policy not to get close to anyone. That way you couldn't feel responsible if they ended up dead.'

'Remember that I put the policy aside sufficiently to move in with you.'

'I know you did, Monique, and I'm happy and grateful that you did. But the echo of what you said comes back to me quite often and it looms especially large each time I try to summon up the courage to talk to you about the future.'

'What is it you want to talk about, Bob?'

'I want to ask you to marry me, but I know you'll just tell me that there's a war on and either or both of us could be dead tomorrow. But to my mind we should put that to one side. Besides, the tide of the war has turned. Let's face it, now the Germans have surrendered at Stalingrad, and now the Americans are so heavily involved, it can only really go one way. Even Churchill agreed with me in his "the end of the beginning" speech after we beat the Afrika Corps at the Second Battle of El Alamein last November.'

Monique seemed to be trying to stop herself laughing, and instead took a drink of her champagne. Then she put it down.

'Yes, Bob, I will.'

'You don't have to answer me now. Give it some thought… What did you say?'

'I said that I will marry you, Bob. I'm not even put off by your quoting Churchill in your proposal, though it was a close-run thing.' She laughed. 'Isn't this where you are supposed to embarrass both of us by getting down on one knee and offering me a ring?'

'Yes, it is, but I have to admit this isn't the most carefully planned thing I've ever done in my life. There isn't actually a ring, but on the positive side that means we can come into Edinburgh tomorrow morning and find one you like rather than one I hope you'll like.'

*

The taxi stopped on the pitch-black street opposite the bungalow. Bob used a torch to count out the fare and the tip for the taxi-driver. As they crossed the road, he heard a car door close a little along the street. He was holding Monique's left arm and could feel her tense. As they approached the front door, Bob brought out his torch again, to illuminate the keyhole in the front door. Then he heard the garden gate open and footsteps on the path. He felt Monique spin round and heard the distinctive sound of her pistol being cocked.

The footsteps stopped suddenly, as if their owner had heard the same sound. 'Group Captain Sutherland, Madame Dubois, it's Taffy Jenkins. I've got a message for you. I'm sorry I startled you.'

Bob shone his torch along the path to see Private Jenkins, shielding his eyes from the glare. He could see to his right that Monique was lowering her pistol. Bob felt relief flood over him. 'Hello, Taffy. I hope you've not had to wait too long for us.'

'Can we get you a cup of tea?' asked Monique.

'No thank you, ma'am. I brought a thermos flask. I've not been waiting long. Captain Darlington received a telephone call in the officers' mess at Craigiehall a little earlier from Commodore Cunningham in London. He would like the group captain to phone him back as soon as possible on his home telephone number. That's the message.'

'Thank you, Taffy, I'm very grateful,' said Bob.

'You're welcome, sir. I'll be off back to Craigiehall now.'

Bob heard the gate close as he opened the front door. 'That certainly got the adrenaline pumping,' he said.

'It did, Bob,' said Monique. 'But when something like that happens, you really do need to remember that you've got a gun too. It could save your life one day.'

'I'd better find out what Maurice wants.' Commodore Maurice Cunningham was head of Military Intelligence, Section 11, and Bob's immediate boss.

It took a little while for the call to be put through, but it was then answered immediately at the other end with an anonymous, 'Hello.' Even with just the one word, Bob recognised the voice.

'Hello, sir, you asked me to call you as soon as possible. I'm calling from home, so this is not a secure line.'

'Thank you for calling back. How soon can you and your female colleague get down to London?'

'It should be light enough to fly by about 7 a.m., sir. If there's a car waiting at Northolt, we could be with you not too long after 9 a.m., certainly by half-past.'

'Both of you?'

'Yes, sir, I've got a two-seater aircraft now.'

'Good, I'll see you both then.'

'Can I ask how long we will be away for, sir? Do we need to pack?'

'You might need to spend a day or two down here, and tell your colleagues that the two of you could be completely out of touch for up to a week.'

'See you in the morning, sir.'

Bob then telephoned Anthony Darlington in the officers'

mess at Craigiehall.

After that he called the duty officer at RAF Turnhouse to ask him to make sure that Bob's Mosquito would be out of the hangar and ready for flight first thing in the morning.

*

'You've no second thoughts then Bob?'

Bob was laying in the darkness of their bedroom on his back. Monique lay against his right-hand side, her head nestled on his shoulder.

'None at all. I'd have asked before today if I'd known what your answer was going to be. I'm just sorry that Commodore Cunningham's chucked a spanner in our ring-shopping plans. Perhaps we'll have time to look for something nice in London.'

'Don't think I'm being in any way presumptuous, Bob, but I have been eyeing up a ring I really like in a jeweller's shop in Rose Street. If it's all right with you, I'd prefer to wait until I can show it to you to see if you like it as much as I do.'

'That sounds great. I know it's only been a few days, but I've really missed you, Monique.'

'I've missed you, too, in lots of different ways. I hope that now we're engaged you're not going to suddenly go off sex.' She trailed her fingertips down his chest.

Bob laughed and took her hand, rolling her over onto her back before leaning over and kissing her. 'That sounds like a challenge to me!'

*

It was much later, though without moving to look at the

luminous dial on his watch, Bob had no idea what time it was. He could hear the ticking of the folding alarm clock, but its face seemed to be turned out of sight. He felt a movement and realised Monique was also awake.

'Are you all right?' he asked.

'Yes, I've just been trying to work out what name I should use when we get married. The obvious answer to that would be "your real one", but I'm not actually sure I've got a real name in the normally accepted sense. I've gone through life putting on and taking off names the way most people put on and take off raincoats. Even now, I'm Monique Dubois in Edinburgh, because that's the cover name I used when I first came to work in Scotland and met you at Sarclet Castle, but I'm Vera Duval as far as MI5 in London is concerned. Yet even that's only a flag of convenience. I was Vera Staritzka when I was born, and became Vera Schalburg not much later, and have had other names including Vera Eriksen when the Abwehr thought I was working for them. And that's if you don't include the names of my two dead husbands. I like "Sutherland", but it's what goes on the paperwork and what I use as a first name that's got me worried.'

'Could you produce a legal set of documents that would allow you to get married as Monique Dubois?'

'Yes, I think so, but only "legal" in the sense of not being open to challenge. They wouldn't be "real" in any absolute sense.'

'If it helps,' said Bob, 'as far as I'm concerned, I'm marrying Monique Dubois. I just never think of you as "Vera".'

'It does help, my love. That's what we'll do, then, and I'll become Mrs Monique Sutherland. Do you think your father would give me away?'

'I'm sure he'd be honoured,' said Bob.

'What about a best man?'

'I'd not thought about it,' said Bob. 'Perhaps Michael Dixon would be prepared to do it.'

'That seems a nice idea.'

There was a long, comfortable silence, though Bob knew Monique wasn't asleep.

'Monique, you worked in MI6 or SIS in London for a while before transferring to MI5, didn't you?'

'Yes, why?'

'Have you ever heard of an SIS Section VII?'

'Perhaps something on their administration side? I'm not sure. Why are you asking?'

Bob gave her a brief account of his day.

'Wow, that's quite a story. I didn't know that SIS had any operations within the UK, to be honest. I'd thought their focus was entirely overseas.'

'Yes, me too. It seems we're both wrong.'

'Assuming your Captain Elphick was telling you the truth.'

'What makes you think he wasn't?'

'I don't, but you have this information from only a single source, and it does seem a very odd setup that he described to you. You have to keep open the possibility that Section VII is just one man's invention.'

'Hell, that would put an utterly different complexion on things,' said Bob. 'Look, we need an early start in the morning and might well have a busy day. He leaned over to look at his watch. It's past 2 a.m. now. We really need to sleep.'

'I'd sleep better after more sex,' said Monique.

'I'm sure that can be arranged,' said Bob.

CHAPTER SIX

Bob always thought that Monique looked especially attractive when kitted out for flight with a sheepskin lined leather flying jacket. Even the leather helmet and yellow life vest looked good on her. He'd told her this once and was quite affronted when she'd called his taste 'weird': having more to do, in her view, with his love for aeroplanes than his love for her. She'd then ticked off on the fingers of one of her hands a list of things she would never be prepared to do in the cockpit of an aircraft, even with him.

Bob's de Havilland Mosquito B Mk IV had been fuelled and was ready to go when they'd arrived at RAF Turnhouse at about 6.50 a.m. after the short drive from the bungalow. It was 'Bob's Mosquito' in the sense that he'd been loaned it by the station commander at RAF Lossiemouth the previous November. It had been languishing there, apparently forgotten and abandoned by the Norfolk-based squadron it was allocated to, since making an emergency landing two months earlier. It had been returned to 'as good as new' condition at Lossiemouth with two new engines and repairs to the undercarriage, but despite it being a very modern and highly capable aircraft, no one seemed interested in giving it a good home.

The deal had been that RAF Lossiemouth would arrange to have the aircraft picked up from Turnhouse after Bob had used it to get himself and Monique there. But it wasn't on their books, and no one seemed bothered, and Bob certainly didn't go out of his way to remind them. It had become something of a waif as a result and Bob saw it as his duty to fly it regularly and make sure it was looked after properly.

Besides, there were times when having two seats was just so much more convenient that having only one: which was all that the Hawker Hurricanes he had previously tended to use to travel round the country could offer.

Monique had flown with Bob in the Mosquito on several occasions. She was aware it was tricky to fly but he'd never told her about the aircraft's most serious vice: that its takeoff speed was considerably lower than the speed at which it could continue to fly if one of its engines failed. What this meant in practice was that if an engine failed before the speed had built up after takeoff, when they would be working at their hardest, then you crashed. It was as simple as that.

Bob felt it was enough that he always held his breath after takeoff, listening intently to the engines as he waited for the undercarriage to retract, which then allowed the speed to start to come up towards a safe level. There was no need to inflict that doubt on Monique.

'Which way are we going, Bob?' asked Monique after they'd taken off to the south-east and were skirting the southern edge of Edinburgh.

'I'd rather hoped for another glorious day like yesterday. It's a shame it's so miserable and the meteorological office at Turnhouse reckons we'll run into squalls and even lower cloud en route. I'm going to do this the lazy way. We'll pick up the main London and North Eastern Railway tracks on the east side of the city and simply follow them to London. I'm aiming to keep below the cloud the whole way. It's how pilots usually navigated when I learned to fly ten years ago, though things have moved on a bit since then. The rule is that you fly to the right of the linear feature you are following. That way you don't collide with anyone following the same feature in the other direction.

'The skies of eastern Britain are incredibly busy these days. If you see any other aircraft, and it's certain you will, tell me. Don't assume I'll have seen them too. Three eyes are better than one.' He smiled, then realised Monique wouldn't see his smile under his mask. 'It's OK, I'm only joking. But I did mean what I said about telling me when you see other aircraft.'

*

Bob had never had reason to get to know London very well, but he recognised Victoria Station from the back of the staff car that had met them at RAF Northolt. Monique knew the city much better, pointing out other landmarks as they passed.

With the Houses of Parliament in view ahead, the car turned right just before it reached Westminster Abbey, another building Bob was able to identify for himself. Not far along the street the car pulled over to the right-hand side of the road and stopped, causing the driver of a coal merchant's lorry coming the other way to brake and beep his horn.

MI11's London offices were in Sanctuary Buildings in Great Smith Street. On a previous visit Bob had noticed a board showing a list of other occupiers of the building in the reception area. He'd been intrigued to see what a disparate bunch they were, including the libraries of the Privy Council and the Foreign Office, as well as the National Savings Committee, whatever that was, the Society for Overseas Settlement of British Women, ditto, plus outposts - presumably, minor outposts - of the Ministry of Pensions, the Ministry of Works, and the Admiralty, amongst others. Notably absent from the board was any mention of 'Military Intelligence, Section 11', which occupied part of the top floor of the building.

Commodore Maurice Cunningham's office was approached through his secretary's and was modest in scale, though large enough to accommodate a desk and a meeting table. The walls were adorned with a series of framed pictures of warships. Most notably the office enjoyed a view out over the street. An army major working for the commodore had told Bob on one of his visits that this was a building where outward-facing offices were prized possessions. The alternative was an office, like the major's, that looked into one of a number of small and very grubby internal wells, and across them into the windows of other people's offices.

The commodore was a man in his late forties with a black beard that was just starting to go grey at the sides. As he greeted Bob and Monique he was, as usual, impeccably turned out in a carefully pressed naval uniform.

'Welcome to both of you, and thanks for coming at such short notice. Let's get some tea laid on. We're expecting one more to join us, Jonathan Waddell, who is one of the deputy directors at the Secret Intelligence Service. He's not keen on it being called MI6, so to keep him happy, let's just stick with "SIS" today. Do you know him, Monique?'

'No, I've heard the name, but I've never met him.'

'Let's sit down at the meeting table,' said the commodore.

'What's it about, sir?' asked Bob.

'There's no point me telling you a second-hand version of the story. Let's wait until he arrives. I let him know when you were picked up at Northolt, so expect him at any moment. In the meantime, how are things in Edinburgh?'

'Well enough, sir. Most of my troops are in Orkney at the moment, following up that mess we stumbled into at the end of last year. I've left Captain Darlington in charge in my absence, pursuing a rather odd case that came our way yesterday.'

'What does that involve?'

Bob gave the commodore a very brief outline of what had happened. 'It was something of a learning experience for me. I'd never heard of the Auxiliary Units before, still less SIS Section VII.'

'The Auxiliary Units are rather old news now, as you seem to have discovered. As for SIS Section VII cells, well, yes, I can confirm they exist, though I have to say that I also only found that out yesterday afternoon when the gentleman who we are waiting for came to see me to tell me about them after SIS had decided they needed to tell you.'

'If that's what's we're here to talk about, sir, it might have been better if I'd brought Captain Darlington to the meeting.'

'No, that's not what I asked you both to come down to London to discuss. Do you mind my asking how things are with the two of you? You told me you were renting a house together. How is that going?'

Bob wondered if the slightly perplexed look on Monique's face was reflected on his own. The commodore, for a navy man, had always seemed very open minded and both he and his boss had been very accepting of the idea of Monique being seconded from MI5 to Bob's team in MI11 despite knowing about their relationship.

'Sorry,' said the commodore. 'I could have phrased that better. We are going to put a proposal to you that would mean the two of you assuming the identities of a married couple. Would you have any problem with that idea?'

Bob looked at Monique.

'If it helps, sir,' she said, 'we got engaged last night.'

'Ah, I see. Congratulations to both of you. There was a time, not long ago, when that might have complicated things immeasurably. But the war has brought about some positive changes and the way the frankly medieval marriage bar is now widely ignored is one of them. Having said that, I believe it's still technically the case, on paper at least, that any female civil servant who gets married must resign her post.'

The commodore saw the look on Monique's face and raised his hands. 'No, of course that's not an issue in these circumstances or for the two of you. It does very satisfactorily answer the question I asked, though.' As if in search of a diversion, he looked at his watch and tutted.

At that moment, the commodore's secretary opened his office door and showed in a tall, heavily built man who seemed to be in his early fifties. The visitor was dressed in an impeccably tailored three-piece suit, and he smiled as he entered. 'I'm sorry I'm late.'

The commodore stood up. 'I'll do the introductions. This is Jonathan Waddell, deputy director at SIS. Jonathan, this is Group Captain Robert Sutherland who is my deputy in MI11, based in Edinburgh, and as you'll have worked out through a process of elimination this is Vera Duval, who has feet in both MI5 and MI11 camps.'

Waddell turned a charming smile on first Bob and then Monique as he shook their hands.

'Have you told them why they are here, Maurice?'

'No, I thought it was better coming directly from you. Take a seat and I'll get some tea brought in. Ah, here it is.'

Once the office door was closed again, Waddell leaned forwards in his chair. 'Have either of you ever been to Stockholm? Call me Jonathan, by the way. Can I call you

Robert and Vera?'

'I prefer to answer to "Bob".'

'And I'm getting used to either "Vera" or "Monique". I'm told you prefer "SIS" to "MI6", Jonathan. Perhaps, for today at least, I should be "Monique".'

'Fair enough, Bob and Monique it is. What about Stockholm?'

'I've never been north of Germany on the continent,' said Bob.

'I've been to Stockholm twice,' said Monique. 'In 1937, and again the following year. As I am sure you know, I was at that time married to Hans Friedrich von Wedel, a senior officer in the Abwehr, and reporting to your SIS colleagues about him and about my own role as an agent in that organisation.'

'Do you speak Swedish?'

'Only up to a point. I speak fluent Danish, having lived in Denmark for six years as a child. The Nordic languages probably look and sound much the same to outsiders, but it's more complicated than that. Danish and Norwegian have almost the same vocabularies, but the words are pronounced very differently. As for Norwegian and Swedish, they have similar pronunciation but use a lot of different words. The result is that Norwegians tend to be pretty good at communicating with either Danes or Swedes, but Danes and Swedes sometimes struggle to make sense of one another. I remember it being a bit of a shock to find that Swedes I encountered in Stockholm thought that Danes talked like they were drunk the whole time. I suppose the short answer is that I can get by in Swedish, but with a heavy accent that's clearly identifiable as Danish.'

'Thank you, Monique.'

'It may be about time we stopped beating about the bush,

Jonathan,' said the commodore.

'Yes, of course Maurice. Two days ago, on Sunday, an SIS officer in Stockholm met an Abwehr officer, also based in the city. The meeting was at the latter's request and the whole thing was done with what our man described as a John Buchan-esque aura of slightly comical secrecy in a rather obscure location away from prying eyes.

'Our man went along mainly through curiosity. The German he was meeting had been based in Stockholm for a year and we knew he was a competent operator who was unlikely to pose any personal threat to our man. After discussing it with his senior officer, our man went ahead with the meeting.

'The two met in an old wooden church that was relocated some decades ago to a sort of history park on an island not far from the centre of the city. After the meeting, the German left first but was shot dead as he emerged from the church.

'Our man was arrested as he tried to leave the park and held overnight by the Swedish Security Service. It seems they'd been tipped off anonymously that SIS had assassinated an Abwehr officer. The Swedish Security Service are quite accommodating in some ways, especially now it's increasingly obvious to them which side is going to win the war, but the one thing they absolutely won't stand for is the belligerents conducting acts of violence on the streets of Swedish cities. We got severely burned in 1940 when the Swedes uncovered a plan by those lunatics in the Special Operations Executive to sabotage harbour facilities in a Swedish port being used to ship iron ore to Germany. Some of the SOE people ended up with long spells in Swedish prisons. The very clear distinction we see between the Secret Intelligence Service and SOE was less obvious to our Swedish friends, and it has taken a lot of effort to rebuild a working relationship with them.

'While they stamp down on anything resembling violence, they are much more relaxed about pretty much every security service on Earth having a significant presence in Stockholm, including the services of the belligerents and of the official or unofficial exiled governments of assorted occupied countries. And then there's the Swedes themselves, of course, who keep extremely close tabs on everything that's happening and have a huge operation in place to tap telephones and monitor other forms of communication. The city is an absolute snake pit, which also makes it a wonderful playground for intelligence officers.

'In this case, thankfully, the Swedes quite quickly realised that whoever had shot the Abwehr agent it wasn't our man.'

'What's this got to do with us, Jonathan?' asked Monique.

'When our man was able to report back, yesterday morning, he said that the German had gone to all the trouble of setting the meeting up simply to pass a short verbal message. Whoever shot the German presumably knew he must have already passed his message but it's difficult to avoid the conclusion he was killed because of it.'

'What was the message?' asked Bob.

'The message was that a prominent member of a secret anti-Nazi faction within the Abwehr would be arriving in Stockholm this Thursday and had proposals to make to the British that were of the utmost importance. The catch was that he would only talk to someone he knew and trusted on the British side. The person who was specified in the message was Vera Eriksen.'

There was a silence in the room.

Then Monique spoke. 'Who is the man who's due to arrive on Thursday?'

'His name is Maximilian von Moser, and we know that he is highly placed on the personal staff of Admiral Canaris, the head of the Abwehr,' said Jonathan.

'The same Admiral Canaris whose plans to kidnap King George were thwarted by Monique and I last year?' asked Bob. 'This sounds a lot like a trap to lure Monique out into the open to me. Remember that she's going to be a prize target for both the Abwehr and the Soviet NKVD and who knows who else. She might be safe here in the UK, which is why she was transferred from SIS to MI5, but she's going to be utterly vulnerable in Stockholm.'

'As it's my life we're talking about, perhaps I should be allowed to fit a word in edgeways,' said Monique. 'The first point is that I do know Maximilian von Moser. I know him well. He was a junior colleague of Hans Friedrich von Wedel when I was married to him, and a much younger and more attractive man. I had a brief affair with him in early 1938. It seems that von Moser has drawn his own conclusions about where my true loyalties lie. Alternatively, it may be that the Abwehr as an organisation has worked out that I was a double agent working for SIS all along. They'd need to have been pretty dim not to.'

'Which just serves to emphasise why you shouldn't go,' said Bob.

'Or, alternatively, it might suggest that this is genuine attempt to make contact,' said Monique. 'The problem is that there's only one way to find out for sure and it's pretty risky.'

'I should perhaps intervene at this point,' said Jonathan Waddell. 'You need to know that what's proposed has caused a heated debated within SIS. For some of us this has unwelcome echoes of what many of us regard as our most inglorious moment. Have either of you heard of the Venlo incident?'

'I see what you mean,' said Monique.

'I haven't,' said Bob.

Waddell turned to look at Bob. 'Between September and November 1939 two SIS officers based in the Netherlands, which was neutral at the time, had a series of meetings with German army officers opposed to Hitler. On the 9th of November 1939, the supposedly dissident army officers revealed themselves to be agents of the Sicherheitsdienst or the SD and kidnapped the two SIS officers on the outskirts of Venlo in the Netherlands, a few yards from the German border, and took them into Germany. During the exchange of fire that preceded their kidnapping, an officer of Dutch Military Intelligence who was liaising with our men was mortally wounded.

'The repercussions were enormous. Information the Gestapo gleaned from our officers severely compromised our operations in Germany. The Nazi government subsequently used the incident to claim that Britain had been involved in a failed attempt on Hitler's life. Perhaps worst of all, the involvement of Dutch Military Intelligence allowed Hitler to claim that the Netherlands had violated its neutrality. This was used as justification for the German invasion of the Netherlands on the 10th of May 1940. They would have invaded anyway but that's not the point. The point was that a failed SIS operation provided the pretext.

'Our concern is that this approach in Stockholm does have a similar feel to it. On balance we've decided, as I said after some debate, that the potential benefits outweigh the risks.'

'Forgive my ignorance,' said Bob, 'but you're going to have to tell me how the SD fits into the German intelligence picture.'

Jonathan Waddell answered. 'The Sicherheitsdienst, whose full name is the "Sicherheitsdienst des Reichsführers-SS" or the Security Service of the Reichsführer-SS, can be thought of as the intelligence agency of the SS and the Nazi Party. With a name like that, you can see why we almost always just refer to them as the SD. They operate within Germany and abroad: with foreign operations conducted by the Ausland-SD or Foreign Security Service.

'There tends to be no love lost between them and the Abwehr. It's the fact that this approach comes from such a senior level within the Abwehr that leads us to want to pursue it further, but the dangers of a repeat of something like the Venlo incident are obvious.

'Turning to practicalities we would propose that if you are prepared to go, Monique, and I emphasise that it can only be your decision, then we will provide you with the best cover story we can in the very limited time we have available.'

'Absolutely not!' said Monique. 'The commodore talked when we arrived about Bob and I assuming the identities of a married couple. You are about to suggest that we go to Stockholm together, with me acting as, I don't know, the wife of a new air attaché in the British embassy or something, aren't you? The commodore already knows, but Bob and I got engaged last night and I am not about to risk the life of my husband-to-be on some damn-fool escapade for which he is totally ill-equipped.'

'Hang on, Monique!' said Bob.

'No, it's true, Bob. You are a wonderful man but you just

don't have the killer instinct you need to survive in a hostile environment. Not so long ago you were faced with an armed man on the top of the tower of the cathedral in Kirkwall. Did you shoot him? No, you lowered your weapon so you could try to "talk sense into him" and nearly got yourself killed. Someone else had to shoot him instead. Then, last night, we both thought we were about to be attacked outside the bungalow. Did you draw your gun? No, you were more worried about your torch while your pistol stayed in its holster. I'm sorry, Bob, but if you came with me to Stockholm, I'd be spending too much of my energy worrying about protecting you because I'd not be confident you could, or would, protect yourself if something went wrong.'

The commodore fiddled with his teacup. 'It might help if we let Jonathan outline what we have in mind so you can both form a clearer view of the potential risks and come to a more informed decision.'

Jonathan leapt in before Monique could speak. 'Thank you, Maurice. What we have in mind is the group captain taking on the role of a senior manager with an aircraft manufacturing company: de Havilland, as it happens. His cover would be that he was travelling to Stockholm to build links with the Swedish Air Force and discuss possible future sales of the Mosquito and other aircraft types with them. His name would be Robert Cadman. His wife, Monique Cadman, would be travelling with him because she's been asked to write a paper comparing social conditions in Stockholm and in London for the Ministry of Information.'

'I know you are the experts,' said Bob, 'but isn't it a little obvious to keep our existing first names for our cover identities?'

'It shouldn't be a problem, Bob,' said Monique. 'Remember that "Monique" is a cover name anyway, and "Robert", forgive me for saying so, is a fairly common name. The major benefit is that it removes any possibility of using the wrong names when talking to one another in company.'

'As I said, you are the experts,' said Bob.

'We did have one concern, Monique,' said Waddell. 'We have considered the possibility that given your history you might be known by sight to some of the residents of the snake pit I referred to earlier and are suggesting a significant change of appearance, specifically the best blonde wig we can find in London. The hope is that by attaching you as an appendage to your husband, and so helping reduce your visibility, we might allow you to meet Maximilian von Moser without anyone else realising what's happening. There is still the concern that this might be a trap, of course, and there is the additional problem that we have no idea who killed the Abwehr agent on Sunday, or why. To mitigate the risks, we would provide security for both of you while you were in Stockholm, but we accept that the whole thing is still a very chancy venture.'

'I'm not keen on the idea of added security,' said Monique. 'To my mind it would simply serve to draw attention to us and compromise our cover. We will both be armed and, despite what I've just said, Bob is a very good shot once he decides to unholster his pistol.'

'As you wish,' said Waddell. 'But the offer's there and you can perhaps decide how to play that once you have got a feel for the place.'

'What about things like papers, clothes and transport?' asked Monique.

It was the commodore who replied. 'In the hope you might

both accept our proposal we are having passports and a few other bits and pieces like British driving licences prepared as we speak and will let you have sufficient Swedish currency for your needs. We will get our friends in the Foreign Office to expedite visas through the Swedish embassy this afternoon. We do need a photograph of you in a blonde wig, Monique, and one of Bob in a civilian shirt and tie. There should by now be someone in my secretary's office ready to sort that out, with the necessary equipment and props. I appreciate clothing is an issue, both for you and for the group captain. If you accept, we will send you off shortly with my secretary and a driver to acquire an upmarket wardrobe of clothes to last you a week and luggage to carry it in. This will be at MI11's expense both in terms of cost and clothing coupons. We'd also equip you with makeup, toiletries and anything else you feel you might need. In the meantime, Bob will head off to the tailor we retain in Savile Row and who made him new uniforms not long ago. He has Bob's measurements and is already working on two business suits, plus some less formal attire, all intended to accommodate his Walther PPK. Bob, I take it you now carry the new one we provided after your first one was damaged?'

Bob nodded, wondering how they'd moved so quickly from discussing whether he and Monique should go to discussing what they would wear.

'Good. We will also sort out an overcoat and shoes, plus socks and underwear and, again, suitable luggage, civilian shaving kit and toiletries and that sort of thing.'

'Hang on a moment,' said Bob. 'When I started in this job, Monique was asked to brief me on highly sensitive intelligence material, codenamed "Ultra". As I recall, and I can almost hear her saying it, one of the conditions of being inducted into the exclusive club of those who know about it was that I had to ensure that I avoided doing anything that gave rise to the slightest possibility of my falling into enemy hands. Now, because a German spy in Stockholm has suggested it would be a good idea, both Monique and I are being placed in very considerable danger of falling into enemy hands.'

'Yes,' said Jonathan, 'we have discussed that.' He put a hand in an outside jacket pocket and pulled out a brown envelope. He opened the envelope and shook it, so its contents slid out onto the wood of the commodore's meeting table.

Bob could see two separate lengths of fine metal chain, each with a pendant attached. The pendants looked a little like small-calibre bullets with rounded ends. Each had a metal cap that sat above a slightly narrower and rather longer lower section.

'What are those?' he asked.

'Those are L-pills, Bob,' said Monique. 'The "L" stands for "lethal". The idea is that you unscrew the bottom sections of the metal outer container from within the top section. Inside there is a rubber sheathed glass ampoule containing potassium cyanide. If you are in danger of being captured you bite down on the ampoule and, hey presto, your secrets stay secret. This really isn't a game we are playing, Bob. If you want proof of that, here it is in front of you.'

Bob felt sick.

'It's OK, Bob, there's always the option of shooting yourself, and me, instead, if it comes to it.' She looked at him with an intensity he'd never seen before. 'I want you to promise me that if you need to, you will shoot me rather than allow me to be captured. If you can't promise me that in a way that makes me believe you mean it, then the whole thing's off.'

Bob looked back at her. 'I promise, Monique.' The sickness was now almost physical.

There was a pause. 'Thank you, Bob. I'm sure you know I would shoot you rather than force you to use one of these pills or be captured.' She turned away from Bob to look at each of the other two men in turn. 'It seems that you have your volunteers, gentlemen.'

The commodore reached over to touch Bob's forearm. 'Are you sure you're happy with this, Bob?'

'Happy isn't the word I'd use, sir, but it will be a hell of a story to tell our grandchildren one day.'

Monique put her hand over her mouth to stifle a laugh, which eased the tension in the room. Then her face took on a more serious look. 'Bob's question reminds me that we may be overlooking something obvious. Is there any information from interception and decryption of Abwehr communications about what's really going on here?'

'No, Monique, we're not overlooking the possibility,' said Waddell. 'The reality is that while Ultra is hugely valuable for seeing the other side of the picture in respect of large-scale events, it can be a bit more hit-and-miss when we are dealing with something much more specific like this, especially if some of those involved are not operating openly within their own organisations. I can tell you that the Abwehr office in Stockholm reported the death of their agent to Berlin early yesterday morning. According to them, the meeting with our man took place at our request. You could interpret that as an indication that their agent did not want to tell those he was working with that he had arranged the meeting, which might support the view that his message was genuine. The Stockholm office of the Abwehr went on to say that although they were still investigating, there was reason to believe he had not been killed by the British. They did not specify what had led them to that conclusion. We think that the Swedish Security Service may also have intercepted and decrypted that message, because not long after we'd worked out what it said, they released our man.

'We have of course tried to establish whether there is any information about Maximilian von Moser travelling to Stockholm in anything we've intercepted and decrypted passing back and forth between different elements of the Abwehr. We've gone back through intercepts from the past week, but it is a little like hunting for a needle in a haystack and, as I said a moment ago, if he is on a private mission as claimed, then we'd not expect to see anything at all on official channels. I can also say that we've seen no mention of the name Vera Eriksen, or any code name which the context suggests might refer to you. If there was an Abwehr-sanctioned plan in place to draw you out and capture or kill you, Monique, we'd have expected to have seen mention of it somewhere.'

'That's fairly encouraging in a sort of "no news is good news" sense,' said Monique.

'I've got two questions,' said Bob. 'As his intermediary was killed, how do we expect von Moser to make contact? And just as importantly, given the shooting, isn't it likely he will call off the visit?'

'Good questions and, frankly, we have no way of knowing the answers to either of them,' said Waddell. 'We can hope that as the German agent chose to contact a particular individual within our operation in Stockholm, von Moser will contact the same individual, a man by the name of Peter Bostock. We will be assigning Mr Bostock to be your liaison officer while you are there and hopefully von Moser will find a way of contacting him when he arrives in the city. Do you have any other questions?'

'Are either of us going to have to actually perform to the scripts suggested by our cover stories?' asked Bob. 'I love the Mosquito, but I'd be hard pressed to try to sell it to anyone who might ask technical questions.'

'No. It will be enough for you to be able to talk in general terms about the aircraft's virtues in a social environment, where you can give secrecy as a reason for not going deeper. We're not planning to put you into actual meetings with the Swedish Air Force or anything like that. The same goes for your cover, Monique.'

'If Stockholm really is the snake pit you describe,' said Monique, 'then it's not going to take some of its residents five minutes to spot that we're not who we say we are.'

'That's probably true. But almost everyone involved in the intelligence community in the city is pretending to be someone they aren't and that's just an accepted fact of life. So long as they don't work out who you really are, and why you are there, it shouldn't matter if it becomes known that Robert and Monique Cadman are not who they claim to be. Is there anything else before you go out and make a large hole in Maurice's budget?'

'Just one thing,' said Monique. 'You haven't told us how we are getting to Stockholm. Last time I looked, there were German-occupied countries between here and there.'

CHAPTER SEVEN

As they passed over Newcastle, Bob could see that the weather was much clearer ahead of them. By the time the distinctive outline of Holy Island came into view, they were flying under blue skies with a bright evening sun illuminating the landscape below.

Monique had been very quiet since they'd left RAF Northolt. Since before then, in fact. She'd said very little when they'd met back at Commodore Cunningham's office and during the drive out of the city.

'Are you all right, Monique?'

She didn't reply at first. Then, out of the corner of his good eye, Bob saw her turn towards him in the navigator's seat, positioned just a little behind his own and to the right of it in the Mosquito's snug cockpit.

'I'm sorry, Bob. I'm just a bit preoccupied by what's ahead of us. At a more mundane level, I'm worried that our luggage is going to be safe.'

'They put our suitcases in a net suspended from the attachments in the bomb bay normally used to hang bombs,' said Bob. 'I'm sure they'll be fine. I hope so, anyway. I've never owned clothing that's even a fraction of the value of what's currently in my case.'

'You and me both,' said Monique. 'I kept thinking Rose, the commodore's secretary, was going to baulk at what I was buying, but if anything she was encouraging me to push the boat out further. I have to say that I'm frankly amazed that you can still get hold of Chanel No.5 in London with the war on and with France occupied, but apparently you can. It's certainly not cheap, though. As it's all part of our rather threadbare cover I didn't want to hold back.'

'I've spent much of the flight wondering how we agreed quite so readily to what was being proposed,' said Bob. 'We both had serious doubts initially.'

'We were bribed with fine clothes and expensive perfume, Bob. All joking apart, I never had any doubts about going to Stockholm myself, despite the obvious risks. What worried me was you being involved.'

'What changed your mind?'

'I'm sorry about what I said this morning, about you not having a killer instinct.'

'Why be sorry, Monique? Every word was true.'

'I know, but it being true didn't make it the right thing to say, especially in front of the audience we had. I could see that I'd really hurt you. Then I realised that if we're going to spend the rest of our lives together, and assuming that's for longer than just the next couple of days, if I went to Stockholm without you, it would be something that could come between us forever. I didn't want to start our engagement by undermining you, and our relationship, in that way.'

'Thanks for telling me, Monique.'

'As we're on the subject, though, you really are going to have to work hard on supressing your tendency to think the best of everyone and every situation you find yourself in. You should have kept your gun pointing at Edward Swanson when you found him on top of that cathedral tower. And you should have drawn your pistol when we thought we were in danger last night. We could easily end up in a situation where both our lives depend on you overcoming your instincts and reacting differently.'

'I know, Monique. I do have a linked question, though. Why did you rule out the idea of SIS providing us with security in Stockholm? Surely that would have been prudent in the circumstances?'

'It just felt like the right thing to do, Bob.'

Bob thought that was an uncharacteristically vague reply for Monique, but before he could press the point, she asked him a question.

'I've been honest with you about my reasons for not objecting, Bob. Now it's your turn. Why did you change tack so quickly during the meeting this morning? I thought you were going to dig in and be really difficult.'

'It's the other side of the same coin, really. If our relationship had been purely professional and you simply reported to me, then I think I might well have argued much more strongly against what is by any standards a bloody silly and extremely dangerous idea. But you don't just report to me. We are a couple. I suddenly realised that if I stopped you going to Stockholm, or really tried to and was overruled, then it would always seem to you, and to the others present, that I'd done it for personal rather than professional reasons. It seemed to me that was something you might always resent and, to echo your thoughts, that didn't seem like a great foundation on which to build our marriage.'

'In other words, we both wanted to object to the other being involved on professional grounds, but neither pushed it for purely personal reasons,' said Monique. 'Good grief, I think we deserve each other!'

Bob could see from her eyes above her oxygen mask that Monique was laughing. He hoped she could tell that he was smiling back.

*

Bob flew low along the coast of Fife until he passed St Andrews on his left and then turned to bring the Mosquito into land from the east at RAF Leuchars, almost straight into a setting sun whose disk had nearly touched the horizon. Having landed, he taxied round the airfield to the concrete parking areas that formed the 540 Squadron dispersal on its north side, in the angle between the two main runways. There he followed signals from an airman to come to a halt not far from what he knew was the squadron office.

Bob followed Monique down the short access ladder from the hatch in the floor of the aircraft.

'Hello Bob!'

Bob turned round to see Wing Commander Eric Gill walking over from the office, a broad grin on his face.

'It's true then. I really did sell the merits of flying a Mosquito to you. Hello, who's this?'

Monique had removed her leather helmet and life jacket and shaken her hair loose.

'Hello Eric, it's good to see you again,' said Bob. 'Can I introduce Madame Monique Dubois, who works with me at MI11? Monique, this is Wing Commander Eric Gill, commanding officer of 540 Squadron, which operates photo reconnaissance Mosquitos from here.'

'Enchanté, Madame Dubois,' said Gill, smiling broadly at Monique.

Bob grinned. 'I remember you had quite a reputation with the ladies when you were a flight commander on 111 Squadron back in the Autumn of 1940, Eric. There's something you should know about Monique. She and I got engaged last night.'

'Congratulations to both of you! A celebratory drink in the officers' mess seems a fine idea.'

'I'm afraid not, Eric. This isn't a social call. Monique and I are due to report to the BOAC office here at Leuchars at midnight. I'm pleased I could catch you on the phone before we left London and I'm grateful to you for agreeing to get your people to give my Mosquito a thorough service. I'm afraid I've not got any of the usual paperwork for the aircraft, so other than knowing she was given two new engines and had her undercarriage repaired after a crash landing at Lossiemouth last September or thereabouts, I really know nothing of her history. Getting the Mossie serviced seemed like a good idea as we were going to be away for a few days.'

'In Stockholm?'

'That's right but keep it to yourself.'

'Rather you than me.'

'What's wrong with the place?'

'Nothing, as far as I know, but the trip is rather interesting.'

'What type of aircraft do they use? asked Bob.

'To date a number of different types have been used to make the run. As you say, British Overseas Airways Corporation, BOAC, operate the service. That's because the Swedes won't allow British military aircraft or crews to use their airfields. Early last month BOAC made their first run in a specially adapted Mosquito, the idea being that the aircraft is much less likely to be caught and intercepted by Luftwaffe fighters based in Norway or Denmark than anything previously used. This has apparently proved highly successful, and I'm told it's on the cards that they'll get more Mosquitos, with deliveries beginning next month. At a more practical level, have you had anything to eat?'

'We flew down to London early this morning,' said Monique, 'and managed a sandwich this afternoon, but otherwise no. As Bob says, we sadly have to decline your kind offer of a drink, but we've got over four hours before we need to report for our flight to Stockholm and I for one am starving.'

'I'll get a driver to take us over to the officers' mess,' said Gill.

'We've also got some luggage that's got everything we need for the trip hanging in a net in the bomb bay,' said Bob, 'in two rather expensive leather suitcases.'

'I'll get someone to take them over to the BOAC office,' said Eric. 'Look let's walk over to my squadron office so I can get things moving.' As they walked, he turned to Monique. 'Has Bob told you how the two of us won the Battle of Britain between us, while on rival Hurricane squadrons at Croydon?'

Monique smiled. 'No, I'm afraid he skipped that part of his life story.'

'He must surely have told you that it was me who taught him to fly the Mosquito?'

'You mean that this infatuation he has with "his" aircraft is your fault?'

'Ah, yes, the Mosquito does seem to have a powerful effect on the people who get to know it. "Infatuation" is a really good word for it.'

*

The BOAC office was a single-storey brick building covered in rather faded camouflage paint behind one of the hangars at RAF Leuchars.

Bob and Monique had taken the opportunity to doze in a

lounge in the officers' mess after they'd finished a thoroughly enjoyable dinner with Wing Commander Gill and, after he came in by chance and then joined them, the station commander, Group Captain More, who Bob had met on his first case with MI11 the previous October.

It seemed the presence of a sleeping group captain had deterred others from using the lounge and as a result the two of them enjoyed well over an hour's sleep before a mess steward had knocked on the frame of the open door to tell them a car was waiting.

As Bob and Monique entered the BOAC office, a man in a civilian pilot's uniform with four rings round his sleeves and a peaked cap on his head looked up from a map on the table he was standing beside. 'Hello, Bob, I assumed "Group Captain Robert Sutherland" was you.'

'This can sometimes be a small world,' said Bob. 'Hello John, how are you? This is Monique Dubois, who works with me in Military Intelligence, Section 11. Monique, this is Squadron Leader John Tickell, who was my second in command on 55 Operational Training Unit at RAF Annan last year, at the time the powers that be decided I should be doing other things instead.'

'Pleased to meet, you, ma'am.'

'Monique is fine.'

'No problem. While we're on names, it's just John or "Captain Tickell" these days, Bob. This is a strictly civilian operation.'

'We had dinner with Eric Gill and Andrew More,' said Bob, 'and we're told that you use a Mosquito now. I've been trying to work out how you would get one passenger in a Mosquito, never mind two.'

'I'll show you presently. First, though, your luggage was delivered earlier, and we need to get you out of uniform. You need to get rid of absolutely everything including your identity discs and your aircrew watch, plus your personal documents and wallet. Put it all in this holdall and we'll keep it securely locked away here until you get back. If you've got some casual clothing available that you can put on under sheepskin lined flying overalls, that would be great. Not shoes, though, we'll be providing boots. It's a three-hour trip, at high altitude, and as a result, and despite the heating system, very cold, so we need to dress to compensate. Here's a bag for you to put your stay-at-home stuff in, Monique.'

Monique was waiting when Bob emerged from the men's toilets. 'I've never seen you in civilian clothing before,' she said. 'I'm not sure a cardigan is quite your thing, and certainly not in that burgundy colour.'

'I agree about the colour, but the idea is that it allows me access to the shoulder holster, which I'm sure meets your approval.'

'And you've removed your identity discs?'

'Yes, ma'am,' said Bob, smiling. 'Though I decided the aircrew watch wouldn't undermine my cover, so kept it on.'

'And I'm wearing this.' Monique held up her left hand for him to see.

'A wedding ring? It fits the cover, I agree, but we've yet to buy the engagement ring!'

'It's only on loan. We can sort out the real thing in due course. On a more serious note, are you wearing the chain with your L-pill on it?'

Bob's smile disappeared. 'I am. As you said earlier, it does bring home the seriousness of what we're getting into.

Shouldn't you be wearing your blonde wig?'

'I did put it on. But it's a work of art and cost someone a lot of money, and someone else a lot of their hair. The thought of stuffing it into a sweaty leather flying helmet for three hours and risking damaging it was more than I could bear. I've got it in a cloth bag I'll carry with me, and I'll put it on as soon as we get there.'

'Does that mean I'm going to have to wait to see you in it? I find the idea very alluring.'

'You fancy the thought of going to bed with a strange blonde, then?' Monique smiled. 'I'm afraid you're going to have to wait until quite a lot later tonight for that.' She seemed to be about to say more, but at that moment John Tickell walked back into the office followed by two men in white overalls who, he said, would look after the suitcases.

Tickell was now fully kitted out for flying. Civilian operation or not, thought Bob, he looked completely indistinguishable from a bomber pilot about to set off for Hamburg or Berlin.

*

By Bob's watch it was 12.30 a.m. when they emerged from the short corridor that led past empty offices into the hangar nearest the BOAC office. There were several Mosquitos in various stages of disassembly and Bob saw his own sitting in the far corner, waiting to be serviced. This was clearly 540 Squadron's hangar.

'We've borrowed this end for our parking area,' said John. 'It wasn't such an issue when we were relying only on types like the Avro York and Lockheed Hudson, but as we've currently only got one Mosquito, we don't want to broadcast whether it's at Leuchars or not too widely, because if it's not here then there's a good chance that it could be somewhere where a well-informed German fighter pilot might be able to find it. We've still got one of the Hudsons parked outside.'

Bob saw that the BOAC Mosquito was camouflaged much like his own, but carried a civilian registration, G-AGFV, in large letters on the sides of the fuselage. From this angle he could see it was in even larger letters across the underside of both wings. The registration was underlined in a long tricolour of red, white and blue.

'I'm still not seeing how we all fit in,' said Bob. 'And where's your navigator?'

'On these flights it's a "first officer", but tonight he's got the night off and you'll take his seat, Bob. Nominally you'll be doing the navigation, which I recall you were rather good at. But don't worry, I know the way, by day or by night. I'll be making the trip back solo.'

'What about me?' asked Monique.

'Are you at all claustrophobic?'

'No, why?'

'Follow me, I'll show you.' He let them both under the aircraft, where the bomb bay doors were open. 'We've converted the front part of the bomb bay into a rather cosy little den for one person. It's felt-lined as you can see, for comfort. There's an oxygen supply in here, which you'll need, and you will be plugged into the intercom. There are also heating controls which I'll show you how to operate, and a reading light. We can additionally provide coffee and sandwiches. Or not as you prefer,' as he saw Monique shake her head.

'What would have happened if I had been claustrophobic?'

'Let's just say that could have been tricky.'

'And toilet facilities?'

'We're all in the same boat as far as that's concerned. That's why I suggested a toilet break before you got all that kit on.'

Bob looked into the space that Monique was meant to occupy for the next three hours and felt deeply relieved that it wasn't him who would have to travel that way. He looked round. 'What are the metal baskets for in the rear part of the bomb bay?'

'Tonight, they're for your suitcases,' said John. 'As often as not, however, they are for the boxes of ball bearings we bring back from Sweden. Our war industry relies heavily on Swedish ball bearings, as does the German war industry for that matter. The amount we can carry does actually make a difference. On the outward trip we'll sometimes carry gold, as bars or sovereigns. The Swedes are very businesslike people and very much prefer cash on delivery.'

*

To Bob's surprise, John started the aircraft while they were still inside the hangar. He then taxied out and round the airfield to line up at the eastern end of the longest runway, which was lit up ahead of them by the beam of the Chance Light, a floodlight located just to the left of the threshold, and by the runway marker lights. After the wheels had come up and the speed increased, Bob found he could breathe again as they turned back towards the North Sea and began their climb. Looking over towards Leuchars, Bob saw all the runway lights go out, consigning the entire area to darkness.

He looked at John, but could see only the vaguest outline of him, illuminated by the dimmed lights from the instruments. 'The only thing I don't like about the Mossie are those few moments after takeoff, when you find yourself listening to the engines and wishing for the speed to increase to the point where a failure isn't going to kill you.'

'Me too,' said John. 'I've talked to pilots on 540 Squadron who say that stays with you, even after months of flying the thing.'

'You do know I can hear everything you are saying over the intercom, don't you?' said Monique.

'Sorry, Monique,' said Bob, mentally kicking himself.

'Is there any way we can change that, so I don't have to listen to the two of you talk about aeroplanes, which is what I suspect you are going to do for the next three hours? It's actually quite comfortable down here and I'd like to try to get some sleep.'

'Yes, we can manage that Monique,' said John. 'But your microphone will still work if you activate it so you can let us know if you have any problems.'

'I will.'

They flew over the edge of a weather front as they crossed the North Sea, the clouds beautifully illuminated from above by the nearly full moon.

'A little cloud is never a bad thing as you near enemy territory,' said John.

'What's our route tonight?'

'In a straight line it's about 685 nautical miles from Leuchars to Stockholm's Bromma Airport, but that takes you over a chunk of southern Norway. We don't like to make things too easy for the Luftwaffe, so rarely travel in a straight line and try to vary our route a little as well. If you take a slight dogleg to the south, you can avoid overflying both Norway and Denmark, and make an approach to Sweden over the Skagerrak. That's what I intend to do tonight. We're still within range of fighter bases in both Norway and Denmark, so need to keep a good lookout.'

'Presumably, that's why you fly at night as well?' asked Bob.

'Usually, we fly during daylight in the Mosquito. We always flew at night in slower, lower and more vulnerable aircraft, and still do when we use them, but we've found that with the Mosquito we can outrun or climb above pretty much anything that tries to come after us. This particular aircraft has been modified in ways that make it, we believe, the fastest example of the type that has yet flown. We would have had to fly this trip at night anyway because of your schedule but I understand it was thought better to wait a few hours until we could arrive in the early hours of the morning rather than before midnight. That way we might catch the Abwehr spy ring at Bromma Airport off guard or, with any luck, literally asleep.'

CHAPTER EIGHT

'It's seeing lights on the ground that I find strangest,' said Bob.

'Yes', said John, 'it takes you back to before the war, doesn't it? We're almost there. The approach to the active runway at Bromma is from the south-east tonight so we'll turn just to the south of the city centre before making our approach. It's the early hours of the morning, yet there's still plenty of light down there.

'Having said that, I did one trip in January in a Lockheed Hudson, and we got to about this point and realised there was hardly a light to be seen anywhere. The Swedes don't take their neutrality for granted and run regular civil defence exercises. You'll see communal air raid shelters on Stockholm's streets for example. That night it had been decreed that the population of the city would practice their blackout drills in case of an air raid. Let me tell you they did very well indeed and gave me the fright of my life. My first thought was that we'd mucked up our navigation to the extent that we were over Oslo or Copenhagen. Then we realised that we'd seen lights on the ground as we crossed southern Sweden to get here.

'My second thought was that without runway lights we'd never be able to land. Fortunately, a quick radio call to the tower sorted that out, but I did have a nasty few moments until the lights came on.'

*

At Bromma they taxied past an airport building and a large hangar, coming to rest just outside its far end, near some offices built onto its side. Two cars were parked nearby.

Bob and John helped Monique out of her compartment. She'd already taken off her leather flying helmet and put her blonde wig on. She said she'd slept almost the whole way over, waking only when she felt the jolt of the landing. They then took the suitcases out of the baskets in the bomb bay and John led the way towards the offices that Bob had seen as they came to a halt. He could see a man in a dark overcoat and a matching trilby hat standing in a window, watching them.

As they entered from a short corridor, the man stubbed out his cigarette and smiled broadly. 'Mr and Mrs Cadman, I'm so pleased to meet you. My name is Peter Bostock and I'm with the British Passport Control Organisation in Stockholm.'

'I'll say my farewells, then, Bob.'

'Thanks, John. Are you heading straight back?' Bob asked.

'I'm going to see if I can get a cup of coffee at this time, then yes, I'll collect your flying kit and make my way back to Leuchars. There's no return cargo this morning apparently, as this trip was a last-minute thing.'

As John walked away, Bob turned back to Peter Bostock. He remembered that Jonathan Waddell had said that 'British Passport Control Organisation' was the cover – he'd described it as 'so thin it's virtually transparent' – used by SIS in various parts of the world. Both Bob and Monique shook Peter Bostock's hand.

Bostock smiled again. 'Can we get you out of your flying kit? I assume you'll have shoes in the suitcases. Then we need to get you through Swedish passport control. I've got a driver and a car waiting and will run you to your hotel. The airport's quite close to the city centre, so it won't take long.

After they'd shed their sheepskin lined overalls and boots,

they donned shoes and coats.

Bostock then led them across the corridor to a neighbouring office. 'Passport control is normally in the main airport building but as the place is so quiet at this time of the morning, they've agreed you can do it here. That also keeps you away from any prying eyes that may still be about, though you can take it for granted that your arrival will be reported by the gentleman we are about to meet to the Swedish Security Service as soon as we leave him. They like to keep tabs on everyone and everything.'

The office was occupied by a man in a black uniform and peaked cap, sitting at a desk and reading a newspaper. He looked up as they entered. 'Hello.' He stood up and walked across the office. 'Can you bring you passports over to this table, please?' The officer took the documents held out by Bob and Monique. He leafed through each in turn, scrutinising the photographs and then looking at them. 'Can I ask why you have come to Stockholm?'

'Business,' said Bob.

'What business?'

'I sell aeroplanes for de Havilland. I'd like to sell some to the Swedish Air Force.'

'And you, Mrs Cadman. Do you always accompany your husband on his sales trips?'

'No, but I've been asked to look at social conditions in Stockholm and write a paper comparing them to London.'

The officer had been making notes and wrote this down as well. 'You both have suitcases. Can you tell me whether you are carrying any of these items with you?' He put a piece of paper on the table in front of them. It had, in English, a list on it that covered obvious things like alcohol and tobacco, plus some less obvious items. Bob had expected to see firearms mentioned but didn't.

'No, I'm not carrying anything on that list,' said Monique.

'Nor I,' said Bob.

'Very well, everything seems to be in order.' The officer stamped their passports, on the opposite pages to their Swedish visas, and then handed them back to their owners. 'Welcome to Sweden'.

*

'The Swedes can be quite helpful these days,' said Peter Bostock, turning round in his seat in the front of the car. 'But never underestimate them. They'll know you aren't who you say you are but will be happy enough to suspend disbelief so long as you behave yourselves.'

'What counts as behaving ourselves?' asked Monique.

'They are fairly broad-minded, though as I found out on Sunday, if they think we are abusing their hospitality by bringing the nastier aspects of the war too close, then they can be altogether less friendly. I assume you are both carrying weapons. Keep them out of sight unless you are going to be able to justify why you didn't to the Swedes afterwards.'

'You talked about our hotel,' said Monique. 'Where are we staying?'

'We sometimes put visitors up at a place called the Hotel Skeppsbron. As the name implies, it's on Skeppsbron, which is the road that runs down the east side of Stadsholmen, the island that's home to Stockholm's old town, more usually known as "Staden mellan broarna" or the "Town Between the Bridges". There's an extremely popular restaurant on the ground floor of the hotel.'

'I visited Stockholm before the war,' said Monique. 'I stayed in a huge place that seemed in competition with the Royal Palace, across on the other side of the stretch of water it looked out over. I think it was called the Grand Hotel.'

'Yes.' said Bostock. 'It lives up to its name but it's not ideal for our purposes. For one thing, they've set up a press room there that's used as a gathering place for foreign correspondents from around the world. Last time I heard, there were nearly 50 journalists based there, plus support staff. It is known, with good reason, as "the listening post of Europe". The other slight drawback is that it's very close to the German legation, so tends to be used a lot by their staff. For both of those reasons it's not good for anyone trying to keep a low profile.'

'Can I ask a stupid question?' asked Bob.

'I've always found those are the ones that work best,' said Bostock.

'Since we left the airport, I've been trying to work out what's wrong about this car, and I've suddenly realised what it is. We are driving on the left, yet this is a left-hand drive car. Is it a vehicle that's been imported from somewhere else in Europe?'

Peter Bostock laughed. 'No, this is a Volvo and was manufactured in Sweden. You've hit upon one of the great conundrums of Swedish life. Although they drive on the left, almost all the cars they use, including those they manufacture themselves, are left-hand drive. I'm not sure of the historical roots, but I was told that the question of incompatibility with their overland neighbours in Norway and Finland, who drive on the right, has been a bone of contention for as long as there have been roads crossing the borders.'

A few moments later he spoke again. 'We've just crossed a

bridge onto the island of Stadsholmen and we'll be at your hotel shortly. I'll show you straight up to the top floor where you have a large corner room with private facilities and a view over the harbour. There is a lift, thankfully. I understand that you don't want our help with security?'

'It seems too much like waving a flag and shouting, "look at us",' said Monique.

'Fair enough if that's your preference. I should say that we've checked your room for hidden microphones, but the fact that it's free of them now doesn't mean it will necessarily stay free of them.

'Given the time, I suggest I return at, let's say, 1 p.m. That will allow you some sleep. I can then take you for lunch. We've got a day in hand before things hopefully start to happen tomorrow. The most useful thing might be for me to give you a Cook's tour of the city this afternoon, so you've got a general idea of the layout and know where some of the key players are located. How does that sound?'

*

'This is extremely nice,' said Monique. 'We seem to be up in the roof and, as far as you can tell in the dark, the view from the window is amazing. It's such a luxury not having to turn off the lights before opening the curtains. Talking of views, you haven't said what you think of me as a blonde.'

'You look great. You remind me of someone, though I can't quite think who. But if I'm honest I prefer the real non-blonde Monique.'

'Thank you for saying so my love.'

'I know who it is you remind me of! Remember that new

film we saw a few weeks back in Poole's Roxy Cinema on Gorgie Road?'

'Casablanca?'

'That's the one. The female lead was a Swedish actress called Ingrid Bergman. In that wig you could almost pass for her in the film.'

Monique laughed.

'What's funny?' asked Bob.

'That solves a mystery I've been puzzling over since you put that coat and hat on at the airport. When you were sorting out your no-expense-spared wardrobe in London yesterday, what decided you to pick that particular coat and that particular hat out of the many that must have been on offer?'

'I don't know,' said Bob, defensively. 'It's been a long time since I've had to choose my own clothes remember. I normally live in my uniform. Why, don't you like them?'

'They wouldn't have been my first choice but that doesn't matter. What matters is that it shows just how much of an impression "Casablanca" must have made on you, which is a surprise given how forgettable a film it was.'

'It was nicely stirring, in an anti-Nazi sort of way. But I agree that it's no "Gone with the Wind". Why?'

'Think back. Humphrey Bogart's character wore a hat and a trench coat just like yours at the airport at the end of the film.'

'You know, I think you're right. I wonder if that was why the elderly gentleman in the tailors seemed amused when I picked them out. Never mind. I like them even if you don't.' Bob smiled.

'If it helps, you're a lot more handsome than Humphrey Bogart, with or without the hat and trench coat.'

'Thank you. And you are a lot more beautiful than Ingrid

Bergman.'

Monique laughed. 'That may be the first time you've ever told me a direct lie, Bob. But I'll forgive you as it was well meant. Anyway, it's time we were in bed. To sleep, I should add. And before you get any ideas, Ingrid is staying on the bedside table. Sleeping in a wig seems about as sensible as putting a flying helmet over one. I do have one request, though.'

'Let me guess. It's that I keep my Walther PPK within reach.'

'You are learning, Bob. Perhaps you'll develop a killer instinct yet.'

Bob found himself wondering whether that really would be such a desirable outcome. He'd only killed one man and he hadn't found it a very pleasant experience. Then he realised what a hypocrite he was being. As a fighter pilot he'd shot down 24 Luftwaffe aircraft. But aircraft are only things, inanimate objects. Some of the crews of those aircraft had escaped by parachute or by making forced landings. But many hadn't. In his quiet moments Bob knew only too well that what he'd really done was kill a large number of young men who were just like himself except for the language they spoke and the country they happened to have been born in.

CHAPTER NINE

They walked with Peter Bostock into the warren of narrow old town streets that lay behind the Hotel Skeppsbron.

Bostock half-turned as he walked. 'It's pushing our luck a little to eat in the hotel restaurant,' he said. 'It's good, but it can get busy and my face is known to some around the city. It's as well to avoid flaunting too openly in your hotel that the two of you are connected to me. But it's not far to a nice little café where the tables are well spaced out. We head off to the left in the square here and it's just down this street.'

The café interior was quite dark and intimate and fairly quiet, and the table they were seated at did seem secluded enough to ensure privacy, so long as they talked quietly.

Monique looked around. 'Jonathan Waddell described Stockholm as a snake pit. How do we know that none of the residents have arranged for us to be listened to?'

'There comes a point when you just have to decide what the acceptable risk is. I have used this place before, but not frequently. I think we can talk privately.'

The food was pleasant enough but Bob couldn't help thinking that, even by wartime Edinburgh standards, it was a little bland. He tried to summon some enthusiasm but failed.

Peter Bostock must have noticed. 'What you need to remember about Sweden is that although it's neutral, it has been profoundly affected by the war in many ways. Food is rationed, like in Britain. Unlike in Britain, though, some of the food sold in restaurants is also subject to rationing, especially anything containing butter, bread, most meats and eggs. Fish, wild game and rabbit are outside the scope of rationing, as are milk, potatoes and other vegetables. Stories abound of substitutions taking place, with badger and squirrel being used instead of more traditional meats. Some Swedes also seem to have taken to eating seagull eggs. No one's seriously hungry thanks to good harvests last year. Otherwise, it could have been a different story. I've got sets of ration coupons here in each of your names so you should be able to dine as you please.

'Sweden has also been hit because of its traditional heavy reliance on imported oil and coal. It might be home to huge deposits of iron ore, but its shortages of basic fuels have been quite crippling. The saving grace there is that it's quite a large country, not much short of twice the size of the United Kingdom, and much of the land area is covered in trees.

'As a result, they have a huge timber industry and wood is now about the only readily available fuel left. As we drive round later you will see long stacks of cut wood beside streets throughout the city. They are intended for domestic and business heating, and for cooking too. You will also see that most of the cars and lorries on the streets, not that there are all that many cars still running, have been converted to run on wood gas. It's used in Britain too, but not on anything like the same scale as here, or in Germany for that matter. Wood is burned in a controlled way to produce a mix of gases that is then fed into a normal petrol engine. Cars that have been adapted tend to be slower, have much more limited ranges and take a while to get ready to go anywhere. But that's better than cars that haven't been adapted, which are left to rot. The only petrol-powered cars you are likely to see on the streets are official or diplomatic vehicles. Most ordinary people get about the city by tram or on their bicycles. Or they walk. The city centre is not so large as to make that impracticable.

'The reliance on wood pulp extends to its use in place of leather and textiles in some cases and as animal fodder. I've even heard stories of it being used to bulk up food.'

'You're really not making this seem any more appetising,' said Bob, smiling.

'Sorry, don't shoot the messenger. Before I finish on rationing it's as well to tell you about alcohol. The sale of spirits is heavily regulated though not primarily because of the war. Sweden's had a strong temperance movement since the last century. For the last couple of decades that's resulted in those old enough to drink spirits being issued with ration books that are stamped whenever they make a purchase. When they run out of spaces for stamps in a given month they must wait until the start of the next month to make a purchase. It's called the Stockholm System or the Bratt System. Beer and wine aren't included in the scheme, but beer in Sweden tends to be very weak and imported wine can be as hard to find as petrol.

'People can buy spirits in restaurants to get round the system, but only if they order a three-course meal. And of course, food in restaurants is itself now rationed. You'll find in some places that they have an utterly inedible meal available that gets served to customer after customer to allow the sale of spirits to be justified. It's quite common to see these meals appearing with previous customers' cigarette butts on the plate along with the cold inedible food.'

'Now that is truly nauseating,' said Bob.

'Indeed. But if I can give you a brief summary, it's that while no one's actually bombed Stockholm, don't assume that the people you see have entirely escaped the effects of the war.'

'Yes, I understand,' said Bob, as a dessert was served that was rather more appetising in appearance than the main course had been. 'I'm sure that the people here are extremely grateful to be out of it, though. Given the reliance of the Germans on Swedish iron ore and, so I was told last night, ball bearings, wouldn't it have been easier for Hitler simply to invade Sweden when he invaded Norway and Denmark?'

'That's a question that was endlessly debated for a while. I think that the simple answer is that he had little to gain from doing so. It wasn't widely publicised at the time, and still isn't, but the Swedes allowed the Germans to transport troops back and forth along Swedish railway lines between the Baltic ports and Norway after their invasion of that country. Later, after the German invasion of the Soviet Union, the Swedes allowed the transport on their railways of an entire German infantry division from the Norwegian border to the Finnish border.

'I'm sure the Swedes didn't relish the idea of dancing with the devil, but they appear to have calculated correctly that if they made some concessions, it would prevent invasion and preserve their neutrality. On the other hand, they have flexed their neutrality in more helpful ways too. They have been hugely supportive of large numbers of Norwegian and Danish refugees and turned a blind eye to resistance organisations being set up in those countries, especially Norway, with links back to Sweden. They are even apparently comfortable with the idea of our friends in the Special Operations Executive running and equipping their Norwegian networks from within Sweden, despite some earlier problems caused here by SOE. Meanwhile, there are many Danish Jews who owe their lives to the safe haven offered by Sweden, and tens of thousands of Finnish children can say the same thing.'

'Jonathan Waddell suggested the Swedes are shifting their stance in the allies' favour now the tide of the war seems to have turned and there is no longer a realistic threat to them from Germany.'

'That's true. It's too early to say yet, but I think the Germans' defeat at Stalingrad last month might be particularly influential. I've got one contact who told me that there are some in the Swedish government who want to see the country actively training Norwegian and Danish resistance fighters. Right, if you've both finished, I'll sort out the bill and ration coupons. There should be a driver and car outside.'

*

Peter Bostock sat in the front again and turned round so he could talk to Bob and Monique, who he'd given a map of the city centre to allow them to follow the route. 'We'll start by retracing our steps from last night, following the road along the shore of this island, Stadsholmen, and round the corner of the Royal Palace. Then we cross Norrbro, the main bridge to Norrmalm, the part of the city to the north.'

The weather was largely cloudy, with the occasional glimpse of patches of blue sky. As they drove, Bob began to recognise the picture that Bostock had painted over lunch. Bicycles and pedestrians were everywhere and the few cars they saw nearly all had remarkably ugly wood gas conversions involving the addition of what in most cases looked like a cylindrical domestic water tank, usually at their rear.

'The first highlight of the tour is the Grand Hotel, which we discussed last night. As you know, Monique, that's the very imposing building on our left. Just beyond it, also overlooking this end of the Norrström, the river on our right which forms part of the harbour, is the home of the German Legation in

Stockholm at Hovslagargatan 2.'

Bob leaned forwards in his seat for a better view and looked with interest at a five-storey plus roof level structure built from a light-coloured stone. It had a large flag of Nazi Germany flying from a flagpole on the roof. Though tall, the frontage of the building was only three bays wide. His view of the far side as they drove past was obscured by a stack of wood that must have been a dozen feet high and over fifty yards long running alongside the road. This wasn't the first stack of firewood he'd seen so far on their drive, but it was the largest.

'As Hitler's embassy in Sweden it doesn't look very large,' he said.

'It gives a rather misleading impression because in plan the building is a triangle and what you see from the road is just an end of it rather than a side. Besides, as we'll see presently, our German friends do have other accommodation in the city. The large building immediately past it, on our left now, is the Nationalmuseum, which is well worth a visit so long as you don't mind the neighbours.'

A few minutes later he spoke again. 'We've now driven round to the other side of what amounts to a peninsula called Blasieholmen, which I've been told was originally a separate island. The finger of water on our right here is Nybroviken, which forms another arm of the harbour.'

He spoke to the driver. 'Alex, can you pull over and stop for a moment? Thank you. I've stopped here to show you the building you can see on the far side of the harbour, the very grand-looking place with two blocks fronting on to the street with a gap between them that gives a view to a third part standing well back.'

'Yes, we see it,' said Bob.

'That's Strandvägen 7. The central part, the shy and retiring part, is where you'll find the offices of the OSS, the Office of Strategic Services, or our American opposite numbers if you prefer.'

Bostock then directed the driver to take them round to the head of the harbour, where they turned left onto a broad shopping street. 'This is Birger Jarlsgatan, said to be one of the longest streets in central Stockholm. Let's slow down a moment. I've brought you here to show you the white stone building we are approaching on our right. That is Birger Jarlsgatan 12, which houses the offices of the British Passport Control Organisation, where I am based.'

'So that's where we find SIS,' said Bob.

Bostock smiled. 'Yes, it is rather futile to try to maintain a pretence that everyone who matters saw through years ago. But we are still officially the British Passport Control Organisation in the city, and we spend at least some of our time on passport work just to maintain the cover.'

The car turned right and seemed to be heading back the way they had come along a nearly parallel road. Then they turned left. 'Now, just to show you what an intimate little city we live in, this is Nybrogatan, and a little further up here on the left, yes, here it is, the large brick building, is number 27. That's where you find the "Bureau Wagner", which is what the Germans call the Abwehr headquarters in the city.'

'Which means that SIS, the OSS and the Abwehr are all located within short walking distance of one another?' asked Bob, looking at the map.

'I did say it was an intimate little city.'

'Why do they call it the Bureau Wagner?' asked Monique.

'It's named after the senior officer, Major Hans Wagner,

who the Abwehr apparently refer to when talking to the Swedes as "Dr Wagner". The Abwehr operation in the city was based in the German Legation until last October, when it moved here. Since then, it has been known as the Bureau Wagner.'

'Wagner's not someone I've heard of,' said Monique. 'Where to next?'

'Next, we take a quick look at what amounts to something of an outlier in the pattern, though still quite close in real terms. The Soviet NKVD is based at Villagatan 7.' This time it took a few minutes for the car to take them to, and then past, a large stone villa on a street a little to the north of the other addresses they had visited. Throughout the journey the vehicle traffic remained light, but the driver was clearly having to pay close attention to the swarms of cyclists.

Monique leaned forwards in her seat. 'Something you need to know, Peter, is that the occupants of that building have as much reason to want the two of us dead as those of the Bureau Wagner.'

'That is useful to know,' said Bostock, 'if not necessarily helpful in terms of ensuring your safety. Let's take a right at this next junction and we'll head south-east along Östermalmsgatan. This time I want to show you where the home team are based, the Swedish Security Service. It's worth bearing in mind that the Swedes run a huge operation to make sure they are aware of what we are all getting up to on their patch. You must assume that every phone call you make here is listened in on, and every telegram and letter is read. Not all of them are, of course, but the only sensible option is to work on that assumption. What's interesting is that while all the foreign agencies operating in the city know about this, very few Swedes do. The service is not publicly acknowledged despite employing, by one reliable estimate I heard recently, over a thousand people.

'They are based in this large complex of grey stone buildings on the left, with the red tiled roofs. This is known to Swedes as "The Grey House" or "The General Staff House". It is also home to the HQ of the Swedish armed forces, but a significant part has been taken over by our friends in the Swedish Security Service.

'Our final port of call is a mile or so to the south-east and a little removed from the other locations I've shown you. The British embassy can be found in the Bünsowska Villa in what has traditionally been the diplomatic quarter of Stockholm. It's an amazing building that looks out over a stretch of water to the island of Djurgården. We can drive by, but we'll not call in. The "real" diplomats of the Foreign Office tend to be a bit sniffy about us "cloak and dagger" types.'

Bostock resumed his commentary when the car was on a broad avenue lined on the right-hand side by large villas. 'Over there is the rear of the British embassy. It's actually much larger than it seems because that's only the smaller of two ranges which are set at an angle to one another. We'll take a right at the end here and travel back on ourselves on a street running alongside the water.' After they'd done so he said, 'That's the front of the building on the right, the brick structure with the curved frontage. They do amazing cocktail receptions but, as I said, don't expect an invitation.

'That's pretty much everything I wanted to show you by way of orientation. What I suggest is that I run you back to your hotel and you can have the evening off. Hopefully things will get more interesting tomorrow. We'll be monitoring any flights into Bromma Airport from Berlin to see if we can identify

Maximilian von Moser on arrival, assuming he comes by air, which is by no means certain. There are other ways he could arrive that would be less visible, so we'll have to see.

'As for this evening, I suggest the two of you keep a low profile in the hotel restaurant. Here are the food coupons I talked about. I've also got a ration book for you, Bob, that will allow you to buy spirits. Will you want one too, Monique?'

'No, thanks.'

'The offer of a security detail is still open if you want it.'

She shook her head.

'If you change your minds just let me know,' said Bostock. 'You said yourself, Monique, that the NKVD and Abwehr would both like to see you dead if they knew you were here. We must also bear in mind that we have no idea who killed Werner Lippisch, the Abwehr agent I met on Sunday, and they must clearly be considered a threat to you as well.'

'Are there no clues at all?' asked Monique.

'The Swedes were fairly quick to conclude it wasn't me, for which I was very grateful, but I have no idea what they based that conclusion on. The problem is that given the nature of what seems to be proposed by Lippisch and von Moser, the list of possible suspects who might want a possibly rogue Abwehr agent dead is a long one.'

'It has to include other elements in the Abwehr,' said Monique.

'That's true. But it's worth also bearing in mind that the key players whose premises I showed you today are only the most obvious elements of the picture. There is also a significant Finnish presence here and official or – more often – unofficial representatives of occupied Czechoslovakia, Poland, France, Norway and Denmark active in the city. Even the Japanese have a finger in the pie.'

'I can see that complicates matters,' said Monique.

'Oh, it gets a lot more complicated than that. There are others who I personally think offer between them the most likely explanation for the death of Werner Lippisch.'

'Who are they?' asked Bob.

'Other German agencies with a presence in the city. For example, we've identified known agents of the Sicherheitsdienst or SD in Stockholm in the past few months. Given the difficult relationship between the SD and the Abwehr, the idea of an element of the Abwehr wanting to make proposals to the British would be of huge interest to them.

'Then we've got an odd organisation called INF III, which apparently provides a personal spy network reporting direct to Joachim von Ribbentrop who, as you know, is the Nazi Foreign Minister. It appears that this network operates in parallel with, but entirely separate from, the Auswärtiges Amt, or the German Foreign Office. We've identified the press attaché in the German Legation as heading up this organisation in Stockholm but suspect that's something not known to his Auswärtiges Amt colleagues in the legation or to the Bureau Wagner.

'Just to muddy the waters further, there's also an arm in Stockholm of the NSDAP/AO, which is the foreign organisation of the National Socialist German Workers Party, better known as the Nazi Party.'

'Good grief,' said Bob. 'What an utter mess.'

'Indeed. What it boils down to is that the list of people who might want to prevent part of the Abwehr cosying up to the British is a long and confusing one. Whoever killed Lippisch might well also want von Moser dead or, if they knew who she really was, Mrs Cadman here. Please be careful this evening.

Anyway, this is your hotel coming up on the right. Here's a note of my home and office telephone numbers. Don't hesitate to call if you have a problem, but remember what I said about phone calls being listened to here.'

CHAPTER TEN

Monique was standing in the bedroom window, which she'd opened wide despite the chill outside. 'I just can't get over that view.'

Bob came to stand behind her and put his arms around her waist. 'It is pretty amazing. I've still got the map we were given by...' Monique had quickly turned to place a finger over his lips to stop him talking, then placed it against her own, in a 'shush!' gesture.

'Ah, yes, of course,' said Bob. 'We've got a couple of hours before we're going to want dinner and if we can't discuss anything meaningful, how are we going to pass the time? There's something I need to talk to you about after today. Should we go out for a walk?'

Monique smiled. 'Perhaps we could walk and talk when the time comes for dinner? More immediately, I'm very taken by the idea of putting the lovely bath we've got in our very own bathroom to good use, assuming the hotel can run to a bath-full of hot water. Then I thought that Humphrey might want to take Ingrid to bed. Though if you'd prefer, I'd be happy if Bob just wanted to enjoy some time with Monique. The bed doesn't seem to creak which is always a good start.'

'That sounds fine by me,' said Bob, 'but let's close the window before the room gets cold.'

The hotel did run to an adequate supply of hot water and the bed didn't creak, even when tested vigorously. Bob initially found himself distracted by the idea that their lovemaking might be being listened to by the Swedish Security Service, but it rapidly became clear that Monique suffered from no such inhibitions. Bob let himself follow her lead and put the idea out of his head. These were the benefits, he thought, of being given a cover as a married couple.

Bob was quite happy that Ingrid had again been consigned to the bedside table before Monique had stepped into the bath. And while he very much liked the trench coat and hat that he had acquired in London he didn't think he'd ever see himself as Humphrey Bogart. On the other hand, he was beginning to think that Stockholm did have more than a passing resemblance to the Casablanca portrayed in the film. Just so long as they didn't find themselves in Rick's Café they'd be fine, he thought, as he trailed his fingers softly up the inside of Monique's right thigh.

*

They walked out of the Hotel Skeppsbron at a little after 6.30 p.m. The clouds had thickened since their earlier drive and there was now a chill, cutting wind coming in from the east, straight off the harbour onto Skeppsbron. Bob was surprised to see how dark it was getting. The clouds didn't help, and the gloom made it feel as if the sun had already set somewhere beyond them.

Both had stopped at the top of the three steps descending from the red stone arch beyond the hotel's front door to the pavement. 'The street lights are starting to come on,' he said. 'I was amazed to see them on our drive in from the airport this morning. They really bring home just what a difference the blackout makes to our lives back home.'

'I'm looking forward to the chance to stroll without any need for torches and with no chance of tripping over or falling down kerbs,' said Monique. 'Good grief, that wind is freezing. The hat and wig help, but not much. Let's cut up the side of the hotel and into the old town. We'll be sheltered there. We might find a café open that sells coffee.'

'Do you really think there could be someone listening in to our room?' asked Bob.

'Probably not, but we have to assume there might be. The Swedes would have had plenty of opportunity while we were out this afternoon to wire microphones in if they wanted to. It takes a fair bit of effort, and it very much depends how curious they are about us. Anyway, it's a good excuse for a walk.'

'Are you going to tell me why you suggested I put on a clean shirt and the more formal of the suits, and why you've picked your best dress?'

'All in good time, Bob.'

They turned left and then walked up a narrow street along the side of the hotel. It took only a short time to reach the 'square' that they had passed through with Bostock earlier that day: which was more triangular than square in shape. As it had been earlier, it was busy with people walking this way or that, singly or in couples. Having looked at the map Bostock had given them, Bob suggested they head straight across the square rather than turn left as they had on the way to lunch. This took them into a narrow, paved street lined with shops. A sign on a wall proclaimed it to be Västerlånggatan.

They had only walked a few yards along the street when Monique surprised Bob by looking over her shoulder and then pushing him sharply to his right, through a square-topped doorway beyond which was a narrow alley. Looking ahead he could see, in the light of ornate lamps attached to the buildings on one side of the alley, the start of a flight of stone steps. It made him think of Fleshmarket Close in Edinburgh, though apparently with fewer steps. The alley was empty, in contrast to the street behind them.

'What are you doing…' He stopped when he saw that Monique was holding her pistol.

'Quiet, Bob, someone's following us. They were out of sight long enough for us to hide in here. Stand against the wall on this side, where you are partly hidden.'

Bob did as he was told then watched as Monique turned back towards the street, pressed against the wall so she would also be hidden by the frame of the doorway built round the entrance to the alley. A figure in a light overcoat and dark hat stopped in the street nearby, his back to them as he looked from side to side, up and down the street. He appeared to be unaware of the alley behind him.

Monique stepped forwards and Bob heard her say, 'Walk slowly backwards,' as she pressed the muzzle of her pistol into the figure's back. Bob was transfixed, but none of the many people passing along the street seemed to notice anything odd. 'That's right. Slowly now. Two more paces.' Then, as the man reversed through the doorway, 'Right, hands in the air where I can see them. Turn round, get your back to the wall.'

Bob saw Monique reach into the top of the man's overcoat. She removed and passed a pistol to him, never wavering in the aim of her own.

'Who are you and why are you following us?' she asked.

To Bob's surprise, the man smiled. 'I think you know that already, Mrs Cadman, or you'd not be speaking to me in English. My name is Neil Prentice and I work for Peter Bostock.'

'It's all right Bob,' said Monique, 'you can give him his

pistol back.'

Bob did so.

'As for you, Mr Prentice, I'd be grateful if you would pass on a message to Peter Bostock. Please tell him that while we are grateful for his concern, when we said we didn't want or need him to provide security for us we really meant it. Your presence following us round, not very expertly if I may say, can only help attract attention to us. I much prefer the idea of knowing that if someone is following me then I can deal with the problem as I see fit, without fear of hurting anyone on my side. You should consider yourself lucky that I half expected you, or someone like you from SIS, to turn up.'

'In his defence, Mrs Cadman, I believe Peter was acting on instructions from London.'

'Tell him that he can stop acting on them. Jonathan Waddell knows we don't want security. I'm not happy he chose to ignore our wishes. OK, I suggest you get on your way, preferably heading back the way you came, and leave us to enjoy the rest of our evening.'

Prentice smiled again. 'I will pass your messages on, Mrs Cadman. I think that perhaps someone's underestimated you.'

As Prentice turned and walked back along the street, Bob felt the adrenaline drain out of his system. 'My God! This might be a good time to find out how the spirit rationing system works. A whisky would go down very well right now.'

'We're going to need our wits about us, Bob,' said Monique. 'But we do need to find somewhere warmer to talk.'

Monique led the way back through the doorway into Västerlånggatan and set off in the direction they'd previously been walking.

Most of the shops were closed but some still had lights on.

There were a number of advertising signs at first floor level projecting out into the street, some of which were also illuminated. Street lighting came from lamps attached to the fronts of buildings or strung on wires between opposite sides of the street. Despite the chill in the air, there were still plenty of people about, some obviously hurrying home after work, others apparently just strolling. Bob noticed there were some children amongst the adults on the street.

'You'd never see anything like this in Edinburgh,' he said. 'People avoid going out in the dark unless they need to. After a long dark winter, this feels a little like coming out of hibernation. Wouldn't it be wonderful to see George Street or Rose Street lit up and busy like this after dark?'

'It would, Bob, but I don't see that happening anytime soon.'

A little further along the street Monique stopped and turned to him. 'This looks ideal,' she said, before leading him into the start of a shopping arcade off to the left. On the near side of its entrance was a café that was open. Monique again led the way. The interior was very narrow, with a small serving area at the front. Large windows looked out from most of its length into the arcade. Monique sat at a table some way along, out of hearing of the serving area. The only other customers were a young couple sitting near the front of the café: the man wearing what looked like an army conscript's uniform and the woman in a white cardigan and red beret.

The elderly man who had been behind the counter when they entered approached their table. There was a longer discussion between him and Monique than Bob had expected in, presumably, Swedish before he departed.

'I was asking if their coffee has ever been near a coffee

bean,' said Monique. 'It seems that roasted acorns and, if you are lucky, chicory is about as close as you'll get in most places in Stockholm these days. "Didn't I know there was a war on?" or words to that effect. He did say that their beer, though weak by the Danish standards he thought I'd be used to, was widely liked. On his recommendation I've ordered two beers.'

Bob thought that the beer was pleasantly refreshing. 'Back in the hotel I said there was something I wanted to talk to you about, Monique. What happened on the way here adds focus to my concern.'

'What's that, Bob?'

'When we were flying up to Leuchars,' Bob paused, '24 hours ago, though it seems longer, I asked why you'd rejected the idea of SIS providing us with security here. Your answer was unconvincing. I've also heard you give your reasons to Jonathan Waddell in London and to Peter Bostock and Neil Prentice here in Stockholm. Though you put more effort into what you said to them, I'm still not convinced you are being entirely honest with anyone, me included.'

Monique took a drink from her beer, then put it back on the table between them. 'I'm sorry, Bob. In my defence I was going to tell you the real reason this evening.' She smiled. 'The good thing is that this suggests you are finally learning not to trust anyone, even me.'

'I'm not sure that is a good thing in the circumstances of our engagement,' said Bob. 'Nor does it seem a good thing when we are sitting here, in a way that feels totally exposed, in a city that a deputy director of SIS described as a "snake pit".'

'If this feels exposed, Bob, then I'm not sure you are going to like what I'm about to suggest. A little earlier you asked why I'd picked my best dress to come out in. Peter Bostock suggested that we spend the evening keeping a low profile in our hotel restaurant. For reasons that I promise I'll explain to you, I think it would be very much better if we went for dinner at the Grand Hotel.'

'You are joking, aren't you?' asked Bob. There was a pause while they looked across the table at one another. 'No, I can see you're not. So that was why you declined the offer of security: so that none of our SIS friends could stick their oar in and stop you dining where you pleased?'

Monique just took another drink of her beer, looking at him and saying nothing.

'No, that's not it,' continued Bob. 'You were against our being given any protection right from the start, from before we had any idea where we were staying or how dangerous the Grand Hotel might be for you. You're going to have to tell me, Monique.'

'You recall I said at the meeting in London yesterday that I know, or at least that I once knew, Maximilian von Moser. What I said at the meeting was true, but it wasn't the complete truth.

'As I said, I did fall for von Moser's charms because he was a much younger and more attractive man than my husband at the time and, as it turned out, a vastly more able lover. I very quickly discovered, however, that he was also an utter bastard. I have known some truly horrible men in my time. Count Sergei Ignatieff, my first husband, was the worst of them, but Maximilian von Moser came a close second.

'Once I'd seen through his superficial charm and beauty and his proficiency in bed, I discovered a man who had the ability to suck the joy out of everyone around him and, if he chose, replace it with fear and dread. When I tried to bring our relationship, by then a few weeks old, to an end he threatened to tell my husband what had been going on behind his back.

'He correctly assumed I'd be naïve enough not to realise that he had far more to lose from my husband finding out about our affair than I had. Hans Friedrich von Wedel had many failings, including his being almost 60 and his near total disinterest in sex with his wife, but he was no one's fool and wouldn't have taken ten seconds to work out that our affair was much more von Moser's doing than mine.

'But I was too young and stupid and as a result of von Moser's blackmail our affair dragged on for another month after I'd tried to end it. Then, one night at his apartment in Berlin, when we'd both drunk a lot of brandy and he was being particularly vile, the reality suddenly struck me. I could simply walk away and there was nothing he'd be able to do about it. We got into a furious argument and he tried to strangle me. I got loose of his grip for long enough to grab a full wine bottle that was standing on a table, and I smashed it against the side of his head. He went down on the floor and stayed there. It was red wine and as the bottle had smashed it was hard to tell in the aftermath what was wine and what was blood, though it was obvious there was plenty of the latter.

'I thought I'd killed him and left his apartment in panic. My husband was away, so I went home and cleaned myself up, then sobered up, then realised that if I had killed him, I'd left a trail of clues that would lead even the most stupid of detectives straight to me.'

'But you hadn't killed him,' said Bob.

'No, I hadn't, but you can imagine how I felt, waiting to find out what had happened but not being able to ask anyone. Two days later I heard that Maximilian von Moser was in hospital, recovering from what was being described as a car accident. He never returned to work for my husband and was posted elsewhere when he came out of hospital. I don't think my husband ever found out what had been going on and certainly not about what happened that night.

'I did see von Moser a year or so later, not long before the outbreak of war, when I was attending a function in Paris with my husband. Even from across a large room it was obvious that he'd remember me every time he looked in a mirror, for he had large scars on the left-hand side of his face, where the wine bottle had smashed as I hit him with it. His attempt to strangle me had cost him his beauty.

'He must have sensed someone looking, for he caught my eye across the room. The look of sheer hatred that flashed across his face had to be seen to be believed, though he quickly had his charming mask back in place.'

It was Bob's turn to drink his beer as he collected his thoughts. 'I'm guessing you think that von Moser named you as a contact because he has a personal grudge against you and sees this as an opportunity to bring you close enough to get even?'

'That must be the reason, Bob. As I've said in the past, the Abwehr probably concluded that I'd been working for the British as soon as they heard I'd not been executed with my two fellow spies after I came ashore in Scotland. Von Moser would know that had put me entirely beyond his reach. But now it seems that he's worked out a way to bring me back within it.'

'Why didn't you say any of this in London yesterday?' asked Bob. 'It would have shown this whole enterprise for what it is and I'm sure the idea would have been killed stone dead there and then.'

'You are overlooking two things, Bob. The first is that if von Moser now works closely with Admiral Canaris, the head of the Abwehr, then there might be something real underlying the approach even if von Moser has chosen to pursue a personal vendetta on the back of it. The second is the possibility that I might want to meet von Moser again.'

'Why would you possibly want to meet him again?'

'To hear what he has to say and, if he's still the same evil man who tried to strangle me in 1938, to kill him. I may have permanently disfigured him in return for what he tried to do, but he still appears in my nightmares. It will be easier to move forwards with the rest of my life – for you and I to move forwards with the rest of our lives together – if I take this chance to resolve a nasty hangover from my past.'

'And you don't want SIS providing us with security because you want to minimise the chance of any witnesses when the time comes to resolve your hangover, as you put it?'

'That's right, Bob.'

'Bloody hell! This is becoming a day full of surprises. I'm not saying I agree that what you have in mind is sensible or right, but you've moved things on to the point where I don't have any choice but to accept the situation you've put us in. I am grateful to you for being honest with me even if it's rather belatedly. The part you've not explained is why all this makes it necessary for us to dine in what seems to be the most dangerous place in Stockholm.' Bob sat back and laughed.

'What's so funny?'

'A little earlier, while we were in bed, it occurred to me that in some ways Stockholm is quite like the Casablanca depicted in the film. But we would be fine, I thought, so long as we stayed clear of Rick's Café. Now you're suggesting we go marching straight into Stockholm's version of it while singing "La Marseillaise" just to make sure everyone notices us. Why?'

'Is that the sort of thing you think about when you're in bed with me?'

'Not usually, no,' said Bob, defensively. Then he realised she was pulling his leg and smiled. 'You have to admit that these are unusual circumstances.'

'I'll forgive you then, Bob, if you'll forgive me for not being honest with you about von Moser.'

Bob realised that any response except a smile and a nod could lead them into difficult territory so, despite his real feelings, he smiled and nodded.

'Look at it this way,' said Monique. 'Von Moser may be a bastard, but he's a clever bastard. If you were in his shoes, would you arrive on the day you'd said you were going to arrive, when the British and perhaps the Swedes are on the lookout for you? I'm betting he's already in the city. I thought it might be worth visiting the Grand Hotel because if he is already in Stockholm, then he's as likely to turn up there as anywhere else.

'To be clear, I'm not suggesting we go there trying to draw attention to ourselves. This wig and the makeup do alter my appearance quite dramatically. I think there's a fair chance that even someone who has good reason to remember my face and who is expecting me to be in the city will be deceived. Von Moser, on the other hand, will find it altogether more difficult to change his appearance because of the scars on his face.'

'What do we do if we see him?'

'I don't know, Bob. That will depend on the circumstances. But it might allow us to find out where he's staying. And it might allow us to take the initiative instead of simply sitting around in the hope that von Moser chooses to get in touch with Bostock tomorrow.'

Bob put his beer back down on the table. 'It would also, of course, cut Bostock out entirely and might allow you the chance to kill von Moser while you still have the element of surprise.'

'That's true, too, but I'd do it in a way that didn't compromise the underlying objective we've been sent here to achieve which is to hear the proposals they – whoever "they" are – have to make.'

Bob wished that he totally believed her, then decided it was time for a change of tone. 'I suppose that if nothing else, dinner at the Grand will prove once and for all whether it's possible to get a decent meal in this city.' He looked at his watch. 'Should we finish our beers, pay for them, and go?'

CHAPTER ELEVEN

Bob and Monique made their way north through Stockholm's compact old town, the 'Town Between the Bridges'. It was a little less busy than it had been on their way to the café, but there were still plenty of people about. The bridge they needed was the one they'd already crossed several times with Peter Bostock.

Once they were out of the old town's narrow streets the wind made itself keenly felt. Like the people they passed, Bob and Monique hunched down into their collars for protection. More than once, Bob felt as if he was about to lose his hat to the wind.

For Bob, the only consolation was that as soon as they started to cross the bridge, the lights of the Grand Hotel came into view, off to the right. Once they made it over the bridge it wasn't too far to the hotel, whose entrance fully lived up to the grandeur of the hotel's name.

As they approached the doors from the pavement, Monique squeezed Bob's hand. 'Act as if you are going into the North British Hotel on Princes Street. And talk English. I'm just the quiet wife: the "appendage," as Jonathan Waddell put it. I'll smile and say nothing unless I have to.'

The uniformed porter who greeted them in the busy lobby, at the top of the short flight of stairs up from the main doors, did so in English. Something about them clearly looked foreign, Bob realised. The man wasn't the least put out to hear that Bob and Monique had no booking but wanted to eat in the hotel's best dining room anyway. He told them where to find the cloakroom and pointed out the way to the restaurant.

What they found was a large and immensely impressive rectangular room that to Bob seemed quite busy: busy enough to be noticeable smoky, but not overwhelmingly so. Drawn curtains along one long side suggested windows, while towards the rear of the room the stunningly ornate ceiling was supported by a line of highly decorated square columns.

Looking around, Bob saw that some of the men were wearing dinner jackets. Most, however, kept him company by wearing lounge suits. A few of the male diners were eating on their own while others, presumably here on business, were sharing their tables with one or more other men. The smaller number of women in the restaurant seemed dressed to impress and most were partnered by dinner-jacketed men. There was a hum of conversation in the room that Bob found comfortable.

Bob and Monique were taken to a table nearly in the centre of the room, but Monique asked, in English, if it would be possible to sit at one that was vacant at the rear of the restaurant, nearer a corner. The waiter seemed about to point out what Bob had already seen: that the table Monique had identified carried a small sign which he assumed meant it was reserved. But then the man was caught by the full force of Monique's dazzling smile and led them over to it, removing the sign as he reached the table.

Monique chose the seat at the rear of the table, the one that Bob realised offered the best view of the body of the restaurant, and smiled again, thanking the waiter in English. He responded by pulling out her chair to help her sit, then unfurling her serviette. Bob sat, unaided, on the side of the table that offered a view down the length of the room, though his view of the near end of it was restricted by the lack of vision in his left eye. The tables were well-spaced, giving every opportunity for private conversation. When asked by the waiter if he wanted to see the wine list, Bob ordered a bottle of soda water for each of them.

'Sorry, Bob,' said Monique, 'I hope you don't mind my having first choice of seats. I just want to be able to keep watch on as much of the restaurant as possible.'

'Is that why you wanted a table nearer the side rather than in the centre?'

'Yes, though as a matter of principle it's better to select your own table rather than take one you've been given. Though that doesn't really matter when you turn up unannounced, as we have here.' She stopped talking as the waiter returned with bottles of soda water and menus which, Bob saw, were in English.

The menu restored his faith in Swedish wartime cuisine, though it also left him feeling grateful that they'd been given a generous quantity of cash before leaving London.

'It looks like the menu gives prices in kronas and in ration points,' said Bob.

'I think the plural of krona is kronor, my love. But yes, you are right. It seems you really can get just about anything in wartime so long as you are able to pay top prices for it. Looking at this, it's difficult to get any sense of how to budget for the rationing. Beef tournedos is 100 ration points, for example, but potatoes and vegetables only have a cost in kronor.'

'I don't know about you, Monique, but it seems to me that the best way to forget there's a war on is to select items that are not rationed. There are several starters that fall into this category, and mains. The venison sounds ideal from my point of view.'

'I think you're probably right, Bob. The fish dishes, depending on what else is in them, are also outside the rationing system. It's less easy for dessert, though, presumably because butter and eggs are rationed. I'm sure they are used to helping visitors unfamiliar with the system.'

'Do you think we're going to be able to manage to eat a three-course dinner?' asked Bob.

'We must. Remember that the point of being here is to see who comes and goes. The longer we can make our dinner last, the better chance we have of seeing von Moser.'

The food, despite the restrictions on wartime supply, was remarkable. They said little to one another over the starter. Bob spent much of the time thinking about what Monique was intending to do and trying to decide how to talk to her about it. If he'd just been her boss, it would be easy. They'd already be at Bromma Airport waiting for a flight back to Leuchars.

But their relationship made things infinitely more complicated. If he pulled rank now, as he felt he should, then he could destroy the future he longed for with Monique. And what if there really were important proposals that needed to be conveyed from a faction within the Abwehr back to London? Aborting the visit could mean losing an opportunity, possibly a major opportunity.

By now, the main courses had arrived and Bob found himself eating the best venison dish he'd ever tasted.

'You don't look like you're enjoying the food very much Bob. It really is vastly better than what we were served at lunch. You should make the most of it while you've got the chance.' Bob realised that Monique was looking at him with concern in her eyes.

'I know, Monique. It really is outstanding. Sorry I've been

so quiet. I've been going over in my head our discussion earlier.'

'You're worried that you're engaged to someone who is planning to kill a man for personal rather than just professional reasons?'

'That's certainly a side of you I don't think I've seen before.'

'Come on Bob, you know I've killed in the past. And since meeting you, for that matter. Remember the German airman in the seaplane?'

'Yes, I do know that. But that was in the heat of war. Planning to kill someone because of an affair that ended badly is quite different. You recognised that yourself in distinguishing between personal and professional reasons.'

'He's an enemy agent who, for whatever reason, is certainly going to want to kill me,' said Monique. 'Can we just agree to look at it that way? That keeps it the right side of the line you've got in your head, a line that I very much understand. I don't think that you should hold against me the fact that I was totally honest with you earlier. I felt I owed it to you to tell you exactly what happened between von Moser and me. But you must accept I was telling you as my future husband and not as the deputy head of MI11 and the man I report to. If we're to have a future together, I have to be able to feel I can be honest with you. I don't want to have to keep secrets from my third husband in the way I kept them from my first two.'

Bob smiled and reached over to put his hand on Monique's. 'I'm sorry. I know I'm marrying the whole person. As are you. We both come with baggage and uncomfortably sharp edges. The only way we're going to be able to deal with that is to talk honestly to each other.' He leaned back. 'Do you really think we're going to manage dessert?'

'Let's see if we can get a coffee first,' said Monique. 'If there's a cup of the stuff anywhere in Stockholm that owes anything to coffee beans, then it will be here.'

The coffee was excellent. As they waited for their desserts Bob returned to a specific issue that had been worrying him. 'When I asked you earlier what we'd do if we saw von Moser, you didn't know. Have you had any more thoughts about that? What will you do if the next man who enters the restaurant has prominent scars on the left-hand side of his face? For the sake of argument, let's assume it's happened. What if it was the man who's just walked in, the tall bald man in the tweed suit?'

'Sorry, Bob, I just believe I'll know if it happens. It would depend on whether he was alone or with other people, and how many and who. I'd just rely on my instincts and hope for the best. Bob, are you listening to me?'

'My turn to apologise, Monique. It's that man I pointed out just now when he came in. I'm sure I've met him somewhere but can't say when or where or why. And I've no idea who he is.'

Monique looked around the room. 'It was meant to be ghosts from my past that we were here to exorcise, Bob. Did you see where he went?'

'He joined a table over on the far side of the room, one with three men already dining at it.'

'Is there any chance he saw you or recognised you?'

'I don't know. There was a moment when I thought I'd caught his eye, but it was very fleeting and I got no sense of recognition from him.'

'Very well. He's got his back to the centre of the room, so there's no chance of him seeing us leave.'

'Is that what you think we should do?'

'Let's enjoy our desserts, especially as they're costing us both kronor and ration points, but as we've already had coffee, I think we should then go. We've given von Moser plenty of time to appear and he's not obliged. I suppose it was a bit of a long shot anyway. I've been keeping a close watch and I've not seen anyone else I recognise either. As fishing expeditions go, a tall bald man in his mid-thirties in an obviously British tweed suit isn't much of a return for the time we've spent here. On the other hand, the company has been lovely and the food magnificent. I think that's the best meal I can remember eating in, well, I don't know how long.'

'That's true,' said Bob. 'The fact that maximum prices are set for restaurant meals at home doesn't really make for outstanding quality, even in the best of places.'

*

Without obviously turning his head to his left, Bob had been unable to see if the bald man had paid any attention to their departure from the dining room. Monique said she'd not seen him show any interest.

They collected their coats and hats from the cloakroom and made their way back into the lobby, which if anything seemed busier now than it had earlier. The same porter they'd spoken to on arrival walked towards them when he saw them approaching.

'Are sir and madam leaving already?'

'Yes, thank you,' said Bob.

'Is this your first visit to Stockholm?'

'Yes,' said Bob. He noticed Monique said nothing.

'Perhaps you don't know that on Wednesday and Thursday nights we have dancing in the winter garden towards the rear of the hotel. With a live band and a magnificent setting, it is an ideal way to spend a few hours in the company of a lovely lady like madam. Before the war we insisted on white tie or black tie, but in this more informal age a suit and tie are more than sufficient.'

Bob looked at Monique. He had already guessed that she'd see this as another chance of spotting von Moser in a large social gathering.

She smiled brightly. 'Thank you, that sounds lovely! Which way do we go?'

*

'You have to admit that the porter's description of a "magnificent setting" was an accurate one,' said Bob.

They'd left their coats and hats in another cloakroom and were now standing on the edge of a vast space that extended up past two floors of windows that overlooked it from surrounding parts of the hotel, to a curved and latticed glass roof which, Bob realised, would provide a huge amount of light during the day.

At ground level the space they were standing in was almost surrounded by arches that gave access to what in a church would have been described as aisles. These were occupied by dining tables covered with white tablecloths and by seating, as was the outer edge of the main floor. A large part of the main space was given over to a dance floor.

At the far end there was a balcony at first floor level. Lighting came from lamps around the edges of the space, set high on the walls, and from lamps on each of the tables.

There were plenty of people sitting at tables, though by no means enough to fill the huge space. Perhaps that was why, Bob thought, the staff seemed so keen to direct guests here who were on the point of leaving the hotel.

A waiter showed them to a table on one side of the main space whose location seemed to meet Monique's approval.

Bob looked at Monique. 'Soda water, or champagne?'

She smiled. 'Let's enjoy ourselves.'

Bob turned to the waiter. 'What champagnes do you have?'

As they sipped their drinks, Monique looked around. 'I should have remembered this place. I was in here more than once when I stayed in the hotel with Hans Friedrich von Wedel in 1937 and 1938. It's odd, though. It's only five or six years ago, but I was struggling to remember the rest of the hotel when we came in. The restaurant we ate in doesn't seem to have changed much. I get the impression a lot more has changed here. I recall the dance floor being much smaller and the place serving primarily as a winter garden. Now it seems to have been given over much more completely to dancing, with just some token bits of garden left.'

'Have you noticed much else that's changed in the city since 1938?'

'There was no food or fuel rationing back then, obviously, though you did still have to play silly games involving ordering food if you wanted to buy spirits in restaurants. I visited the Abwehr offices in the German legation a few times during our visits. As we heard earlier, they've since moved. Otherwise, no. I think I've seen more of Stockholm today than I saw in two visits of maybe a few days each back then. I don't believe we visited the old town, for example, and we certainly didn't spend time driving past the NKVD offices or the British embassy!'

At that point, the lights around the side walls of the winter garden dimmed, leaving the space attractively illuminated by the lights on the tables. A band that Bob hadn't noticed struck up on the far side of the space and people began to get up from tables and drift towards the dance floor.

Bob looked at Monique, who burst out laughing.

'You know, Bob, I've no idea whether you dance or not.'

'I always thought I cut something of a dash at Auxiliary Air Force functions and City of Glasgow Police social nights in my earlier years, but that may have been optimism born of too much beer. And I've not been on a dance floor since before the Battle of Britain started. How about you? Oh, Christ, sorry, I forgot. How many years did you spend as a professional dancer?'

'Too many, Bob, and it was all quite a long time ago. But I'm happy to give it a go if you are.'

Bob was distinctly nervous as they stood up, though he felt better as he led Monique onto the dance floor. After a few clumsy moves the years started to slip away and he found himself remembering steps he'd forgotten he ever knew in the first place. It helped that Monique seemed a natural teacher, quietly and patiently coaching him as they held one another. Bob was grateful that the winter garden wasn't full. There were plenty of people on the dance floor but there was enough space to enjoy the dancing without continually worrying about bumping into other dancers.

They stayed on the dance floor until the band stopped for a break and the main lights came on again. Monique led Bob back to their table, a broad smile on her face, then poured them both some champagne.

'You dance very well, Bob.'

'And you flatter very well, Monique. I have to say, though, that I can't remember when I last had that much fun.' Bob saw the look on Monique's face and guessed what she was about to say. 'With my clothes on, I should add.'

'I'm sure there are dances in Edinburgh we could go to, you know,' said Monique. 'I found that relaxing and enjoyable. And you really are quite good given how out of practice you say you are.'

'Hello, I'm sorry to intrude, but I thought I recognised you earlier.'

Bob looked up, startled, to see the bald man from the restaurant standing beside their table.

The man continued. 'You don't remember me, do you? I'm Francis Lutterman. These days I'm the Stockholm correspondent for The Daily Express. You are Squadron Leader Robert Sutherland, aren't you? Back in October 1940, I interviewed you when you were the commanding officer of a Hurricane squadron based at Croydon. The interview had been set up to mark your being awarded a second Distinguished Flying Cross a couple of weeks earlier but, in the meantime, you'd achieved the feat of shooting down five German fighters in a single day.'

Monique stood up. 'Perhaps you'd better take a seat, Mr Lutterman.' As he did so she looked at Bob. 'Do you remember Mr Lutterman, Bob?' When Bob nodded, she turned her attention back to Lutterman. 'I'd be grateful if you could keep Bob's identity to yourself. We are in Stockholm as Bob and Monique Cadman. You may know he was shot down, from what you say not long after you interviewed him, and severely injured. He now works for the de Havilland Aircraft Company and is here to try to sell aircraft to the Swedish Air Force.

Given his war record and the fact he is quite well known, we are here under assumed names. I should perhaps add that if any word of his real identity leaks out, then you will be held to account for it under the Official Secrets Acts.'

'Wow, you don't waste any time in getting to the point, do you Mrs Cadman? You're not quite who you want to appear to be either, are you?' Lutterman held up his hand in a placatory gesture. 'Don't worry I'll not be publishing anything that compromises either of you. I just thought it would be nice to catch up with you, Bob. I did hear you'd been shot down and wounded and just thought it was a pleasant surprise to see you here.'

Bob looked quizzically at Monique, then back at Lutterman. 'I don't want to seem ungrateful for your concern, Mr Lutterman, but there's really very little I can tell you about myself or what I've been doing since we last talked.'

'That's all right. I'd be happy just to talk about what you both think of Stockholm, entirely off the record. And your bottle's nearly empty. I can replace it, courtesy of The Daily Express, so long as you don't mind my sharing it with you.' He smiled again as he looked back and forth between them. 'Or, of course, I could just gracefully admit defeat and stop spoiling your evening. If you ever do want to get hold of me, I'm based in the press room here in the Grand Hotel. The telephone number is on my card.' He laid a card on the table in front of each of them, then stood up and walked off back towards the rest of the hotel.

Monique smiled. 'I thought of a lot of different things that might happen tonight, but I have to admit that wasn't one of them. Right, I get the sense the band are getting ready to play again. Do you want to stay for more dancing or would you prefer to set off on a cold, if thankfully not very long, walk through the old town to our hotel?'

'If I'm honest, having my cover blown quite that easily has shaken me.'

'Don't worry about it, Bob. Lutterman values his position far too much to compromise either you or me. Not that he knows anything very compromising when you come to think about it. Just put him out of your mind.'

'Fair enough,' said Bob. 'Lutterman was right about our champagne, though. It looks like there's enough left for about half a glass each. Can I suggest we finish it off, then consolidate our newly discovered shared passion for dancing for a little while longer before collecting our coats and braving that wind again?'

'That sounds like a perfect end to a really quite extraordinary day.'

CHAPTER TWELVE

When Monique threw open the curtains of their room next morning it was to let in the bright sunlight of a beautiful day.

'Look at it now, Bob! I'll never get tired of this view.'

'Yes, it's even better with blue skies. But then for a pilot pretty much anywhere is better with blue skies.'

They'd returned to their hotel the previous night by a different route through the old town, coming round the east end of the Royal Palace after crossing the bridge and then following a street that ran parallel to Skeppsbron that afforded them some shelter from the wind. Bob had the sense that this would have been a quieter street anyway than the one they'd used on the way out, and this was particularly true much later in the evening.

At one point Monique had pulled him into a deep doorway for a passionate kiss. He'd seen her looking past his head, back up the street they'd walked along. He hadn't been surprised. He'd had an unsettling sense they were being followed. She'd said there was no one there and laughed it off as excessive caution. Bob had still felt uneasy and he knew that she had too.

After a rather functional Scandinavian wartime breakfast, they returned to their room. The view from the window was just as good, but Bob sensed and shared Monique's restlessness.

'As I see it, Monique, we can't just hang about here, avoiding talking about anything that matters and waiting for the gentleman we saw yesterday to get in touch, or not, depending on whether anyone has contacted him.'

Monique smiled. 'We certainly can't spend the day in convoluted discussions like the one you've just started, Bob.

Let's go out for a walk. It's a beautiful morning. When we see a telephone kiosk, we can call our friend to ask, in a guarded way, if he has any news for us. Now I'm doing it.'

'Looking at the people cycling along the street and walking on the harbourside, it doesn't look very warm, despite the sunshine.'

'Don't worry, Bob. If we survived the cold wind on our outing last night, we'll be fine this morning. Grab your coat and, if you must, your hat.'

As they passed the reception desk the middle-aged lady who seemed to be something of a fixture there called out 'Mrs Cadman,' followed by something in Swedish.

Monique turned and, while Bob waited in the doorway, had a short exchange with the woman, who then pulled out an envelope from beneath the counter and handed it over.

'What is it?' asked Bob, as Monique led the way out onto the pavement outside.

'Let's cross over the road to the harbourside and find out,' she said. 'Ferries seem to leave from the steps over there. There ought to be a seat we can use.'

'Perhaps a telephone kiosk, too.'

Monique led the way to a wooden bench with views out over the harbour and opened the envelope she was holding. There was a single page letter inside, and Bob watched the colour drain from her face as she read it.

'What's the matter?'

'This was delivered by hand to the hotel reception a quarter of an hour ago, just after we went back up to our room from breakfast. The envelope is addressed to "Mrs Cadman". The man who delivered it was foreign, she thought German, and said it was urgent. The receptionist was about to get someone to bring it up to our room when we came down.' Monique handed Bob the letter.

It was handwritten and in German. Bob translated it a little haltingly as he read it out loud. 'My dearest Schatz. I am so pleased you accepted my invitation to come to Stockholm. I must say how beautiful you look as a blonde. Meet me in Riddarholmskyrkan at 10.30 a.m. this morning. Please ensure you do not involve the Secret Intelligence Service. If it makes you feel more comfortable you may bring that fool who is posing as your husband. I do so much look forward to meeting you again. Your loving M.'

Bob looked up at Monique. 'Do you recognise the handwriting as von Moser's?'

'Sorry, no. We didn't work closely together, and our relationship wasn't really built on romantic letters that, in any case, my husband might find. I've already told you what I saw in him. I think he wanted me because he liked the idea of knowing he was cuckolding my husband even if he had to keep that knowledge to himself.'

'That means it's possible that this might have been written by someone else.'

'Not really, Bob. To my mind, the "My dearest Schatz" makes it pretty certain that he wrote it.'

'What's the significance of "Schatz"? I think I've come across it before but I'm not sure I know what it means.'

'It means "treasure" or "sweetheart". It's a common term of endearment in Germany.'

'Is that what he used to call you?'

'No, von Moser didn't use endearments. That's the point, really. He did, just once, call me "Schatz". It was while he was trying to strangle me and just before I was able to grab the bottle of wine that saved my life. Using that greeting in the letter is a way of showing me that it really is from him, but also that he is still thinking about what happened. I read it as a threat that would be understood only by me.'

Bob felt a shiver running down his spine. 'This is getting extremely dangerous, Monique.'

'Yes, but I'm not going to underestimate von Moser and I guarantee he's still arrogant enough to underestimate me, even after what happened the last time we met.'

'Let's talk about that when we've a better idea about what he's got in mind,' said Bob. 'The first thing we need to do is to find out where Riddarholmskyrkan is and what it is,' said Bob. 'Do you fancy asking that policeman over there, by the ferry landing?'

'I can tell you it's a church, from the name,' said Monique. 'But the "where" is trickier. Asking a policeman risks word of where von Moser wants to meet getting back to SIS or the Swedish Security Service, if either of them start looking for us here.'

'Have you got a better idea?'

Monique walked over to where the policeman was helping a woman with a large pram up a set of stone steps from a ferry that had berthed while she and Bob had been talking. Other passengers had flooded ashore, leaving the woman struggling. Once she'd made it to the level of the harbourside, the policeman seemed happy to speak to Monique. Bob guessed from his arm gestures that where they wanted to be was back in the old town.

Monique rejoined him on the bench. 'Von Moser wants to meet in the Riddarholm Church. It's apparently on the small island of Riddarholmen, which is on the far side of this island,

Stadsholmen, and connected to it by a bridge. The policeman wanted to tell me the history of the Swedish monarchs who have been buried there but I was able to get away without causing offence.'

Bob had been looking at their map of Stockholm. 'I think this is it, here. Yes, you can see the name. It's not far.' He looked at his watch. 'We should be fine for time. How are we going to play this? There's a telephone kiosk over there. We could tell Peter Bostock what's happening, though only at the risk of also telling the Swedish Security Service.'

'I'm not sure "we" should be playing this at all, Bob. First and foremost, we mustn't involve Bostock. Partly for the reasons we discussed last night, but also partly because the letter explicitly says not to involve SIS. I don't want Bostock lumbering in and frightening von Moser away. That man of Bostock's who was following us wasn't very good and if that's the quality of the people he has available, he's not going to be much help.'

'I can't say I like that, but I do understand it.'

'I'm not sure you're going to like this part, either. I think you should stay here while I go to meet von Moser. What worries me is that he's obviously been watching us. He knows I'm a blonde now, for example, and he's aware that we have a cover as a married couple and the names we are using. He also knows where we are staying. He could be watching us now or have someone watching us. No, don't look round. It's just that I can see no good reason why he would say you can come with me. It feels like he's setting up some sort of trap for the two of us.'

'You have to remember, Monique, that he's supposed to be here to pass on an important message intended for the British government. That could be legitimate. He may have changed over the past few years. Many of us have.'

'I don't believe that evil bastard is capable of change,' said Monique.

'In that case it might help if you to have someone with you who von Moser has discounted as a fool. You talked about the likelihood he'll underestimate you. We already know he's underestimated me. You and I have discussed my limitations when it comes to a killer instinct, but I like to think I'm no one's fool.'

Monique smiled. 'No, you're not Bob. Besides, you're not going to give way on this, are you?'

Bob felt it best not to reply as he returned Monique's smile.

'Come on,' she said. 'Let's go and look at this church. If we can get there a little early, it will give us a chance to spot any traps. Bear in mind that's what von Moser would expect me to do, though, and remember that he could have someone following us, just to make sure we're doing as he instructed and not involving SIS.'

Bob stood up, relieved that Monique hadn't put him in a position where he'd had to insist that he accompany her against her wishes.

He looked at the map again. 'We can start by following the route we took last night, up past the café we had our beers in. Then we cut across to the west.' As they re-crossed the road a thought struck him. 'If von Moser called you "Schatz" as he was trying to strangle you, what did you call him as you hit him with the wine bottle?'

'I don't know, Bob. Probably "Mistkerl" if I called him anything at all.'

'Ah, I did pick up what that means on my youthful trip

down the Rhine. The bargemen I rode part of the way with gave me a good grounding in the less genteel side of the German language.'

*

'I'm pleased there are plenty of people about,' said Monique. 'But it still feels very exposed.'

They were walking arm in arm along a pavement separated by railings from the embankment of the waterway to their left, which ran between the island of Stadsholmen and the neighbouring smaller island of Riddarholmen. The church they were interested in had been very obviously in view for a little while. Immediately ahead of them was the bridge between the islands. The road crossing the bridge could be seen continuing across a broad cobbled area to the north of the church before disappearing out of sight beyond a building.

The exterior of the church seemed to Bob to be an odd mix of styles. As they walked across the bridge to the island, he was looking at it from the north-east. The most prominent feature, literally, was the tall red brick tower at the far, or western end, which was topped off by what seemed an impossibly narrow and impossibly tall black latticework spire. Much of the rest of the church was also made from the same red bricks as the tower. The exception to this was a large domed extension at the near end of the north wall which dominated the view from their angle of approach. This was made of very light-coloured stone and was much more highly decorated than the rest of the building. The effect was a little incongruous, as if a chapel built in Rome for an altogether different setting had somehow been transported to Scandinavia and grafted onto a church that it didn't suit at all.

There were a few cars and other vehicles, either travelling back and forth or parked in the square to the north of the church but, as was the case elsewhere in the city, most people were on foot or riding bicycles.

'There's a door over there,' said Monique. She pointed towards another extension on the northern side of the church which, because it was also in red brick, Bob hadn't paid much attention to.

'Are we just going straight in?' he asked.

'What else is there to do? Hang on, there's a note on the door. It seems they're doing some work inside and you can't get in this way. Visitors are supposed to use the door at the west end, beneath the tower.'

Bob turned to move in that direction but stopped when Monique reached out to touch his arm.

'Hang on, Bob. This doorway's not deep, but it shelters us a little from the view of the people in the square. Cock your Walther PPK and put it in your right-hand coat pocket with the safety catch on. That way it's still safe, but you can react much more quickly if the need arises. If I remember rightly, the last time you shot someone it was with a gun in your overcoat pocket.'

Bob smiled to ease the tension he felt. 'Yes, but that wasn't my coat, and I really don't want to spoil this one.'

'Much better that you spoil it with a shot you've fired than with a shot someone else has fired.'

'Funnily enough that was pretty much what King George said when I gave him back his coat, complete with bullet hole, last September,' said Bob.

One of the pair of large wooden doors at the west end of the church stood open and Bob led Monique into the space beyond, his right hand in his coat pocket, holding his pistol. With his left hand he removed his hat.

Beyond the door was a space beneath the tower, which opened out into the large nave of the church. This was reached by descending a set of half a dozen stone steps.

Bob stopped at the top of the steps, and Monique caught up with him, standing beside him. He could see a few people in the church. They included a family group with two children looking at something on the north wall, two couples, two women deep in conversation, and two individuals, a man and a woman. All appeared to fit the role of interested visitors.

He looked at his watch. 'We're still early. At least that allows us to have a look round and get a feel for the place. It looks like we've got a nave here with a narrower chancel beyond it. What doesn't seem to fit with any pattern I'm familiar with are the multiple side chapels.'

'The policeman said this place has been used to bury Swedish monarchs for centuries,' said Monique. 'I'm wondering whether "bury" is a loose expression that actually means building another chapel onto Riddarholm Church and putting the family coffins into it.'

They were now standing in the centre of the nave. 'I think you're right, Monique. There are chapels built onto both the north and south walls, and all seem to have tombs on display in them. There's another one over there, at the west end, next to the tower. This one, on the south side, seems to have been built in a way that obscures the view of the interior from the nave, but otherwise it fits the pattern.' Bob walked over to it. 'Yes, there's an oblique set of steps leading up beyond the iron gate and you can just see a tomb and windows.'

He returned to where Monique was standing. 'I'm less clear what all the dark brown panels lining large parts of the walls are about.' He was looking at a series of decorated boards, each perhaps 18 inches wide and rather more from top to bottom that were arranged in vertical rows around the walls.

Bob had lodged his hat in the top of his coat and reached out to take Monique's arm, but she shook it free. He realised it was the hand she'd have in her coat pocket holding her gun. 'I'm sorry Monique, but we might as well play the part of tourists.'

'Yes, you're right Bob, but I do want to keep this hand free.' She walked over to the north side of the nave to look at some of the boards Bob had commented on. 'They seem to be the crests of notable people. They refer to generals and admirals and various others. That one is for "Elliot Joh. Erik." Apparently, he was "president," though I don't know of what, as I don't think Sweden has a president. Each crest comes with two dates. The second might be a date of death, in his case in 1927, but the first is usually too close to it to be a date of birth. His is 1905. Perhaps we should explore the chancel?'

Monique led the way into the narrower eastern end of the church. The lower parts of the walls, up to the bottoms of the windows at a height of perhaps eight feet above the floor, were almost entirely covered by commemorative boards like those they'd looked at in the nave.

Bob checked his watch and saw they still had a little time in hand. He looked around. Most of the visitors seemed to be in the nave, though the two women were closer, taking notes from the information on the crested boards on the north wall of the chancel.

'There are two more of these burial chapels on the south

side,' he said. 'These seem larger and grander than those in the nave.'

'There's a set of steps here,' said Monique. 'Just before you get to the two large tombs in front of the altar. I think they lead down into that large chapel that was so prominent from the outside.'

Monique again led the way, down stone steps that led to an arched doorway blocked by a metal grill. Lights in the underground room beyond brought a glow from a series of gilded tombs.

'Wow,' said Bob. 'I wonder if this was what Howard Carter felt like when he found Tutankhamun's treasure. Some of the tombs are only child size.'

They spent several minutes just gazing into the burial space of the chapel. Then Monique looked at her watch. 'It's time,' she said. 'Let's go back up and meet von Moser. I recall him being a very punctual man.'

As Bob climbed the steps back up to the chancel, he could feel the sweat on his hand as it gripped his Walther PPK in his pocket. Monique was ahead of him and emerged from the staircase a few seconds before him.

As his head came up above the floor level of the chancel, he heard a voice from his left, his blind side, greeting Monique. 'Hello, Schatz.'

Bob could see Monique was already looking towards the speaker. Once he was at the top of the steps, he also turned to look. He saw an athletically built man of a little above average height with closely cropped blond hair and strikingly blue eyes in his mid-thirties. The man was wearing a dark raincoat. The scars Monique had given him seemed to comprise one running from just in front of his left ear right down to the side of his chin with a second, smaller, scar that ran from the side of his nose and met the first in the middle of his cheek.

Von Moser smiled coldly. 'Please, let's keep calm. I'm speaking in English so you both understand that I mean you no harm. I am sure you are both armed and would ask that you respect the sanctity of this beautiful building. Let's avoid any unpleasantness in the church.'

Bob looked round to see that the two women were no longer in the chancel. It looked as if they had gone to look at the panels in the nave. Other visitors likewise seemed to be in the main body of the church. The only people in the chancel were the two of them and von Moser.

'We are here to take delivery of a message, Herr von Moser,' said Monique. 'A message that is apparently of importance to the British government.'

'There's no need to be so formal, Vera. You never used to be. It was always "Max" back then. Does the so-called Mr Cadman here know about you and me? Yes, I see from his lack of response that he does. Anyway, enough of the small talk. I do have a message for you.' He pulled an envelope out of his pocket and offered it to Monique.

Monique took it, then opened the envelope and removed what seemed to Bob to be a single handwritten page of letter paper. There was quiet as she read, broken only by the occasional sound of a passing car or lorry coming in through the windows. Then she looked at Bob and he was shocked to see tears in her eyes.

'What's wrong?'

'I'm sorry Bob, but I'm going to have to leave with Herr von Moser.'

'You can't!'

'I'm sorry, I have to. Please don't try to stop us.'

Von Moser smiled. 'This is a charming little scene if I may say so. Now if you'll excuse us, Mr Cadman, your wife and I must be leaving. Stay here until we are out of the church.'

Bob wanted to do something, anything. Mostly he wanted to shoot von Moser. He came as close as releasing the safety catch on his pistol. But he felt paralysed by the pleading look in Monique's teary eyes before she turned to walk beside von Moser towards the west end of the church.

Bob knew that with a lead of the better part of the length of the church, there would be little chance of him working out where they had gone, especially if they had a car outside, which is what he'd have done if he'd been in von Moser's shoes.

As soon as the west door closed, Bob ran as if his life depended on it – as if Monique's life depended on it – to the alcove behind the door in the north wall of the church. Paving slabs had been lifted in the alcove, but it was still possible to unbolt the door. Thankfully, the large key was in the lock, and he was able to unlock and open the door sufficiently to squeeze through.

Bob looked wildly around. A black car had emerged from beyond the west end of the church. Bob could see there were two people in the back seat. He couldn't positively identify them as Monique and von Moser but felt it had to be them. He shrank back into the doorway, though he knew that if either was looking this way then they'd see him.

As the car drove behind a small group of vehicles parked next to the road to the north of the church, Bob realised that there were two men standing and smoking beside one of them. Both had soft peaked caps and Bob realised from some he'd seen queueing outside the Grand Hotel that their cars were taxis.

He ran over. 'Do either of you speak English?'

'I do, sir,' said the younger of the two.

'Do you see the black car just crossing the bridge to the old town. I want to follow it. I need to know where it's going.'

The taxi driver laughed. 'People only say that in films.'

'Well, I'm saying it now and I'll give you three times the normal fare if you keep them in sight.'

'Get in.'

As they crossed the bridge back to Stadsholmen the driver said, 'They've turned left. I think they must be intending to cross the bridge to Norrmalm.' A few moments later he said, 'Yes, look. You can see them on the bridge a little ahead of us.'

'Can you get any closer?'

The taxi driver laughed. 'You'll be lucky. You can see that car runs on petrol. In case you hadn't noticed, this one runs on wood gas. If that driver sees we're following and puts his foot down, then there's no way we can keep up.'

A short while later the driver spoke again. 'I think you're in luck. They've just turned for Stockholm Central Station. Three times a cheap fare is still a cheap fare, but I wish you luck.'

The taxi came to a halt in front of the station and Bob pushed some notes into the man's hand as he opened the door.

'That's more than you said.'

'Keep the change, and thanks,' said Bob.

Stockholm Central Station was an impressively long, white building with a main entrance in the centre of its longest frontage. Bob had seen von Moser's car – what he hoped was von Moser's car - driving away as the taxi pulled in.

As Bob stood outside the station, he had no idea where von Moser and Monique had gone. Into the station was the obvious answer. Bob entered, to find himself in a huge arched space with the light coming through glass panels in the roof reflected from the light-coloured floor. Though vast, the station was quite busy and Bob feared he'd simply not be able to see von Moser and Monique amid the mass of other people, all of whom seemed to be wearing coats and hats of one sort or another.

Then he remembered that von Moser hadn't been wearing a hat, or obviously carrying one, in the church. He might have left it in the car but, if he was bareheaded, it might make him easier to pick out.

As it turned out, it was Monique's blonde wig that Bob saw first, some distance away, and he realised she'd not worn her hat that morning either. She was walking away from him and von Moser was beside her, carrying a leather bag.

Bob walked as fast as he could without drawing attention to himself. He wasn't far behind them when von Moser showed tickets to an inspector and the two of them passed onto a platform where a train was waiting. He saw Monique look back and briefly caught her eye. It seemed to him that she smiled when she saw him and then she emphatically shook her head and mouthed the word 'no', before turning to walk alongside von Moser towards the train.

Bob stopped and watched as they boarded the train. The sign above the ticket gate said 'Göteborg'. Trying to avoid people rushing for a train that seemed imminently due to depart, Bob asked a railway worker where the train was going. He was directed to another man who spoke English. By the time he'd had it confirmed that Monique and von Moser were on a train bound for Gothenburg, the whistles had blown and the train was pulling away in an impressive display of steam from the engine.

He turned and walked back towards the station's main entrance, then stopped. Patting his pockets produced some change and he went over to one of a line of public telephones. Then he found the note that Peter Bostock had given him with his numbers. It took what seemed an age to be put through.

'Hello Peter. It's Bob Cadman. I'm calling from a public phone so will keep this short. I've got a problem and need your urgent help. Yes, extremely urgent. I'm at Stockholm Central Station. Thanks. I'll wait for you outside the main entrance.'

CHAPTER THIRTEEN

'What the hell did you think you were doing?'

Bob was sitting in the smoky office of Simon Smith, head of the Stockholm office of the British Passport Control Organisation and the senior SIS officer in the city. Heavy net curtains prevented much of a view out into the street outside, or one in from the buildings on the opposite side of the street, Bob realised. The office didn't really live up to the fine exterior of Birger Jarlsgatan 12. There was no room for a separate meeting table, so Bob sat on the opposite side from Smith of a careworn wooden desk, which was turned end-on to the window.

Peter Bostock sat at the end of the desk away from the window. Bob had declined the offer of tea though the two SIS officers were drinking theirs, between drawing on their cigarettes.

'It seems to me that you've utterly messed up the job you were sent here to do,' continued Smith, angrily. 'I'm going to report back that not only have you failed to take delivery of the Abwehr's message, which was the whole point of the exercise, but you also declined our offer of protection, rejected the protection we did provide, took wholly needless risks against our advice, and that as a result your colleague is now missing, presumably in the hands of the Abwehr. I'm told that in real life you are a pilot with the RAF. I sincerely hope that you are a good one, because you can take it from me that your career as an intelligence officer is over.'

Bob had been thinking through this moment, or one very like it, since seeing Monique's shake of the head on the railway station platform.

'There are a couple of things you have perhaps failed to consider, Mr Smith.'

'What are they?'

'The first is that as deputy head of MI11, I outrank you and am therefore the senior intelligence officer currently present in Stockholm.' Bob wasn't entirely sure that was correct but thought it unlikely that Smith would be sure either.

He continued. 'The second is that the situation is very much still live, and it would be helpful if we could work together to get the job done rather than indulge in pointless recriminations at this stage. I understand why things appear the way they do to you, but your position really isn't very helpful. Perhaps we might start by working out the practical steps we should be taking. When we've done that, I will happily fill you in on the background, so you've got a clearer understanding of why I chose to proceed as I did.'

Smith looked across the table at him, still obviously angry. Bob looked back, passively. He'd thought that Smith's job should make him a pretty good poker player and was surprised to see the doubt show quite so transparently on the man's face, a good couple of seconds before he spoke.

'Very well. What would you have us do, Mr Cadman?'

Bob worked hard to keep the relief he felt from showing on his own face. Monique always said he was too easy to read. This wouldn't be a good time to let Smith and Bostock know how profound his concerns were. He knew that if he played his cards right, he might just be able to help Monique and buy a little time to come up with a vaguely credible explanation for what had happened. In his heart of hearts, he knew that he had indeed, as Smith had put it, messed up the job he had been sent to do. But it wouldn't help anyone, least of all Monique, to admit that to Smith.

'As you know, I saw von Moser and Monique getting on a train bound for Gothenburg. Do you have people there who can keep watch for them when they arrive and find out where they are going and what they are doing?'

'I'm ahead of you, Mr Cadman. The trains do make intermediate stops, but we've been in secure contact with our people in Gothenburg, a married couple. If von Moser and Mrs Cadman are still on the train when it arrives there late this afternoon, then my people will do exactly as you suggest. I also have three of my men catching the next train for Gothenburg to back up the efforts of those who are based there.'

'Thank you, I'm grateful. I also wish to go to Gothenburg myself.'

'I very strongly advise against that. To put it frankly, I can do without you getting involved because I don't think you can help. I believe that your relationship with Mrs Cadman goes rather beyond your cover as man and wife. Am I right?'

Bob nodded.

'To my mind that makes you the last person we want involved and that would be true whoever you were and whatever your rank in the intelligence community. I'm not sure you'll take my word for that, however, and would suggest that we each report back what's happened to our superiors in London and let them decide whether you should go to Gothenburg or not. You can draft and send a secure cable to Commodore Cunningham from here as soon as we've finished our meeting. You have my personal word we'll not look over your shoulder, literally or metaphorically, in your communications with MI11, though I accept it's your choice whether you believe me or not.'

'Thank you,' said Bob.

'That's agreed then. So that I can provide my superiors in SIS with a full account of how we have arrived at this very sorry state of affairs, perhaps you could fill me in on the background. Why did you refuse our help and keep us in the dark? And why did the two of you go to the Grand Hotel last night? Yes, Mr Cadman, of course I know you were there. You were warned against it, yet you went anyway. Finally, I need to know what led to your colleague getting on a train to Gothenburg with Maximilian von Moser.'

'That's reasonable. I should start by suggesting you call me Bob. The first thing you may not know, but really need to know, was that Monique and von Moser had an affair when she was married to Hans Friedrich von Wedel, a senior officer in the Abwehr and von Moser's boss at the time. This happened early in 1938 and it ended when von Wedel discovered what was going on and accused Maximilian von Moser of seducing his wife. The result was that von Moser was sent to work elsewhere, under a very dark cloud.

'It seems von Moser continued to carry a torch for Monique. Of course, it must subsequently have become obvious to the Abwehr that she had been a double agent working for SIS all along, but by that time she was beyond their reach in Britain, where she transferred to MI5 and was more recently seconded to MI11.

'It remains to be seen what lies behind the approach that the German agent made to Peter here, and why that led to the agent being killed. But I hope that what we've done will enable us to find that out. Monique's view, which I shared, was that if we allowed your people to trail us round Stockholm then von Moser might simply never get in touch. She certainly didn't believe that after the last Abwehr agent was killed, von Moser would try to use your people as intermediaries a second time. She and I agreed that the only option, albeit a risky one, was to try to see if von Moser was already in Stockholm. She felt her wig and makeup would conceal her identity sufficiently to allow us to spend some time in what seemed the most likely place in the city to find him, the Grand Hotel. Clearly someone reporting to you saw through her disguise or knew what the disguise was. Otherwise, you wouldn't have known that we were there last night.'

Smith laughed. 'Actually, it was you who was recognised, Bob.'

Bob filed that thought away for future reference. 'Setting that aside, it appears that von Moser or someone working with him did identify Monique at the Grand Hotel. She didn't see him, though. She said he was easy to recognise because of large scars on his face caused by a road accident just after they split up. We both had the sense that someone was following us on our way back to our hotel last night, though if they were, they were doing it very well.

'Then, this morning, a letter was delivered for Monique at the hotel, addressed to her as Mrs Cadman. It was from von Moser and asked her to be at Riddarholm Church at 10.30 a.m. It explicitly instructed her not to involve the Secret Intelligence Service.'

'Did she recognise the writing?' asked Smith.

'No, she said she'd not seen much of his handwriting. But the letter did address her by a term of endearment he had always used for her. She was sure it was from von Moser.'

'Then the two of you went to Riddarholm Church together?'

'Correct. When we met him, it was obvious that von Moser had never overcome his feelings for Monique, or "Vera" as he called her. He said it was vital that she accompany him to meet someone who had a message to pass on to the British government, but that she had to go alone with him.'

Smith stubbed his cigarette out in an already full ashtray on his desk. 'How did you feel about Monique going off alone with a senior Abwehr officer who is apparently still besotted with her?'

'At a personal level I felt just as you'd imagine I would feel. At a professional level it seemed the best way to get to the bottom of things and bring about a positive result. Monique had indicated to me, without von Moser seeing, that she felt she should go with him. I was faced with a choice between letting her go or accepting that the whole thing was off.

'Von Moser asked me to stay in the church until they had left. They went out of the west door. I then managed to get out of a door that was closed for repairs on the north side of the church and got a taxi that was parked nearby to follow von Moser's car. I thought it would lead me to the rendezvous with this other person. Instead, it led me to the railway station. The rest you know. I can only assume the person von Moser wants Monique to meet is in Gothenburg.'

'Yes, I can see that,' said Smith. 'There's also the possibility that this whole thing may be just a ruse whose objective was always to return Monique to the tender mercies of the Abwehr. Gothenburg is just a boat ride across the Kattegat from German-occupied Denmark. It would be relatively easy for them to force her to make the crossing once she was there. Having said that, if that was the intention, then they might have been better going to Malmo, from where the crossing to Denmark is very much shorter.'

'I got no sense of von Moser having ulterior motives, and I'm sure Monique didn't either.'

'No, I suppose von Moser still having feelings for her does argue against that.'

That depended, Bob thought, on what those feelings were. But he put that on one side.

Smith looked at his watch. 'I don't think there's much more we can do until we hear from Gothenburg, and that won't be until quite a bit later. I am grateful to you for the background Bob, as it will allow me to set out a rather more balanced picture in the report I now need to wire back to SIS in London. As I said, please feel free to use our facilities to wire your own report to MI11. If the considered opinion in London is that you should travel to Gothenburg, then we can arrange it, though probably not until first thing in the morning. Can I offer you a car to take you back to your hotel?'

'Thank you but no, Simon. I think I perhaps need a walk to clear my head. Will you let me know when you hear something from your people in Gothenburg?'

'Yes, and when we receive replies from London, though I do need to know where you are to be able to get in touch with you. Perhaps it would be simplest if we could reconvene here at 8 p.m. to see if there's any news by then. You know, Bob, I wish I could be confident you're not simply going to walk out of here, go straight to the railway station and catch the next train to Gothenburg. Can I ask for your word that you'll wait until we hear back from London?'

'You have my word, Simon. Besides, I need to write my cable to Commodore Cunningham.'

*

Bob had worked hard to ensure that the account he had written for Maurice Cunningham was entirely consistent with what he had told Simon Smith. He knew that if things did go badly wrong, then Smith's assessment of Bob's future prospects as an intelligence officer was an accurate one. The best he could do in the meantime was pick a defensible story that contained as few lies as possible and stick to it. If, however unlikely it seemed now, everything worked out well, the lies were small enough not to stand out too obviously. If things didn't work out well, his career would be the least of his worries.

Having emerged from the rather anonymous doorway of Birger Jarlsgatan 12, Bob turned left and walked down to the end of the street, almost as far as the spur of the harbour. He then cut across a park and walked along a street that ended up running along one side of the Grand Hotel.

The porter in the main lobby, not the same one who had been on duty the previous evening, directed Bob to the press room. This was busy, with seemingly large numbers of people coming and going, or typing, or talking on telephones. He was able to find someone who could tell him that Francis Lutterman was out, but that he was expected back. Bob was offered a cup of tea and asked to wait in a lounge area. Despite the clamour in the press centre, Bob had the impression that the hotel was much quieter than it had been the previous night.

Bob had absolutely nothing else to do until the evening so felt that sitting in the press room's lounge drinking what turned out to be very good tea and reading newspapers was as good a way to pass the time as any. He had no desire to return to his hotel room and knew he'd feel at a loss wherever he was. He kept thinking over Monique's response on reading the letter von Moser had given her in the church. He could make no sense at all of what she'd done, despite his mind going round and round the same pointless loops.

The seats were comfortable, and Bob must have dozed. He woke with a start when he heard someone say, 'Hello Bob.'

He looked up to see Francis Lutterman standing over him.

'Hello Francis.'

'It's Frank to my friends. I hear you came in looking for me a little earlier.'

'Yes. Is there anywhere we can talk without any chance of being overheard?'

'In Stockholm? Hardly. You know what they say about walls having ears. Well, it's nowhere truer than here. I'd suggest a seat on the harbourside, but it is getting rather chilly out there. The hotel bar is likely to be quiet at this time of the afternoon and the coffee in there is the best in Stockholm. With a choice of plenty of tables, we ought to stand a fair chance of a private conversation.'

The bar was large, quiet and attractive but Bob wondered how it managed given everything he'd been told about Sweden's approach to alcohol.

They took a table that was neither at the edge of the room nor near the actual bar and Bob ordered two coffees.

'What was it you wanted to talk to me about?' asked Frank.

'I'd like to know who you told about seeing me in the hotel last night,' replied Bob.

'Straight to the point, Bob. Fair enough. Your companion last night, Mrs Cadman, said enough to lead me to believe she might be SIS. I mentioned seeing the two of you to a contact in the Passport Control Organisation who I bumped into a little later. I had some faint hope of finding out more about why you were here but learned nothing. That's the extent of my story. And before you ask, no, I'm not going to tell you the name of the contact I spoke to.'

'I understand that. What I need to know is whether you talked to anyone who might then have, wittingly or otherwise, passed information on to the Abwehr. Particularly information about the name I'm using.'

'No, of course not Bob. Look it might help if you understand how things work here. I'm guessing you're not actually in Stockholm to sell aeroplanes. No, don't answer that. With your background and with the approach adopted by the lady you were with last night when I recognised you, I'm guessing you have something to do with military intelligence. Don't answer that either.

'If I'm right, then someone will already have told you that a significant part of the economy of the city sometimes seems to be propped up by intelligence agencies of just about every nation on Earth trying to work out what all the others are doing and what's going on in the northern European countries that Sweden has such good links with.

'Those links also make this an especially attractive place for the world's press. Sorting out the wheat from the chaff can be a real task a lot of the time, but there's probably more raw information flowing through Stockholm than through any other city in Europe. There are refugees constantly arriving here from just about anywhere you care to mention, all of whom have stories to tell. Then there are the diplomats and their intelligence colleagues, many of whom are happy to talk to the press when it suits them. Finally, having large numbers of reporters here is in many ways a resource in itself. We tend to feed off one another a lot of the time.

'It's fair to say that there's a divide between reporters from Axis powers and those from allied nations, but we try to maintain civil relations and do sometimes help each other out with basic information. I'd never socialise with a German correspondent, for example, but I might tell one what Churchill's date of birth was if he asked. But you can be assured I said nothing to anyone other than my SIS contact about seeing you last night.'

'OK, thank you Frank.'

'Can I ask why you wanted to know?'

'Are you prepared to talk on the basis that this conversation never took place?' asked Bob.

'Yes, if that's what you want.'

'I do. It's just that someone followed Monique and I back to our hotel last night. I think they were with the Abwehr and knew our cover names.'

'Are you all right? Where is Mrs Cadman?'

'Yes, we're fine. Monique has had to go out of the city today, which has given me scope to indulge my idle curiosity.'

'You're not staying in the Grand, then?'

'No, in a hotel over in the old town.'

'Look if you're still here, I'd be happy to take the two of you to what will be a great party in the old town tomorrow night being thrown by a friend of mine. Things always loosen up a little on Friday nights in Stockholm and there are some in Swedish society who like to prove they do know how to spell "bohemian", despite the alcohol laws. It's the best chance you'll get to see that Sweden isn't all as dour and serious as it usually paints itself.'

'I'm not entirely sure where I'll be tomorrow.'

'That's not a problem. Telephone me tomorrow, any time up to the end of the afternoon, if you are interested and I'll let you have the address.'

'Thanks, Frank, I'll give it some thought.' Bob had already given it all the thought he was going to, but didn't want to appear rude by rejecting the invitation outright.

*

Bob ate dinner alone in the restaurant of the Hotel Skeppsbron. He ate mainly because it passed a little time. He realised he'd eaten nothing since breakfast and, though not at all hungry, had the sense that he ought to have dinner. He'd have been hard pressed afterwards to say what he'd eaten.

After dinner he went out and spent time wandering the streets of Stockholm. The weather had changed for the worse. It was much milder than the previous night, or even earlier that afternoon, but there the good news ended. The wind had strengthened and swung round to the west, and it drove frequent rain showers across the city, some of which were heavy.

Bob's trench coat proved better than he'd feared at keeping out the rain and although it was soaking when he arrived at Birger Jarlsgatan 12 a few minutes before the agreed time, he was relatively dry.

They reconvened in Simon Smith's office. Bob accepted the offer of coffee but having tasted it he immediately regretted his decision. Curtains had been pulled over the windows to make sure there was no chance of anyone seeing into the illuminated office through the nets that Bob had seen earlier. As before, both Simon Smith and Peter Bostock immediately lit up cigarettes, giving Bob a depressing sense of déjà vu.

'What have we got?' he asked.

'First,' said Smith, 'I want to show you a cable we've received that's been jointly addressed to you and me from Jonathan Waddell and Commodore Cunningham.'

Bob took the piece of paper that Simon passed over the desk.

'You'll see it is short and to the point and has two main elements,' said Smith. 'They say that you should stay in Stockholm for the moment and that you are not permitted to go to Gothenburg. I'm sure you'll dislike that outcome and I'm sorry about that, though as you know I also believe it is best that you remain here.

'I'm even sorrier about the second point they make. You will see that I am instructed to take all steps necessary to make sure that Mrs Cadman does not fall irretrievably into German hands. They are quite clear that if we can locate her then we must guard against any attempt to move her from Sweden to Denmark. They accept that taking her to Gothenburg may be part of the Abwehr's efforts to communicate with us, but they have also said that if we believe she is about to be moved by sea from there to Denmark, or moved south to Malmo, from where a crossing to Denmark would be easier, we must try to rescue her. If we cannot rescue her, then we are ordered to kill her.'

After the discussion about L-pills in London, Bob had seen this coming. The rational part of his brain had been fully expecting it. But that made it no easier to bear hearing Simon Smith say the words. He wondered for a moment whether the dinner he'd eaten at the hotel would make any more of an impression when he saw it a second time. Then he realised that he had to act with total professionalism. Any sign of weakness now could lead to his being ordered back to Britain and that would leave him even more powerless than he already felt.

'OK,' he said. 'I see that. Have your people in Gothenburg reported back?'

Bob saw Simon Smith and Peter Bostock exchange glances before the latter spoke.

'Yes. Mrs Cadman and von Moser arrived on the train you saw them board in Stockholm. They seemed relaxed and happy, "acting as a couple", apparently. They were met by a car that took them to a large house in an exclusive area on the edge of the city. The house stands in its own large garden so we know very little about it yet and can't make any moves, certainly not until the three additional men we've sent to Gothenburg are established. I understand the weather's particularly bad there this evening and there's some hope this might allow our people to get close enough later to see what's going on inside the house without being detected. That's all I can tell you, I'm afraid.'

Simon Smith put his cigarette down. 'As I see it, the good news is that they stayed on the train all the way to Gothenburg and as a result we know where they are. Now we just need to play a waiting game. As Peter said, we might get better information when we've got a full team on the job.'

'Will you keep me in touch?' asked Bob.

'Of course. Perhaps we should gather again at, say, 2 p.m. tomorrow and Peter and I can bring you up to date with developments. If anything important comes up in the meantime we'll contact you at your hotel, or leave a message there simply asking you to "get in touch with William". Can I offer you a car to take you back to your hotel? Last time I looked, the weather wasn't great out there.'

'It's not, but while I'm grateful, I'd prefer to walk.' Bob saw the look on Simon Smith's face. 'Don't worry, I'm not about to disobey a direct order by going to Gothenburg.'

Once he was in the old town, Bob followed the route to the hotel that he'd taken with Monique the previous night. There was no sense of being followed this time, but when he reached the doorway in which she'd kissed him he paused, then doubled over and was violently sick.

He wiped his mouth with a handkerchief as he straightened up, looking around and hoping that no one had seen what had happened. A young couple had just come into view from ahead of him. Bob moved swiftly away from the evidence of his weakness, being careful not to step in it. He wasn't really looking forward to reaching the hotel. He didn't think he'd be getting any sleep.

CHAPTER FOURTEEN

Bob had left the curtains of the room open. He'd slept a little, eventually, but had forgotten that the sunrise here was much earlier than he was used to in Edinburgh. There was no sun shining into the room but, even with the grey clouds that Bob could see from the bed, the light had woken him early.

Looking out of the window revealed that the day he'd woken up to was what at home he'd have called 'dreich'. It was raining, though not heavily, and there was a slight mist that partly obscured more distant parts of the view out over the harbour. It was a scene that perfectly matched Bob's mood.

For want of anything better to do, Bob pulled a chair in front of the window, wrapped a blanket round himself, and watched those parts of Stockholm he could see though the mist coming to life. He dozed for a while, awaking with a start to realise that by any normal standards he'd now slept in. There was still time to get ready and go down to the hotel restaurant before the breakfast service ended, which is what he did.

As he had at dinner, Bob wondered why he'd bothered. Despite what must have been a very empty stomach, he had to make a conscious effort to eat. Duty done, he returned to the room and pulled out the map of Stockholm.

2 p.m. seemed a very long time away. He knew that it was possible there would be news earlier, but the idea of sitting at the hotel and waiting, just in case, was simply unbearable.

Bob looked at the map again, an idea starting to form at the back of his mind. Another quick look out of the window confirmed his recollection that taxis waited on the far side of Skeppsbron hoping to pick up passengers disembarking from the ferries. There were two there now. He also realised that the early morning mist had cleared and the rain had stopped.

The trench coat and hat hadn't fully dried since the previous night, but Bob knew he'd miss them if he didn't wear them. He donned them and then took the lift to the ground floor and crossed Skeppsbron to where there were now three taxis waiting.

The trip to Bromma Airport didn't take long and Bob tipped the taxi driver generously. He found it interesting to compare what he saw now in daylight with his fleeting impressions gained in the dark very early on the morning he and Monique arrived, two days and it seemed like half a lifetime ago. The road from the city centre approached from behind the end of the main airport building. This was a long, mainly two-storey structure with what might have been a viewing area on the roof and a glazed control tower sitting atop the near end. Beyond the main building he could see the side of the large hangar in front of whose far end the Mosquito had parked on arrival.

There were several taxis and other vehicles outside the airport building and a good few people milling about on the pavement and, he then discovered, inside. Some were carrying suitcases while others seemed to be waiting, perhaps to meet passengers arriving on an incoming flight.

He wasn't surprised to see that there was no obvious mention of British Overseas Airways Corporation on any of the information signs in the main airport building. Bob was guessing that the office where they'd had their passports stamped, attached to the far end of the hangar, was the one normally used by BOAC, but it seemed as well to check.

He saw a desk carrying a sign for AB Aerotransport, the Swedish government-owned airline. A young woman at the desk smiled brightly as he approached and directed him, in fluent English, to go out of the door at the end nearest the hangar and to make his way from there.

'Visitors are supposed to follow the path leading round the rear of the hangar to the offices at the far end, but as you're on your own and without luggage I'm sure no one will mind if you take the shorter route along the front of it.'

Bob needed no second invitation. He was fascinated by the aircraft he could see parked along the far side of the concrete hardstanding in front of the hangar, and by those he was able to see inside as some of the sliding doors had been pulled open. He looked up to try to work out how the extremely broad span of the building supported itself given the absence of obvious columns along its front edge. He realised there was a diagonal truss pattern forming a lateral support above the hangar doors, as if the hangar had been the work of a bridge-builder.

Once he reached the offices attached to the far end of the hangar, Bob entered by the door they'd used when they had arrived. He'd not noticed in the dark, but there was a slightly crude wooden sign above the door proclaiming, in white lettering, this to be 'British Overseas Airways'. The corridor and offices beyond the door seemed deserted.

Bob entered the room where their passports had been checked. After waiting a few moments, he called out, 'Hello!'

There was no reply and he was about to leave when he heard footsteps. Bob turned towards the sound to see a grey-haired man in his fifties come into the room. He was wearing an airline pilot's uniform with the four gold stripes of a captain round his wrists. He said something Bob didn't catch in Swedish.

'I'm sorry,' said Bob. 'Do you speak English?'

'With a Birmingham accent, since you ask, just as you speak it with, let me guess, an Edinburgh accent?'

Bob smiled. 'Yes, right first time. Hello, I'm Bob Cadman. I flew over with John Tickell from Leuchars early on Wednesday morning. I'm at a bit of a loose end in Stockholm today and popped in on the off chance that John might be about. I take it from the absence of any of your aircraft parked outside that he's not?'

'Hello Bob, I'm pleased to meet you. I'm Neil Bartholomew. I manage the BOAC operation here. As you've guessed, you're out of luck. We are expecting the Mosquito in tonight and John may be rostered as the captain. I'd have to check. But that will be the first inbound flight from Leuchars since a Lockheed Hudson made the trip out here and back again the night before last. We had another Hudson flight planned for last night, but the weather further west took a serious turn for the worse yesterday afternoon. There were severe storms over the North Sea and, according to the meteorological office here, everywhere this side of it, including much of Denmark, southern Norway and western Sweden.

'If it was as bad as they were saying, I doubt if anyone has flown anything over the North Sea since the middle of yesterday. We certainly haven't and I know the Swedes, who fly a parallel service from here to Dyce near Aberdeen under the AB Aerotransport banner, have also been grounded. It's still not great over there, apparently, but we've had a telex in from the office at Leuchars this morning saying the RAF meteorological people there expect it to ease sufficiently by mid-evening to allow flying to resume.'

'That's fair enough. It was something of a long shot anyway. If you do see John later, can you pass on my good wishes?'

'Of course. Look, I've got time on my hands because of the weather. I've given our people the morning off, as you might have noticed. I'd be happy to treat you to a cup of coffee back in the main airport building.' He must have seen the doubt in Bob's mind reflected on his face and laughed. 'No, don't worry. Bromma Airport is seen as Stockholm's front door to the world. They serve real coffee here. Let me get my coat.'

Bartholomew locked the office door as they left. 'Anything that might be of interest to the Abwehr is securely locked away in my safe, but you can never be too careful. We have something of a gentleman's agreement here, strictly enforced by the Swedes. The Abwehr pays very close attention to what we are doing, and SIS pays very close attention to the comings and goings of our friends in Lufthansa, which is little more than an arm of the Luftwaffe in civilian clothing these days, making them no different from us, really. But it's strictly "look don't touch".'

'You've not had any instances of sabotage? It was the first thing I thought of when John said there was an Abwehr spy ring at the airport.'

'Thank God, no. Though we are extremely careful whenever we've got an aircraft on the ground here, especially if it's here for any length of time. That's particularly true of our newest and best toy, our Mosquito. We are pretty sure, however, that every time one of our aircraft takes off from here, news about it is quickly passed to Luftwaffe fighter units based in Norway and Denmark. We have had instances of their trying to hunt down particular flights. The Mosquito is rather changing the rules of that game, thankfully.'

As they walked back across the front of the large hangar,

Bartholomew half-turned to Bob. 'I was in early on Wednesday and saw John before he flew back to Leuchars after bringing you over. He didn't break any confidences, but I gather that you flew together on an operational training unit last year?'

'He flew. I mainly shuffled paper. I've not flown operationally, or even all that regularly, since being shot down at the beginning of November 1940.'

'He said you were a highly decorated squadron commander during the Battle of Britain and a very successful fighter pilot.'

'Right up until the moment I wasn't quite successful enough, unfortunately. Hello, what's this?' Bob stopped to watch an ungainly silver and black three-engined airliner land from the south-east. There was a broad red band across its fin carrying a black swastika on a white background. 'I may be rusty, but I know a Junkers Ju 52 when I see one.'

'That's right. That will be the Lufthansa flight arriving from Berlin. Their flights to Stockholm don't run the same risks of interception as ours, so they can afford to fly aircraft that look a little more like airliners. And their schedule has obviously not been disrupted by the storm to the west.'

The two men stopped as they reached the front corner of the main airport building. The aircraft was taxiing in from the runway and came to a stop not far away from them, on the opposite side of the concrete hardstanding and facing towards them.

After the three engines had stopped, the wheels were chocked, and a short set of steps was wheeled by two men in overalls up to the left-hand side of the fuselage. A dozen or so passengers disembarked before being directed by a member of the crew to walk over to a door in the front of the airport building, near where Bob and Neil were standing.

Two other members of the crew then emerged from the aircraft. One had a heavy limp.

Neil Bartholomew laughed. 'I tell you what, Bob. Have you ever seen a Ju 52 close to?'

'No. If I had it would have been through my gunsight, but it's not a type I've encountered in the flesh, so to speak.'

'I'd like to introduce you to someone.'

Bartholomew led the way over to the aircraft where the three crew were in discussion. As he approached, the man who was clearly giving instructions to the others turned towards Neil and Bob.

The frown on his face was swiftly replaced by a smile. 'Hello Neil! How are you?'

'Hello Oskar. It's good to see you. Can I introduce you to Bob? Bob's a fellow pilot and he was just saying that he'd never seen a Junkers Ju 52 up close.'

'Hello, Bob. Any friend of Neil's is a friend of mine. Wait a moment, will you?' He turned to his colleagues and Bob heard him asking them to be ready for a briefing for the return flight an hour later. Oskar was a short, heavily built man in his early thirties. From the way he moved, Bob thought that his limp might be the result of an artificial right leg.

Oskar turned back. 'Do you want to have a look inside, Bob? It's what you'd call basic, but it gets the job done.'

'Yes, please.'

*

'Tell me this Bob,' said Neil, 'have you had a better cup of coffee in Stockholm?'

'I dined at the Grand Hotel on Wednesday night, if that

answers your question.'

'Fair enough, I concede defeat, but this has to be the second-best cup of coffee in the city.'

'It's certainly better than anything you'll find in Berlin,' said Oskar, quietly, as if not wanting to be overheard.

The three men had found a table by a window in the first-floor café that offered a view out over the aircraft parking area and runway.

'Thank you for taking the time to show me round the Ju 52,' said Bob. 'I know you'll need to be making your return trip to Berlin soon.'

'There's always time to talk about aeroplanes with a fellow enthusiast. It's not actually a bad plane to fly. Have you ever flown anything like it?'

'I flew a Sunderland flying boat once, as co-pilot,' said Bob 'I also flew a Dornier Do 24, another flying boat, for a short flight. To my mind the smaller an aeroplane the better. Though I'd make an exception to that rule for the Mosquito, which is exquisite despite having two engines.'

'I agree with you about small aeroplanes,' said Oskar. 'I've never got over my true love, the Messerschmitt Bf 109.'

'You were a fighter pilot?'

'Yes, until this happened.' Oskar patted his right leg with the palm of his hand. It made a hollow sound.

'Were you shot down?'

'No, at least I can say the RAF never got me. Of all the stupid things, it was a landing accident. I was a flight commander on a squadron based in northern France and three of us crossed the Channel just as the sun was setting to see what we could find. It was winter, so we lost the light quite early. My two colleagues were inexperienced and became separated from me.

'At one point I thought I'd nearly collided with one of them, but then realised the wing shape I could see against the twilight sky above me was wrong. There I was, over Kent, with a Hawker Hurricane flying on the same westerly course just above me and no more than 25 metres ahead of me. My first concern was that there might be others, but I weaved a little to check behind and as far as I could see he was alone. As I dropped back to give myself space to take the shot, he turned, but it was clear he had no idea I was there, so I was able to follow and close again and give myself the easiest kill I ever achieved. A short burst was all it took. The poor devil went straight down and after I'd avoided flying into him, I was able to watch the trail of sparks and then flames all the way down to the ground. The explosion lit up the countryside.

'I was feeling quite pleased with myself by the time I got back to my base in France. Especially as I'd been able to radio back while crossing the Channel and learn that my colleagues had returned safely. Perhaps I was a little too pleased with myself. I've always said it was an overactive mole digging up the grass runway. But whatever the reason, my landing went badly wrong and the aircraft flipped over, which is never a good thing in a Bf 109. They were able to get me out, but my right leg was a hell of a mess and I later lost it. I've been flying rather larger aeroplanes ever since.'

'Do you remember the date?' asked Bob.

'How could I possibly forget? It was the 1st of November 1940.'

Bob put his coffee down on the table and sat back in his chair. 'On that day, not long after dusk, I was flying a Hawker Hurricane alone over Kent. I was flying west towards my base at Croydon. It was my second flight of the day. I'd shot down a Messerschmitt Bf 109 fifteen minutes after sunrise that same morning and if I'm honest I was very tired after a long day and an intensive couple of months. I never saw the aircraft that shot me down but I'm wondering whether it was yours.'

'It has to be, Bob,' said Oskar. 'There couldn't be two incidents like that in the same area at the same time. That would be far too much of a coincidence.'

'You mean like the two of us meeting here today?'

Oskar laughed. 'Very true, Bob.' Then his face took on a more serious expression. 'I always tried to avoid thinking about the crews of the aircraft I shot down. I suppose you did too. I must say that I'm happy you survived.'

'Thank you. I'm not sure how, but I somehow got out before my plane hit the ground. I didn't get away with it entirely. An injury to the side of my head lost me the sight in my left eye and I've not flown operationally since then.'

'It seems we both paid a heavy price for our meeting that evening. I suppose there's an irony about that. How do you feel about me now that we've met? Do you hate me for what I did to you?'

'Of course not, Oskar. I think you and I are probably very alike. If our positions had been reversed, I've have done the same thing.'

Oskar looked at his watch. 'Perhaps you are right. It has been amazing to meet you Bob, but I must go. Should we exchange names and addresses so that if we make it through the war, we might find one another again and share a proper drink to celebrate our survival?'

'I'll leave my contact information with Neil when I return to Britain,' said Bob. 'I'm sure he'd be happy to send yours on to me.'

Neil Bartholomew nodded. 'I'd be honoured to.'

*

As Bob had suspected, there was a viewing area on the airport roof and Neil took him up to watch the Lufthansa aircraft take off at the start of its flight back to Berlin.

'That must have been a hell of a shock, Bob. I knew that Oskar was a fighter pilot during the Battle of Britain. But the idea that the two of you might have met, so to speak, never occurred to me. I feel rather sorry for my part in your being confronted with what must be a very unpleasant memory.'

'Don't be,' said Bob. 'I quite often have nightmares about being shot down. In part I think that's because I knew so little about what really happened and how it happened. As far as I was concerned, it just came out of nowhere. Now I've met Oskar, I can see in him someone who enjoys a nice cup of coffee, just like me, and someone happy to shoot down any enemy aircraft that presents itself, also just like me. I rather hope that having met him and heard his side of what happened, I might be able to sleep a little better in future.'

*

Bob called Peter Bostock from a public telephone in the airport.

'We've been looking for you, Bob. Are you back at the hotel? If so, I'll send someone to pick you up. We need to talk as soon as possible.'

'No, I'm calling from Bromma Airport.'

'Pardon?'

'Bromma Airport.'

'All right. We'll get a car to you.'

'It will be quicker if I get a taxi,' said Bob. 'I'll be there as soon as I can.'

CHAPTER FIFTEEN

Simon Smith didn't look as if he'd got a lot more sleep than Bob the previous night. They sat on opposite sides of a table in what Bob assumed was a meeting room in Birger Jarlsgatan 12. One beige side wall carried two large maps, one of the Scandinavian countries and the other of southern Sweden. The opposite wall, the one with the door in it, carried a large street map of Stockholm. The room had no windows and was lit by two light fittings hanging from the ceiling.

Bob wondered whether the change of scenery was so they could discuss something on one of the maps. Or perhaps it was just that the ashtrays in Simon Smith's own office were full to overflowing and the man had decided that it was easier to meet somewhere else than it was to empty them.

Smith was, inevitably, smoking now. 'I hope Peter will join us in a moment, Bob. After you telephoned, we got a further signal from our people in Gothenburg and he's waiting while it's decoded. That shouldn't take much longer. It's probably a silly question, but what were you doing at Bromma Airport?'

'Shouldn't I have been there?'

'Don't be so prickly, Bob. I was simply making conversation while we wait.'

'Sorry, Simon. I find it hard to wait about with nothing to do. You said yourself that if my career in intelligence doesn't work out, I might need to fall back on piloting. I was just looking at the BOAC and Lufthansa operations there to see what my options might be.'

'Seriously?'

'No, not seriously. But flying's been in my blood for a

decade and it seemed as good a place as any to spend the time until 2 p.m.'

'If you'd stayed at your hotel, we could have had this meeting earlier.'

'But then we wouldn't have seen the latest signal from Gothenburg.'

Smith frowned, then smiled. 'Touché. Did you find the airport an interesting place?'

'I suppose you could say that. I had coffee with the manager of the BOAC office and a Lufthansa pilot he knows who, it emerged during conversation, was almost certainly the man who shot me down over Kent at the beginning of November 1940.'

'I take it you are joking?'

'No, this time I am being serious.'

'That must have been awkward,' said Smith.

'Not as awkward as you might think. We agreed to meet after the war, assuming we both survive, so we can have a proper drink together.'

'That seems very forgiving.'

'There's nothing to forgive. We were just two fighter pilots doing the same job. He saw me and I didn't see him and that's all there was to it. He didn't come out of it much better than I did, to be honest. He crashed on landing back at his base in northern France and lost his right leg.'

'I assume you did nothing to compromise your cover in talking to this German pilot?'

'Don't worry, Simon. We kept it on strictly first name terms. We'll exchange contact information via the BOAC office manager when I've finished in Stockholm.'

Peter Bostock came into the office. 'I'm sorry to keep you

waiting. As you'll hear, the latest signal does rather change the picture painted by the one we got earlier this morning.'

'Let's take things chronologically,' said Smith. 'Peter, can you first talk us through the earlier signal, which you and I have discussed, and then you can brief both Bob and I on the most recent one. I should warn you, Bob, there is something in the first signal that you will find hard to take.'

Bostock stubbed out a cigarette, then sat back in his chair. 'As Simon said, we got a signal from our people in Gothenburg earlier this morning. It reported that the three men we sent down joined up with the couple we have based in Gothenburg after they arrived last night. It seems the weather was atrocious all night. This had the advantage of allowing the team to get quite close to the house in the dark. They had no means of listening in on anything going on inside, and for the most part the curtains were closed, blocking any view in.

'There are three people in the house, von Moser, Mrs Cadman, and the driver who met them at the station in Gothenburg, who isn't known to our people there, suggesting he's not a local Abwehr man. None of the three left the house last night after arriving there from the station. The third man cooked dinner. Either there were no curtains in the kitchen, or he chose not to use them.

'The curtains were again not used, initially at least, when they all retired to bed. We don't know where the third man slept, but it did become clear that von Moser and Mrs Cadman were intending to share a bedroom on the first floor.'

Bob felt as if he'd been kicked in the stomach. 'Can I ask what that's based on?'

'The lights came on in an upstairs room, presumably a bedroom. Our people were obviously at a lower level behind cover in the garden so couldn't see far into the room, but they did see von Moser and Mrs Cadman stand together in the window, looking out, though probably without seeing much as it was dark outside and light in the room. They embraced and kissed, and then von Moser closed the curtains.

'Then, this morning, our people saw Mrs Cadman open the curtains of the room while wearing a dressing gown. It was light by this time of course. She disappeared from view, and a few moments later there was a glimpse of von Moser crossing the room near the window, apparently unclothed, though only the upper part of his body could be seen from outside.'

Smith stubbed out another cigarette. 'Thank you, Peter. I'm sorry, Bob, I'm sure that's not what you wanted to hear. That's why we've been trying to get hold of you. I've drafted a cable back to London saying that there must now be a real risk that Mrs Cadman is intending to go over to the Abwehr. Or perhaps that she's worked for them all along as this would be a very peculiar time to change your allegiance in that direction, whoever you were. The cable recommends that we raid the house in Gothenburg with a view to taking her into custody and preventing any possibility of her going to Denmark. I understand that the weather last night was bad enough to stop just about anything sailing across the Kattegat from Gothenburg to German-occupied Denmark. I think we must accept the possibility that it was their intention to hole up in that house only until later last night, then sail over to Denmark, and the weather stopped them. We're trying to find out when it's due to improve.'

Bob heard himself talking in a slightly disembodied voice. 'I'm told that the RAF meteorological people in Scotland think the weather will have improved sufficiently by mid-evening to allow a flight to be made from Leuchars to Bromma. I imagine that means sailing across the Kattegat will be possible this evening or tonight, too.'

'Thank you. That gives us a timescale we've got to work to in clearing our lines with London.' Smith looked at his watch.

'Hang on, Simon,' said Bostock. 'I think you both need to hear what's in the second signal before passing advice back to London.'

'Yes of course, Peter.'

This time Bostock referred to the first of two pieces of paper he was holding. 'It seems that not long after the first signal was sent, things started to happen in Gothenburg. First, von Moser left in a taxi that collected him from the house. He was followed to the harbour area of the city, but we lost him after he got out of the taxi. Gothenburg harbour is the largest in Sweden, indeed, anywhere in Scandinavia, so that's disappointing but perhaps not surprising. It's worth also saying that only one member of the team tailed von Moser because we've made clear to them that Mrs Cadman is much more important. They know we need to keep enough focus on her to prevent her being taken to Denmark against her will or travelling there of her own accord.'

'Von Moser going to the harbour does seem to imply that our theory about their intending to sail to Denmark together might be correct,' said Smith.

'It could equally imply that they are, as we initially believed, in Gothenburg because they are waiting to meet someone,' said Bob. 'Von Moser's movements are consistent with him arranging to meet someone who is now expected tonight rather than last night.'

'That's true,' said Smith, 'but that's hard to square with the apparent intimacy between von Moser and Mrs Cadman.'

Bob struggled to hide behind a professional mask and let none of his real feelings show. 'I accept that. But whatever von Moser's feelings for Monique, I genuinely believe that she loathes him. It's true that she entered a relationship with him back in 1938 based on mutual attraction, but she then rapidly came to hate him. He stopped her ending the relationship by blackmailing her. She eventually called his bluff and told her husband herself what had been going on. If she shared von Moser's bed last night, then you can be sure it was because she's trying to gain an advantage over him.'

The problem with telling lies, thought Bob, was that you need to remember them well enough to build convincingly on them if the need arose.

'There is more, which might help clear things up a little,' said Bostock.

'Very well, Peter, tell us the rest,' said Smith.

'Some time after von Moser left by taxi, Mrs Cadman and the other man left in the car they'd arrived in. They went to a department store in the centre of the city, where Mrs Cadman shopped for clothes.'

'Clothes?' asked Smith.

'Remember she only had what she was wearing when she went to Gothenburg,' said Bob.

'Having a female agent on the ground helped greatly,' said Bostock, looking again at the papers in his hand. 'Apparently the other man wasn't comfortable getting too closely involved in the lingerie department and this enabled our agent to talk very briefly to Mrs Cadman without it raising any alarms. The other man was well out of earshot so, while standing next to her and appearing to look at something herself, our agent was able to say, in English, "I'm SIS, do you need help?"'

'What was Monique's reply?' asked Bob.

'She said, and I quote exactly, "No, I'm fine, keep clear. Tell Bob that Max is SD." At that point it seems the man watching her got twitchy and told Mrs Cadman in German to hurry up and get what she needed because they had to leave. She complied. Our agent's best guess was that she bought a couple of blouses and enough underwear for a few days.'

There was a silence in the room while Bob digested what he'd just heard. He assumed that Smith was doing the same thing.

'I don't mind admitting that I'm a little out of my depth here,' said Bob. 'Peter, on the initial tour you gave us of Stockholm, you told Monique and I that you'd identified agents of the SD in Stockholm recently. You said that there was no love lost between them and the Abwehr. Back in London, Jonathan Waddell told Monique and I that Maximilian von Moser is highly placed on the personal staff of Admiral Canaris, the head of the Abwehr. Yet Monique was sure enough about Max's affiliation to the SD, and sure enough about its importance, to make that the one thing she told your agent in Gothenburg.'

Smith lit another cigarette and drew on it deeply. 'It is possible that von Moser is using his position in the Abwehr to feed information about their activities back to the SD. Either way I find it highly significant that Mrs Cadman has passed this on to us. I don't pretend to understand what the hell's going on in Gothenburg, but to my mind this makes absolutely clear that she's on our side and not on theirs.'

'There is still the risk that she could be taken to Denmark against her wishes,' said Bob. 'I think you should order your people to go in and rescue her immediately.'

'I'm sorry, Bob,' said Smith, 'but that makes no sense at all. The one person who might understand what's really happening is Mrs Cadman herself, and she has explicitly rejected our offer of help. I think we must trust her judgement and abide by her wishes. We also need to guard against her being taken anywhere against her will, of course, but for the moment I think we have to continue to watch and wait.'

'But...'

'Bob, I understand your position, but you have to ask yourself whether what you are feeling is reasonable professional concern for a colleague or something else. It's open to you, of course, to make recommendations to London that differ from mine, but I honestly think that will simply make it look like you are allowing your judgement to be clouded by personal feelings.'

There was silence in the room as Bob looked past Smith's head at the point where Gothenburg was shown on the large map of southern Sweden. He knew that Smith was right. He also knew that he desperately wanted to find a reason to prevent Monique sharing von Moser's bed for a second night. It wasn't the thought of the two of them having sex that worried him most. He didn't like the idea but knew he had to trust Monique. To his mind the fact that she had asked the SIS agent to pass her message on to him, by name, meant everything. No, what worried him most, as the only person in the room who knew the true nature of the relationship between Monique and von Moser, was that she was in mortal danger. And that was true whoever von Moser was really working for.

'Bob? We need to tell London what's happening.'

'You are right, Simon. You can tell them that I support your view that we need to let things run for the moment.' Bob looked at his watch.

'I'll do that. Do you want to stay here this afternoon and evening to see how things develop?'

'To be honest, I'm a bit of a fifth wheel on the wagon here and, in any case, I need to catch up on sleep from last night. Will you contact me at the hotel or leave a message there if anything else happens? If I've not heard anything from you by then, I'll telephone Peter in the morning.'

'Yes, we'll certainly keep you in touch. Do you want a lift to your hotel?'

'No thanks. Walking gives me time to think. And thank you for not asking this time, but please rest assured I'm not about to make my way to Gothenburg.'

*

As Bob walked along the side of the Grand Hotel an idea started to form. Perhaps he couldn't do anything to help Monique, but he certainly wouldn't do her, or himself, any good by spending the evening and night going round in exhausting mental circles as he worried about her plight. Bob therefore turned and headed for the hotel entrance.

Frank Lutterman was on the telephone when Bob approached his desk in the Grand Hotel's busy press room and waved a friendly greeting, then pointed at a chair next to his desk.

When Frank put down the telephone, Bob smiled. 'I didn't know you spoke Swedish.'

'I don't think you'll find many Swedes who agree that I do. What can I do for you, Bob? You look like you've seen a ghost.'

'I suppose I have. A little earlier today, I met the man who shot me down in November 1940.' Bob saw the interest in Frank's eyes. 'And before you say anything at all, yes you can have the exclusive, but only after the war.'

Frank slumped back in mock disappointment. 'Is this a social call, then?'

'It is, in a way. You talked about a party taking place in the old town tonight. Monique is still out of town and I'm at something of a loose end, so if the offer's still open...'

'That's a shame, I'd rather hoped to get to know Mrs Cadman better, but yes, the offer's still open.' Frank picked up a pen and wrote on a notepad on his desk, then tore off the sheet he'd written on and handed it to Bob. That's the address. It's in one of the narrow parallel streets that run back from Skeppsbron. That's the road that runs down the east side of Stadsholmen, the island that the old town stands on. I've also given you the name of the lady whose party it is, Birgitta Davidsson. She's a sculptor and the party will be taking place in her studio. The downside of that is that you are honour-bound to buy any work-in-progress you break after you've drunk too much.'

'As a guest, am I expected to contribute? I know alcohol is hard to come by in Stockholm.'

'Perhaps we can help one another out there,' said Frank. 'Have your SIS colleagues... Apologies, that's not a fair way for me to approach this. I'll start again. When you arrived, were you given a ration book for spirits?'

'Yes, but I've no idea how it works in practice.'

'That's where we can help each other out. These ration books work quite oddly, as the amount each person is allowed per month depends very much on their social status and income. And on their gender. Women are given smaller rations than men. I'm guessing you'll have been given a relatively generous allowance, though that will still only amount to a few litres of spirits per month. My own ration book tends to be worked quite hard. It goes with the job. What I'm proposing is that you lend me yours and I will use it to buy your month's allocation of spirits, which I will take to the party as a contribution from both of us.'

'That sounds fair,' said Bob as he retrieved the book from inside the stiff covers of his passport. 'Here you go. What time do things kick off?'

'I think you'd describe it as "late until much later". On past experience, I'd suggest you turn up any time between 9 p.m. and 10 p.m., though if you left it until the early hours of tomorrow morning, I think you'd find it was still going strong.'

CHAPTER SIXTEEN

Bob was still a little distance away from the main entrance to the Hotel Skeppsbron when he noticed a black car parked outside it on the hotel side of the road, facing towards him. He could see there were two men inside. Without being too obvious, he undid the top button of his trench coat. His Walther PPK wasn't cocked, but there was no way he could remedy that without his actions being seen by other pedestrians or by the men in the car.

He was a few yards away when the front passenger door opened, and a man got out on the side of the car away from the pavement. Bob was again struck by the oddity of a nation that drove on the left doing so in left-hand drive cars.

'Hello, Mr Cadman?'

The man was wearing a dark overcoat, a dark hat and a scarf pulled up round his neck, but despite not being able to see much of him, Bob thought he looked familiar.

Bob slid his right hand into the top of his trench coat and the man raised his hands.

'I mean you no harm. I just want to talk.'

'Peter Sinclair!' exclaimed Bob. 'This is becoming a day for surprises.'

'It's Charles Young, now. I'm told that everyone listens in on everyone else in Stockholm, so I'll not suggest we talk in your hotel. I did see a bench over on the harbourside and the weather's not bad. That might suit our needs.'

Peter Sinclair, or Charles Young, sat down on the bench that Bob had shared with Monique the previous morning and seemed to be looking at the crowd of people getting on a ferry nearby. 'It's quite something to be in a city that's not at war.'

'Yes, it is a very refreshing change,' said Bob, sitting next to him. 'I'd ask what you've been doing since we last met in September, but I assume you've spent part of the time recovering from the wounds you received at Strathmore Lodge.'

'How did you know?'

'We found blood on the rear seat of the car you were in. It had to be yours. The paratroopers guarding Hess also put two bullet holes in the windscreen of the car.'

'Yes, it wasn't a very pleasant experience. It was made worse because the U-boat that evacuated us had to hold station off the Caithness coast until things were resolved. As a result, I didn't get more than basic medical assistance until we got to Kiel, five days after I was shot. It was very touch-and-go for a while. I'd been hit in the chest and lost part of my left lung because of the delay in receiving effective treatment. But I'm not looking for sympathy and we're not here to exchange pleasantries.'

'Why are we here?' asked Bob. 'I suppose you know that you are viewed as a traitor back in SIS?'

'Yes, that's inevitable. But let's turn to the present. I'm here because I have a problem which I think you may be able to help me resolve to our mutual advantage.'

'Why me?'

'For reasons I'll explain.'

A gust of wind caused Bob to shiver. 'Tell me more.'

'Since early January I have been attached to the staff of Admiral Wilhelm Canaris. After his efforts to end the war last September were thwarted, largely by you as I understand it, the admiral has been trying to find different routes to the same end.

The need for this has become more pressing because of wider events like the loss of the Battle of Stalingrad. Germany is now obviously going to lose this war, sooner or later. Canaris's goal is to ensure that the nation is not utterly destroyed in the process.'

'And that's a goal you share?'

'My aim, as it was when we last met, is to bring about peace between Britain and Germany. I don't believe that any objective assessment would judge me to be a traitor against Britain, but I suppose you'd expect me to say that. Anyway, I'm sure you know that Admiral Canaris is the head of the Abwehr. He is also no supporter of Hitler and the band of psychopathic lunatics who keep him in power. The admiral has a proposal he wishes to put to the British government, but he needs a means of conveying it that he can rely on. The situation is especially difficult because there are many, in the Abwehr and elsewhere, who would view what is proposed as treason against Germany.'

'You have my full attention,' said Bob.

'The plan is for a meeting to be set up to allow Canaris's proposal to be communicated back to the British government. Responsibility for setting up the meeting was given to a close and trusted member of the admiral's staff, Maximilian von Moser. His view was that he should select the British courier for the message himself and chose a woman who the Abwehr knew as Vera Eriksen. She subsequently defected to Britain and is believed to be working for MI5. I should say that there are some in the Abwehr who think she was a double agent working for the British all along, but that's not what matters now. What matters is that von Moser knew her and felt he could trust her for this role. With that in mind, a member of the Abwehr office in Stockholm approached a member of SIS here and asked that

Vera Eriksen come to Stockholm. Canaris's name wasn't mentioned for obvious reasons: the idea was simply that she should meet von Moser.

'The problem we have is that von Moser came to Stockholm on Wednesday and yesterday he simply disappeared off the face of the earth. The Abwehr agent who first made contact was shot and killed after talking to the SIS agent and our concern is that something similar has happened to von Moser. As I said, there are many people in Germany, and doubtless Germans here in Stockholm, who would like to stop Canaris's initiative from succeeding.'

'I'd repeat my earlier question. Why are you talking to me?'

'We heard that an aircraft from Scotland landed at Bromma Airport early on Wednesday morning with two British intelligence agents on board, a man and a woman travelling as Mr Robert and Mrs Monique Cadman. Given the timing it seems highly likely that Mrs Cadman is Vera Eriksen, though it appears from the description we were given that she has gone to some lengths to change her appearance since she was with the Abwehr. Then, on Wednesday night, this couple turned up at the Grand Hotel and Vera Eriksen was identified from her current description by one of the Abwehr agents supporting von Moser and then, discreetly, by von Moser himself. The couple were followed back to their hotel, the Hotel Skeppsbron just over there. The plan was that the following morning von Moser would have a note delivered to Mrs Cadman setting up a meeting with her, which in turn would lead to a meeting between her and Admiral Canaris. We know that the note was delivered, but then von Moser disappeared.'

'The admiral is planning to come to Stockholm himself?'

'Yes, which shows you how important this is to him as

that's a huge personal risk. To be frank it would have been much simpler if he'd simply entrusted the message to von Moser or to me, but he felt that it would be a sign of his personal commitment if he came to Stockholm. When von Moser dropped out of sight, the admiral asked me to come here to find out what had happened. I was on this morning's Lufthansa flight from Berlin. I must admit that it gave me a hell of a fright to see you standing by the airport building with a man in uniform. Then I realised it was an airline pilot's uniform, and you appeared not to notice me anyway, even though I walked within a few yards of you.'

'That was pure coincidence, I had no idea you were on the plane. You've still not told me why it's me you are talking to.'

'It is obvious that Robert Sutherland and Robert Cadman are one and the same man. Given the circumstances of our last meeting, I am prepared to bet not only that Vera Eriksen and Monique Cadman are the same woman, but also that the Monique Dubois who I met in Caithness in September is just another of her aliases.

'It is in the British interest to hear what Admiral Canaris is proposing and I am talking to you because you might know what has become of von Moser and perhaps Mrs Cadman as well, as I note that she is nowhere to be seen today. I am also talking to you because I believe you can, if necessary, act as the courier for Canaris's message in her place. I just want one or both of you to meet him and listen to what he has to say, then put a question back to London and meet him a second time to give Canaris the answer.'

'Is he in Stockholm already?' asked Bob. 'Was he on that Junkers Ju 52 with you?'

'No. It seemed important to try to find out what had

become of von Moser first. Do you know?'

'Yes, I do. There are two pieces of information von Moser obviously didn't pass on to Canaris when he suggested that Vera Eriksen be nominated as the go-between. The first is that the relationship between them ended very badly. Back in early 1938 von Moser blackmailed her into continuing to cheat on her husband after she wanted to finish her relationship with him. As you probably know, her husband was a senior Abwehr officer who was killed in 1940, leaving her a widow. Anyway, the relationship between Monique and von Moser deteriorated to the point where, during an argument, he tried to strangle her. To save herself she gave him those scars on his face.'

'I was told they were the result of a car crash.'

'That's what everyone was told. The scars were inflicted with a wine bottle. It seems von Moser isn't the forgiving type and, despite the passage of time, he viewed Canaris's need to make contact as a means of drawing Monique back within his grasp.'

'You mean to tell me that his whole approach has been driven by a desire for personal revenge?'

'Apparently so. Monique and I met von Moser in a church in the old town yesterday morning, after she'd received the note that you mentioned from him. At the church he gave her a handwritten letter which upset her. I don't know what was in it. She then left with him. I was able to follow them as far as Stockholm Central Station where they boarded a train after Monique had indicated she didn't want me to follow any further.'

'Where was the train going?'

'I don't think it would help for you to know,' said Bob. 'Some friends of mine are keeping watch on where they are staying, and I don't want you sending in an Abwehr team to muddy the waters further. Brief contact has been made with Monique and it seems she does not wish my friends to intervene.'

Bob could see that Young, as it was perhaps best to think of him, wasn't happy with that. Bob could also see that he had accepted he had little choice in the matter.

'Very well. You said there were two pieces of information that von Moser kept to himself. What was the other?'

'When contact was made with Monique, she said that von Moser was with the SD.'

There was a long silence and it seemed to Bob that Young's face had gone white.

Eventually the man spoke. 'Do you have anything to back that up?'

'Absolutely nothing. But it seems to me that Monique thought that fact was sufficiently important that she used her one chance to communicate with my friends to pass it on. She would not have done that unless she was absolutely certain about it. Additionally, someone drove von Moser and Monique from the church to the station. If it wasn't an Abwehr agent who could already have told you where they'd gone, then who was it? It's known that there are SD agents in the city.'

'That really does give us a problem,' said Young. 'The SD and their masters in the SS would love to have evidence that Canaris is guilty of treason. They have ambitions to take over the Abwehr altogether. If von Moser is their stooge on Canaris's staff, then they must have pretty much everything they need already. My problem is that communications with Canaris are not straightforward. I can't use the normal Abwehr channels, for obvious reasons, and most alternatives can be listened in on by the Swedish Security Service. Canaris is due to arrive within the next 24 hours. I'll not tell you how. If I can make contact, then I suspect he will wish to press on anyway. Are you prepared to meet him when he's in the city? It's important that you tell no one in SIS what's happening until after you've heard what he has to say. That reduces the chance of a leak. You have to accept that proceeding in this way, with you dealing secretly via a known "traitor" like me, could raise doubts about your own loyalty.'

Bob thought about that. Young's proposal had its attractions, as it would ensure that SIS were not distracted from their focus on Monique in Gothenburg. He could also see no way in which what was suggested might make Monique's position worse than it already was. Realistically, he thought Canaris had to be planning to arrive on tomorrow morning's flight from Berlin, assuming they operated on a Saturday. He wasn't sure how long it took to sail across the Baltic by ship or travel overland via Denmark, but he had the feeling it would be too long for the admiral's needs.

'I'm happy to go ahead on the basis you suggest.'

'Very well, I'll be in touch with you here at your hotel at about lunchtime tomorrow.'

CHAPTER SEVENTEEN

Dinner at the hotel was no more enjoyable than the previous night's had been. Bob found the thought of Monique being with von Moser was going round and round in his head to the exclusion of almost everything else. The rational side of his mind knew that what he'd said to Smith earlier was correct. If Monique had shared a bed with von Moser, then it was calculated by her to gain an advantage over him. But the irrational side of his mind had all sorts of other ideas which were was exceedingly difficult to quell.

After dinner, Bob walked clockwise round the edge of the island of Stadsholmen, the island that housed the old town. It used some time and as he approached the end of his circuit it allowed him to locate the street where the party was due to take place, not far north of his hotel. If he was honest, he was having second thoughts about going. With Monique in real danger in Gothenburg it felt deeply disloyal and uncaring to be going out with the intention of enjoying himself. In the end he concluded that wasn't what he was doing. He was looking for a distraction to help keep him sane. Spending an entire evening and night in his own company, constantly worrying about Monique, would do no one any good.

Back at the hotel, Bob parked himself on the chair in front of the window and looked out on the lights of a city at peace, a sight that he still found very strange.

*

The address Frank had given him turned out to be a four-storey building on the south side of the street he'd located earlier, one of those running at right angles to Skeppsbron. Bob arrived a little after 9.30 p.m. The substantial wooden door from the street was ajar and there was a handwritten sign that he could just make out in the light from the streetlamps. Making it out and understanding what it said were two different things. Fortunately, the written instructions were accompanied by a stylised drawing of stairs with arrows that suggested partygoers were meant to proceed to the top of the building.

This he did. There were two doors off the top landing. One was closed. The other was slightly open and carried another handwritten sign. This one said 'Välkommen!' the meaning of which Bob thought he could work out. There was the sound of music coming from inside.

Beyond the door was a short corridor with three closed side doors. A table taking up half the width of the corridor was covered in coats. Bob put his, wrapped around his hat, beneath it. The door at the far end of the corridor was open and he followed the music to and then through it.

Bob emerged into a large double-height space that was, self-evidently, an artist's studio, or perhaps, given its size, a studio used by several artists. The floor area was generous. There were three very tall multi-pane windows on the north wall, and the sloping ceiling had skylights, also angled to the north. In daylight this would be a beautifully lit room. Now, the uncurtained windows and the skylights simply gave a view out over the street or up to the night sky above.

Bob's first reaction was that the party had yet to start but, when he looked more carefully, he realised the size of the studio was deceptive. There must have been twenty or more people there already, though the space could easily have accommodated several times as many.

The walls were covered with paintings and bookshelves and there were large numbers of ceramics or carved objects of every shape and size on shelves or on tables around the sides of the space. It looked like work benches and whatever else it was the usual occupants of the space used to create their art had been pulled to the end furthest from the windows and covered in dustsheets. In front of them were tables carrying bottles, glasses and plates of simple canapés.

The big band dance music he'd been able to hear from the landing outside was coming from a large radiogram standing in front of a window. It looked a little incongruous, as though it didn't normally live in the studio. The area in front of it had been set aside as a dance floor, though the three couples currently dancing seemed a little self-conscious, as if hoping others would join them.

At first sight the people were a reasonable balance of genders and a range of ages from early twenties to elderly. Casual dress predominated, but there were a couple of other men in suits, so Bob didn't feel like he stood out too much.

One of the men in suits was Frank Lutterman. He smiled and waved when he saw Bob, then left the group he'd been with and walked over to him.

'Let me get you a drink, Bob.'

'Thanks, Frank. What is there?'

'Come over to the drinks tables. The poison of choice is brännvin, which literally means "distilled wine", though it has more to do with potatoes or grain than wine. That's what the Swedish rationing system is really intended to control and partly, thanks to your ration book, there's enough to go round. Here's your book back, by the way. I'm afraid you'll not be able to use it again until the start of next month, though that's only a few days away.'

'Is brännvin any good?'

'The stuff I brought along is, it's high-grade vodka, those bottles at the back. Outside, in the rest of Stockholm, you can find a range of qualities, including some ghastly stuff made from wood cellulose. The idea is to drink it straight, from these small shot glasses.'

'That sounds a great way to get very drunk very quickly,' said Bob, doubtfully.

'That's why the Swedes have been rationing it so rigorously for the past 20 or so years. At the time, rationing was a liberal alternative to total prohibition, which our friends in the USA went in for at about the same time. You'll find quite a few Swedes, those who think the rationing is too restrictive, regret that Sweden didn't go in for a similar form of prohibition, on the grounds that it would have broken down by now, as it did in the States.'

'Is that beer over there?'

'It is. It's weak beer, but pleasant enough. There's a bottle opener over here, and some glasses unless you prefer to use the bottle.'

Bob looked around. It seemed from the few people he could see with beer that it was acceptable to drink it direct from the bottle, so he opted to do likewise.

'The party has still to get going, really,' said Frank. 'I think you'll find that most people speak English. Most importantly, let me introduce you to our hostess.' Frank was looking to Bob's blind left side and Bob turned, realising they'd been approached by an attractive woman with short blonde hair and aged about 30. She was a couple of inches shorter than Bob and had on a blue and beige striped blouse that was fastened at the neck with a brooch, over a grey skirt. She had a cigarette in her hand.

Her grey eyes sparkled as she smiled. 'Is this your Scottish friend, Frank?'

'It is. This is Bob Cadman. Bob, this is Birgitta Davidsson, whose studio and party this is.'

'Others also use the studio, but I live here, certainly. "Bob" is an unusual name.'

'It's short for "Robert", Birgitta.'

'I prefer Robert, may I call you that?'

'Yes, of course.'

'If you'll excuse me for just a moment,' said Frank. 'I'll leave you two to get acquainted.'

Birgitta smiled as she watched Frank move back towards the small group he'd been with when Bob had arrived. She nodded towards them. 'The beautiful dark-haired lady over there, the one Frank's talking to now, is called Anastasia Sorokin. She's recently arrived as one of the Stockholm correspondents of Pravda and I think that Frank is trying to get into her bed.'

'Given his age, I thought he'd be married.'

'He is. But his wife is in England and he's in Stockholm, so what do you expect? I've warned him that if he succeeds there will probably be an NKVD photographer hiding in the wardrobe, but his brains seem to have moved from his head to his balls.'

'You said other people use the studio,' said Bob. 'Is much of the work on display here yours?'

'I moved the best works out for the party, but a few of the pieces of sculpture are mine, like that one, and that. What do you think?'

'I'm intrigued,' said Bob. 'That piece there, like a crouching animal with the head turned so it's looking backwards through eyes you've drawn on, that looks like it could have come out of an Egyptian pharaoh's tomb.'

Birgitta smiled. 'That wasn't what I had in mind, but now you've mentioned it I can see what you mean. Do you know much about art?'

'Very little, I'm afraid. I was a Glasgow policeman who became a fighter pilot who now sells aeroplanes. Some of the finer things in life might have passed me by during that process.'

'Frank tells me that you sell military aeroplanes.'

'That's true. Do you have a problem with that?'

'Not at all. With the world gone mad, I can't imagine that people build or sell any other sort of aeroplanes now. You must remember, though, that mine is a peace-loving nation. We've not taken part in any war since 1814, nearly 130 years ago, and I think that has hugely influenced the way we look at ourselves and at the world. The current lunacy has led to conscription and shortages in Sweden, but we at least don't live in daily fear for our lives.'

'No, I can't tell you how different it feels, being in a city that's not at war.'

'Frank also told me you were a highly successful fighter pilot.'

'If success is measured in terms of shooting down the other side's aeroplanes and killing their young men, then I suppose I was. But then I was shot down myself and my injuries stopped me flying operationally.'

'That makes you quite an exotic creature in a place like

Stockholm,' said Birgitta.

'For all the wrong reason, perhaps,' replied Bob.

At this point Frank appeared again and pulled Bob over to introduce him to Anastasia Sorokin and two other correspondents from the Grand Hotel press room, an American with the Washington Post and a man working for a Finnish newspaper that Bob hadn't heard of before.

Anastasia wandered off to talk to a young man who'd come into the party. The others carried on a conversation about how long it would take the Soviets to roll the Germans back completely, now they'd started the process at Stalingrad. After getting another beer for himself and a vodka for Frank, Bob found the other two men had also moved on.

'Anastasia has disappeared,' Bob said, looking around.

'Sadly, yes,' replied Frank.

'Birgitta seems to think you are in danger of getting yourself into deep water there,' said Bob.'

Frank smiled. 'Birgitta can be very direct sometimes. She may be right about Anastasia though. Why else would she show any interest in a clapped-out old correspondent ten years older than herself? That said, it would be a lot of fun finding out.'

People continued to arrive at the party and by 1 a.m. the studio was quite crowded. Bob had the sense that a limited stock of dance records was being played in a cycle on the radiogram. The steadily increasing numbers making use of the dance floor didn't seem to mind.

Bob had found himself talking to quite a few different people during the evening and had realised that Frank had been right about this being an ideal way to gain an insight into Swedish society, or one part of it at least. But now he was wondering whether it was time to leave.

There was a tap on his shoulder. 'You are on your own, Robert.'

Bob turned round to see Birgitta had approached him from behind.

She had an unguarded smile on her face that suggested she'd not held back from the brännvin, though she didn't appear drunk. 'Do you dance at all?'

'Sometimes, but I was about to leave.'

'Nonsense. If I've got my timing right, my friend is about to put on some slow music especially because I told her I want to dance with you.'

She had got her timing right and the music changed exactly to order.

Bob laughed. 'How can I resist an invitation like that?'

Birgitta took his hand and led him to the dance floor, where she turned to face him and pulled him into a tight embrace. There was an immediate look of surprise on her face, and she released him and took a step backwards before reaching out a hand to tentatively touch the left side of his chest.

'Is that a…'

Bob put his finger to his lips. 'Shush, Birgitta. If that means you don't want to dance with me, I fully understand.'

She pulled him close again and spoke quietly into his ear. 'No, it was just a surprise, that's all. As I said earlier, mine is a peace-loving nation and not many people carry guns.'

After three dances, Birgitta surprised Bob by briefly kissing him, then she led him off the dance floor. In a quieter corner she leaned close to him. 'Robert, I have to ask if you would help with an artistic project I've been pursuing on and off for the past year.'

'What is it?'

'I'm producing a series of figures inspired by real people. They model for me while I do some initial drawings, and later I work the drawings up into finished objects. I'm doing different kinds of people and, ever since I started, I've wanted to produce a figure of a warrior. Being Sweden, true warriors are not easy to find. I did wonder about using someone from the Norwegian resistance who I met here in Stockholm. But while he's a warrior now, back in Norway before the war he was a fisherman. You are much more what I've been looking for.'

'I'd love to help Birgitta, but I don't know how long I will be in Stockholm. It may only be a day or so.'

'Can I at least show you what I have in mind Robert? Follow me. I've moved some of the figures I've completed to another room to protect against accidents at the party.'

Despite his increasing misgivings, Bob followed Birgitta out of the main studio space. In the corridor, she opened the side door closest to table the coats were on and led him into the room beyond.

'But this is your bedroom.'

'I have to live somewhere, Robert, and this seemed the best place to keep my figures.'

Much of the floorspace was given over to a large bed. Bob was initially distracted by the sight of Birgitta hurriedly picking up items of clothing discarded on the bed and floor, but then his attention was attracted by a table against the wall on the side opposite the curtained window.

On it were placed four figures, each perhaps two to three feet in height. He wasn't sure if they were ceramic or carved. They seemed to be roughly human in form, but with elongated necks and distorted heads, and in odd poses. The largest was crouching and combined the extreme stomach and neck musculature of a male athlete with impressively prominent female breasts and a head that seemed to have been inspired by a quizzical duck.

Birgitta saw him looking. 'What do you think?'

'They're certainly unique,' said Bob.

She laughed. 'That's a word people use about works of art they don't like.'

'It's not that I don't like them. I think it's just that I don't understand them.' Bob realised that he was becoming increasingly adept at telling lies the more he practiced. If he was honest, he didn't think that Birgitta needed a human warrior to model for the figure she wanted to produce. She simply needed to look at some of the garish images that he'd occasionally glimpsed in newsagents on the covers of cheap science fiction magazines. Tact prevented him saying so.

'I could do the sketches I need right now. You'll have to take your clothes off, of course.'

'Pardon?'

'You can see that none of the figures are actually wearing suits,' she said, smiling.

'I'd have to think about that,' said Bob, wishing that the floor would open up and swallow him.

'Oh, Robert, don't be coy. Let me be totally honest with you. I do want to use you as a model but I'm sure you must know that's not the only reason I've brought you to my bedroom.'

Birgitta had unfastened the brooch closing the neck of her blouse and now pulled the garment over her head, revealing a black brassiere underneath.

'Hang on, Birgitta. I'm married!'

'So is Frank, but that's never been a problem for him. Nor

for most men, for that matter. Can you unfasten the clasp at the back?'

Bob felt himself freezing, like a rabbit caught in a car's pre-war headlights.

'No matter, I can do it myself.' Birgitta removed her brassiere and turned to face him with a smile on her face. He found himself wondering if she'd modelled the breasts he'd noticed on the largest figure on her own.

'I could do with a hand undoing the zip on my skirt, though. It can be quite awkward.' She turned her back to him and looked over her shoulder, smiling.

Bob felt as if he'd lost the power of free will as he took two steps towards Birgitta and reached out for the top of the zip she was pointing at, in the middle of her lower back.

CHAPTER EIGHTEEN

Monique watched as Max undressed, carefully folding his clothes or hanging them on the back of a chair. She'd always thought he was a beautiful man. He still was. Even the scars she'd given him, though destroying any ideal of perfect classical beauty, seemed to lend him a sense of intrigue and allure. She doubted if he ever thought of them in that way though.

He was four years older than her, and the past five years had done nothing to diminish or dissipate his impressive physique, which still made her think of a picture she'd seen in a newspaper of Michelangelo's statue of David. Unlike David, Max had what she'd always thought of as the ideal amount of body hair, much darker than the blond hair on his head. There was enough of it to clearly signal his masculinity and add some texture to the touch, but not so much that it ever created the impression, with the lights on or off, that she was bedding a gorilla.

There was another difference. Unlike Michelangelo's David, Max was well-endowed. Not as well-endowed as he used to sometimes think he was, but better than her idea of average. He was also, when he was trying to impress or when he could be bothered, an exceptionally good lover who took care to find out exactly what a woman wanted in bed and provide it for her. The previous night's experience suggested that skill might have deserted him at some point during the preceding five years: or perhaps it was just that he didn't feel the current circumstances made it worth bothering.

She'd always thought it a tragedy that such a nearly perfect body was home to such an utterly repellent human being.

As Max walked towards the bed, Monique could see that he was already semi-erect.

For her part, Monique was doing her best impression of Manet's *'Olympia'*. She'd first seen this inspirational painting as a young teenager after her parents had moved to Paris. Whenever she'd been back to the city since, she'd made renewing her acquaintance with Olympia the first thing she'd done after arriving and the last thing she did before leaving. She knew that the critics of the day had hated it when it was first exhibited in 1865. But for her there was something that drew her into the painting like no other she'd ever seen. As she'd grown older and experienced some of life's darker offerings, she'd increasingly come to see herself as Olympia. There had been times when she'd been able to survive only by, in her mind, becoming Olympia and letting Vera stand to one side and watch.

So now, reclining naked on the bed, she almost unconsciously mimicked the painting by crossing her lower legs and moving her left hand, so it covered her pubic hair. If the situation had been different, she'd have laughed at her own actions, but this was no time for laughing.

'The game's over, Max.'

'What are you talking about, Vera?'

'This morning, after you left and before Ernst took me shopping, I picked the lock on your leather case. I found my father's journal and his Danish passport. It was a mistake to leave them where I could find them so easily. The last entry in the journal was written in August 1941. The passport expired late last year. He's dead, isn't he?'

Max had stopped walking and she found it hard to read the

expression on his face as he stood and looked at her. What she'd said had obviously taken his mind off sex.

He finally spoke. 'I always made the mistake of underestimating you, Vera. It seems I've done it again. No one can expect to be the last surviving relative of a traitor to the Third Reich and not face consequences. Your father was arrested in Paris a week after the two men you went ashore with in Scotland were executed by the British as spies. That they had died while you had, it seemed, disappeared without trace, was compelling evidence of your treachery. Your father was interrogated to see what he knew about it. It was thought unlikely he knew anything, but it seems he had a weak heart, so we will never know for sure one way or the other.'

'That must have given you great satisfaction.'

'I had nothing to do with it. I didn't even know about it until months afterwards. I was having a drink with an ex-colleague who had taken part in the arrest of your father. He remembered that I'd known you and was full of the story that you were a traitor. The only thing they didn't know for sure was whether you'd been turned by MI5 after you'd been arrested in Scotland, or whether you'd been a double agent all along.

'I had to think about that. The more I thought about it the surer I became that you'd been working for the British from the beginning. That might explain why you'd married that dotard von Wedel, something I'd never understood. That way you could spy on him. I even wondered if it went back much further, to when you were married to that Russian count you once mentioned to me. No matter. I'm sure you'll be happy to tell all soon enough.

'Anyway, I took the opportunity to get hold of your father's journal and passport from this ex-colleague, and a vague plan began to form. That's when I had the letter written in a reasonable copy of your father's handwriting. You'll have realised it was very non-specific about dates and locations.'

'How about you, Max? Were you with the SD all along, working for them from within the Abwehr?'

'Oh no, that only happened after we had our last little encounter. I felt there had to be something better than the Abwehr, and it turned out there was.'

Max sat on the side of the bed and reached over to stroke the outside of her right breast with his finger.

It was as much as Monique, or Vera, or Olympia could do not to physically recoil. She knew that if she did, it would show Max the depth of her fear of him. Max was a man who enjoyed fear in others. It was important that he didn't see hers.

'I'm curious Max. Did you really believe that you'd be able to convince me to sign up as an agent for the SD, spying on the British, just using a letter that you'd got someone to cook up based on what they'd learned of my father's handwriting from his journal? That's what you seemed to suggest at first last night.'

Max laughed. 'No, of course not. You'd never have contemplated such a move without physical evidence that he was still alive and in our hands. The letter was only ever intended to get you to agree to come to Gothenburg. I knew you had to come. You couldn't refuse and risk the possibility it might be genuine.'

'Which means it was all play-acting when you talked about my father arriving in Gothenburg in the middle of the night on a fishing boat that it turned out had been prevented from sailing from Jutland by the storm?'

'The boat was real, and the storm was all-too-real. Your

father's presence on the boat obviously wasn't. What you must realise is that this has nothing to do with turning you into an agent for the SD. It has everything to do with returning you to Germany, via Denmark, so the SD can use you to demonstrate to those who need to know just how ineffective the Abwehr has been for many years. The fishing boat was due to come last night, just as it's now due to come later tonight. But its task is to collect you, not to deliver your father.'

Monique had hoped that once she got Max talking, he would keep on talking.

He didn't disappoint. 'You've not eaten or drunk anything that Ernst has given you today. That's a shame, as it would have ensured you'd have been nicely compliant and had an easy journey back to the fatherland. As it is, we're going to have to tie you up and carry you like a sack of potatoes.'

He stroked her breast again. 'Still, your choosing to stay awake does give me a final chance to enjoy that beautiful body of yours before it's ruined in a Gestapo torture cell or a concentration camp. You are still extremely beautiful, you know, Vera, despite the passage of five years.'

Monique moved a little, to make it slightly harder for Max to reach her. 'You do disappoint me, Max.'

'Why's that?'

'Since seeing my father's journal this morning I've been thinking this was all about personal revenge. I've long known you hated me for stealing your beauty and I thought you'd finally decided you were man enough to do something about it. But no. You've got me in your power and what are you intending to do? You're intending to rape me, then tie me up and hand me over to the SD or the Gestapo to do your dirty work for you. I thought you had more guts than that.'

Max stood up and turned to face her. 'I'm not a rapist!'

'Yes, you are. Do you think I willingly got into bed with a monster like you last night? I might have smiled and feigned orgasms twice, but you were blackmailing me, and that made it rape, just as much as it would be tonight. Let's be realistic, would I have come within 500 metres of that face of yours if you hadn't been holding the life of my father over my head? What woman in her right mind would?'

The flash of fury that crossed his face gave Monique less warning than she'd hoped for and when he lunged it was with one fist rather than two hands as she'd expected. The blow caught her on the right side of her stomach and left her gasping for breath as she lay on her back. That gave him time to leap onto the bed and kneel astride her body as his hands gained a grip on her throat.

This, at least, she had been expecting, but she was in the wrong place. She needed to be further over the bed. There was nothing she could do here, and she felt her throat already being fiercely constricted. In desperation she reached down and grabbed his balls with one hand and squeezed them hard. He grunted and released his grip while he fought to release hers.

Monique threw her body sideways. Max was caught by surprise, but with his greater weight and strength quickly had her pinned down on her back once more, and again he reached for her throat with his hands.

This time, though, Monique was where she wanted to be. With her left hand she reached up under the pillow and felt the handle of the knife she'd taken from the kitchen that morning, now within reach. She pulled it out and in a single slashing motion opened a deep wound that ran right across Max's midriff. She felt something hot and looked down to see that his intestines were tumbling out of the huge gash she'd made and forming a pile on her own stomach. At the same time there was a smell that made her want to gag. Max's hands never made it to her throat a second time. Instead, he wrapped his arms round himself, as if trying to hold his insides in, and let out a high-pitched scream.

Monique didn't think, she just wanted to stop that scream. She made a second slashing motion and this time cut open his throat from one side to the other.

The fountain of his blood momentarily blinded her but at least she'd stopped him screaming. He was still kneeling astride her, but he toppled sideways onto the bed when she pushed him.

Monique knew she had no time to lose. She rolled out from underneath his leg, briefly wiped her eyes with a piece of bedding, then ran over to where Max had left his clothes. They'd taken her gun from her in the car after leaving the church. But she'd seen Max take his holster off when he'd undressed. She found his pistol but the blood on her hands meant they were slippery. It took her two attempts to pull back the slide to cock the weapon.

When Monique looked up, she realised she had taken too long. Ernst had heard the scream and was standing in the doorway with his gun pointing directly at her.

As her eyes met his, a look of absolute horror crossed his face and his gun wavered. Monique shot him twice in the upper body without raising Max's pistol. Ernst was thrown sideways against the edge of the doorframe and then collapsed to the ground. Judging by the pool of blood that seemed to form immediately, she didn't think he'd be any more trouble to her.

Off to one side, Monique caught a flash of movement and

turned, to see a reflection of herself in the mirrored door of the wardrobe. She'd witnessed some dreadful sights in her time, but now understood the look on Ernst's face when he'd seen her. She was naked and covered, literally, from head to foot in blood and worse, with the only relief from the red being the patch she'd cleared round her eyes. Monique was transfixed by the sight.

She was only released from the spell by the sound of running footsteps and then there was more movement in the doorway of the room. Monique swung her gun back to see a woman standing and looking at her, apparently almost as horror-stricken as Ernst had been.

The woman raised her hands, one of which carried a gun. 'Monique! You're safe! Put the gun down! We met in the shop this morning.'

Monique recognised the woman and realised she was speaking in English. She lowered the pistol, but still held it in her right hand.

The woman came over to her. 'You've been injured. Where are you hurt?'

'It's not my blood. It's his.' Monique gestured towards Max.

The woman moved nearer the bed. 'Oh, Christ. I'll not bother checking him for signs of life. And the one by the door is looking very dead, too. Come on, let's get you into the bathroom. I'll help you get cleaned up. I've got colleagues in the hallway. I'll send them downstairs to preserve your modesty, then they'll get to work sorting this place out. I'm Hilda by the way, I'm with SIS.'

'My fingerprints will be on the knife and the gun. And all over this place.'

'Don't worry. Just put the gun down on the floor and leave everything to us. Are those your clothes over there? It doesn't look like they were hit by any blood, which is a blessing.'

'There's also my blonde wig,' said Monique, pointing towards the dressing table. 'It's as well I was playing Olympia and not Ingrid tonight. All this blood would have wrecked the wig.'

It looked as if Hilda was about to ask what Monique meant but then decided against it. She turned and walked out into the upper hallway. Monique followed, leaving a trail of Max's blood across the floor as she went.

*

It was perhaps not surprising that the front door of the Hotel Skeppsbron was locked. Bob pressed the buzzer to summon the night porter. It took a little while. When he opened the door, it looked as if the man had been asleep.

Bob apologised in English and then, oddly, in German. He wasn't sure why he'd done that.

'Mr Cadman, yes?'

'Yes, I'm Mr Cadman.'

'Passport?'

'Pardon? No one's checked that before.' Bob didn't want to start an argument so showed the night porter his passport.

'Good!' the porter disappeared behind the reception desk, then emerged with an envelope. Inside was a brief hand-written message asking him to contact William.

Bob turned to the night porter. 'Is there a telephone I could use? It's urgent and I'm happy to pay.'

The meaning of this did seem to translate and Bob was

shown a telephone in the small office behind the reception desk.

Peter Bostock's office number was answered by a voice that simply said 'Hello, duty officer speaking.'

'Hello, it's Bob Cadman. I've had a message to get in touch.'

'Hello Mr Cadman, it's Neil Prentice. We met if you remember. I've got a message for you but can't pass it over the phone. Are you at your hotel?'

'Yes I am.'

'I'll drive over. I'll be with you in ten minutes, fifteen at most.'

'I'll wait outside. Can you just tell me if it's good news or bad?'

'It's good news, Mr Cadman.'

The night porter was happy to let Bob have a key to the hotel front door, successfully conveying the conditions that he made sure it was locked when he came back in and that he returned the key to the place the porter had specified. Bob went outside to wait while, he assumed, the night porter went back to bed.

Prentice took not much more than ten minutes and pulled up on the far side of Skeppsbron. Bob crossed the empty road and got into the front passenger seat.

'Thank you for driving over. What have you got for me?'

'Mrs Cadman is in a safe place in Gothenburg with our people. Things came to a head earlier tonight and she killed both Maximilian von Moser and the other man. Our people were keeping watch and went in to clear away any evidence before the Swedes find out what's happened.'

'Is Monique all right?'

'I understand she's in perfect physical health.'

'When will she be coming back to Stockholm?'

'The idea is for her to accompany the men we sent down to Gothenburg back by train tomorrow morning. She's likely to be in the city by early afternoon. We'll let you know when she's back and obviously you can take part in her debrief with Simon Smith.'

'No, as my officer in MI11 she'll talk to me first and then we will jointly brief Simon.'

'I'm not sure he's going to like that, Mr Cadman.'

'Simon understands that as deputy head of MI11, I am the senior British intelligence officer currently in Stockholm. He doesn't have to like my preferred approach, he merely needs to comply with it. I'd be grateful if you could pass that on. You can sugar-coat it as much as you like, but he must know that what I've said is not up for debate. Now, I've had an exceptionally long day and intend to catch up on some sleep.' Bob looked at his watch. 'I have something planned after lunch, so will be out of touch. I will then contact Simon and have my meeting with Mrs Cadman if she's back.'

'I'll pass all that on, Mr Cadman.' From the slightly amused look on Neil Prentice's face, Bob got the sense there wasn't going to be much sugar-coating at all when his messaged was conveyed to Simon Smith. He wondered what Smith had done to upset Prentice.

Bob felt a deep sense of relief flooding through him as he watched the car turn in the road and drive back the way it had come up Skeppsbron. Monique was safe! Not only that, but she'd killed von Moser. So long as she said nothing to SIS that contradicted the carefully embroidered story he had told them – and Commodore Cunningham in MI11, he reminded himself –

then their careers had also been retrieved from the dark pit they'd dropped into when von Moser took Monique onto a train bound for Gothenburg.

Bob wondered whether, if he was otherwise occupied when the time came, Simon Smith might try to debrief Monique anyway. He wasn't sure he trusted the man to comply with a clear order that he didn't like. Then he realised that even though he had no way of warning Monique, she'd say nothing at all to SIS without talking to him first.

Bob re-crossed Skeppsbron, hoping the key he'd been given really would unlock the front door to the hotel. He didn't want to have to wake the night porter again.

CHAPTER NINETEEN

The knock on the bedroom door broke into a dream. It wasn't THE dream, the nightmare, the one that Bob had remembered so vividly on waking so often since November 1940. The one that brought back the emotions and sensations of fighting desperately to get out of his catastrophically damaged Hurricane in the dark before it plummeted to the ground. The one that left him sweating, even on the coldest night.

No, this dream felt as if it had a similar setting, but something was quite different, and the details were impossible to retain as he awoke. He spent a second wondering if meeting Oskar might really have taken the nightmare away, then another wondering whether it was sensible to respond to the loss of something that, on occasions, had profoundly distressed him with what felt rather like regret.

Then the knock came again on the door. Bob sat bolt upright, then leaned over to take his Walther PPK out of his holster, which was on the floor beside the top of the bed. Monique always complained that he never kept his pistol close enough and would have been pleased with him if she'd been here. Monique! The realisation struck him that she was safe, and he felt almost euphoric.

Now he just needed to make sure he stayed safe. There were two dressing gowns hanging on the back of the door and Bob put one on before standing to the side of the door and calling out, 'Hello.'

'Mr Cadman, I have a message for you.'

To Bob, the voice sounded like a passable impression of the middle-aged Swedish lady who was often on the reception desk. He opened the door, while keeping the ready-to-fire Walther in his dressing gown pocket.

It was the receptionist. 'There was a phone call for you. He left this message.' She handed over a folded piece of paper.

He opened it. It was short and to the point. *'Bob. I will pick you up at your hotel at noon. Charles.'*

He looked up at the receptionist. 'Thank you. Tack!'

She smiled and turned towards the lift.

Bob checked his watch to find he had an hour to get himself ready.

*

Bob realised that both courtesy and professional ethics demanded that he should put Major Peter Sinclair to one side and think of Charles Young in terms of who and what he now was. Bob understood fully why SIS would view as a traitor one of their officers who had plotted against them and who had very nearly had King George abducted by German commandos. He also understood that Sinclair had done what he'd done through a misplaced idealism, though that would be unlikely to save him from the gallows if he were ever unwise enough to turn up in London. Sinclair's scheme had failed, thanks to Monique and to a lesser extent to Bob himself, and he found he bore the man no personal ill-will.

He wondered if Charles Young felt the same way about him. Bob's initial reaction, on hearing in London of von Moser's close links with Admiral Canaris, was that the whole idea of Monique/Vera being used as go-between was a convoluted trap intended to snare her. As it turned out, it had been, but not in the way Bob had thought. It occurred to him that by agreeing to go off with Charles, on his own and without telling SIS, he was putting himself entirely at the mercy of Canaris's faction within the Abwehr. If their agenda was something other than he'd been led to believe, then he was walking into a trap himself.

But some chances seemed worth taking and though he'd been looking for reasons to dislike the man, Bob realised that at a personal level he trusted Charles Young.

He still felt extremely nervous as he stood just inside the front door of the hotel a minute or two before the appointed hour. Then he saw a black petrol-powered car pull up on the opposite side of Skeppsbron. As he went out into the drizzle and crossed the road, Bob saw Charles Young get out of the side of the car nearest to him, realising this meant there was at least one other person, the driver, in the car.

'Let's get in the back together, Bob. There's someone I want to introduce you to.'

The driver wore a coat that Bob thought was very similar to his own, but no hat.

As Bob got in, the man turned round in his seat and smiled, then extended a hand. 'Hello Mr Cadman. My name is Stig Sandström and I'm a deputy director in the Swedish Security Service.' He must have seen the doubt on Bob's face because he smiled again. 'Yes, we do actually exist as real people.'

'I'm sure you do, it's simply that I hadn't expected to meet any of you, and certainly not today.'

'Can I start by asking whether anyone knows what you are planning to do?' asked Sandström. 'Have you told SIS you are meeting Admiral Canaris?'

'No, I decided to trust Charles and keep that entirely to myself, though I have to admit that standing there inside the hotel doorway just now I was beginning to wonder whether that was a wise decision.'

'Thank you, Bob,' said Charles Young.

'Good,' said Sandström. 'You will be able to report back afterwards, of course. To explain my involvement, I should perhaps say that Admiral Canaris has long been an acquaintance of the head of the Swedish Security Service, Carl Holmlund. They came to know one another not long after the admiral took over the Abwehr at the beginning of 1935, rather before Carl was promoted to his current role. Over the years, Admiral Canaris has evolved from a fervent supporter of Hitler and the Nazis into someone who opposed the moves that brought about this war, and latterly into someone who is actively – though of course secretly – opposed to Hitler continuing in power. Carl's personal links with him have allowed us to observe this process closely. Matters are now coming to a head. You'd have to be blind not to see how the war is going, though it seems the Nazis are indeed still blind to it. Meanwhile, however, the admiral's position has become a very tenuous one. Though head of the Abwehr, he cannot rely on or trust many parts of his own organisation, while other parts of the Nazi security machine are increasingly trying to take over the Abwehr in its entirety. They nearly succeeded when Reinhard Heydrich ran the SD and the Gestapo. His death last June prevented that happening at the time, but the issue is again being discussed. I understand that the admiral has now additionally become aware of a new threat arising from the betrayal of a close and trusted advisor who, it turns out, has been reporting to the SD. As a result, he's in grave danger.

'In response, the Swedish government last night decided to take the unique step of directly assisting the admiral. He travelled from Berlin to Stockholm this morning on an otherwise empty "repositioning" AB Aerotransport flight that "diverted" to a Swedish military airfield rather than landing at Bromma. It was felt there was too much risk of his being recognised on a Lufthansa flight or at a public airport. We have also provided a secure venue for his meeting with you. He has been assured that the venue is free of any listening or recording devices, and I make that same assurance to you, though it matters much more to him.

'I have also been instructed to pass on to you the request that when you report back what Admiral Canaris has to say, you make explicit that his initiative has the full support of the Swedish government, at the very highest levels.'

'You already know what he is going to say?'

'Of course. Though anyone who's been immersed in international developments over the past couple of months could probably make a reasonable guess. This meeting isn't really a question of content and I expect it to be rather short. Rather it is a question of the admiral demonstrating to those you will be reporting to that he is prepared to risk his life, in the hope that influences their response. The Swedish government's decision to throw its weight behind him is likewise intended to try to influence their deliberations.'

'Thank you for being so open with me,' said Bob.

'If you like, you can think of what I've said as setting the meeting in a context that will help you write the report that we want you to write. Anyway, let's go. We don't want to be late.' Sandström turned back and put the car in gear.

Bob recognised parts of the route they took. 'Isn't this the way to the British embassy?'

Sandström laughed. 'You can be sure that's one place the

admiral will not be visiting today. Though he'd probably prefer to show up there than at the German legation.' A few minutes later they turned off the route Bob recognised and crossed a bridge.

'We've crossed onto the island of Djurgården,' said Sandström. 'This has traditionally been Stockholm's playground. This large building to our right is the Nordic Museum of Cultural History. The slightly odd thing is that most of the west shore of the island, pretty much everything beyond the museum, is now one of our largest naval bases. To show what I mean by odd, the military occupation of this end of the island is interrupted by the Gröna Lund amusement park, which is coming up on our right. On our left is the Skansen open-air museum park. Both are very popular with Stockholmers wanting a day away from the centre of the city. It was in Skansen that the Abwehr agent was shot and killed last Sunday. That was a beautiful day and there were quite a few visitors to the island, especially to Gröna Lund. Given the weather, I doubt if they have opened today. We turn off just down here.'

Bob leaned forwards to look through the windscreen. The car had turned right off the road they'd been following and almost immediately stopped at a checkpoint manned by armed men in naval uniform. There was a brief conversation which ended when Sandström showed a pass and the barrier across the road was lifted. A sharp corner brought them onto a narrow wooden bridge, which had a further checkpoint at its far end. Again, they were allowed through.

'This is the island of Beckholmen,' said Sandström. 'It's been an important centre for shipbuilding and ship repair for the last century and is now operated by the Swedish Navy. It's only small and a fair proportion of the surface area is occupied by three dry docks. We're here partly because of the security that the navy presence gives the island, and partly because of this.'

The car had climbed steeply up a small hill beyond the bridge and was now approaching what looked like a tiny classical mansion, just three bays wide by two storeys high, with small single-storey extensions on either side. The face they were approaching had a window each side of a central door, and three more on the upper floor. It was topped off by a shallow triangular pediment. There were two naval guards standing outside the door and Bob could see more, in pairs, patrolling the garden. The Swedes seemed to be taking security very seriously.

'This is the dockmaster's house and is ideal for our needs,' said Sandström.

After the car had come to a halt beside two others parked near the front door, Charles led the way into the house. The hall that lay beyond the front door wasn't large, but two men were waiting there. Bob's attention was drawn to a distinguished-looking man in his fifties with silver hair and bushy eyebrows.

Charles Young made the introductions. 'Admiral Canaris, may I present Mr Robert Cadman?'

'Actually, sir,' said Bob, 'as you are here at great personal risk, it's only fair you know who you are talking to. Cover name aside, I'm Group Captain Robert Sutherland and I'm the deputy head of Military Intelligence, Section 11, based in Edinburgh.'

The admiral smiled. 'I'm pleased to meet you, group captain, and thank you for being open with me. Tell me, is Maurice Cunningham still head of MI11? No, don't reply, though I can see you know him.'

If this was the admiral's way of trying to impress Bob, he had succeeded.

The second man had the sort of hard-to-describe anonymity that suggested he'd be a good intelligence officer. Bob wasn't surprised when Sandström introduced him as Carl Holmlund, the head of the Swedish Security Service.

'I'm pleased to meet you, group captain. We've set up a meeting room in here.' Holmlund turned to the admiral. 'Do you want to lead the way, Wilhelm? We'll follow.'

The dockmaster's house may have been small, but it did have a room at the rear of the ground floor that was large enough for a nice wooden table that could have accommodated ten rather than five. The day was sufficiently gloomy to ensure there was no problem looking into the light coming in through the windows, so Bob was happy to sit opposite Admiral Canaris, who had taken the chair in the centre of the side of the table nearest the windows. Charles Young sat to one side of the admiral and Carl Holmlund on the other. Perhaps to even things up a little, Stig Sandström chose to sit to Bob's right.

After coffee had been served – very good coffee, Bob noted – it was Holmlund who opened proceedings, welcoming both the admiral and Bob to Stockholm and emphasising that there were no recordings being made of their conversation.

Bob raised a finger. 'Is there any objection if I make notes?'

'None at all,' said Canaris.

Bob saw Holmlund tense as he reached into his jacket, then relax as he produced a small notebook, rather like those he had used as a policeman in Glasgow. An outside top pocket produced a pencil.

'Very well,' said Canaris. 'What I have to say will not surprise anyone in this room, but what is important is that I say it. Carl has known me quite a long time and if I were not present would probably tell you that there was a time when I believed Hitler was a force for good in Germany. That's probably why I was given this job in 1935. Four years later I advised against the actions that brought about war in 1939, but my advice was overruled. By then I was no longer among Hitler's favourites and the feeling was reciprocated. However, I kept my job, despite the efforts of powerful men to deprive me of it. How long that will remain true is unclear. My enemies within the Third Reich seem to become more numerous and more powerful by the day.

'For my part, I have become increasingly sickened by many of the things being done in Germany's name by the Nazis, both on the battlefield and elsewhere. I am not alone in that. I believe that given sufficient assurances by the allies, it would be possible to overthrow Hitler and replace him with a leader with a totally different outlook.'

'You mean yourself, sir?' asked Bob.

'Initially, yes, though I have no wish to become a politician permanently. The aim would be to oversee a change to a proper democracy.'

'What do you mean by "sufficient assurances", sir?'

'Ah, that is the only question that really matters. I need to know on what basis the allied powers would accept the surrender of Germany in the circumstances I describe. If I am to attract the people who I need to take part in this process, I need to offer them something better than what is already on the table. You will know that the Casablanca Conference between Prime Minister Churchill and President Roosevelt took place two months ago. The result was an agreement between them that the allies would only accept "unconditional surrender" from the Axis powers. This was the phrase used by Roosevelt at the concluding press conference and he has since repeated it in a radio broadcast.

'My problem is this. An allied demand of "unconditional surrender" gives no incentive at all to the many in Germany who would oppose Hitler if they felt there was a better alternative available. I believe we can rid ourselves of the man if we can offer Germany a more honourable and more palatable alternative. I also believe it is in the interests of Churchill and Roosevelt to reach a reasonable settlement with the quite different Germany I am describing. If they do not then, from where I sit in Berlin, there seems every chance that the Soviet Union will take over the whole of German-occupied Europe, all the way to the Atlantic coast. That cannot be a desirable outcome for the British or the Americans. A negotiated peace with Germany by Britain and America would leave us with viable forces in eastern Europe able to prevent that wider Soviet takeover. At the heart of all this is a simple question. Would the allies offer Germany more favourable surrender terms if the country were led by someone other than Hitler, someone prepared to work with them to achieve a lasting peace?'

Carl Holmlund coughed to clear his throat. 'As I think you already know, group captain, I have been instructed to tell you that the Swedish government entirely supports the initiative being taken by Admiral Canaris and strongly urges the British government to respond constructively to the question he has asked.'

'Thank you,' said Bob. 'I can do no more than promise to pass on your question and the arguments you have made in support of it. I will also report the position of the Swedish government. I have met Winston Churchill personally and I hope he will consider carefully what I tell him. I am afraid I have no idea how long it is likely to take to receive a substantive response that I can pass back to you.'

'Perhaps I can help there,' said Canaris. 'I am sure Mr Churchill will want to consult President Roosevelt. With that in mind, I have agreed with my Swedish friends to return immediately to Berlin, before my absence is noticed. Can I ask that when you are able to provide a response, you inform Carl Holmlund, then arrange to come to Stockholm? This is of course my highest priority, so I will ensure I return to meet you again.'

'That sounds reasonable, sir.'

'Thank you. Carl, before you take me back to my plane, may I have a private word with the group captain and Mr Young? It's about the internal Abwehr problem I told you about.'

'Yes, of course, Wilhelm. Stig and I will wait in the hall.'

When the door closed, Canaris leaned forwards. 'Do you have any word about Maximilian von Moser, group captain?'

'Yes, sir. He's dead. I don't know any details, but I understand both he and a colleague of his who was with him are dead.'

'And are you sure he was working for the SD, as you told Charles?'

'I trust the source completely, sir, but again I know no details.'

'Thank you, group captain. We will take a hard look at what he's been doing when we get back to Berlin but if what you say is correct then you may have saved me a great deal of trouble and I am grateful. I understand he used my wish to hold a meeting as a means of abducting a colleague of yours who he had a historical grudge against. How is she?'

'Thank you for asking, admiral. She is safe, but I've not been able to talk to her yet.'

'If, as Charles tells me, she was a double agent working against the Abwehr, perhaps I shouldn't feel as pleased as I do to hear that. But there are many who would regard me as a traitor too, so I'm not well place to make judgments of that sort. Please pass on my best wishes to your colleague when you see her.'

'I will, sir. I don't often surprise her, but I think I might with that.'

CHAPTER TWENTY

'Where the hell are you?' asked Smith.

Bob looked round. 'I'm in a telephone kiosk on a street corner just opposite the city end of the bridge that leads over to the island of Djurgården. Is Monique with you yet?'

'She is but she's refusing to tell me anything until you're present, and you've done a disappearing act.'

'Well, I've reappeared. And as I recall, I gave specific instructions that you were not to try to talk to Monique until I had done so.'

'We need to talk about who gives instructions to who in my city,' said Smith.

'We do, though I suspect you mean "to whom". Right now, though, you'll find it very much to your advantage to do what I tell you to do.'

'Now listen, Bob…'

'No, you listen, Simon. You are going to get into a car with Monique, just the two of you. Then you are going to come and pick me up. Sooner rather than later would be preferable because its's raining and people are going to start getting unhappy if I spend much longer in this kiosk. First, though, you are going to contact the British ambassador and ensure that whatever he's doing right now, he makes himself available to see us.'

'I can't do that!'

'I'm sure that you can. As head of SIS in Stockholm you must have a means of emergency contact that puts you at the top of his priority list. I am ordering you to make use of that to set up an immediate meeting with the ambassador. And before you say I can't do that, I just did. And bear this in mind. This is my responsibility and you are simply doing what you've been told to do by a senior officer. If the ambassador is unimpressed after he's heard what I've got to say, then it's not you he's going to be unhappy with, it's me. That would get me out from under your feet really rather quickly.'

'Very well, we won't be long.'

*

Monique had thought a step ahead and was sitting in the rear of the car, with Smith driving.

The simple joy that lit up her face when he got into the car was the best thing that Bob had ever seen. He hoped his feelings were as transparent to her. They embraced as Smith pulled quickly away from the kerb, a manoeuvre accompanied by a chorus of disapproving cycle bells.

'I'm sorry, Bob,' he said, after a moment. 'I don't want to intrude as I know this has been a difficult time for both of you. But it's only going to take a couple of minutes to get to the British embassy and I really do need to have some idea of why we are going before we get there.'

'That's fair enough,' said Bob. 'The headlines are that I've just come from a meeting with Admiral Canaris that was set up by the Swedish Security Service. I need the ambassador to ensure that the cable I must now write setting out a question from Canaris and the views of the Swedish government finds its way to Winston Churchill's desk by the most direct and secure route possible. Will that do?'

Monique spluttered and Bob could see she was fighting to hold back laughter.

There was a moment's silence from the front of the car. When Smith spoke, it was clear his anger had dissipated. 'I apologise Bob. It seems I've misjudged you.'

*

'Sir Fabian, this is Group Captain Robert Sutherland, deputy head of Military Intelligence, Section 11, based in Edinburgh, and this is Madame Monique Dubois, who works with him. Bob, Monique, can I introduce you to Sir Fabian Saunders, British ambassador to Sweden?'

Bob had thought the exterior of the British embassy was impressive on the tour that Peter Bostock had given them. It turned out that the interior was even more so, while the marble-floored and walled office used by the ambassador himself was little short of palatial.

The ambassador ushered them towards a surprisingly ordinary meeting table set in front of an unlit marble fireplace. Over the fireplace was a large painting of King George, in naval uniform. Around the other walls were paintings of British landscapes.

'I had to bring to a premature end a meeting with the American ambassador when I got your message, Simon. Can someone tell me what this is about?'

'I think that falls to me, Sir Fabian,' said Bob. 'I've just met Admiral Canaris and need your help in passing his message to Winston Churchill.'

There was a pause before the ambassador spoke. 'I have to admit that wasn't what I was expecting to hear. But you can be assured you have my complete attention, group captain. Perhaps you need to tell me the full story?'

Bob carefully talked the ambassador through the background to Canaris's visit to Stockholm and then recounted the meeting itself. The ambassador asked for points of clarification here and there, but for the most part simply listened.

'What it boils down to is this, sir. Monique and I successfully undertook an investigation for the prime minister last September so my name will probably attract his attention, but I need you to help me find the best way of making sure that we can get a cable through the system and onto his desk.'

The ambassador laughed. 'Twenty-five years in the diplomatic service and a knighthood, and when perhaps the most important diplomatic initiative the world has seen in nearly four years of war happens right on my doorstep, my role is to act as a glorified postman! Perhaps I can do a little more. I am at least quite a good diplomat and words are my business. I'll get my secretary to come in and, based on what you've just told me, perhaps you and I can between us dictate the contents of a cable. This can be addressed via the Foreign Office in a way that ensures it quickly gets to the Prime Minister. She can then type it up. You will get the final say on the content, but I may be able to advise on the best approach to take. The cable will be sent from me, as the ambassador, which will give it maximum momentum in the Foreign Office, but it will be framed as a message from you to Winston Churchill, as that will ensure maximum impact when it gets to him. How does that sound?'

'It sounds ideal, Sir Fabian.'

Bob had expected the process to be cumbersome but, in the event, it proved much easier than he had feared. The result, in far less time than if he'd been writing it himself, set out what he wanted to say, but in a considerably more accomplished way than if he'd actually been writing it. The ambassador, true to his word, had been able to suggest ways of improving what Bob was saying without distorting its meaning.

Monique and Simon had been sitting on the opposite side of the meeting table watching the process and drinking coffee. As the typed-up text of the cable was getting a final read through, Bob saw them talking quietly together.

'Can we offer a suggestion?' asked Monique.

'What's that?' asked the ambassador.

'That the cable be copied to Commodore Maurice Cunningham in MI11 and Jonathan Waddell in SIS, with a note that Simon Smith has been party to its production.'

The ambassador laughed again. 'That's an expression worthy of a diplomat, Madame Dubois. Your suggestion makes sense, though.'

'Yes,' said Bob, 'that way we kill three birds with one stone and make sure that everyone is kept fully involved.'

Sir Fabian looked at his watch. 'If you are sure that you are happy, Bob, we'll get that coded and sent. I should have said it earlier, but well done. We should get some sort of initial acknowledgement tomorrow. I know it will be a Sunday, but there is a war on, and I don't think that Winston is known for taking weekends off. As Canaris said to you though, I'm sure a full response will take rather longer.'

*

'Thank you, Simon, I'm grateful,' said Bob, as the car pulled up outside the Hotel Skeppsbron.

'Just to confirm, we'll see you both at 7 p.m. at Birger

Jarlsgatan 12 for a full discussion about Gothenburg?'

'That's right,' said Bob. 'That will give us a chance to catch up ourselves and make up for the fact that I've had nothing to eat so far today.'

As the car drove away, Bob turned to Monique and embraced her, then kissed her deeply. 'I'm so glad to have you back.'

'I'm so glad to be back. I don't want to spoil the moment, but I've had nothing to eat since an early breakfast and you said you'd eaten nothing at all. Can we put this bag in the room, then go and find somewhere we can eat and talk?'

'Isn't that the bag that von Moser was carrying at the station?'

'Yes, but he had no further use for it, and I needed something for the clothes I'd bought.'

*

Monique had been right. The little café in the arcade that ran off Västerlånggatan, the one they'd enjoyed a beer in on Wednesday, also sold food. It turned out that it wasn't great food, but Bob was growing used to the idea that in Stockholm food from just about anywhere except the Grand Hotel was largely functional.

Again, the place was quiet and though two other tables were occupied, they made sure there was no one within hearing.

'It might be best if you went first, Bob. I need to know how you explained away my going off with von Moser. I know you must have said something to explain it away, because if you'd told them the truth, that you allowed me to override your caution and the SIS offers of protection as I did, then they'd have recalled you to Britain.'

'It was looking quite bad, to be honest. That was when I started playing the "I outrank you" card with Simon Smith to unbalance him. As far as the story of our exploits in Stockholm was concerned, I went for the least change from the truth I could manage which still gave a credible and justifiable story. I told Smith and Bostock that you'd had an affair with von Moser in early 1938, that it ended when your husband found out and sent von Moser away, and that von Moser had never got over his feelings for you.'

'That last part is true,' said Monique, grimacing.

'That's the point,' said Bob. 'I wanted to keep things as true as possible but make changes that resulted in a totally different interpretation. Once your mutual desire for revenge was taken out of the picture, everything else took on a changed complexion.

'I went on to say that you and I had gone to the Grand Hotel against SIS advice – which Smith already knew - because we didn't believe von Moser would use them as intermediaries again and we hoped to find him there. That's just about it. I think everything else I told them was true. It just shows how little you need to change to turn a story completely on its head. I should add that I made the same slight changes to reality when I submitted my report to Commodore Cunningham. That didn't feel good, but it was necessary for consistency.'

'That was very well done, Bob. We'll make a practiced liar out of you yet. Which, in case you're wondering, is a good thing. Look, we've got plenty of time. Now we've got the key points covered, why don't you talk me through everything that's happened from your end?'

Bob talked while they finished an unmemorable meal and drank pleasant, if weak, beer. Monique reacted only three times, to put her hand on his when he was talking about meeting Oskar, to raise her eyebrows when he told her about Peter Sinclair turning up, and with an astonished 'really?' when he said that Admiral Canaris had asked him to pass on his best wishes to her.

There was a slightly uncomfortable silence after Bob finished talking. Monique negotiated with the barman for two more beers. Then she sat back down at their table and leaned forwards towards him. 'I get the sense you are trying to work out how to tell me something else, Bob. Would it have anything to do with that distinctive perfume I've noticed on your suit jacket whenever I've got close to you?'

'You're right, Monique. There is something I've not mentioned. As I told you, I went to see Frank Lutterman on Thursday afternoon, to find out whether it was him who'd told SIS that I'd been in the Grand Hotel with you. In passing he invited me to a party being held in the studio of a sculptor last night. I wasn't going to go, but in the end decided it might just stop me going insane with worry about you.'

Bob went on to tell Monique the entire story. By the time he finished she was laughing.

'What's so funny?' he asked.

'I can't believe you fell for a variant on the old "Would you like to come up and see my etchings?" line. Artists have been using that to snare their victims for decades. And if I understand you correctly, having pulled down the zip of her skirt for her, you came to your senses, bid your farewells and walked out, leaving the poor woman half naked and with a zip she might not have been able to get back up? That's not very gentlemanly.'

'Would it have been better if I'd stayed and helped her get completely undressed?'

'I'm pulling your leg, Bob. In any case, you say you went and found Frank and told him what had happened before you left. Something tells me he'd have been able to render any assistance she might have needed. While he might not have been her first pick for the night, I think you'll find that he feels he owes you a favour.'

'I hope you're right. You do believe me, don't you, Monique?'

'Of course, I do Bob. Our relationship is nearly perfect in many ways, but one thing that does sometimes worry me is a fundamental imbalance when it comes to trust.'

'What do you mean?'

'I'm not sure how or why, but I can tell whenever you are edging away from the truth, however slightly. You've never lied to me, except that comment about my being more beautiful than Ingrid Bergman, but I know that if you did, I'd be able to tell immediately. You may have suddenly become much better at telling lies to SIS and to Commodore Cunningham than in the past, which is commendable, but I can still read you like a book.'

'What's wrong with that?'

'There's nothing wrong with it, Bob, except that it doesn't work the other way. I've told many more lies in my life than you ever will, to many different people in many different circumstances. At times I have literally lived lies. I've never lied to you, even though you had your doubts at the time Hess was assassinated, but I know that I could lie to you, and you would be none the wiser.'

'But I trust you not to. We love each other and we're getting married. Trust is what makes the whole thing work.'

'Yes, I know that you trust me. Sometimes the responsibility that comes with that can be quite scary. What I mean by an imbalance is that the question of me trusting you, or not, doesn't really arise. If I know whether you are telling the truth, then I don't have to choose, as an act of faith, whether to place my trust in you, in the way you have to in me.'

'I understand what you're saying, Monique. I'm not sure what to do about it.'

'I don't think there's anything either of us can do about it and I'm not saying it's a major issue. I just wanted you to know, because I love you, that it is something that sometimes worries me.'

'Fair enough, I do understand and thank you for telling me.' Bob looked at his watch. 'However weak that beer, I don't think we can risk a third drink before going to bat against Simon Smith. I've not been looking forward to this, but I think you now need to tell me your story, Monique. Why did you go off with von Moser and what happened in Gothenburg?'

Monique looked at what was left of her beer, and then back across the table at Bob. The darkness he'd sometimes sensed just behind her eyes was as close to the surface as he'd ever seen it.

'No, it's not something I've been relishing either,' she said. 'But you need to know, both as my boss and as the man I love. If I'm honest, I'm having trouble working out where to start.'

'How about with the letter that von Moser gave you in Riddarholm Church?' asked Bob.

'Thank you, yes. The thing you need to know is that I never had much family. My adoptive mother died of cancer in Paris when I was seventeen. My elder brother Christian joined the Danish army when the family was living there. I was 10 at the time and I believe he stayed in the army. We were never very close and lost touch. He was killed during the supposedly bloodless German invasion of Denmark on 9 April 1940. I never discovered the circumstance. I of course travelled to Scotland in September that same year and lost any chance of finding out. That left my adoptive father, who I had last heard of living in Paris in the summer of 1940.

'Anyway, the letter von Moser gave me was in my father's handwriting and in Danish, his first language. It was signed by him and was addressed to me as "Dear Vera". It was undated. It said that my father was in the hands of the Gestapo because of my betrayal in defecting to the British and that he would be killed if I did not do what I was told. The letter, it said, would be given to me by Maximilian von Moser and that it was important that I fully cooperated with him. That was about it.'

'Did you think it really was from your father?'

'Once I had a chance to think about it, I was very unsure. It had been a long time since I'd seen my father's handwriting, but it did look right. On the other hand, the contents were far from convincing. I felt the only option I had was to play along and see if I could work out whether it was real or not. I should warn you that in my mind, "playing along" meant doing whatever it took to appeal to von Moser's ego in the hope he would let something slip. That meant putting aside the circumstances in which we'd tried to kill each other and pretending I was falling under his spell again.

'We were met in Gothenburg by a man called Ernst. He drove us to a large house perhaps half an hour's drive from the railway station. That's all I can tell you, though I know that by the next day at least, SIS were able to find the house.'

'After I'd seen you get on the train to Gothenburg, they met it at the other end and followed you both from there.'

'That was nice work, Bob. I'd thought there was no way you could follow us from the church. It was such a joy to see you at the railway station. I hope you understand why I told you not to follow us any further. Von Moser would have had no qualms killing you if he'd seen you again.

'We stayed in the house that evening. Max had a half-hearted and very unconvincing go at trying to persuade me that, based on the letter alone, I should agree to become an agent for the SD. He later said the letter was only ever intended to get me as far as Gothenburg, and I think that rings true.

'I told Max there was no way I would work for the SD until I'd met my father and seen for myself that he was alive. Max would have known I'd never cooperate without hard evidence, so this was simply a way of staying in character. Max responded by saying that my father had been due to be on board a fishing boat leaving Jutland later that night, and that I would have been able to meet him when the fishing boat landed in Gothenburg in the early hours of the morning. The bad weather we'd been experiencing since arriving in Gothenburg had prevented the boat from sailing and the decision had been taken to move everything back by 24 hours. I'd therefore be able to see my father the following night.

'In order to continue to play to Max's ego I went to bed with him on Thursday night. I felt that until I knew the truth about my father, I had to do anything it took, even that, to get Max off his guard. I'm sorry, Bob.'

Bob reached over and took her hands in his. 'I'm only glad I've got you back. I already knew, anyway. The SIS team were keeping close watch on the house and had concluded the two of you were sharing a bed from what they could see while curtains weren't drawn. When they reported that back to Smith, I elaborated on my initial story by telling him that you loathed von Moser because he'd blackmailed you into continuing your relationship with him in 1938 and that your husband had found out about the affair because you'd told him. I said you could only be sleeping with von Moser in order to gain an advantage over him.'

'It just goes to show,' said Monique. 'I had no idea anyone was watching on the first night but on principle did try to reveal what was happening to the outside as much as I could. Max valued his privacy rather more, so I only had limited success.'

'Forgive me asking a practical question,' said Bob, 'but I did see your diaphragm in our bathroom in the hotel on Thursday night.'

'You're worried about a small Maximilian running amok? God forbid! At a practical level, Max used condoms on the two occasions we had intercourse, so there's no fear of that. He was a fastidious man so I suspect kept himself clean in other ways, but if not, then the condoms will have helped there too.'

'That thought hadn't crossed my mind,' said Bob. 'But I suppose that is reassuring.' He wasn't certain how reassured he really felt. 'How did you explain away your L-pill? He must have had an idea of what it was.'

'I simply took it off and kept it in a pocket. I was beginning to think I might need it if I couldn't come up with a better idea. Things got more interesting yesterday morning. Max went off in a taxi. He said he was going to check the arrangements for the fishing boat bringing my father over from Jutland that night. I suspected, of course, that the whole thing was a ploy to get me onto a boat bound for Jutland, but again had to play along.

'After Max had gone, I picked the lock on his bag. Inside, beneath its floor, I found my father's journal and his Danish passport. The journal hadn't been written in since August 1941, the month the two men I landed in Scotland with were executed by the British as spies. The passport expired late last year. I took that to mean my father was dead but until I could confront Max, I couldn't be certain.

'Later, Ernst took me out to remedy the fact I had no clothes in Gothenburg other than those I was wearing, and a woman from SIS made brief contact in a shop. I asked her to stay clear and to tell you Max was with the SD. Max was out for most of the day. I was now reasonably sure they were planning to take me to Denmark and, on the pretext of an upset stomach, avoided consuming any food or drink they gave me to avoid being drugged. I only drank directly from the tap.

'Last night we went to bed quite early, again with Max and I sharing a room. As he came to get into bed, I told him I had found the journal and passport and goaded him into losing his temper to loosen his tongue. It worked. He confirmed my father had died while being interrogated in Paris after it had become obvious that I was a double agent. He confirmed that the plan was to get me into the hands of the Gestapo, so that once they'd extracted my story it could be used by the SS and SD against the Abwehr. He also said he'd only begun working for the SD after I'd scarred his face.

'I then taunted him about his face and the way it must scare women away. As I'd hoped that caused him to lose control and attack me. He's a strong man, and a quick one, and he almost succeeded in strangling me this time, but I was able to get loose sufficiently to reach a knife from the kitchen that I'd hidden under a pillow earlier. I was operating on pure adrenaline and instinct by this point, and I used the knife to eviscerate Max and then to cut his throat. It made a hell of a mess, most of which ended up on me.

'I got his body off me and was able to get to his gun, which I used to kill Ernst, who had come into the room after hearing Max's screams. Then Hilda, the SIS officer I'd met in the shop, came in and helped me get myself clean. That's about it. The SIS team cleaned up the house as far as they could, but given the extent of the mess decided to burn it down. I was told this morning that as it was built of wood there's almost nothing left. I also heard this morning that the SIS agents put the two bodies in weighted sacks and sank them in the Kattegat off Gothenburg last night.'

'My God, Monique. Are you all right? That must have been a truly horrific experience.'

'I've got a large bruise on the side of my stomach where Max punched me. And there's this.' Monique removed a scarf she'd been wearing to reveal obvious bruising on her neck. 'But believe me, Max ended up looking much worse.'

'How are you feeling about it now?'

'What I'm having trouble coming to terms with is the idea that the Gestapo killed my father because of what I'd done. I always knew the choices I made in my life could have consequences, of course, but hearing that vague fears and concerns had become real was a shock.' Monique looked across the table at Bob and he could see she was crying. He reached out for her hand, knowing there was nothing he could do to console her.

Then she smiled and used her free hand to wipe away her tears. He wished she'd given herself a little more time to grieve.

Perhaps that would come later.

Monique continued. 'Except for hearing about my father and having to go to bed with Max we've not done badly. You managed things wonderfully here and saved our careers. A couple of days on your own in a foreign city and you appear to have transformed yourself into a highly effective intelligence officer who's managed to surprise everyone. And you just about avoided falling into the web that the lady sculptor had woven for you.

'For my part I've now resolved my problem with Max once and for all. It's funny that one of the last things I said to him was that I expected him to have more guts than to let the SD or the Gestapo do his dirty work for him. Within a couple of minutes, he was proving that he had more than enough guts to go round.' She laughed in a slightly forced way.

Bob smiled with her, though it was a struggle. He looked at his watch. 'Let's pay our bill and take a slow walk to our meeting with Simon Smith. I think it may still be raining but that's fine with me if it is with you.'

CHAPTER TWENTY-ONE

'Hello, it looks like we've got company,' said John Tickell. He was looking to the right, past Bob in the navigator's seat.

They were well above a solid blanket of cloud but there was a more broken layer above and around them. Bob caught a glimpse of the aircraft John had seen, apparently on a converging course from the north and a little above them.

'That's another Mosquito, isn't it?' asked Bob.

'It is. Given the blue colour I'd guess it's a photo reconnaissance aircraft, probably from 540 Squadron and on its way back to Leuchars, like us.

Bob watched as the aircraft closed in on them, then took up station just off their right wing. The pilot waved. Bob could see the navigator looking at them from his seat on the far side of the cockpit and a little behind the pilot's.

'Give them a wave, Bob.'

Bob did so. 'Do you often meet them while making your crossings?'

'Occasionally. They know to keep a lookout for us. He'll keep radio silence until we're much closer to Scotland, but it looks like he fancies some company for the trip home, which is fine by me.'

Bob gazed out at the second Mosquito. Until the previous October he'd only seen the type at a distance and on the ground, but he'd still come to think of it as one of the most beautiful aeroplanes he'd ever seen. Then he'd flown in one from Leuchars and fallen in love. If his memory of the registration was correct it was the very aircraft that he was looking at now. This was the first time he'd been able to see the type at close range in flight and to his mind it was pretty much the perfection of the aircraft designer's art. It just looked so right.

As he watched, spellbound, Bob wondered how things would work out over Canaris's question to Churchill. A messenger from the British embassy had come to the hotel early that morning to say there had been a reply in the early hours from the prime minister's private secretary. He had thanked Bob and the ambassador for the cable and said that the prime minister hoped to have a reply for Canaris later this coming week.

That was no surprise. It was, after all, pretty much what Canaris himself had expected.

Bob and Monique's meeting with Simon Smith and Peter Bostock the previous evening had concluded there was nothing further they could do in Stockholm for the moment. The meeting had gone well. Bob knew in his heart of hearts that it could so easily have been quite different. Monique had recounted events in Gothenburg. She'd stuck largely to the truth, omitting only any references to past enmity between her and von Moser. The female SIS officer had already reported on Monique's horrific condition when they'd found her and the state of von Moser's corpse, so Smith and Bostock had known what to expect.

They'd concluded at the meeting that things had been tied up quite neatly with one exception. They still had no idea who killed the Abwehr agent who'd met Peter Bostock the previous Sunday. This had concerned Monique and the two SIS agents. Monique had suggested that it might have been arranged by von Moser through the SD, simply to ensure the British treated the message that had been passed more seriously. Bob wasn't sure it really mattered any more, though hadn't said so given the views of the three more experienced intelligence officers in the room.

The meeting had wound up with farewells and an agreement that Simon Smith would cable BOAC at Leuchars to arrange for their transport back to Scotland the next morning.

Bob and Monique had an early night. She'd diverted his gentle advances, saying she just needed him to hold her, which he did. Bob thought that Monique had got some sleep during the night, though he'd been woken twice by her sobbing. She'd not wanted to talk about what was upsetting her. To Bob's mind it took little imagination to realise that her experience with von Moser and learning about the death of her father would leave a deep impression on even the most hardened of souls. He'd done the only thing he could and held her tight while she wept, feeling the tickle of her tears running down the side of his chest.

Neil Bartholomew hadn't been in the BOAC office at Bromma Airport when he and Monique had arrived that morning. Bob had known he'd have another chance to see him and leave a contact address for Oskar when he returned with Churchill's answer to Canaris, which was probably better anyway from a security point of view. He'd decided to give Oskar his parents' address but no surname. The Swedes had again provided someone to stamp their passports in the BOAC office, which again avoided the need to use the main airport building. The process was even more perfunctory than it had been on arrival. Bob had wondered whether the Swedish Intelligence Service was now actively working to smooth their way.

The second Mosquito stayed in formation until they were

perhaps 30 miles from Leuchars and well into their descent.

Then the radio crackled into life. 'Hello Bob, welcome home!' Bob looked across to see the other pilot had unfastened his mask, exposing his face.

'Hello Eric. Thanks for the welcome.'

'I'll see you on the ground Bob. Last one down buys the drinks!'

With that, the blue Mosquito pulled away and not long afterwards disappeared into a layer of cloud ahead of and below them.

'I thought you said on the outward trip that this was the fastest Mosquito that's yet flown, John.'

'It is, Bob, but it's not BOAC policy to engage in air racing. Not unless the other aircraft has a black cross on its side and a swastika on its tail. Besides, I might be looking for a job from Wing Commander Gill at some point. I'm not about to embarrass him by demonstrating that my Mosquito is faster than his.'

*

'It feels strange to be back in uniform,' said Bob. He was standing in the BOAC office at RAF Leuchars.

'If I'm honest, I'm quite happy to consign Ingrid's golden locks back to their bag,' said Monique. She seemed more rested than she had earlier. When they'd extracted her from the little cabin in the bomb bay of the Mosquito, she said she'd slept on the way over.

'Hello you two!' Bob turned round to see that Eric Gill had come into the office. 'I've got a car outside and can run you round to your aircraft, which we've serviced for you.'

'Thanks for the welcome just now, Eric. There wasn't any need to come and meet us though.'

'I'd been on an operational flight taking holiday snaps over the Norwegian coast. I heard before I left that you were due back today so when I saw you I thought I'd close in and say hello.'

After Bob had said his farewells to John Tickell, warning him that they'd have to return to Stockholm at some point in the next week, they followed Eric Gill out to the car.

'I'm very grateful to you for giving her the once-over, Eric,' said Bob as they pulled away.

'You should know there's been a debate about ownership of your aircraft while you were in Stockholm, Bob. One of my flight sergeants took it upon himself to try to get hold of the aircraft's records from the squadron it was allocated to before it crash-landed at Lossiemouth. He felt, and I agreed, that we should ensure that the servicing was not only done properly but that it was recorded properly as well.'

'Ah, I was rather hoping not to remind them of its existence,' said Bob.

'It did result in a phone call from the squadron's commanding officer, demanding the aircraft's return. I explained the circumstances to him, and we came to a mutually satisfactory agreement.'

'What was that?' asked Monique from the rear of the car. 'Obviously, it's still here because you said you were taking us to it.'

'Yes, it is, Monique. We agreed to transfer the aircraft from its previous owners to 540 Squadron, on the basis it would then be formally loaned to MI11 for your use, Bob, and usually based at Turnhouse. That way everything's above board and all the servicing records can be properly maintained, once we've caught up with what was done to her at Lossiemouth.'

'That was very generous of them,' said Monique.

'They didn't come out of the discussion completely empty-handed. We agreed that the squadron commander and five of his colleagues would fly up to Leuchars next month for a couple of days' golf. The best course in the world is just across the River Eden estuary from us, in St Andrews. It suits me because I've not been playing enough golf, despite the temptation on the doorstep. We're going to turn it into a sort of inter-squadron challenge, though the details are still to be worked out. You'd be very welcome to join in as part of the 540 Squadron team, Bob.'

'I'm very grateful, Eric, but I never learned to play and St Andrews doesn't strike me as the place for a novice.'

'I'm surprised they are still playing in wartime,' said Monique. 'I'd thought any open areas had been covered with obstacles to prevent aerial landings or turned into allotments.'

'Apparently a deal was done which allowed the Royal and Ancient Golf Club to have a say in the placement of ditches and obstacles on their courses. I've seen it said that the result is a better test for the golfer, though I never played there before the war so can't directly compare. At least if your ball ends up in one of the trenches they've dug across the fairways, you can lift it out without penalty.'

*

The short flight back to RAF Turnhouse passed without incident and once there, Bob arranged for the Mosquito to be towed into a hangar to protect it from the Scottish elements. His staff car was where he'd left it at Turnhouse, and they drove to Craigiehall. The MI11 offices were empty so Bob and Monique worked together to produce a report of their trip to Stockholm for Commodore Cunningham which they then took to Craigiehall's post room to ensure it would get to London as quickly and securely as possible.

It had turned into a nice afternoon. Bob looked at his watch. 'Everyone else has taken Sunday off, so I don't see why we should be any different. I'm sure there's a pile of papers in my secure cabinet that I should be looking at, but they can wait until tomorrow. We could have a late lunch here or at the officers' mess at Turnhouse, or we could just go back to the bungalow in Featherhall Crescent and have a lazy afternoon. I'm not sure I remember what one of those is.'

'Is there anywhere we can go and talk, Bob? I'm not sure I'm up to jumping straight back into happy domesticity right now and I'm certainly not hungry. I did a lot of thinking last night when I couldn't sleep, and I need to talk things through with you.'

*

'Do we have to climb that?' asked Monique.

'It's not as bad as it looks,' said Bob. 'The stile here gets us over the fence from the road, and then, admittedly, it's a steep pull up that track. But it's not far up to the skyline and then it levels out to a gentle uphill walk over a grassy field for a couple of hundred yards. My father used to bring me here when I was young.'

'Am I going to think it's worth it when we get to the top?' Monique was smiling, which Bob took to be a good sign.

'The view is amazing. I personally guarantee you'll not regret the climb.'

At the top of the hill, beyond the field they'd crossed, Bob led Monique up a final rise on top of which was a jumble of large boulders and a single tree. There was no one else in sight. 'Welcome to Cairnpapple Hill.'

'What is it?'

'No one knows for sure, though it's obviously an ancient barrow of some sort. It's not the site itself that is the main reason to come here though: it's the views.'

Monique stood on a high point close to the tree and slowly turned through 360 degrees. 'I see what you mean. The air's a bit murky in places but you are right. The views are amazing.'

'It's said that on a clear day you can see right across Scotland from here,' said Bob. 'Though as that means looking beyond the smoke from the chimneys of Lanarkshire and Glasgow to the west and from those of Edinburgh to the east, I suspect that may only be a theoretical "clear day". Certainly, I never saw the mountains of the Isle of Arran when I came up with my father and there's no way you can today. It's still rather special though. At least without much wind it's warm enough to park ourselves on that boulder over there, which looks ideally shaped to form a seat.'

There was a long silence after they'd sat down.

Bob eventually felt he had to break it. 'What's wrong, Monique? I can understand that hearing about the death of your father would have been hard to take. And I can understand how shocking what happened with von Moser must have been. But since we had our meeting with Smith and Bostock last night, I've had the sense of an increasing distance between us. Is it because of Birgitta Davidsson? You said you knew I was telling the truth about her. Nothing happened between us. Not what she wanted, anyway.'

'No, Bob, I've not been worrying about you and the lady sculptor.'

'What do you want to talk about, then?'

'It's two things that connect together, Bob. They are both things we've talked about in the past, but they are both things that come into much sharper focus for me after the past couple of days.'

Bob put his right arm round Monique's shoulders but felt her pull away slightly and removed it. 'I'm sorry Monique, I didn't mean to overstep the mark. I think you'd better just come out with what's worrying you.'

Monique drew up her knees and placed her chin on them, with her arms wrapped round her lower legs. 'We talked about this on the night you proposed to me Bob. At Dunrobin Castle last September, you tried to persuade me to see you again after I returned to London, and I told you that I'd been a bad omen for the men I got close to. My first husband was shot as a spy in Russia and the second was killed in a car crash in Berlin.'

'And I recall you telling me that you were better off without both of them.'

'That's true, but it's not the point. The point is that I've jinxed every man I've ever cared for. As you reminded me before you proposed, I said back then that I'd made a point of not getting close to anyone for quite some time, as that way I couldn't feel responsible if they ended up dead. Somehow, I've lost sight of that with you and allowed my love to overcome my common sense. As a result I allowed my fixation on personal revenge against von Moser to overcome my professional judgement, and yours, to the point where it nearly cost you your career and me my life.'

'But it didn't. I was able to reinvent reality enough to give you the time you needed to come out alive and make sure von Moser didn't.'

'Yes, and I'm deeply grateful. My point is that you should never have been placed in a position where you needed to do that. And meantime I've discovered that this jinx of mine led to the death of my father, while being interrogated by the Gestapo. I'm responsible for that, just as I've been responsible for so many other dreadful things in my time.'

'I seem to recall that the last time we had a conversation like this, in Orkney, you said you'd accepted a secondment to my team in MI11 because you hoped it might give you a chance to put the past behind you and find some of the happiness that had always eluded you.'

'That's true, but if von Moser proved anything, it's that my past is just too complex and dark to ever put behind me.'

'Are you saying you've not found happiness over the past few months?' asked Bob. 'Winter in Edinburgh during the blackout may not be the most joyous of times, but I know I've been happier than ever before, and I hoped you were too.'

'I have been Bob, but that's the point. Thinking about things last night, I found I was terrified I was going to jinx you too. I don't know how I'd survive if something happened to you because of me.' Bob saw Monique shiver as she pulled her legs more tightly towards her body.

'What you're saying is that you're so afraid of losing me that you want to give me up? Sorry, Monique, that makes no sense at all. We love each other and that's all that matters. To hell with everything else and everyone else.'

'That's only part of it, Bob. The other part ties in with what

I've been saying about your killer instinct, or your lack of it, and your basic decency, or your excess of it. You might have been able to lie to SIS and to Commodore Cunningham about what happened in Stockholm, and that really is progress. But part of me wishes you were enough of a bastard to have taken that lady sculptor to bed and then convincingly lied to me about it afterwards.'

'Hang, on, Monique. I've got a distinct memory of you telling me once that you were sick of falling for men who were bastards and were only giving me another chance because I might be different. It seems to me you're setting this up so that I'm damned whatever I do or don't do. I thought you loved me because I was the sort of man who'd be faithful to you, the sort of man who would tell you the truth.'

'I'm sorry, Bob, I'm not sure I really expressed that very well. What really worries me is the sense that I feel responsible for you, the sense that I need to make good any shortcomings in your own sense of self preservation. I've talked, doubtless until you're utterly sick of it, about what happened on that cathedral tower in Kirkwall, and about the relatively trivial incident when Taffy Jenkins was waiting outside the bungalow.

'While we were in Stockholm, I'm not sure I ever totally relaxed. I had the sense that not only was I looking over my shoulder the whole time, but that I had to look over yours for you too. I'm not sure I can go through the rest of my life feeling that I must do that.

'Fundamentally, Bob, you and I just have different outlooks because we've had utterly different lives. You are a nice decent man who needs to find a nice decent woman to marry and have children with. I'm neither nice nor decent. Do you know what I felt when I sliced von Moser's guts open and then cut his throat? I felt elation. Not just relief, but something close to actual pleasure at what I was doing to him. That's not natural for anyone. And I felt the same when I saw the look of horror on Ernst's face and knew that the sight of a naked woman covered in blood had caused him to freeze just long enough to allow me to kill him too. That's who I am Bob, and I can't see how there's any place for someone like me in your world.'

'Come on, Monique, this is the anger and the shock and the sorrow talking. I'm sure that if you had a couple of days to think things through, you'd come to a different conclusion.'

'There at least we agree, Bob.'

'What do you mean?'

'I'm sure I must be owed leave. I can't remember when I last took any. What I intend to do is telephone Yvette in London this evening and if she's there this week I'll go down by train in the morning and spend a few days with her. Hopefully, that will give me the perspective you and I both think I need.'

'I have to say that I was thinking more along the lines of spending the next couple of days buying that ring you'd seen in Rose Street and telling my parents we're engaged,' said Bob. 'What do we say about that to the people who already know?'

'There's no need to say anything at all,' said Monique. 'We can decide what to do about that when we've talked again. And in case you're wondering, I want you to let me know when we need to go back to Stockholm. You only got involved in that because of me and professional pride and my love for you both demand that I see it through to the end.'

'I'm sure I'll manage without you looking over my shoulder for me, thanks, Monique. By common consent I did fine on my own once you and von Moser had taken each other out of the picture. Besides, do you know how totally inconsistent you're being? One minute we're not compatible because you need to look after me, and the next you're insisting you look after me some more. I'll be fine on my own in Stockholm, Monique. You go off and enjoy Yvette's company.'

'Oh, come on Bob. I've told you there's no need to worry about anything happening between Yvette and me.'

'And you've also told me you could lie to me without my knowing, and you're probably right. This is one of those moments when that imbalance of trust you talked about comes into play. And right now, my capacity for trust is feeling distinctly diminished.'

'Oh, come on, Bob, grow up. This really isn't the time.'

The two of them sat without speaking for a long time before Bob stood up. Monique then did likewise.

They drove in silence back to the bungalow in Featherhall Crescent. Though it was still only early evening, Monique said she was tired and went to bed in the spare room. Bob realised they'd not eaten since breakfast. There was no answer when he knocked on the spare room door, so he walked to the fish and chip shop on St John's Road, hoping against hope it was open on a Sunday night. It was, and he brought back two fish suppers wrapped in newspaper. Monique still wasn't responding to knocks on the spare room door, so he ate alone and threw hers in the dustbin once it had gone cold.

CHAPTER TWENTY-TWO

Bob didn't hear Monique leave next morning. He assumed she'd telephoned for a taxi to take her to Waverley Station. He'd been under the impression that the first London train left rather later in the morning, but perhaps she'd gone early to avoid him. She'd not come into their room for any of her belongings, so unless she'd gathered things together while he was out buying fish and chips, it appeared that she'd simply travelled with what she'd packed for Stockholm.

Bob knew that there was nothing edible in the house, so he decided to drive to the officers' mess at RAF Turnhouse for breakfast. That also put off the moment when he'd have to turn up at the MI11 offices at Craigiehall without Monique, something he was dreading.

Before leaving, he went through the kitchen to the back door, to check he'd locked it after going out to the dustbin the previous night. It was only as he was about to leave the kitchen that he noticed a small pile of documents, with an envelope on top, in the centre of the kitchen table.

The envelope was addressed to 'Bob'. He ripped it open.

'My Dearest Bob

'I'm sorry to leave with yesterday's argument still hanging between us. If we are to have a life together then we both need to be certain it's the right thing to do. I know that you have that certainty and I know that I've hurt you by telling you of my doubts. I'm so sorry about that. I love you so deeply and hurting you is the very last thing I want to do.

'Perhaps that's one of the reasons I need some time to think things through. If we leap into marriage and it turns out we

aren't right for each other, then I'll have hurt you far, far more than I've hurt you now. My first two marriages were dreadful mistakes and I desperately want to make sure that my third, and your first, isn't likewise destined for disaster before it even begins.

'I'll not repeat what I said on that hilltop yesterday, but we are fundamentally different people in so many important ways. A large part of me thinks that you can, and should, do better than me. I hope a little distance will allow us both to reflect before we decide what to do next.

'I have left my father's journal, his passport and the forged letter with this note. Would you mind locking them away safely in the office?

'When you hear about going back to Stockholm, call me at Yvette's. Her number is Belgravia 1508.

'Your loving Monique.'

Bob picked up the documents and took them, with the note, through to the lounge. He sat for a while in the armchair nearest the window, reading and re-reading Monique's note. He kept focusing on the thought that she was leaving the door ajar. There seemed less finality in what she said in the note than he'd taken from what she'd said on Cairnpapple Hill.

He felt torn. Part of him simply wanted to weep. He had wiped away a tear in the kitchen when he'd first read the note. Another part of him felt angry about what seemed to be Monique's inconsistent, almost contradictory, position. Perhaps when he went back to Stockholm, he ought to make a point of calling on Birgitta Davidsson. If Monique really wanted him to show he could be a bastard, that would be a good demonstration. Then he realised that trying to take a woman to bed merely for dramatic effect was something he could never do, either to Birgitta or to Monique. Besides, if he turned up on Birgitta's doorstep after the way he'd left her the last time they'd met, there was every chance she'd simply tell him to get lost.

Bob folded Monique's note and placed it between the pages of a copy of John Buchan's *The Thirty-Nine Steps* that was amongst the books on the bookshelf in the lounge. It somehow seemed an appropriate place to leave it. He placed her father's documents carefully in his briefcase.

*

Bob had been right. The pile of paper in his in tray was depressingly large. His secretary, Joyce Stuart, provided a cup of tea as soon as he arrived but, as usual, Bob's first thought was to find ways of evading his paperwork.

'Who's in the office this morning, Joyce?'

'It's pretty much a full house, sir.'

'Can you ask everyone who's available from the three teams to join me in here, please Joyce? You too, if that's possible.'

Bob knew from experience that the meeting table in his office could just about accommodate eight at a push, so long as a couple of extra chairs were carried across from Monique's office. He then took up position at the head of the table.

While he waited, he looked around his office. He had finally stamped a little of his personality on the room. He'd got their army landlords to redecorate and with Monique's help had located some nice aviation paintings which he'd had hung on the walls. In a nod to the realities of the job, he'd also had a large map of Scotland and northern England placed so it covered most of the wall behind his desk, from floor to ceiling.

Bob's teams filed in, most carrying cups of tea. His deputy, Lieutenant Commander Michael Dixon, was followed in by Petty Officer Andrew MacDonald. Captain Anthony Darlington and Sergeant Gilbert Potter occupied the opposite side of the meeting table to their naval colleagues. Last in were his Royal Air Force team, Flight Lieutenant George Buchan and Sergeant Peter Bennett. They took two of the remaining chairs, leaving the last for Joyce Stuart.

'Thanks to all of you for coming in. When I've spoken, I want to do a quick run round the table to find out what I need to be immediately aware of, but first I want to bring you up to date with what Monique and I have been doing over the past week. I should start by emphasising that nothing I'm about to tell you should go beyond this room. I know you all well enough to be sure I can absolutely rely on your discretion.

'I am sure that Anthony will have told you that I telephoned him last Monday night to let him know that Commodore Cunningham had asked Monique and I to travel to London early the following morning. We duly flew down and met the commodore and a deputy director of SIS, or MI6 if you prefer.

'To cut a long story short, the commodore asked us to travel to Stockholm to act as couriers for a message from a faction within the Abwehr that was said to be of importance to the British government.'

'Why you, Bob?' asked Michael Dixon.

'That's a good question. It's complicated, but the idea was that I was going along simply to provide cover. It was Monique who had been nominated by the senior Abwehr figure who was said to be behind the approach as his preferred courier. It seems he and Monique knew one another before the war. The whole thing appeared highly dubious, but Monique was keen to proceed as it was possible there really was a chance of opening a valuable channel of communication.

'Anyway, we flew up to RAF Leuchars on Tuesday evening and from there to Stockholm in the early hours of Wednesday morning. We familiarised ourselves with the city on Wednesday afternoon and evening and the other side made contact on Thursday morning. I'll not bore you with the fine details, but it turned out that we'd walked into a trap set by the SD, the intelligence agency of the SS. Their aim was to discredit the Abwehr by capturing Monique and playing on her past role as a double agent for SIS in arguments about the Abwehr's future within the Nazi regime.

'They were able to get her as far as Gothenburg with a view to taking her to Denmark and then Germany. Things were a little touch-and-go for a while, but Monique was able to wreck the SD plan with some help from an SIS team. In her absence from Stockholm, I found myself nominated as the first reserve courier by the opposition Abwehr faction. On Friday I attended a meeting hosted by the Swedish Security Service with a very senior Abwehr officer. I passed back a message from him to the British government and expect to have to travel back to Stockholm later this week to deliver a reply. That's about it.'

There was silence round the table. To Bob's surprise it was Joyce Stuart who spoke first. 'If you'll forgive me saying so, sir, that raises a lot of questions you probably don't want to answer. Could you tell us how Monique is, though? You were a little vague there, but it sounds like she might have had a hard time. It's obvious to all of us that she's not here today.'

Bob smiled. 'I'm sorry, Joyce. I should have said without you having to ask. She's physically fine despite, as you say, having had quite a hard time. The SD officers holding her in Gothenburg both ended up dead. We arrived back at Leuchars yesterday and she came into the office to help me write our report for Commodore Cunningham. We've agreed, however, that she could do with a few days' leave and she left this morning to stay with friends in London.'

'Thank you, Bob,' said Michael Dixon. 'You didn't have to tell us any of that, but I'm sure I speak for all of us in saying how grateful we are to be kept in the picture.'

'That's no problem. Anyway, now it's your turn, Michael. How was Orkney?'

'A lot better than the last time we visited, Bob. As you know, the four of us flew up on Monday. We flew back on Friday afternoon. George and I spent most of Saturday writing a report which you'll find amongst your papers. We also sent a copy to Commodore Cunningham as he was involved last time and we didn't know when you were due to return. Suffice it to say that we found a totally different ethos on the naval side of things. There had been lots of changes of personnel and we learned that the corruption and other problems had been found to be even more extensive than we'd discovered on our visit in November. This time we found a few minor procedural issues which we highlighted to the new group of naval senior officers there, but nothing that was of any real significance. Meanwhile, the army and RAF commands had also taken a close look at their operations to discover whether any of the serious issues we found on the naval side had spread across services.'

'What was the conclusion there?' asked Bob.

'That a few individuals who'd had close working links with naval colleagues needed urgent postings away from Orkney, which has happened, but nothing to compare with what was going on amongst naval personnel on the islands.'

'Thank you,' said Bob.

'You haven't asked him the really important question, sir,' said Petty Officer Andrew MacDonald.

Bob smiled, with a little effort. 'Thank you for reminding me, Andrew. How did things work out with Betty Swanson, Michael?'

The Lieutenant Commander blushed.

'She said "yes",' said Andrew MacDonald. 'We all took Michael out on a tour of some of Edinburgh's pubs on Saturday night to celebrate.'

'Not all of us,' said Joyce, smiling.

'Congratulations to both of you, Michael. I'm so pleased for you. Let's talk about practicalities as soon as you want. The offer of the spare room at Featherhall Crescent is still open.' Bob hoped he'd been successful in concealing the hurt he felt at Michael's news. It was wonderful, for both Michael and Betty, but it brought Bob and Monique's uncertain position into very sharp and painful focus.

'Thanks, Bob,' said Michael.

'How about you, Anthony? It seems an awfully long time ago, but I left you in the middle of an investigation into the activities of Sergeant Edgar Ross at Dundas Castle, which had led us into some rather murky waters involving Auxiliary Units and SIS Section VII cells.'

Bob paused and looked around the table. 'For others present, I need to emphasise that no mention of those latter units should go beyond this room. I'm not sure I've really come to terms with the idea that we've got not one, but two entirely different private armies operating on our doorstep without our knowing. And then smallpox was also, metaphorically speaking, thrown into the mix.'

Captain Antony Darlington sat back in his chair. He looked to his left and Bob saw him catch Sergeant Gilbert Potter's eye. The sergeant stood up and left the office, closing the door behind himself. Anthony then looked back at Bob. 'You'll find a full report amongst your papers sir, not yet copied to Commodore Cunningham for reasons that I hope will become clear. The headlines are that Sergeant Edgar Ross seems to have gone off the rails following the death of his wife Mary during the smallpox outbreak in November. Things appear to have been compounded by the stroke suffered by his last remaining comrade in the unit at Dundas Castle, by the wider uncertainty about the future of the Auxiliary Units, and by a lack of clarity about whether his job at Edinburgh Castle would exempt him from call-up once the exemption previously conferred by his membership of the Auxiliary Units had been removed.

'It can only be speculation, but it seems that Sergeant Ross suffered some sort of mental breakdown without anyone who knew him realising. Why this should have led him to assault Corporal Barbara Mallory at Dundas Castle nearly a fortnight ago is anyone's guess. The only good news I've got is that Corporal Mallory has regained consciousness and it's hoped she'll make a full recovery. We can likewise only guess why he was creeping around the castle grounds a week later when he was shot. But there's no suggestion that anyone else was involved in his activities.'

'Does that mean it's case closed?' asked Bob.

'Not quite, sir. You remember that you asked us to look at Sergeant Ross's place of work and home? We found nothing in his office in Edinburgh Castle. When we searched his home, we found a few documents that relate to his wife's role in her SIS

Section VII cell.'

'Have you notified Captain Elphick?'

'No, sir. I thought you might want to do that after you've had a chance to look at what we found.'

'Is that what Gilbert's gone out to fetch?' asked Bob.

'No, sir. The SIS stuff will wait. Gilbert went to get some other things we found in Sergeant Ross's flat from the safe. These were much more interesting, and I think may need your fairly immediate attention.'

As if on cue, Sergeant Potter came back into the room. He sat down next to Anthony Darlington and placed a small canvas bag he'd been carrying on the table. He undid the bag and removed from it three small black felt pouches and a rather larger but otherwise similar pouch. These he also placed on the table after putting the canvas bag down on the floor beside his chair.

'You're certainly good at building up tension,' said Bob.

'Oh, you've seen nothing yet, sir,' said the sergeant. He picked up one of the small pouches, opened it and placed an ornate ring on the table.

Bob looked at Anthony Darlington. 'May I?'

'Be my guest, sir.'

Bob picked up the ring and looked at it, turning it so it caught the light from the window. 'I'm no expert, but this looks like a gold ring with a very large setting which houses a big red stone surrounded by small white stones. The red stone has had a cross engraved into it. Not a religious cross, but more like a Swiss flag, with the arms meeting in the middle. What am I meant to make of it?'

'Try this, sir,' said Gilbert Potter, placing a blue enamelled object on the table.

Again, Bob picked it up. 'From the loop at the top I'd say it's a pendant. It's largely covered on both sides by blue enamel. Once side has the symbol of a man carrying a cross on it, surrounded by white stones. Are they diamonds? Were the stones on the ring diamonds as well, surrounding a large ruby? The other side of the pendant has the symbol of a thistle on it. That's surrounded by an inscription, NEMO ME IMPUNE LACESSIT. Isn't that something to do with Scottish royalty?'

'It's Latin for "No one provokes me with impunity",' said Joyce Stuart. 'That was the motto of the Royal Stuart dynasty of Scotland. It appears on the badges of a number of Scottish army regiments and, as here, on the Order of the Thistle.'

Bob whistled. 'What the hell have you found, Anthony?'

Joyce stood up. 'If you wait a moment, I'll show you, group captain. In the meantime, it would be helpful if Gilbert could reveal the final two items.'

As she left the room, Gilbert Potter placed on the table a much larger pendant, this time a depiction of a beautifully enamelled and bejewelled horseman on a white horse, complete with a spear. 'Group Captain Sutherland, can I introduce you to St George? St George, meet Group Captain Sutherland.'

Then he opened the largest of the four felt pouches and gently slid out onto Bob's office table what looked like a jumble of gold and enamel.

Anthony Darlington placed his hands on the table, clasped together. 'I should tell you, sir, that we found the canvas bag containing the four pouches and their contents in a drawer containing underwear and socks at Sergeant Ross's flat. He may have been going through a breakdown, but he was keeping on top of his laundry.

'Neither Gilbert nor I had the faintest idea what they were, though it was obvious they were something special. We brought them back here and laid them out on this table, much as they are now. It was Joyce who told us what we were looking at.'

'What are we looking at?' asked Bob.

Joyce Stuart had returned to the room and as she sat down, she placed a large blue hardback book on the table. 'You need to know that my husband is very keen on history,' she said. 'Having been born with the name Stuart, he's always been especially interested in the history of the Stuart dynasty, which spelled its name "Stewart" with an "ew" until Mary Queen of Scots moved to France and had the spelling changed to ensure it would be correctly pronounced there. Before the war he took me to visit Edinburgh Castle. At that time, the Honours of Scotland, the Scottish crown jewels, could be viewed by visitors.'

'I once visited as a teenager,' said Bob. 'It wasn't long after they'd opened the Scottish National War Memorial so I must have been about 15 or 16. The Honours of Scotland were on display in a nearby building.'

'That's right,' said Joyce. 'But I'll wager that all you can remember are the immediately impressive items like the crown, the sceptre, the sword of state and so on.'

'I didn't know you were the betting type, Joyce, but you've won anyway.' Bob smiled and sat back. 'There were quite a few other items on display as well, weren't there? I can't remember any details though. Are you saying these are part of the Honours of Scotland?'

'These are the known as the Stewart Jewels, spelled the old way,' said Joyce. 'They were all my husband was interested in when we visited so they stuck in my memory. The ring you looked at first is the Coronation Ring and the ruby was apparently used in the coronation of James II of England and VII of Scotland. The pendant is the Thistle Badge. Its origins are unclear, but it may date back to Charles I. The last two items are called the Garter Collar and Great George, and the St George pendant hangs from the gold and enamel collar. They've been dated back to the late 1600s. All these items appear to have been bequeathed in 1807 to the Prince of Wales, the future King George IV, by Cardinal Henry Stuart who, until his death, had been the last of the line of Jacobite claimants to the Scottish and English crowns.'

Bob whistled again. 'They must be priceless. What the hell were they doing in Edgar Ross's sock drawer?'

'We know he worked in the clerk of works' office at Edinburgh Castle,' said Anthony. 'Joyce told us about reports that the Honours of Scotland were removed from display in the castle and taken to a place of safety at the beginning of the war. We've also been able to establish from notes and charts we found in the flat that his late wife, Mary Ross, seemed to have had an interest in the Jacobites, and in particular in the Polish Sobieski family, who according to one book we found had links through marriage to Prince James Francis Edward or "The Old Pretender". It's not beyond the bounds of possibility from what I've seen that she believed she was descended from the Sobieski family. There are claims some of them came to Scotland in the last century.

'Either way, if we have a man whose job made him privy to the hiding place of the jewels and whose wife believed she had a family link to their origin and had recently died in tragic circumstances, it's not that hard to see how Edgar Ross might have decided to steal the Stewart Jewels. It's all very improbable, but what we're looking at is even more improbable.'

'I understand all that,' said Bob. 'But how sure are we that these really are the Stewart Jewels?'

Joyce Stuart slid the blue book across the table towards Bob. 'See for yourself, sir. I got this from the Edinburgh Central Library. It's supposed to be retained in the library for reference but being in military intelligence does have its advantages.' She opened the book at a bookmark. 'There are two full pages of photographs here, with a set of colour drawings on the next two pages.'

Bob looked at the drawings and then the photographs. 'I never doubted you, Joyce, but it's good to have such clear confirmation. Hang on, this photograph seems to show the panel with the thistle on the pendant being hinged upwards to reveal a miniature portrait of a woman. Does ours do that?'

Joyce Stuart picked up the Thistle Badge and carefully inserted a thumbnail. 'Do you mean like this, sir?'

'Exactly like that. That's simply beautiful. Does anyone outside this room know about this?'

'No, sir,' said Anthony Darlington. I called on police help to search the operational base at Dundas Castle. We found nothing of interest beyond a hammer that is almost certainly the weapon that was used to attack Corporal Mallory. But I felt we could do a more careful job in the flat if Gilbert and I did it ourselves. The only people who know about this are Edgar Ross himself and the eight of us here. And he's not able to tell anyone.'

'Perhaps we should tell someone,' said Bob. 'Joyce, can you get hold of the office of Lieutenant General Sir Charles Gordon, who, as well as being general officer commanding the army's Scottish Command, is also the governor of Edinburgh Castle. Please tell his aide de camp or whoever you can talk to that I need to see him, that he needs to be on his own, and that it is a matter of the utmost urgency. That ought to attract his attention. Anthony, can you come with me please? Bring the bag with the jewels and the library book. Can you also find Taffy Jenkins and get him to bring the car round please Joyce? We'll be outside the front door in five minutes.'

As Joyce left his office, Bob watched Gilbert and Anthony putting the objects back in their felt pouches. This felt much more worthwhile than tackling his backlog of paperwork, he decided.

CHAPTER TWENTY-THREE

'The message I was given emphasised the need for urgency, group captain. You've piqued my interest and I hope you aren't going to let me down now you're here.'

Lieutenant General Sir Charles Gordon was sitting at his desk. Even seated, he was a large man who Bob suspected was used to intimidating those around him by his very presence. Add in the finery of a general's uniform and a very grand wood panelled office in Edinburgh Castle and the sense of power he radiated was palpable. Bob found himself hoping that the general would indeed feel that the meeting had been a good use of his time.

'Can I introduce Captain Anthony Darlington, sir? He joined MI11 from the Commando Basic Training Centre late last year.'

'Pleased to meet you, captain. Let's not stand on ceremony. Let's sit down over here and talk.' He gestured towards a group of soft chairs gathered round a coffee table in a corner of his office. 'Ah, here's the tea. Good.'

After the tea had been served and the orderly had left the office, General Gordon sat forwards in his chair to pick up his cup. 'I know you spoke to Brigadier Blackett a week or so back about the Auxiliary Units, Sutherland. If that's why you've come to see me today, I'd prefer to involve the brigadier in this meeting.

'There is a link, sir, but it's a tenuous one. I need to talk to you in your role as governor of Edinburgh Castle and I think it would be best if you hear what I've got to say before you decide who else to involve.'

'Very well, Sutherland. Say your piece.'

'The starting point was a shooting at Dundas Castle near Queensferry a week ago, sir. A female sentry with the RAF barrage balloon squadron based there shot an intruder who didn't obey a command to halt. The week before, another female sentry there had been attacked and severely injured, so they were on high alert.

'Following a trail left by the wounded man led us to an Auxiliary Unit operational base hidden in the grounds of the castle. The man had died because of the wound he'd received. He turned out to be a Sergeant Edgar Ross who was a member of the Auxiliary Units. From what we've been able to establish he had suffered some sort of breakdown following the death of his wife from smallpox in November, and perhaps because of the wider run down of the Auxiliary Units and uncertainty about his future.'

'I've still to see what this has to do with me.'

'Edgar Ross's main occupation was in the clerk of works' office here at Edinburgh Castle. When we searched his flat, we found several items that I think will be of interest to you, sir.'

Bob looked across at Captain Darlington, who gently unwrapped the objects and placed them on the general's coffee table.

There was a long silence while the general stared at the objects on the table.

'You're going to have to tell me what these are, Sutherland.'

'We believe they are the Stewart Jewels, sir, part of the Honours of Scotland.'

'My God! They can't be! The Honours were securely hidden away well before I was posted to Edinburgh. My predecessor in this job told me that in 1939 they were moved for protection to a cellar beneath the Crown Room, which is where they'd been on display before the war. Then, with the threat of invasion seeming very real, they were moved again, I think in May 1941. They were hidden away in some long-forgotten and deeply buried part of the castle where no one would ever think of looking for them. What I thought amusing about the story was that the only copies of the plan of where they had been hidden were sent for safe keeping in sealed envelopes to the king, to the governor-general of Canada and to the secretary of state for Scotland. That seemed a very odd way of doing things, but who was I to come along afterwards and question it?'

'Does that mean you don't know where they are meant to be hidden?' asked Bob.

'That's exactly what I mean, Sutherland. Can we take this a step at a time? How sure are you that these are what you think they are?'

Anthony Darlington opened the library book and, having gently moved the jewels to one side, placed it in front of the general. 'Here you go, sir. There are photographs on these pages, and colour drawings over the page here.'

Bob watched as the general peered intently at the pictures, then picked up the ring and compared it with a colour drawing. He could almost read the general's mind as he picked up the thistle pendant and used his nail to flick open the cover to reveal the picture beneath, as depicted in the photograph that Bob had noticed earlier.

Then General Gordon picked up his cup of tea and drank a little, before replacing it on the table.

'Very well, you've convinced me. My problem is that I

need to find out whether this is all that is missing, but I can't because I don't have a copy of the plan of where the Honours are hidden.'

'Might your clerk of works know, sir?' asked Bob.

'I spoke to the castle's clerk of works, a Mr Hector Williamson, last week,' said Anthony Darlington. 'That was before we found these, but I did ask him how long he'd known Edgar Ross. From what he said, Ross had been at the castle since before the war and was by some margin the longest serving member of a small office of three men, counting the clerk himself. It seems Ross's role with the Auxiliary Units, which was not known to the clerk, who simply knew "he had something to do with the Home Guard", gave him stability in his job. Other members of the office had served for short periods before leaving to join the forces. Hector Williamson himself has only been in post since last summer. Previously he'd been doing a similar job at the Palace of Holyroodhouse. His predecessor had retired and moved to Cornwall to live with his daughter. The third member of the team is a young lad not long out of school who expects to be joining the army soon.'

The general coughed. 'What you are saying, captain, is that neither of the other two would have been here in May 1941 and that the only man who might know anything is in Cornwall. We might be able to reach him by telephone, but this isn't something I want to trust to public telephone lines. I should add that my predecessor was killed in a plane crash in Egypt late last year so isn't able to assist either. It is helpful to know that Ross was working here at the time the Honours were hidden, though. Someone must have done the actual work of moving and hiding them. I can't imagine for an instant that my predecessor would have got his hands dirty himself. Our assumption must be that Ross has known all along where the hiding place was and at some point, presumably recently, but we've no way of knowing that for sure, decided to take the Stewart Jewels for himself. Who knows about this?'

'No one outside my team at MI11,' said Bob.

'Good. I'm feeling torn between two rather contradictory requirements. On the one hand I want to make sure no word of this leaks out, but on the other I urgently need to discover whether these are the only part of the Honours of Scotland that were taken by Ross, or anyone else for that matter.

'I'm rather hoping that a copy of the plan being in the possession of the secretary of state for Scotland means it's here in Edinburgh, presumably in his offices in St Andrews House. If I can get hold of that plan, then I can find out if anything else is also missing. The optimist in me hopes that if these jewels are all that's gone, then we can simply put the Honours in a rather safer place in the castle, invasion no longer being a realistic possibility, and pretend that none of this ever happened. The pessimist in me realises that if more of the Honours are missing then I might find myself very quickly posted to somewhere much less desirable than Edinburgh. You know, I've read that the men who designed the secret passageways in pyramids were killed to keep their lips sealed once their pharaohs were entombed. This experience rather shows why that might have been a wise thing to do.'

'Can we help, sir?' asked Bob.

'I'm very grateful for what you've done so far, group captain. I will pay a personal call on the secretary of state if he's in Edinburgh, or on the senior member of his staff in Edinburgh if the secretary of state is in London. I'm going to have to explain what's happened, but I suspect that they will realise that my career isn't the only one in danger here and cooperate with what I have in mind. Once I've got the plan, I'll let you know. It's only fair that as your team found the jewels you witness what happens next.'

'Thank you, sir. We'll be back at Craigiehall. Your people know how to get in touch. What do you want to do with these?' Bob gestured at the Stewart Jewels.

'If you can put them back in their bags, captain, I'll make sure they are locked away in a safe. The book has served its purpose, you can take that away with you.'

'Perhaps you might want to hang on to it for the moment, sir,' said Captain Darlington. 'Just in front of the section I showed you are similar images of the other component parts of the Honours of Scotland. This may be the nearest thing we have to an inventory of what should be hidden in the castle.'

*

Bob had a sandwich that Joyce had brought him from the canteen for lunch and turned his attention to his in tray.

He looked at his watch occasionally, wondering how Lieutenant General Gordon was getting on. As the afternoon drifted by and Bob's pile of paperwork slowly diminished, he concluded that he wasn't going to be hearing anything more about the Honours of Scotland.

It was just before 5 p.m. when Joyce put her head round Bob's office door. 'There's a telephone call for you, sir.'

Bob picked up the handset on his desk. 'Sutherland speaking.'

'Hello, it's Charles Gordon here.'

It took Bob a second to work out who was calling him.

'Hello General Gordon. How are things going?'

'The plans I needed – it turned out there were two of them - were held in London, not in Edinburgh, but the secretary of state's office agreed to have photographic copies made. These have been flown up to Edinburgh this afternoon and I now have them in my possession. It appears that finding out what I need to know isn't going to be straightforward. I have briefed my clerk of works but given what one of the plans suggests, he and I agree we are going to need at least a couple of men with picks and shovels, and I really don't want to spark rumours here at the castle that there's a problem.'

'You're wondering whether I can bring along people who already know, to help recover the rest, sir?'

'That's exactly right, Sutherland. It's not an order, but I would be extremely grateful.'

'No problem, sir. I'll see what I can do. When do you want us?'

'Again, I want to keep things quiet. If you could arrange to arrive at the castle at 7 p.m. there should be far fewer people about.'

*

Bob knew that Anthony Darlington had made a point of staying close by in expectation of the general's phone call and was pleased to find that Sergeant Potter was also still in the army team's office with him. Gilbert Potter was a large and powerful man who took to the idea of a treasure hunt with enthusiasm. The RAF team was out of the office, and Lieutenant Commander Michael Dixon had left for the day. He'd told Bob earlier that he needed to pursue a hotel management job that

Betty Swanson had applied for in Edinburgh. It would be something for her to do while she looked to purchase a business in the city with the money that she'd made from selling the remaining three-quarters of the St Magnus Hotel in Kirkwall.

On the other hand, Petty Officer Andrew MacDonald was still in the office and seemed keen to prove his strength with a pick or shovel.

Gilbert and Andrew ate in the sergeant's mess at Craigiehall while Bob and Anthony enjoyed the slightly elevated atmosphere of the officers' mess. Bob wished there was somewhere they could all go and eat together but had long since come to recognise that the British class system was deeply embedded in all its military services.

It had turned into a nice evening when the car, with Andrew driving, stopped just outside the castle's main gate and Bob showed his pass. The sentry raised the barrier and they drove on. Immediately beyond the gatehouse they were flagged down by a man wearing a set of blue overalls and a tweed cap. Bob's first impression was that he seemed to be in his late forties.

'Group Captain Sutherland?'

'Yes.'

'I'm the clerk of works, Hector Williamson. Can I squeeze in the back so I can show you where to go?'

'Of course,' said Bob.

'Before we drive off, can I draw your attention to this massive, curved wall that extends far above us and dominates the eastern approaches to the castle? It's got a series of large gun embrasures round the top. You'll understand why I've shown you that in a few moments.'

Bob leaned forwards from the rear seat to try to see through the windscreen, but only really got a sense of the structure once the car had turned right to continue its progress through the castle and he could look up through the side window.

The clerk of works directed Andrew to drive to the top of the castle, beyond the barracks and through the narrow gateway that gave access to the upper ward. Bob had seen armed guards in the lower ward and by the barracks, but the upper ward seemed deserted.

'Keep on going, past St Margaret's Chapel on the left, until you come alongside the Scottish National War Memorial on your right. This is it here. Park by the end wall. Right, before we get out, I'll try to orientate you. The building directly ahead of us, connected to the War Memorial by that high arch, is the Royal Palace, which includes the Crown Room where the Honours of Scotland were displayed before the war. To its left, and ours, you'll see a low wall. Beyond that is the rear of the upper surface of the Half-Moon Battery, built in 1571. It was the lower part of the outer face of the Half-Moon Battery that I drew your attention to from the main gate. You can think of it as semi-cylindrical in shape and built to provide a platform for a set of large guns intended to make this side of the castle impregnable.

'Let's get out now. Can we walk over to this set of railings which extend out from and then run parallel to this back wall of the Half-Moon Battery? You'll see that beyond them is a lower-level passage, open to the sky. This can be accessed by the steps you see descending from the gate on our left, though that is kept locked. Even with the Honours no longer on view we still get lots of visitors to the castle, especially to the War Memorial and St Margaret's Chapel, but we don't encourage them to go down there.'

Bob looked around. There was no one at all in sight at this

time of the evening. He and Monique had visited the upper part of the castle as tourists the previous November. It felt very different now.

Williamson continued. 'The two heavy wooden doors you can see down there, on the rear wall of the battery, give access to the upper parts of a much older part of the castle that we can talk about later. For the moment, all you need to know is that we will shortly be emerging from a door that's not visible from here in the cellars of the Royal Palace into the far end of that passage, and then going through the left-hand of the two wooden doors down there.

'If you'll now follow me under the arch over there into Crown Square, I'll take you into the Royal Palace. That's right, now just go up those steps, please.'

Bob found himself in a rather shabby room that had no windows. In the gloomy artificial light, he saw it was home to two large glass cases. The cases were home to a collection of clay pipes and old coins and there was a notice saying that these were archaeological finds from around the castle. There were two maps hanging on one wall, one of Edinburgh and the other of the castle itself.

Lieutenant General Sir Charles Gordon entered by another door. 'Good evening, group captain and thank you for coming. This, believe it or not, is the Crown Room, where the Honours of Scotland were displayed until 1939. I've often thought we could make more of it than we do in their absence. It's quite common to see visitors leaving with disappointed faces and perhaps that shouldn't be a surprise.

'Anyway, if you could follow me down the steps accessed from the back of the room, we'll descend two flights to the cellars.'

The general led the way down to an ill-lit lower floor and then into a room with a vaulted ceiling and stone walls. Bob saw that along one side were lined up two picks and a shovel and two different sizes of crowbar, as well as half a dozen paraffin lamps.

'Hector has gathered together everything we think we'll need,' said the general,' and I've got the library book and the all-important copies of the plans, though it might be best to leave the book here for the moment. We will exit the Royal Palace via the door at the end of this corridor.'

Bob picked up the shovel and a lamp and others also gathered up equipment. Hector unlocked a door which Bob saw opened into an arched passageway. A few yards away this became the open passage they'd looked down into shortly before. The clerk of works led them past one wooden door on their right to a second. He removed a large padlock from an iron hasp then used another, much larger, key to unlock the door itself.

'Out of curiosity,' said Bob, 'why this door and not the one we came past?'

'That one opens onto a sheer drop,' said Hector. 'After the general showed me the plans earlier, I came on a little reconnaissance on my own. I doubt if anyone's been in here since May 1941 – no one who should have been here, anyway - and it seemed as well to get an idea of the lie of the land. I also wanted to work out which keys fitted which doors from the large collection in my office.' The door squealed as he pushed it open. 'Perhaps I should have oiled the hinges while I was at it. There's a flat area just beyond the door where we can light the lamps. Then we need to scramble down a few feet to the floor of the room.'

Once they were inside with the lamps lit, Hector closed the outer door.

Bob could hear a dripping sound and looked up to see the shape of a small grid in the roof against the evening sky. 'What's up there?'

'That's drainage from the upper surface of the Half-Moon Battery. It drains into its own interior, which seems an odd way to have done things. I'm not sure why it's dripping given it's been dry today but, as you can hear, it is. What you need to remember is that we have now moved back two centuries in time. Entombed within the 1571 Half-Moon Battery are the surprisingly extensive remains of a much older structure, a tower house called David's Tower built in the late 1300s.

'I would urge great caution. We are in the surviving parts of a large building that is completely contained within the later defensive structure. It would originally have risen considerably above the height of the Half-Moon Battery and I saw enough earlier to know that in places putting a foot wrong could see you fall all the way to the bottom, which I suspect is on a level with the main gate where we met.'

'Can I have your attention?' asked the general. 'The Honours were hidden in two different locations and one of them is meant to be in a cavity they dug into the rear wall of this room. Captain, could you hold up your lamp so we can see the plan more clearly? I think the location is just over there. There are no signs of disturbance, but I suppose you'd expect they'd have taken care to cover their tracks.'

Bob watched. 'If you've got this huge, buried structure, it seems a bit lazy for them to have hidden the Honours in the very first room you come into from the populated parts of the castle.'

'I have to admit that thought crossed my mind too, Sutherland,' said the general. 'But this is definitely the room the first plan relates to. The second requires us to go a little further into the structure, though not as far as you might expect. Do you fancy your chances with one of the picks, sergeant? For my money, the plan is showing the cavity to be about here.' The general drew a cigar shape perhaps three feet long on the rear wall with a piece of chalk.

'Of course, sir,' said Gilbert Potter.

'It will be quicker with two,' said Andrew MacDonald, 'if that's OK with you, sir?'

The general stood back while Gilbert and Andrew used the picks on the two ends of the shape he'd drawn.

Bob was no expert, but it seemed to him that progress was slow. If they were digging in the right place, then whoever had hidden part of the Honours here had made a good job of sealing the hole back up again. After a little while he could tell that Andrew's initial burst of energy had dissipated. He saw the general had noticed too and was looking around the room. Then, to Bob's amazement, the general took off his jacket and laid it out of the way, on the higher piece of floor near the entrance and placed his hat on it.

'Give me your pick, petty officer. I think this is a job for the ex-rugby forwards in the room.'

Bob thought the general had to be in his late forties or perhaps early fifties but in riding boots and breeches held up by braces he cut an impressive figure, easily as large physically as the much younger Sergeant Potter and still displaying plenty of muscle. As the digging restarted, Bob realised that a general wielding a pick was one of the more surreal sights he'd seen in his life, and he wished that Monique could have been here to share it with him. It only took a few more minutes before Sergeant Potter broke though into a void in the wall.

'There's a long wooden chest in here,' said General Gordon. 'Let's remove the last of the stone with the crowbars. We don't want to damage anything.'

A few minutes later they had the chest on the floor of the room.

'It still seems securely fastened,' said the general. 'Good, that will do in here. Petty officer, I'd be grateful if you could remain here with this chest while we move on to the second hiding place. I don't want anyone stealing it from under our noses when we've come this far.'

'Yes sir, of course.'

Bob could see that Andrew was disappointed.

'Right, where to now, Hector?' asked the general.

'We need to go down the passage on this side of the room, sir. It descends several steps before arriving at a stout wooden door.' He led the way, unlocking the door and going into a continuation of the stone passage beyond it. 'According to the second plan, we now need to descend these stone steps to our left, which lead down below this sharply pointed lintel. Don't go any further along the passage we've been following. I discovered earlier that the floor drops away just along there. There's another locked door down these steps and this was as far as I got earlier because I couldn't find the key for it.'

General Gordon spoke from behind. 'Perhaps the sergeant could do the honours with one of the crowbars? Don't worry about damaging the door.'

It didn't take Gilbert Potter long to persuade the door to open and he then led them into a stone room with a vaulted ceiling, perhaps twenty feet long. In the light from the lamps

Bob could see several features including an old fireplace, or the space for one, at the far end. In the most distance corner there was an opening in the right-hand side wall.

The general was looking at his plan. 'According to this, there's a latrine closet through that opening. That's the second hiding place.'

'In a latrine closet?' asked Bob.

'Apparently not in the latrine itself, but beneath the floor immediately in front of it.'

The latrine was in a very much smaller room. The general had others hold their lamps to provide illumination from the main room while he went in with Sergeant Potter.

'It's supposed to be this central flagstone, sergeant. Can someone pass in the smaller crowbar?'

Bob glimpsed the flagstone being lifted.

'There's a large wooden chest in the hole below,' said Sergeant Potter, and a smaller wooden box next to it, placed on its end to fill the space.'

'Let's get them both out and into the main room,' said General Gordon.

'The smaller one's been smashed open and replaced with the broken end downwards so that wasn't obvious,' said Gilbert.

It was clear that the fastenings on the larger chest were undisturbed. They placed the smaller box on top of it and opened it.

'It's zinc-lined,' said General Gordon. 'Although it's been opened, there are still two felt pouches in here, like the others, though they hardly fill it.' He picked up the larger of the two and tipped its contents onto his hand. 'It's an utterly magnificent necklace. There must be hundreds of diamonds in it. There's a picture of this in your library book. Time to take stock, I think. With the two large chests apparently still securely fastened and this beauty still in the box that has been opened, I begin to hope that Ross really was only interested in the Stewart Jewels. Let's take what we've found back to the cellars of the Royal Palace and make a proper assessment.'

*

'It was good of the general to break out the Cognac,' said Gilbert Potter as Andrew MacDonald drove down the castle esplanade in the darkness.

It was exceptionally fine Cognac,' said Anthony Darlington. 'I suspect he felt it was a small price to pay for saving his career. You could feel the relief radiating off him when it became more and more clear that only the Stewart Jewels had been taken. That will allow him to place the full set of Honours under guard and pretend that none of this ever happened.'

'Would he really have lost his job?' asked Gilbert Potter.

'They'd have wanted to blame someone,' said Bob. 'Rank may have its privileges, but it has its responsibilities too, and he's the governor of the castle.'

'I have to admit,' said Andrew, 'that the sight of a general taking off his hat and jacket to wield a pick is one that will stay with me always. He did a pretty good job too, alongside Gilbert here of course.'

'Can you drop me off at the bungalow in Corstorphine on your way out to Craigiehall?' asked Bob. 'I'd be grateful if whoever's in first in the morning could send Taffy Jenkins out to pick me up as my staff car is at the office.'

The car pulled away, leaving Bob standing on the pavement

of a darkened Featherhall Crescent. The idea of going into an empty house really didn't appeal, but he'd already eaten so the diversion of a walk to the fish and chip shop wasn't available. He went in and made sure the blackout curtains were closed before switching on the light in the lounge. Then he removed the copy of John Buchan's *The Thirty-Nine Steps* from the bookshelf and sat down on the sofa to read Monique's note again, wondering if he could be bothered to light a fire.

CHAPTER TWENTY-FOUR

The Tuesday seemed to pass very slowly. The only good thing about it was that Bob was finally able to get on top of his paperwork. The report that Michael Dixon and George Buchan had produced following their trip to Orkney was excellent and showed how much had changed there. To Bob's mind it went a long way to justifying the existence of his Edinburgh outpost of MI11. But for his team's visit in November, a great deal that was rotten might have stayed hidden from view. He was pleased Michael and George had sent a copy of their report directly to Commodore Cunningham.

Bob also wrote a report for the Commodore on the outcome of their investigation into Sergeant Edgar Ross. In it, he touched on wider thoughts he'd had about the curious lingering but apparently pointless existence of the Auxiliary Units. He also flagged up what Anthony Darlington had gleaned about the organisation of SIS Section VII cells from the documents he'd found at the Ross's flat.

When they'd discussed it, Bob and Anthony had concluded that Mary Ross wasn't meant to have such documents at home. This was confirmed by Captain John Elphick, who Bob had invited in for a meeting with Anthony and himself early on the Tuesday evening. Bob assured him that nothing in the documents had gone any further. All three of them knew he was lying.

Bob stayed late in the office on Tuesday, largely to put off the moment when he'd have to go back to the bungalow. After leaving Craigiehall he decided to dine in the officers' mess at RAF Turnhouse, partly for the same reason and partly because he knew he needed to eat, even though he didn't feel very hungry. As he arrived, he bumped into Wing Commander Bernard Spencer, the station commander at RAF Turnhouse, and the two dined together before retiring to the bar for drinks with some of the station's senior officers.

After a longer time in the bar than anyone had planned, Bob felt he'd drunk too much to drive home, so spent the night in a room in the mess before returning to the bungalow in Featherhall Crescent early next morning for a shave and a change of shirt and underwear. He was struck by how cold and abandoned the bungalow felt and knew he'd have to do something to make it more homely before Betty Swanson and Michael Dixon were ready to move into the spare room. He realised he'd not thought to ask Michael what had happened with Betty's job application and when she'd be likely to be heading south from Orkney.

It turned out that Michael was away from the office on Wednesday with Andrew MacDonald, visiting and assessing security at naval facilities on Clydeside.

Bob spent the late morning and part of the afternoon accompanying Flight Lieutenant George Buchan and Sergeant Peter Bennett on a visit to RAF Grangemouth. The visit was pre-planned, and George didn't seem to mind Bob attaching himself as a supernumerary. As he'd told George, he'd flown from RAF Grangemouth for a short period at the beginning of the war and was interested to see how the place had developed since then.

Bob had done his pre-war flying with 602 (City of Glasgow) Squadron of the Auxiliary Air Force at Abbotsinch near Glasgow. As war approached, their Hawker Hind biplane light bombers were replaced by Supermarine Spitfires and they became a fighter squadron. On the 6th of October 1939 the squadron mobilised for war and moved to RAF Grangemouth. They'd only stayed for a month before being posted to RAF Drem in East Lothian. It was while flying from Drem, first with 602 Squadron and from May 1940 as a flight commander flying Hawker Hurricanes with 605 Squadron, that Bob had achieved his early kills and gained his first Distinguished Flying Cross. But his war had begun at RAF Grangemouth.

It was now the base of a Spitfire operational training unit charged with training fighter pilots. Bob was embarrassed to find himself viewed as something of a celebrity after the wings and medal ribbons on his tunic provoked some obvious questions.

The commanding officer asked over lunch whether he fancied a flight in a Spitfire. Bob was sorely tempted but remembered how long it had been since he'd flown one. He also remembered that it was a less forgiving aircraft than the Hurricanes he'd flown later and much more recently, and recalled that some pilots had found landing the Spitfire especially tricky, though he'd never had a problem himself. He regretfully declined, though if George and Peter hadn't been there to witness the outcome he might have replied differently.

RAF Grangemouth had changed significantly since he'd flown from it in 1939. Tarmac runways had replaced the grass strips that Bob had used and there were quite a few buildings he didn't recognise. He was struck, however, by the way the focus of the airfield remained the large and impressive pre-war watch office, flanked by two enormous hangars.

In the car on the way back to Craigiehall, George Buchan assured him that his presence on the visit had been a help rather than a distraction. Bob hoped that he meant it.

Back in the office, Bob looked through the new additions to his in tray without detecting anything that needed his immediate attention. He therefore told Joyce he was taking what was left of the afternoon off and drove into Corstorphine to get three new front door keys cut for the bungalow.

Bob then looked at the advertising cards in a newsagents' window and found two local women offering to clean houses. One gave an address just round the corner from the shop, so he went and knocked on her door. Mrs Edith Grant was a slim, dark-haired woman who seemed to be in her late forties. Within five minutes she'd sat Bob down in her kitchen with a cup of tea. Within five more minutes he'd heard how her son was in the RAF, servicing bombers on an airfield in Lincolnshire, and how she'd been widowed the previous year when her husband had dropped down dead as a result of a heart attack. It seemed that one of her sisters now lived in Wales and she had a niece who was serving in the Women's Royal Naval Service on the south coast of England.

Before he'd met Mrs Grant, Bob had been wondering about the wisdom of allowing a stranger unsupervised access to the bungalow. Now he'd learned her life story in fifteen minutes and knew where she lived, he felt no such qualms.

To make sure he wasn't going to offend any moral sensibilities he explained to Mrs Grant that he and Monique worked together and, though not married, also lived together; and that he was expecting a colleague and his fiancée to move in as well. He didn't say anything about his own and Monique's possibly engaged status.

This left Mrs Grant undaunted, so Bob asked how much she charged. The hourly figure she suggested didn't seem very much at all, so to her obvious delight he offered half as much again, paid in cash and in advance. They agreed that she'd visit the bungalow every Thursday morning, starting the next morning. Bob warned her that they'd not been the most regular of house cleaners since moving in, and she might need to put extra time in initially. He also told her that the bedding in the spare room might need changing and that he thought there were spare sheets in the airing cupboard. Then he paid her for eight hours' work and gave her one of the new front door keys.

Back at the bungalow, Bob decided he wasn't going to put his newly employed cleaner out of a job before she'd even begun, however tempting it was to try to get the place looking better before she arrived the next morning.

He did, however, spend some time looking at bills to work out how much coal they'd used since moving into the bungalow. This confirmed his impression that they'd used rather less than a quarter of their annual ration in the three coldest months of the year. A quick trip out to the coal bunker confirmed his recollection that they'd had a delivery a couple of weeks earlier and had plenty available.

Bob therefore took off his jacket and put on an apron he found on the back of the kitchen door and spent some time cleaning out the fires in the main bedroom and lounge, and the coal-fired boiler in the kitchen. Having done that, he laid rolled-up newspaper and wood ready to light in the fires in the lounge and both bedrooms and made sure the coal scuttles for each were full. Then he got the boiler going as that was the best way to take the chill off the entire house and heat some water.

By the time he'd finished Bob felt in need of a bath.

Afterwards he walked to the fish and chip shop on St John's Road. Back at the bungalow he sat in the warm kitchen and enjoyed his dinner more than anything he'd eaten for several days.

After eating, Bob made sure the blackout curtains were closed before sitting in the lounge. He wondered about lighting the fire, but then remembered why he and Monique had tended to use either the boiler or the fires. There really wasn't any need for both.

Bob opened a copy of the Edinburgh Evening News that he'd bought at the newsagents earlier but found it hard to concentrate and put it on one side.

*

He must have dozed because the sound of the telephone brought him back to reality with a start.

Bob looked at his watch as he went through to the hall to pick up the phone. It wasn't far short of 10 p.m.

'Hello.'

'Hello, is that Bob?'

Bob recognised Commodore Cunningham's voice. 'Hello sir. Yes, it's me. What can I do for you?'

'I'm sorry to call at this time, Bob, but I need you to get yourself down to RAF Northolt first thing in the morning. Can you be there by 9 a.m.?'

'That will be no problem, sir.'

'You should pack on the assumption you'll be away for a few days.'

'Am I going to the same place as last time, sir?' asked Bob, conscious he was speaking on an insecure line.

'That's right, so you'll need everything you took then. Listen, Bob, it's important that you aren't late at Northolt. You can be early, but not late. I'll meet you there.'

'Don't worry, sir. I'll see you in the morning.'

Bob looked at the phone after replacing it in its cradle. He felt like he'd been marking time since getting back to Edinburgh. He was relieved that he could finally go back and finish the job in Stockholm.

Bob went and fetched his notebook from the bedroom. Then he put a call through to the officers' accommodation at HMS *Lochinvar*, the Royal Navy shore base at Port Edgar on the River Forth, where Lieutenant Commander Michael Dixon stayed.

'Hello Bob. What's happened?'

'Nothing to worry about, Michael. I've just heard from Maurice that I'm off on my travels again first thing in the morning.'

'Same place as last time?'

'That's right.'

'Is Monique going with you?'

'I don't know. I need to talk to her as soon as I've finished talking to you.'

'It would be better if she did. The two of you work well together.'

'We'll see. Look Michael, you're in command while I'm away. I'm not aware of anything especially pressing that needs your attention in my absence but if anything comes up that you're not sure about, speak to Maurice Cunningham. I know he'll be happy to advise.'

'Thanks, Bob.'

'I didn't see you today to ask how things are going with Betty. When's she due in Edinburgh?'

'She got the job she applied for and is sailing over to the mainland late tomorrow so she can catch a train down from

Thurso at 8.30 a.m. on Friday. It's a bit of a trek and I gather that after a change at Georgemas to put her on the train from Wick, and another in Inverness, she's due into Waverley Station a few minutes after half-past-nine on Friday night. It makes me glad we travelled by air.'

'It's really good news about the job and that you can start your lives together,' said Bob. 'I've had front door keys to the bungalow cut for each of you. I'll leave one of them just inside the access hatch at the front of the coal bunker, on the left. If I were you, I'd pick it up tomorrow or during the day on Friday. Scrabbling round in the dark late on Friday night might not create a good impression. I'll put the other one by the telephone in the hall. I've also got a local lady in to clean the place tomorrow and the fires are ready to go. There's a coal-fired boiler in the kitchen you'll need to get to grips with too, but I'm sure you'll manage. I'm not sure when I'll be back but make yourselves at home in the meantime. You need to be aware that there's no food in the house.'

'I'm really grateful, Bob. Are you sure about this?'

'Absolutely.'

'Thank you. Have a safe trip.'

Bob looked at his watch after ending the telephone call. He knew that he should ring Monique at Yvette's flat to let her know what was happening. He knew how angry she'd be to be excluded from the trip. On the other hand, she'd had an appalling experience in Gothenburg and really deserved a longer break. He also thought it significant that Maurice Cunningham had made no mention of Monique, while he'd explicitly sought her inclusion last time.

Bob knew, though, that however much he tried to rationalise it, what was really stopping him picking up the phone and asking the operator to put him through to Belgravia 1508 was simple stupid pride. If Monique really thought that he was incapable of operating independently of her then this seemed the perfect way to prove her wrong.

Instead, Bob called the duty officer at RAF Turnhouse to make sure his Mosquito would be ready for flight first thing next morning. Then he telephoned his parents. His mother was already in bed, but after a brief conversation with his father Bob drove the short distance through the blackout to their house at Cramond and had a much longer talk with him. Bob told him about Edgar Ross and the SIS Section VII cells, and about the Stewart Jewels. Mainly, though, he talked to his father about Stockholm and about Monique.

Bob found it hugely helpful to have cleared the air with his father. He'd been feeling guilty about not getting in touch since returning from Stockholm but had felt paralysed by the situation with Monique. For the most part his father listened quietly. He did, however, offer the thought as Bob was leaving that he was a 'bloody fool' for not ringing Monique to let her know about the return trip to Stockholm.

Bob again looked at the telephone in the hall when he got back to the bungalow. It was very late, but not too late to telephone Monique. After a moment's indecision, he left the telephone untouched and after packing his 'Stockholm wardrobe', as he thought of it, and checking he had his false papers, he went to bed.

CHAPTER TWENTY-FIVE

Bob had his suitcase placed in the net still hanging in the Mosquito's bomb bay. As he pulled his flying jacket, leather helmet, life vest and other equipment out of the cockpit access door, he realised that Monique's kit was there too. With a pang of guilt, he pushed it all through into the nose compartment of the aircraft, where it would be out of the way and unlikely to move around.

It was a pleasant morning with high scattered cloud and, give or take the smoke from early morning coal fires, the visibility was excellent. Bob found the thought of simply following the main railway line to London unexciting, so instead he stayed low after takeoff and took a more westerly route that took him low over the tops of the Moorfoot Hills and over Hawick. He then followed the spine of the Pennines, still as low as the topography allowed.

He knew the uplands of northern England, though attractive and benign on a bright morning like this, had seen the premature and usually fatal end of all too many training flights over the past few years. Take a low cloud, stuff it full of hill, add a lost aircraft and you had a recipe for disaster. It was a sombre thought.

Once he reached Derbyshire, he climbed to a more sensible height for the rest of the flight down to RAF Northolt. Given Commodore Cunningham's concern about timing, Bob made sure he was early. He landed at Northolt just after 8.40 a.m. and taxied as instructed by radio to a parking area close to the control tower.

After he'd ensured the wheels had been properly chocked

and the aircraft was safe, Bob stood on the concrete apron to remove his flying kit, which he bundled back onto the floor of the cockpit. He decided the suitcase was safe where it was. He assumed he'd be flying back north to Leuchars later for the flight to Stockholm. Then he arranged for the aircraft to be refuelled.

As he turned away from the airman he'd been speaking to, Bob saw a black saloon car approaching. Commodore Cunningham got out of the driver's side and walked over to greet him.

'You made good time then, Bob.'

'Yes sir. You were keen for me not to be late, so I built some slack into the flight plan.'

'That's good, Bob. That gives us a chance to talk before the main event. Get in the car, will you? Preferably in the back.'

Bob watched, puzzled, as Maurice got into the front of the car, then did as instructed.

'Hello Bob.'

'Monique! I didn't expect to see you here.' There was a pause, then he added, 'I am glad to see you, though.' It was only after saying it that he realised he meant it.

'You didn't think you'd deprive me of another dinner at the Grand Hotel simply by neglecting to telephone Yvette, did you?'

'Perhaps it would help if I talked and the two of you listened for a moment,' said Commodore Cunningham. 'Bob, you'll have noticed the absence of a driver. I wanted a chance to clear the air in private, just the three of us. Monique came to see me on Tuesday and explained that things had become a little strained between the two of you. I told her I wasn't in the least surprised. Both of you went through difficult experiences in Sweden, in different ways, and you both did superbly well, again in different ways. It was only to be expected that the stress of the experience would spill over into your relationship in one way or another. As someone who's come to know both of you quite well, I'd simply say this. You need to give yourselves a chance to digest what happened and move on. Whether you do that separately or together is up to you, though the romantic in me rather hopes you'll find a way of overcoming the current difficulties in your relationship.'

Bob started to say something but Commodore Cunningham, who had turned round to face them from the driving seat of the stationary car, held up a hand. 'Hang on, Bob, I'm not finished. At the end of the day, I'm not here as your friend or your adviser, I'm here as head of MI11 and your boss. As your boss, and this goes for both of you, I'm here to tell you that I require the two of you to pull together to make this return trip to Stockholm a success. I believe that the two of you work very well together as a team and it's important that you remember that now.

'This isn't a matter for debate. I need the two of you to show a unified front this morning and keep that going when you are back in Stockholm. It's perhaps unfortunate in the circumstances that your cover is as a married couple, but it made sense at the time and can't be changed now. I expect the two of you to be wholly professional in maintaining that cover as far as the rest of the world is concerned. If, after your bedroom door is closed, one of you ends up sleeping in an armchair, that's up to you. That same romantic in me hopes it doesn't come to that, but that's really none of my business. Do you understand what I've said, Bob?'

'Yes, sir.'

'How about you, Monique?'

'Yes, sir.'

'Good.' The commodore looked at his watch. 'You and I both built spare time into this morning's schedule, Bob. I wanted to ensure we could have this discussion. We are due to attend a meeting in the operations block here at RAF Northolt beginning at 9.30 a.m. I'd say we've got time to get a cup of tea and give you a chance for a toilet break after your flight before the meeting begins.'

As the commodore set the car in motion he glanced back. 'Thank you for the report you jointly produced about your first trip to Stockholm. One thing puzzled me, Bob. Did Canaris say how he knew my name and position?'

'No, sir. I think he was just showing off.'

'Oh well. Perhaps he keeps track of naval officers who, like him, have made a career in intelligence. I'm sure it's nothing to worry about.'

*

Seen from the path that approached from the road, little was visible of the operations block, or 'Building 27' as the roadside sign stuck into the grass called it. Bob had been in the building before, some years earlier, and knew it was in the form of a large single-storey brick structure with a reinforced roof. This wasn't obvious because it was surrounded by protective grass-covered earth embankments sloping up to brick retaining walls, which were separated from the actual walls of the building by a gap of a few feet. The path led to a doorway set into the grass embankment. Beyond it, Bob followed Monique and the commodore into the operations block itself.

It seemed the meeting room was along a corridor to the right. The commodore poured teas for the three of them at a table set up at the end of the room.

'Bob, Monique, welcome!'

Bob looked over to see Major General Sir Peter Maitland, the Director of Military Intelligence, bearing down on them in his dress uniform. Bob saluted.

'Hello, sir.'

Bob noted with interest that Monique's shift away from the use of the name 'Vera' seemed to have registered even at the highest level of military intelligence.

Maitland gestured towards the man who had followed him into the room. 'I believe you know Jonathan Waddell of the Secret Intelligence Service.'

Bob nodded and smiled at Waddell. Monique walked over with her tea to talk to him.

That left Bob standing with Maitland and Commodore Cunningham. 'This seems a large meeting room for just the five of us,' he said.

'We are expecting two more,' said Maitland. 'Winston thought you were doing a lot of running round the country and beyond on his behalf. He said it was the least he could do to make the trip out to Northolt with his private secretary.'

'Nice try, sir, but I've been up quite a long time and I'm awake enough to spot an April Fool's Day joke when I see one.'

Commodore Cunningham spluttered into his tea while Maitland looked at his watch and smiled. 'I think you might find the joke's on you, Bob.'

At that moment the door opened and the familiar figure of Winston Churchill walked in, smoking a cigar and wearing the uniform of an RAF air commodore. He was followed by an army colonel, who Bob assumed was his private secretary. The colonel poured tea while Maitland introduced Bob and Monique to the prime minister.

'I recall that the group captain and I met last year,' said Winston, 'though you were a wing commander at the time. And you must be the lady whose quick thinking and decisive action prevented the king falling into enemy hands during that same investigation. I'm extremely pleased to meet you, Madame Dubois.

'I have to ask, group captain, what do you think of the new addition to my uniform? I learned to fly while first lord of the admiralty before the last war, but I was talked out of flying solo on safety grounds so never qualified as a pilot. I've been the honorary air commodore of 615 Squadron since 1939 and to mark today's 25th anniversary of the creation of the RAF the Air Council has, with the king's approval, awarded me honorary pilot's wings. I'm sure you'll give me an honest answer to a question that's been slightly troubling me. How will real pilots feel about my wearing your wings?'

Bob looked at the prime minister's chest. Above multiple rows of medal ribbons, only some of which he recognised, Churchill was wearing, half-hidden behind the lapel of his uniform jacket, the distinctive wings of an RAF pilot.

Bob didn't need to think twice about the answer that immediately came to mind. 'Deeply honoured, sir. The fact you value what we do enough to want to wear that uniform with those wings will be welcomed by everyone else who wears it, and the wings.'

'Thank you, group captain. That puts my mind at rest. I know you've both got a busy day ahead of you. Perhaps we should start? I'll take the seat in the centre of this side of the table, and I suggest the two of you sit opposite me. Others can sit where they choose, though Mark has some documents I might want to refer to, so will sit next to me.'

'Mark' was clearly the army colonel, thought Bob as he followed Monique round to the far side of the table.

'May I take notes, sir?'

'Of course, group captain. I should start by thanking you for the cable you sent after your meeting with Canaris. Yes, I'm sure Sir Fabian Saunders had a hand in it too, but you managed to get a real sense of the occasion and the conviction behind what Canaris said through any diplomatic filter that was then applied to it.

'I've asked to meet you because I would like you to convey my response to Admiral Canaris. I should say immediately that what I have to say is going to be viewed as profoundly discouraging by the admiral. What I have to say could, indeed, be set out in a short cable that the ambassador could pass on to the Swedish Security Service for onwards transmission to Canaris. That would save everyone, the two of you especially, a lot of time and trouble. But I do respect the admiral's position and I believe that as he has made his approach in person, so to speak, I should reply in like manner. I want you to be able to say that you discussed this with me face-to-face and that the response you give to him is the one I personally asked you to give. You will need to frame my reply to the Swedish government in similar terms. I respect the position they have taken, but for reasons I will explain to you, and I hope you will explain to them, I cannot accede to their request to offer a deal to Admiral Canaris.

'Although Admiral Canaris is going to be disappointed by what you tell him, I suspect he's not going to be particularly surprised. You said in your cable that he talked about the Casablanca Conference in January and our agreement that we would only accept an end to the war based on the unconditional surrender of the Axis powers. He also referred to President Roosevelt's statements on that subject at the end of the conference and subsequently.

'Since receiving your cable I have been in communication with President Roosevelt. For your information only, no notes please, I asked the president whether there was scope to offer Canaris any hope along the lines he was seeking, and I sought to persuade the president of the desirability of doing so. The president is adamant that there can be no movement from the stated position. I learned during the conference that the origin of the phrase "unconditional surrender" was in a communication General Ulysses S. Grant made to a Confederate general during the American Civil War, and Roosevelt is totally committed to enforcing it now. If I am entirely honest with you, and again within these four walls only, the speed with which he reached that position and the firmness with which he stuck to it in Casablanca did surprise me at the time. I am less surprised that he is unprepared to shift his position now.

'The other thing you need to understand, again between ourselves, is that in our relationship with the United States I am cast firmly in the role of the ardent lieutenant. I am now certain that the allies are going to win this war. But you must remember why that is. Firstly, it is because we bought time in the early years of the war. The rescue of so many of our young men from the beaches of Dunkirk was nothing short of a miracle. And then you, group captain, and the rest of the "few", brought about another miracle during the Battle of Britain. But we were still alone in Europe. The second reason we are certain to win the war is that Hitler was misguided enough to think he could succeed where Napoleon had failed and conquer the Soviet Union. That has now come back to bite him with a vengeance. But the third and most compelling reason why we are going to win this war is because the Americans are now fully committed to it. The simple truth is this. I may think what I will, but unless I can persuade President Roosevelt of the wisdom of a particular course of action - and I have had my successes - then I do what he wants.

'Before you say anything, I entirely understand the points made by Admiral Canaris about the desirability of encouraging the opposition within Germany and about the danger from the Soviet Union after Germany is defeated. But, and again this is strictly for your ears only, President Roosevelt is less convinced on both counts and my hands are therefore tied.

'I understand that you may feel you are about to embark on a wasted journey, but I hope you both understand why I am asking you to make it anyway. Is there anything you wish to say?'

Bob looked across the table. 'Simply that I'm grateful to you for taking the time to explain your position so thoroughly, sir. You can be assured that we will pass your reply on to Admiral Canaris and the Swedish government with the assurance that it follows careful consideration on your part.'

'Thank you. I believe the two of you now need to fly to Scotland for your onward flight to Stockholm. The ambassador in Stockholm is this morning notifying the Swedish Security Service that you are on your way with an answer. I hope you will not have to wait in Stockholm for too long before meeting Admiral Canaris. On the other hand, there are probably worse places in which to have to pass a day or two. Please let me know how the meeting goes, though I think that's rather pre-ordained. Good luck and a safe journey to both of you.'

With that the prime minister got up and walked out, followed by the colonel. Everyone else also stood up.

After they'd gone there was silence in the room, which was broken by Major General Sir Peter Maitland. 'I think perhaps you need to look on the bright side.'

'Is there a bright side, sir?' asked Bob.

'The best I can offer is that you seem likely to have a more enjoyable visit to Stockholm than Admiral Canaris.'

*

They were approaching Doncaster, following the railway lines, when Monique spoke for the first time. 'Thanks for bringing my flying kit with you, Bob. Had the commodore tipped you off that I'd be coming along?'

'I ought to lie to you, just for the practice, but the honest answer is that I'd forgotten it was in the aircraft until I opened it up this morning. Pushing your kit into the nose compartment was the easiest way of dealing with it.'

'Please, Bob, can we put aside the way we're both feeling? As I said in my note, I am sorry I've hurt you. But you need to remember that I'm also feeling very raw. Not directly because of you, before you ask.'

'I'm sorry, too, Monique.'

Monique looked at him. 'I have to say that the reply we're going to Stockholm to deliver isn't the reply that I hoped we'd be delivering. I'm sure you must feel the same.'

Bob nodded. 'Yes, I had dreams of being the means by

which the war was brought to an early end. You and I both know that what Canaris said about the threat of the Soviets has a ring of truth to it. But we are small cogs in a huge wheel and must move when we're told and in the direction that we're told to move in. I suppose what I found rather shocking was hearing the prime minister saying much the same thing about his own situation.'

'You have to respect his honesty in explaining his position to us in the way he did.'

'Yes, but it shows how much the world has changed in such a short time.'

They lapsed into silence until they were passing over York.

'I do have one question for you, Monique.'

'What's that, Bob?'

'Did you mean what you said earlier about dinner at the Grand Hotel tonight?'

'Absolutely. And since then, I've heard both the prime minister and Sir Peter Maitland instructing us to enjoy our visit to Stockholm. Or words to that effect.'

Bob laughed. 'Here's a thought, Monique. You know what day it is today, don't you?'

'Yes, it's Thursday.' There was a pause, then Bob saw her eyes light up. 'And they have dancing in the winter garden on Wednesday and Thursday nights!'

'My thought exactly.'

CHAPTER TWENTY-SIX

Monique was standing in the window. 'That was all extremely easy. A smooth flight and no questions asked when they stamped our passports in the BOAC office at Bromma Airport. And here we are again, in the same room in the same hotel with the same view. Do you think there's any way I can fold that view up and put it in my suitcase? I'd love to take it home with me.'

Bob walked over and stood next to her. 'If you could, I'd certainly help you carry it. Hopefully, this time Peter Bostock will realise we mean it when we say we don't want his people trailing us. I'd hoped he might have news of Canaris, but we have to remember it was only this morning that the Swedes were told we were coming.'

Monique laughed. 'He wasn't happy when you told him we'd be visiting the Grand Hotel later, but I think the local SIS has come to accept you do outrank anyone they've got in Sweden. At least he could assure us our room here is free of listening devices, for the moment at least.'

Bob turned to face Monique. 'Last time we found ourselves with a couple of hours on our hands before dinner we put it to good use. We started with a bath if I remember correctly.'

Bob saw the expression change on Monique's face and his heart sank.

She turned to face him. 'You've got to understand how difficult this is for me, Bob. But if I let what that bastard did to me govern my life then he'll have won, even from the grave. Please be gentle, though. I'll run the bath. Let me put Ingrid back on the bedside table first.' She removed her blonde wig, then went through to the bathroom.

As he helped her soap herself, Bob could see that the bruises on her stomach and neck, though still obvious, had faded. The warm water and gentle action of the soap caused her to relax, and he wondered how she'd respond if he approached the more sensitive areas of her body.

Monique clearly enjoyed her breasts being washed for rather longer than was strictly necessary. As Bob slowly slid the soap down her lower stomach she gasped and clenched her legs together. He stopped moving. Then she opened her eyes and looked at him with an expression he found very hard to read. He looked down her body and realised that she had allowed her legs to float invitingly apart. He resumed his slow journey with the soap.

They'd discovered on their previous stay that the bed didn't creak, even when worked hard. This time their lovemaking was so slow and gentle it would have been unlikely to cause even the most sensitive of beds to complain.

Afterwards, Bob lay on his back looking at the sky through the uncurtained windows. As on the flight from Leuchars, it was an attractive combination of fluffy white clouds set against a blue background.

Monique had draped herself across his chest. He wondered if she'd fallen asleep, then realised she was crying.

'Are you all right, Monique?'

'I'm better than I was, Bob. Thank you for being so kind and gentle. I've been terrified that you'd find my body abhorrent because I had sex with von Moser.'

'Hang on, of course not. The last night we were in this room, the night before we flew back to Scotland, I wanted to make love to you, but you asked me just to hold you.'

'I know, Bob. But that was just too soon for me and since then I've become more and more sure you'd reject me. It may not be sensible or logical, but that hasn't prevented the fear being very real. I was afraid I was going to lose you.'

'Oh, Monique. Why didn't you say something about that when we were talking on Cairnpapple Hill? I just got the message from what you said that I didn't measure up to your requirements and you were rejecting me because of it.'

'I'm sorry, Bob. I was so afraid of being pushed away that it seemed better to distance myself first. I thought it might hurt less if I did it that way. I don't think it has.' She slid her hand down his body, much as he done earlier with the soap on hers. She laughed. 'It seems that absence really does make the heart grow fonder. Do you mind if I climb on top of you?'

Bob didn't. This time the bed had to do much more to earn its keep.

Afterwards Bob dozed. He woke to see Monique standing naked in the window.

'You're really brightening up the day of any ship's captain out there in the harbour with a telescope,' he said.

'There are lots of windows along Skeppsbron. I can't imagine that anyone's going to pay any attention to this one. What time is it? From the colour of the clouds, I get the feeling the sun's setting behind us.'

'It's 6.30 p.m. I think you're right. It will be getting dark before long.'

'What time do you think we should set off for dinner?'

'Should we give it another hour? It's not going to take all that long to walk to the Grand Hotel. A leisurely dinner followed by some dancing should round off what's been a perfect afternoon and evening.'

Monique returned to bed and lay next to him. 'We need to make sure we don't go back to sleep.'

'I'm sure we won't,' said Bob. 'Monique, do you mind if I ask you a really personal question?'

She smiled. 'In the circumstances I can hardly object.'

'Stop me if I upset you, but what you said earlier about von Moser made me wonder how you've been able to cope with what happened.'

'You mean how I've coped with having had sex with him?'

'Yes.'

'Do you remember what you got me for Christmas?'

'That large book about the French Impressionists?'

'That's right. Have you looked at it at all?'

'I've leafed through it but, as you know, art isn't really my thing.'

'I'm not trying to catch you out. I wanted that particular book because it's got a double page reproduction of a painting I love, *'Olympia'* by Édouard Manet. It's a painting of a nude woman reclining on a bed and looking directly out at the viewer. In the background is her maid, holding a bouquet of flowers and looking at her.'

'Yes, I did see that one,' said Bob. 'She particularly attracted my attention because I thought she looked quite like you, though perhaps her hair isn't quite as dark. I didn't want to comment on the likeness because... well...'

Monique laughed. 'Because she's obviously a prostitute and the viewer of the picture is cast in the role of her client? It's a provocative painting, certainly, and caused a huge stir when it was first exhibited.

'I first saw that painting in Paris just after my family had moved to the city when I was still quite young. I fell in love with it instantly and I visited as often as I could whenever I was in Paris. God knows where it is now, probably in Berlin if it's not too racy for Nazi tastes.

'The thing is this, Bob. You know that I've been through some very difficult patches. I've slept with lots of men in my time, and some women. Some of them I slept with because I liked them and a few of them because I loved them, even if I never told them. Others I slept with because I had little say in the matter or because circumstances meant that I needed to. My first husband viewed me as his property, to be used or abused as suited his drug dealing and spying activities. I learned quickly how to use the attraction that others so often felt for me to my advantage, and I made good use of that skill once he was out of the picture.'

Bob rolled onto his side and placed a hand on Monique's shoulder. 'You don't have to tell me this if you don't want to.'

'I do want to, Bob. I think you should know. The important point is that it was never Vera who went to bed with the people I didn't like or love, it was always Olympia. I gave her an imaginary personality, based on the painting, and she became a real person for me and stood in for me when things got hard to deal with.

'It wasn't Monique or Vera who had sex with Maximilian von Moser last Thursday night, a week ago tonight, it was Olympia. Having said that, it was most definitely Vera who killed him on the Friday night.

'This may all seem a little mad to you, Bob. It may actually be a little mad. But it's how I've otherwise stayed relatively sane over the years. Just so you know, I intend to ensure that last week's outing was my last ever appearance as Olympia. I'm also trying to get Vera out of my life.'

'I noticed that Sir Peter Maitland called you Monique this morning, and the prime minister called you Madame Dubois.'

'I suppose you can look on that as paving the way to my becoming Mrs Monique Sutherland, if you'll still have me after the last week.'

'I'm not sure about the last week, but after the last couple of hours, how could I possibly resist? Seriously, of course I still want to marry you, Monique.'

She rolled towards him and kissed him, then broke away. 'I think we may need to get ready, Bob, before we find ourselves distracted again.'

'It seems we'll have two engagements to celebrate in the office,' said Bob.

'Did Betty say "yes"? That's wonderful.'

'On that subject, Monique, you need to know that Betty and Michael are moving into our spare room, probably tomorrow night. I know we talked about it and agreed to it, but it's happened rather sooner than I expected.'

'The poor girl! The bungalow's in a hell of a state! And the bed in that room's been slept in! That's no way to welcome her to Edinburgh.'

'I went out yesterday and hired a locally-based cleaning lady. She'll come every Thursday morning, hopefully having started with a good few hours this morning. I asked her to change the sheets in the spare room. I also got keys cut for Michael and Betty.'

'My, you have been busy, haven't you? I'm not sure why we didn't think of getting a cleaner earlier. Come on, let's get dressed.'

*

It was obvious that even on an enjoyable night out, Monique wasn't going to let her guard down. Again, it took the deployment of her dazzling smile to have them seated at a table she thought was acceptable in the Grand Hotel's restaurant. Bob realised that although Olympia and Vera were facing retirement, Ingrid was still alive and well and easily capable of bowling men over.

'What are you worried about?' he asked.

'Nothing in particular, Bob. We just need to remember there could easily be people in this room who would want you or I dead if they knew who we are and why we are here.'

Bob had done an assessment of their stocks of Swedish kronor and looked at their ration cards before setting off. 'What do you want to eat and drink, Monique? If we're to follow orders, I think we really need to push the boat out.'

'Let's stick with soda water for the moment and crack open some champagne while we're dancing later. But I agree with you about the food, Bob. We don't know when we're going to get an opportunity like this again.'

Monique was on sparkling form and the food really was magnificent. If possible, Bob's dinner surpassed even the one he'd eaten in the Grand Hotel the week before.

*

The winter garden seemed rather busier than it had on the Wednesday of the previous week.

The band was playing when they entered, and Bob and Monique moved straight to the dance floor. After several dances, which Monique threw herself into with abandon and Bob thoroughly enjoyed, the band took a break. He took

Monique's hand and led her to what seemed to be almost the last empty table, where they ordered champagne.

They'd just finished their first glass when Monique sat up. 'Look over there, Bob. That's Frank Lutterman.'

It seemed Frank had seen them too, for he made a beeline towards their table. As he neared it, Bob was appalled to realise that Frank was holding Birgitta Davidsson by the hand.

'Hello Bob. Hello Monique. Do you mind if we join you? There don't seem to be any vacant tables left.'

'Of course not,' said Monique. She turned to look at Birgitta. I'm pleased to meet you. I'm Monique Cadman. I take it from the look on my husband's face that you are Birgitta Davidsson?'

Birgitta smiled back. 'Yes, you've guessed correctly, Monique. You're right though, your husband doesn't seem pleased to see me.' She burst out laughing and Monique joined in.

'Just so you know,' said Monique, 'he's told me what happened at your party.'

'You are a lucky woman, Monique. Not many husbands are as faithful as yours. I did all I could to tempt him, but still he walked away.'

'Hang on,' said Bob, 'I'm sitting here, you know.'

Monique smiled at him. 'Don't worry, Bob. The circumstances demand that we inflict just a little embarrassment on you before we all share a drink and talk about something else.' She turned to look at Frank. 'Is the fact that the two of you are obviously together a result of Bob telling you what happened before he left the party?'

Frank beamed a bright smile. 'It is. I went to see if Birgitta was all right and, well, you know. The two of us have been friends for some time, but we'd never taken it any further before. I really owe you a favour Bob. Let me order another bottle of that champagne you're drinking.'

Bob couldn't help laughing. He saw Monique smile at him, then wink, something he didn't think he'd ever seen her do before.

CHAPTER TWENTY-SEVEN

'The look on your face was priceless!' They were crossing Norrbro, the bridge back to the island of Stadsholmen, and Monique was holding Bob's arm.

'I have to admit that I was a little shocked,' said Bob. 'Birgitta was the last person I was expecting to meet.'

'She's a lovely person and extremely attractive. I can see why you were tempted.'

'I thought she and Frank seemed happy together.'

'I'm not sure he'll keep up with her. Besides, isn't he married?'

'Birgitta told me so,' said Bob. 'She also said that doesn't seem to bother him much. At the start of the party, he was trying to woo a young Soviet journalist, but I think she went off with someone else.'

'I suspect Birgitta will have given him the shove by next week, but I daresay he'll have happy memories of their brief time together.'

As they reached the south-east corner of the Royal Palace, Monique stopped Bob and kissed him.

'Was that an "I love you" kiss or an "I think we're being followed" kiss?' he asked.

'Both, Bob. There was a slow-moving car going the other way on the far side of the bridge. I think it's the same one that's just passed us. Certainly, they were both dark and both were petrol rather than wood gas powered. What are our options for getting back to the hotel?'

'As it's a mild night I was going to go back the way we came, straight along Skeppsbron. It's the most straightforward route and probably the shortest. But that would be very convenient for anyone following us in a car because it's open and they could hang well back and still keep us in sight. The alternative is to take a right here and then the first left and go along the road that runs parallel to Skeppsbron. We walked that way last Wednesday night to keep out of the wind.'

'Yes, and someone successfully followed us then without my identifying them, which isn't encouraging. I recall that road as being very quiet and accessible to cars, both minus points in my book. What about the road that we walked up to the café in the arcade, the one where I caught Neil Prentice following us?'

'That's a little over towards the west side of the island, but not too far. It's consistently been the busiest street we've encountered in the old town; I suppose because of the shops and cafés. It's late now, but if there are any people about, they are likely to be there rather than anywhere else. And I think the street's pedestrian only, which would be a problem for our friends in the car if they are following us.'

'That's settled, then. How do we get there?'

'We go up this hill, the one in front of the Royal Palace. From memory we go to the top, then try to head as near diagonally left as the street pattern will allow until we find the one you want. The far end of the street emerges in that open area just behind the hotel.'

Västerlånggatan, the street they had in mind, was a little busier than the other parts of the old town they'd walked through, but not much. The arcade that housed their café was closed. Monique stopped in a doorway to kiss Bob again.

'There's definitely someone following us, on foot this time. When we stopped, he stopped. Don't look round Bob. He's got himself out of sight but he's wearing a light-coloured overcoat and a dark hat.'

'Could it be one of Bostock's people?' asked Bob. 'Surely he'd have more sense. It could be the Swedish Security Services making sure that everything goes smoothly.'

'Or it could be the Abwehr or the SD or the SS or the Gestapo or god only knows who else out to kill us to prevent a deal being done with Canaris.'

'There is no deal.'

'You and I both know that, but none of them do. Let's carry on walking. First, cock your pistol and put it in your coat pocket and keep your hand on it.'

As they approached the entrance to the alley where they'd taken Neil Prentice, Bob could see a car parked a little beyond, on the opposite side of the road and facing them.

'I thought this street was meant to be for pedestrians only,' he said.

'If you see a policeman, tell him. I really don't like this, Bob. We've still got one man behind us and that could be the car I saw earlier.'

Bob heard the car start up and saw the headlights come on. He shielded his right eye just in time to avoid being blinded.

'In here, Bob,' said Monique, dragging him by his left arm into the entrance to the alley.

'What now?' asked Bob as they pressed themselves against the wall.

'I don't know.'

'I had a quick look at this alley while you were scaring Neil Prentice last week. You can see most of it from here. There's a level section for maybe 50 yards, then there are stone steps, I'm not sure how many, where it gets very narrow. As you can see there are lights at regular intervals attached to the walls of the buildings on the right so the whole place is well lit. The alley does curve to the left a little, as you can also see, so if you stay next to the wall on the left it cuts down the chances of your being seen from the other end of the alley, wherever you are in it.'

'I don't suppose you know what's at the top of the steps, do you?'

'Only from the map. I looked afterwards out of curiosity. It's a street that runs parallel to the one we were in, though obviously at a higher level.'

At that moment there was the crack of a pistol being fired nearby and the sound of a piece of wall just above their heads being splintered off.

'I don't know where they're firing from, but we can't wait here,' said Bob. 'Run to the bottom of the steps, Monique, but keep as far to the left as you can. I'll be right behind you.'

As Bob ran there was another shot and he felt and then saw his hat fly off his head. He turned to see the man Monique had described, standing in the alley twenty yards behind him with his arm outstretched.

Bob fired without thinking and the man collapsed to the ground. He remembered something that Sergeant James, his firearms instructor at RAF Turnhouse, had told him and muttered to himself, 'One fired and six left.'

'Are you all right, Bob?'

'I'm fine, Monique. I got one of them.' He realised his hat was on the ground at his feet and, without thinking, bent down and picked it up and then put it back on his head.

'Bob, if you provide cover while I run up the steps to the street, then I can do the same for you. If you stay on your left and I'm on the other side, I'll have a clear shot at anyone who tries to get you while you're on the steps without you getting in my line of fire.'

'That sounds good, Monique. Now's probably as good a time as any.'

Bob turned and pointed his gun back along the alley, pressed against its sheltered side. A man in a dark coat appeared, holding a pistol, and Bob fired, but missed. The man fired back then moved out of sight to the inside of the curve of the alley.

'Two fired and five left.'

'I'm at the top, Bob.'

Bob turned and set off up the steps as fast as he could go. He heard a scream and looked up, to see Monique looking to her right, his left, and lit up in the headlights of a car. Time seemed to slow down to a crawl. He saw Monique raise her pistol, but before she could fire she was hit by the car and knocked clear of the narrow segment of the street that he could see. The car stopped. It couldn't have been travelling very fast when it hit her, because its rear door was in line with the top of the alley. As he reached the halfway point of the steps, Bob saw two men manhandling someone, presumably Monique, into the rear of the car. He stopped to take a shot but realised the chances of hitting her were too high and held his fire.

The man behind him in the alley didn't hold back and Bob felt a bullet pass close by the right side of his head before hearing it strike the face of one of the steps ahead of him. Bob knew he needed to reach the car before it pulled away. He also knew that a few more steps would change the angles so that the man behind him would be unable to fire without risking hitting the car.

The car pulled away as Bob was still three steps from the

top. He burst out into the narrow street and saw that it sloped steeply downwards to his right: in the direction the car was travelling. Bob fired instinctively at the back of the car, then realised that was where Monique would be. He heard running footsteps behind him and turned to see the second man was only a few steps from the top and raising his pistol. Bob shot him in the head.

'Four fired and three left.'

Bob turned back towards the car, which was picking up speed as it went down the street. He knew, he hoped, that the driver would be sitting on the left. Monique was in the back. She was probably injured, and he had to take the chance that she'd not be sitting upright in the middle of the rear seat. Then he remembered the promise he'd made to her in Commodore Cunningham's office, to shoot her rather than allow her to be captured. He hoped he wasn't about to keep it. He aimed using two hands, as he'd been taught at RAF Turnhouse, and fired a single shot. 'Five fired and two left.'

The car seemed to carry on picking up speed, but then it veered to the right and bounced off the stone frontage of a building before rebounding and striking a glancing blow on the opposite side of the street.

Bob set off in pursuit at a run. He thought the continuing series of impacts with the buildings should be slowing the car down, but there was no obvious evidence of it. In the street lights he could see there was a T-junction at the bottom of the street with a building directly opposite. He thought it inevitable the car would carry on straight across the junction before ploughing head-on into the building on the far side. But it stopped short of where he expected it to with a loud crunch and an impact that momentarily lifted the rear of the car off the ground and slewed the vehicle round to the right.

As Bob arrived at the car, he realised that the junction was more complex than he'd thought. There was an upper-level road crossing the end of the street with, beyond it, a lower-level road, separated by metal railings and by very substantial square stone supports. The car had run its front right corner into one of these supports and had been stopped dead in its tracks, wrapping itself round the support. The front seat passenger had been thrown forwards through the windscreen and was lying motionless, partly in the car and partly on the bonnet.

Bob pulled at the handle of the right-hand rear door of the car, the one he'd seen Monique bundled into. Even with the adrenaline pumping though his body the door wouldn't shift. Then he caught a strong whiff of petrol and redoubled his efforts. This time the door opened, albeit crookedly. He could see Monique crouched in front of the rear seat on his side of the car. The smell of petrol was now overpowering. She was facing away from him and he grabbed a large handful of the back of her collar and heaved. He'd just about pulled her clear of the car when a man who'd been sitting bent double and unmoving on the far side of the rear seat turned and lurched towards him, reaching out for Monique. Bob shot him in the face.

There was a dull whoomphing noise and the whole car ignited. Bob part carried and part dragged Monique for twenty yards until she was completely clear. He became aware of screaming from the front of the car and could see movement on the bonnet in the flames. It seemed that the front seat passenger had recovered consciousness from the crash to find himself in an inferno.

'Six fired and one left.'

Bob knelt down. 'Monique, are you all right?' He felt the

side of her neck and was reassured by a strong pulse, but she was otherwise unresponsive. 'Come on Monique. I've only just got you back. You can't leave me now.'

Bob became aware of the sound of footsteps and looked up to see two men in overcoats and hats running up the street towards him. He realised he only had one round left and regretted that he'd not stopped to reload his pistol. But if he'd done that, he might not have got Monique out of the car. From his kneeling position Bob raised his pistol towards the nearest man. They'd not know how many rounds he had left and perhaps he could use that to his advantage.

'Group Captain Sutherland! No! We're friends. Lower your gun.'

Bob thought about it for a moment. The accent sounded Swedish rather than German. Who knew who he really was? Then it clicked.

He lowered his Walther PPK. 'Stig Sandström? I must say I'm pleased to see you. Monique's been injured, can you get her an ambulance, please?'

'Help is on its way. I'll make sure she's cared for. Are you all right?'

'I'm fine.'

Bob saw Sandström look beyond him and pivoted to follow his gaze. The second Swede had run past Bob but was now backing away from the fiercely burning car, his arms protecting his face from the flames. Bob guessed he'd tried and failed to help the man on the bonnet.

'Can you give me your gun, please, group captain?'

'Yes, of course. I'm sorry we've brought the war to your lovely city.' Bob handed over his weapon, then looked down at Monique.

Her eyes were open, and she had a puzzled look on her face. 'What's happened, Bob?'

'You're alive, that's all that matters. Don't try to move.'

EPILOGUE

There was an attractive black-haired young woman sitting by Monique's bed when Bob entered the room. She smiled and said something to Monique in Swedish, then stood up and walked out.

Bob walked over to the bed. 'How are you, my love?'

'I've been better if I'm honest Bob, but I was lucky. They weren't trying to kill me; they just used the car to knock me down and leave me unable to defend myself. I have two cracked ribs on the right side which have been strapped up. It's not certain if that's from when the car hit me or from when it crashed. I've also got a large bump on the back of my head. The doctors think that might be from someone hitting me with something hard, perhaps with a pistol, before they dragged me into the car. They're worried about concussion, but I wasn't unconscious for long so they're hopeful it will be fine. The main thing is that there are no indications of any internal injuries and I've got the same number of arms and legs as I started with so, as I said, I've been lucky.'

'Thank God for that at least.'

'Ingrid did less well, I'm afraid. She got rather badly singed when the car ignited. I'm told she might have helped soften the blow on my head a little, so I'm grateful to her.'

Bob realised for the first time since entering her room that Monique wasn't wearing her blonde wig. 'I'll miss her, but not nearly as much as I'd have missed you, Monique.'

She smiled. 'How did it go with Canaris this morning? I'm sorry I missed the meeting.'

'I wouldn't be if I were you. It was a rather sad affair. We said our hellos. I passed on Winston's messages to Canaris and to the Swedish government. Canaris and the Swedes both expressed their disappointment, which I promised to convey back to the prime minister. The whole thing had the sense that everyone involved was just going through the motions. I'm sure Canaris knew full well there was no chance of Winston, or more accurately Roosevelt, being flexible, but he'd asked the question because it was the only thing left for him to do. I think the Swedes are realists, too, but as a matter of principle they felt they ought to support Canaris's initiative.

'Anyway, Stig Sandström, he's a deputy director in the Swedish Security Service, then took me from the dockmaster's house, where the meeting was again held, to the British embassy and Sir Fabian Saunders and I produced another joint cable that he sent back to London. It was rather shorter than the last one. Sir Fabian asked me to pass on his best wishes for a speedy recovery, by the way.'

'That man you just mentioned, Stig Sandström, came to see me here in hospital first thing this morning,' said Monique.

'What did he want?'

'It was a charming and very gentle interrogation about what happened last night. We've done nothing wrong by the Swedes and I told him the complete truth, as far as I could remember it until I got hit by the car.'

'He ran me through the same hoops when he came to the hotel this morning to tell me Canaris was on his way,' said Bob. 'I can understand that they want to know who started the shooting. As you say, it wasn't us and the physical evidence will bear that out. I'd like the chance to talk to him again before we leave about what happened last night and what they know about the men involved. Have the doctors said anything about when you can travel?'

'I've asked and they've gone into long explanations about the uncertainties of head injuries. The best I've been able to get is that they won't physically stop me leaving if I rest until this evening. I think they are being over-cautious, and I certainly believe that the sooner we get back to Scotland the better. The bad news, for you at least, is that when I described the passenger arrangements in the Mosquito, they said I'd be marginally better travelling in a seated position than lying down, and much better travelling where someone could keep an eye on me rather than on my own in the bomb bay.'

'Ah, I see. Fair enough, I suppose. You've never had a problem sleeping in the Mosquito's bomb bay and I could do with catching up on some after last night. Even when I got back to the hotel, with the pair of bodyguards the Swedes insisted on providing, I didn't get a lot of sleep.'

'I was aware you were here for quite a while after they'd brought me in. Thank you, Bob. Incidentally, I've got a fairly good idea of what the Swedes think happened last night, if you're interested.'

'Of course. How do you know?'

'You saw Ellena when you arrived. She's with the Swedish Security Service and has been assigned to protect me while I'm in hospital. She was keen to talk. It's early days, but she says that it looks like what happened last night was an attempt by an SD team to abduct me. The Swedes are aware that the SD presence here has been strengthened in the past few days. I've had time to think about it and my guess is that they may have been in the country looking for Max. They'd know their house in Gothenburg had burned down and would want to find out what had happened and where he was. They'd be particularly keen to find out what I knew about him, and, I imagine, to resurrect his scheme to take me to Denmark.

'Building on what Ellena told me, I suspect I was identified at Bromma when we arrived yesterday, even though we stayed well clear of the main airport building, or at our hotel, or possibly, though the timing would have been tight for the SD to pull together a team, at the Grand Hotel.'

'Hang on,' said Bob. 'Could the Swedes be listening in on this?'

'Ellena says not, but you are right that we need to be a little guarded in what we say. Anyway, the problem the Swedes have is that you didn't leave them very much to work with. According to Ellena, the view in the Swedish Security Service is that you are a hero who single-handedly wiped out almost the entire SD team.'

'I'd not put it quite like that.'

'Really? Let me tell you what Ellena told me. According to her, the SD team had two radio-equipped cars and five men. The assumption is that by the time they made their move, they knew where we were staying and intended to abduct me and probably kill you as we walked along Skeppsbron.

'It seems they thought on their feet when we took a detour and set a trap that involved driving us into the bottom end of that alley and waiting for us to emerge at the top end. I know you shot one of their team in the alley, and Ellena confirmed that a badly wounded man was found there. He's not yet able to answer questions but it's hoped he will before long.

'Apparently the Swedish Security Service had been alerted that something was going on when they picked up radio traffic between the two SD cars while we were still in the Grand Hotel. It took a little while for its significance to be recognised, which is why they arrived on the scene too late to be of help.

'Ellena's account of what happened after the first man was shot was rather incredible, but I assume it was based on what you'd told Stig Sandström backed up by the forensic work the Swedes have been able to do. She said that you killed an SD agent at the top of the steps, then killed the driver of the car, while it was accelerating downhill away from you in the dark, with a single shot to the back of his head that had passed through the rear window. You then shot and killed an SD agent who was trying to stop you getting me out of the burning car. Another of their team died in the fire.'

'It was something like that,' said Bob. 'I wasted a shot in the alley, and then another that hit the back of the car before I began thinking straight. And the car only started burning after my last shot ignited the petrol fumes that I suspect had been caused by my earlier wild shot hitting the fuel tank.'

'Ellena told me they found one round left in your Walther PPK, which meant you'd fired six. Is that right?'

'Yes.'

Monique sat up and winced, reaching for her side. 'Which means that with six rounds you shot and killed three men, caused the death of a fourth and wounded a fifth?'

'When you put it like that, Monique, it sounds very brutal. It was very brutal, to be honest. But I knew that if I let that car get away, I'd lost you forever. I simply couldn't allow that to happen.'

Monique smiled. 'I'm deeply grateful, my love. And I promise never, ever, again to complain about your lack of a killer instinct.'

Bob returned her smile. 'Well, at least that's something. I need to talk to Peter Bostock or Simon Smith about arranging our trip home. I see no reason why they can't get the Mosquito to come over and fly us out tonight. I get the sense the Swedish Security Service strongly shares your desire to see us gone from Stockholm. As do I, for that matter. Incidentally, you need to know that as well as your injuries and Ingrid's demise, we suffered another casualty last night.'

'Who was that?'

Bob held up his hat with his finger and thumb poking through holes in the back and top of the crown. 'Not "who" but "what". I'm going to keep it as a souvenir, but I'm not sure I'm going to be able to wear it again.'

AUTHOR'S NOTE

This book is a work of fiction and should be read as such. Except as noted below, all characters are fictional and any resemblances to real people, either living or dead, are purely coincidental.

Likewise, many of the events that are described in this book are the products of the author's imagination. Others did take place.

Let's start with the characters. Some of the military and intelligence personnel who appear between the pages of this book occupy posts that existed at the time, but nonetheless they are all fictional. This is significant because the military units and intelligence organisations mentioned were usually doing what I describe them as doing at the time the action takes place. Minor characters are also entirely invented.

Some characters could be associated with real people because of their roles, such as the British ambassador in Stockholm and the governor of Edinburgh Castle. Again, the characters who play those roles in this book are not based on their real-life counterparts and are fictional.

Group Captain Robert Sutherland is also an invented character, though he has a career in the Royal Air Force that will be recognised by anyone familiar with the life and achievements of Squadron Leader Archibald McKellar, DSO, DFC and Bar. Bob Sutherland's family background and pre-war employment were very different to Archibald McKellar's, but the two share an eminent list of achievements during the Battle of Britain. Squadron Leader McKellar was tragically killed when he was shot down on the 1st of November 1940, whereas the fictional Group Captain Sutherland was only wounded when he was shot down on the same day, allowing him to play a leading role in this book and its three predecessors.

And Madame Monique Dubois? She is a fictional alias for a real woman. The real Vera Eriksen, or Vera Schalburg, or take your pick from any number of other aliases, had a story that was both complex and very dark. She disappeared during the war after the two German spies she landed with at Port Gordon on the Moray Firth were tried and executed for spying by the British.

A flavour of Monique's story emerges from the pages of this book but to get a fuller picture you should read my first novel, *Eyes Turned Skywards*.

Two real historical figures do appear in this book. Winston Churchill of course existed. His role at the Casablanca Conference in January 1943 was as described here, as was his relationship with President Roosevelt. The president's firm adherence to the principle of 'unconditional surrender' was also real. The phrase 'ardent lieutenant' was used by Churchill in a conversation with a journalist after the Casablanca Conference to describe his relationship with Roosevelt.

It's also true that Churchill was awarded honorary pilot's wings for his air commodore's uniform to mark the 25th anniversary of the creation of the RAF on the 1st of April 1943. His presence that day at RAF Northolt is an invention.

Admiral Wilhelm Canaris was a real historical figure who served as head of the Abwehr from 1935. He later became a key figure in the German opposition to Hitler. In 1943, Canaris did meet SIS agents to ask whether Churchill would offer terms for peace if Hitler was deposed. The meeting took place at a convent in Paris rather than, as in this book, in Stockholm.

Churchill's response was delivered two weeks later and was as uncompromising as the one given to Canaris by Bob Sutherland in Stockholm. In February 1944, less than a year after the events in this book, Admiral Canaris was sacked and the Abwehr was absorbed into the SD. Admiral Canaris was arrested for plotting against Hitler on the 23rd of July 1944 and executed on the 9th of April 1945.

Military Intelligence, Section 11, or MI11, was a real organisation which had a responsibility for military security. Its organisation and other aspects of its operations described in this book are entirely fictional. Sanctuary Buildings in London exists, and at the time was much as described in this book, even down to the list of wartime occupants, though its use by MI11 is imaginary.

The Security Service (MI5) and the Secret Intelligence Service (SIS or MI6) both existed, and both continue to exist at the time of writing. SIS operations in foreign cities during the Second World War tended to be under the cover of the Passport Control Organisation as described here. The SIS operation in the Netherlands in 1939 that became known as the Venlo incident actually happened and the Special Operations Executive did try to sabotage Swedish port facilities in 1940, to the severe detriment of relations between Britain and Sweden for some time afterwards. The lethal L-pills referred to were very real.

The incident on the 20th of February 1943 when an MI5 operation inadvertently provoked diversionary Luftwaffe bombing raids on Fraserburgh and Peterhead did take place.

The various German intelligence agencies referred to in this book, including the Abwehr, the SD, INF III and NASDAP/AO were real. The Abwehr in Stockholm operated under the guise of the Bureau Wagner. The Swedish Security Service was also real, and they operated generally as described here. Their role in helping Canaris is fictional.

The Auxiliary Units were set up and operated much as described in this book and their UK and Scottish HQs were at Coleshill House in the Vale of the White Horse and at Melville House in Fife. Each patrol had an underground operational base as described here. The presence of one in the grounds of Dundas Castle is an invention.

SIS Section VII cells also existed, though even now very little is known about them.

Let's now turn to places that appear in this book.

RAF Northolt was (and is) a military airfield close to London. The operations block, 'Building 27' was externally much as described, though its internal arrangements are imaginary.

Craigiehall was taken over by the army during the war, and later became the main army headquarters in Scotland. It remains an army base at the time of writing. The presence there of part of MI11 is fictional.

Edinburgh is of course a real city and it suffered from an outbreak of smallpox in October and November 1942.

Edinburgh Castle did serve as the headquarters of the army's Scottish Command during the Second World War. The Honours of Scotland are today on display in Edinburgh Castle, as they were before the war. They were moved to a cellar in 1939, and then, to guard against possible capture in an invasion, hidden in the remains of David's Tower in May 1941. The locations of their hiding places were as described here, and the remains of David's Tower can still be found entombed within the later Half-Moon Battery, though they are only partly accessible to the public. The further move of the Honours of Scotland in March 1943 is fictional, as is the theft of the Stewart Jewels.

The North British Hotel in Edinburgh became the Balmoral Hotel some decades ago, while The St Magnus Hotel in Kirkwall is an invention.

Dundas Castle exists and is today a magnificent family home and exclusive use venue, where my younger daughter celebrated her marriage to her Texan husband in 2016. During the war it was taken over by the RAF to become the headquarters of a barrage balloon squadron. The events that take place there in the book are all fictional. The descriptions of the house and grounds are generally accurate.

Melville House in Fife is real and is now a private home. During the war it served as the Scottish HQ of the Auxiliary Units.

Featherhall Crescent in Corstorphine exists, divided into northern and southern arcs, and it is home to bungalows like the one lived in by Bob and Monique. Theirs is a typical example rather than a specific house. Coal rationing did take place during the war.

Cairnpapple Hill exists, though as it was only excavated in 1947/8 much of what can be seen there today was not visible in 1943. My description comes from a photograph taken of the top of the hill in 1929.

RAF Turnhouse existed and later became Edinburgh airport. RAF Leuchars also existed and continued in use as a military airfield until 2015, when it was transferred to the army.

During the war, the British Overseas Airways Corporation operated a service between Leuchars and Stockholm's Bromma Airport carrying passengers and, amongst other things, ball bearings. The route has been variously known, at the time or since, as the ball bearing run, the Stockholm express, the Stockholm line and the Stockholm run. At the time Bob and Monique flew to Stockholm, BOAC had just received its first Mosquito and the adaptations made to carry a passenger were much as described here.

It is worth noting that Sweden also operated an air service from Stockholm to Dyce, near Aberdeen, while Norwegian exiles flew large numbers of their nationals, who had crossed the border into Sweden, to Britain for training. Later in the war the USA started its own air service between Britain and Sweden.

My description of wartime Stockholm is as near as I can make it to the real thing, drawing on multiple sources and a personal visit. Having said that, when an author is 'playing away' there is inevitably greater risk of misunderstandings or errors.

Food and spirit rationing in Stockholm operated much as described, and wood gas was used to power most vehicles.

The layout of wartime Stockholm is as described, complete with the locations of the various intelligence agencies, the British embassy and the German legation. Those premises are now used for other purposes, including as a magnificent villa (the old British embassy) and a hotel (the old German legation). Where they appear, building interiors are largely imagined.

The Grand Hotel is much as described, and its role as 'the listening post of Europe' was commented on at the time. The presence of the press room and the Wednesday and Thursday night dances in the winter garden are factual. The detail of the press room is imagined, but there is a photograph showing the winter garden in 1943.

The old town of Stockholm was (and remains) much as described. The modern visitor will know it as 'Gamla stan'; but that's only been its official name since 1980. Until then it was 'Staden mellan broarna' or the 'Town Between the Bridges'. Streets and buildings are much as described including the arcade and the café, which I have assumed existed back then as they do today. Hotel Skeppsbron is fictional, but its location uses that of a real (as it happens) German restaurant.

Riddarholmskyrkan or Riddarholm Church is real and was as described; as, generally, was Stockholm Central Station. The island of Djurgården continues to be the city's playground. The large naval base has gone, to be replaced in part by the Vasa Museum, but the dockyards on the island of Beckholmen remain, as does the dockmaster's house there. Its internal arrangements are imagined. Skansen and Gröna Lund still exist, as does the old wooden church of Seglora kyrka. And there are still ferries connecting Djurgården with the old town.

Bromma Airport continues to operate, though now mainly for domestic flights. The descriptions of it are based on wartime photographs.

The anonymous 'alley' that twice features in the book, most notably in the climax, is Mårten Trotzigs Gränd or the 'Alley of Mårten Trotzig' and is much as described. There are 36 steps at the upper end and the alley narrows to just 90cm wide, making it the narrowest street in Stockholm and a tourist attraction in its own right.

To conclude, in my view it is the duty of a fiction writer to create a world that feels right to his or her readers. When the world in question is one that is as far removed in so many ways, some predictable and others not, as 1943 is from today, then it is inevitable that false assumptions will be made and facts will be misunderstood. If you find factual errors within this book I apologise and can only hope that they have not got in the way of your enjoyment of the story.